The Pippington Tales

Book 2

The Lady
And
The Frog

By

L. Palmer

Copyright

Copyright © 2017 by L. Palmer

Printed in the United States of America

ISBN

KDP: 978-1-961446-08-3
IngramSpark: 978-1-961446-00-7
IngramSpark Hardcover: 978-1-961446-01-4

http://lpalmerchronicles.com/published-works

The Lady
And
The Frog

Chapter 1

Jack Kingston whistled along with the squeak of his bicycle wheel, taking in the bright afternoon as he rode down North Lane. In the distance, Pippington's factories churned out their daily smoke and the new electric trolley clanged its way across the city. Both seemed to belong to a faraway place as Jack passed mansions hidden behind brick walls and wrought iron fences masked in vines and flowers.

Jack knew too well the estates hidden beyond these decorated barricades. He spent his days battling grime on stain glass windows, liberating marble rain gutters from debris, and slashing away overgrown wisteria vines. When the day was done, he rode back across the city, past midtown's granite buildings, through a few neighborhoods of small brick houses, to the cramped apartment he shared with his brother Henry. He preferred spending his evenings at dance halls, but most nights he settled down to study. He usually ended the evening resting his head against a book, hoping the words would fill him as he slept.

Soon, he would be done with the university and free of these odd jobs all cobbled together. In his coat pocket was the letter announcing his acceptance into the Officer Training Academy for the Pippington Police. He would arrive home tonight and smack the letter on the table. Henry would read it and see Jack was meant to have a life of action instead of sitting at a desk, staring at balance sheets all day.

If Jack did everything right, he would graduate from the Academy with honors and earn his way onto Inspector Gertrude McCay's team. He would stand in his slick and polished uniform, joining the Inspector on the front page of *The Pippington Times*.

Today, however, he had to weed the gardens at the Bradford School for Girls. No respectable newspaper would cover that story, no matter how heroic Jack's efforts were against stubborn morning glories.

He reached the corner of North Lane and Pinafore Street, when a top-hatted gentleman puttered by in a polished motorcar. Mud spattered across Jack's legs. He grunted as he wiped at the added layer of grime on his trousers. His jobs might be dirty, but the headmistress of the Bradford School still expected a level of tidiness.

As he slapped the mud off his hands, a sorrowful moan echoed from the garden hidden behind the nearby fence. Jack wiped his fingers on his worn coat. Whoever was in trouble, he didn't have time to stop and help.

He placed his foot on the pedal. A loud, hiccupping sob forced him to pause.

A quick look wouldn't waste too much time. He followed the echoes of weeping to a vine-ridden brick wall and pushed aside overgrown greenery to uncover a decorative hole in the fence. His forehead wrinkled as he peeked at the green garden beyond with a geometric pattern of roses lining a pathway.

Another sob drew his eyes to the young woman at the end of the pathway. She sat at the edge of a stone well, her golden hair draped around her slender shoulders. The airy layers of her pink gossamer gown fluttered as she wept. Her delicate hands covered her weeping face. Jack wished she would look up and give a full glimpse of her beauty.

He rubbed his neck as he stepped toward his bicycle. Looking was an intrusion. She was a lady at a fine mansion. Some servant would come along and help. Besides, he had hours of work yet to do at the

Bradford School.

The young woman howled out a mournful sob. An ache spread through his chest. Jack couldn't leave a girl in such a poor condition. He wasn't Henry and didn't need to stick to time like he was glued to a minute hand.

Leaning against the fence, Jack called through the opening, "You all right there, miss?"

The lady raised her head and the air left Jack's chest. He had thought Adeline Winkleston was the finest beauty in Pippington, but he had been wrong. The young woman's face was perfect in its symmetry, her cheekbones pronounced, yet soft, her nose just rounded enough, her lips full.

He swallowed. "Can I help you, miss?"

"Who's there?" Her sapphire-blue eyes widened as she glanced around the garden.

Jack leaned his bicycle against the fence and used the vines to climb up. Seated on top, he gave her a friendly smile. "Don't mean to intrude, miss, but it sounds as if you've got some trouble. Anything I can do?"

The lady looked to the house. "My father doesn't like strangers coming into the garden."

"That I can do something about." He jabbed his thumb toward his chest and grinned. "The name's Jack. What's yours?"

"I am Cassandra." She dabbed her face with a lace handkerchief. "Please, be careful up there."

"I'll be all right. Tell me how I can help."

Cassandra turned away as a sob shuddered across her shoulders. "No one can help me. It is lost."

Jack leaned forward. "What've you lost? I'm good at finding things."

She clutched her handkerchief as she stared forlornly into the well. "When my dear mother passed away, her last gift to me was a gold bauble. I-I dropped it in the well." She whimpered. "It is lost, just as my mother is lost to me."

Jack's smile faltered as he scratched his head. "Must be precious, then."

He eyed the well before grabbing a nearby branch and swinging to the ground. "Fortunately, I'm an expert at climbing down wells."

Cassandra stood, her hands shaking. "You should leave before my father sees you. The bauble isn't worth you getting into trouble."

"Not to worry." Jack waved his arm. "I'll have it out faster than you can blink."

He looked into the well shaft. The sun gleamed across the water's surface. Floating on top was a golden ball small enough to fit in the palm of his hand. The well was wider than most of the ones he was hired to clean, with plenty of space for his narrow shoulders. He pulled off his jacket and ran his fingers through his hair. It was already out of place, despite combing it that morning. Well, if he looked heroic enough climbing down the well, she wouldn't notice his hair.

The crank squeaked as he lowered the bucket. It splashed in the water and floated next to the gleaming bauble. Jack locked the crank in place and gripped the rope. He gave a grin and wink to Cassandra before swinging himself into the well. As he descended, he kept his hand against the wall to slow himself. He tried not to cringe as his hands slid on slimy moss and old patches of algae.

Frogs croaked from the bottom of the well, growing louder as Jack approached. There were dozens of bulbous eyes staring up at him. The frogs jumped from stone to stone as if warning each other. Jack rested his feet on a ledge near the water's surface. Once at the top, he should offer to come back and clean the well. It would be a good opportunity to see this girl again.

Holding onto the rope, he crouched down and wrapped his fingers around the bauble. With a grin, he stood and shouted, "I've got it. See, no trouble."

"Would you please put it in the bucket?" she said. "I wouldn't want it to fall."

Allowing himself a happy whistle, he dropped the bauble into the bucket. As it left his hand, he began to fall. The world around him warped as if he were looking through a bulbous lens. His skin grew cold and he splashed into the water. His body felt strange as he kicked to the surface. The well expanded, growing large and vast around him. He reached to grab the ledge, but his hands were slick and mottled green. The bucket rose from the water as Cassandra turned the crank. Jack hopped onto the nearest rock and opened his mouth to call to the girl above, but a long croak erupted instead. Panic rose as he looked down at his webbed feet. He pivoted, seeking a way out, when he found himself nose to slimy nose with another frog.

Henry Kingston's cane tapped along the pavement of North Lane. He looked down at his pocket watch as the gas street lamps flared to life. Nearly seven and still no sign of his brother Jack. He was going to be late for his evening with Evelyn Havish. She would understand, and might not even notice in the tumult of her family's home. However, punctuality was essential. If all went well, he would soon take her hand and help her rise above her family's station, just as he had risen over his own.

He grunted as he shoved his watch into his pocket and limped on. He would have a firm talk with Jack once he found him. Jack had seemed more responsible these past few months, finally shaking off the dust of the family farm and digging into his odd jobs and university exams. Such signs of maturity had taken two years of living with Henry, but they seemed to evaporate with each step Henry now took.

Perhaps Jack had fallen on old habits and drifted off from

appointments to follow some childish daydream. The young man's head was full of fantastic ideas and he believed every rumor of magic or adventure. Henry knew the only real mystery in life was why people were doltish enough to believe in magic.

Leaning on his walking cane, Henry tried to relieve the pressure on his left leg. The leg bent at a slight, odd angle just below the knee. Some days the ache was nearly unbearable. Today, it throbbed lightly, which was more of an irritation. At least he had ridden the electric trolley most of the way from his apartment. The contraption had saved him a little time in his search for his brother.

Henry took a few steps, when he saw the gleam of a bicycle handle poking out from behind some vines. He pulled back the cascade of greenery and glared at his brother's bicycle leaning against the brick fence. Everything seemed in place and in good condition, but there was no explanation for Jack's absence.

A mournful cry broke out from the other side of the fence, followed by a louder-than-polite sob. Henry pushed aside the cold, slick vines until he found a decorative opening revealing the garden beyond.

A young woman of no more than twenty was seated on a bench by a well, her hair and dress indicating a good sense of grooming. Her appearance and manner of weeping reminded him of the girls who flitted around Harold Mackabee, his employer's son. They were drawn by the scent of future wealth. Such females ignored Henry and his aura of middle-class stability.

"Oh," she cried. "If there were only someone to help me."

"Pardon me, miss," he said.

She sat up in affected surprise. "Who was that?"

"Hello! My brother's bicycle is here. Have you seen a young fellow by the name of Jack?"

"If only I had." Her shoulders drooped. "Have you lost someone, just as I have?"

"I believe he has lost himself. Have you seen anyone who might be my brother?"

"Climb the fence so I may look at you."

"I don't climb fences, nor would I, if I could. Don't you have a gate or door?"

A pause was followed by rustling. A row of vines pulled back like a curtain, revealing a wrought iron gate, a rusted chain wrapped around the lock.

"My father locked the gate before he left." She dabbed her cheeks with a lace handkerchief.

Henry analyzed the chain as he scratched his narrow, angular chin. "And there is no spare key?"

"No. I have no way to open it." She leaned her head against the fence as tears rolled down her cheeks.

"I suppose you should discuss it with your father when he returns." Henry straightened his glasses. "Pardon me, but if you have not seen my brother, I must be going."

He began to wheel Jack's bike away.

"Wait!" she said. "Was he a tall young man with dark, unruly hair?"

Henry paused. He would rather not rely on such a flighty young woman to learn his brother's fate, but he saw no other source of information. "You have seen him?"

"I think so, but—" She leaned back her head and sighed, "My head is so clouded with worry. If you could help me, I might remember."

Henry frowned. "And what is your trouble?"

"My dear mother passed away long ago, and—"

"That is unfortunate."

"Her last gift to me was—"

Henry held up a hand. "Please, miss. I do not wish to be entangled in your personal affairs. Unless there is something I can do quickly, I must be going."

"I dropped my mother's final gift, a golden bauble, in the well."

She burst into a sob. "It is lost and I shall never have it again."

"Is that all?" He looked up at the four-story mansion overshadowing the garden. It was too large to be empty. "Don't you have a gardener or workman around who can help you?"

She shook her head. "They are all gone for the day. Please sir. I cannot bear to lose it."

Henry tapped his fingers on his cane before glancing at his pocket-watch. On the farm, many things fell into wells, and most on purpose. His brothers were lithe enough to shimmy down the dark shafts, but his crooked leg kept him from such exercise. Instead, he had developed some tricks as a boy to fish his sisters' dolls out of wells.

From the toolbox attached to the back of the bicycle, he pulled out a small crowbar. He twisted it in the rusted chains and pushed his weight into it. After a second or two, one of the links broke. The chain chinked to the ground and the gate creaked as it opened. Wheeling the bike with him, he followed the young woman to the well. He glanced down the shaft. The dimming sunlight reflected off a golden ball floating on the water's surface. The shaft, however, was lined with algae and other muck while frogs croaked loudly below. The well could use a good cleaning.

From the front of the bicycle, he removed the wicker basket. He unhooked the bucket from the well's rope and replaced it with the basket. With the basket secure on the hook, he lowered the rope. He ignored the young woman watching in fascination. The wicker basket dropped into the water and Henry let it sink. With a few tugs of the rope, he maneuvered the basket beneath the bauble. He jerked the basket up, capturing the bauble.

The young woman's blue eyes were wide once the basket reached the top of the well. Henry set the basket on the edge of the well and pulled a handkerchief from his pocket. Using the cloth, he picked up the bauble and held it out to the young woman. She stared at it as if her mind had temporarily vacated her body. Hoping she was well,

Henry set the ball on the bench. He would rather not explain standing in a strange garden with a fainted woman.

Folding his handkerchief back into a precise square, Henry said, "Your well seems to be infested with frogs. I would recommend getting someone to dredge it out for you. If I find my brother, I might send him over. He is quite good at this sort of work." He pulled a business card for his office at Mackabee and Sons Accounting Firm out of his coat pocket. "I do not have his card on me, but here is mine."

Her eyes blinked as if waking. A warm smile spread as she took the offered card.

"Now, miss, do you remember seeing my brother?" he said.

"I believe— oh, it was so many hours ago, and I have been so worried about my bauble. Ah, yes. I believe he saw a girl he knew and went off walking with her."

The creases of Henry's frown deepened. Her answer seemed the truth, yet was simple enough she should have remembered it easily. He grunted as he straightened his coat. "Thank you, miss. Have a good evening."

He tucked his cane under his arm and began moving the bicycle toward the gate. The young woman hurried forward and stood in his path.

She held out her hand, her fingers dangling. "Thank you, Mr. Kingston. I cannot tell you how grateful I am for your assistance."

He stared at her manicured nails. She seemed to expect a kiss to the hand, but such an expression was far too intimate for their brief acquaintance. Instead, he touched his fingers to hers and gave a quick half-bow. Her fingers started to curl around his, but he pulled his hand away. "Good night."

As he exited onto the street, she slowly closed the gate. He lowered the bicycle seat a little before climbing on and riding away. He had to shift his leg to keep his left foot on the pedal, but cycling was faster than walking.

He turned off North Lane as the bells clanged a quarter after seven. He muttered under his breath. Even at his best speed, he was already fifteen minutes late. Evelyn would still accept his visit, but so excellent a woman deserved better.

Cassandra leaned against the gate as she watched Henry Kingston disappear around the corner. Few men spoke to her as he did. The daring embers of hope rose in her breast. She needed to learn more of this young man and discover the depth of his merit.

She pulled a cord and let the cascade of vines fall over the gate. Strolling to the garden shed, she ran her finger across his simple business card. No fuss or finery. Only a few square letters stating his name, employer, and office address. She would have to plan her next approach carefully.

Entering the shed, she slid the card into the bosom of her corset. She picked up the long-poled net and walked to the well. The frogs' croaking became cacophonous as she lowered the net. She pursed her lips, trying not to think of how many of these slimy creatures she would have to kiss until she found Jack Kingston.

If Jack remained missing, however, Henry may ask too many of the wrong questions. She needed to undo the bauble's work and send Jack home. Then, she would create an opportunity to see Henry Kingston again.

Chapter 2

Evelyn Havish built a rhythm as she slid the scraper across the lye-soaked griffinhide. The steady beat helped clear her head, but worries over Henry Kingston's next visit kept seeping through.

Tonight, just as most Tuesdays for the past six months, Henry would arrive at her home. They would thread through the crowd of friends and relatives until they found a quiet corner. He would sit with her, leaning forward, his eyes focused on hers while they discussed the day's news, emerging scientific theories, and historical events. As they sat a little closer, the conversation would turn to childhood triumphs and sorrows, their own dreams, and, in rare, sweet moments, a possible future together.

He was different from the men her brothers sent. Those fellows pretended to listen while shifting close enough to put an arm around her. If feeling bold, they would steal a kiss. She had left a few with a red mark across their cheek and one with a black eye.

Yet, she wished Henry would be a bit less of a gentleman. On their Sunday walk, they often rested on a park bench to relieve his crooked leg. He would sit close for a while as they talked. Eventually, his hand would nearly cup hers. Each time, a flutter would rise in her breast only to puff away as he would pull back his hand and stand. They would then walk back arm-in-arm, Henry keeping a respectable distance between them.

She paused from scraping to wipe her forehead with her sleeve. Shutting her eyes, she tried to anchor herself back to a month ago when her sister-in-law, Daisy, had been at the hospital bringing her third child into the world. Evelyn had sent Henry a note canceling their evening before rushing over to Dan and Daisy's apartment to watch the other two children.

At seven o'clock, a knock echoed at the door. Dressed in a stained apron, her hair in a loose bun, the three-year-old screaming out a tantrum and the toddler on her hip, she opened the door. There stood Henry and his brother Jack.

"Your mother said you might need assistance." Henry was dressed in his usual fine suit.

The evening lightened as Jack sang with the children while cleaning the windows. Henry pulled off his suit coat and rolled up his shirt-sleeves, joining Evelyn in the kitchen. He spent the evening close by her side, keeping up a light conversation as they washed the mound of dishes.

Once all was cleaned, Evelyn put the children to bed. Henry hesitated by the front door. As she came to say goodnight, he touched her arm, concern in his brown eyes. A warmth she had never experienced before rose within her.

"We can stay a little longer, if you'd like," he said.

She found herself nodding and sitting beside him in front of the fireplace, closer than they had ever sat before. Jack was nearly invisible as he sat in a chair in the corner, reading one of Daisy's romantic adventure novels. Her exhaustion from the day's hustle and bustle crept up on her as she and Henry talked. Her eyelids drooped and she rested her head against Henry's shoulder. His arm wrapped around her, holding her secure and safe. A peace filled her, and, for those brief moments, a whole future of evenings sitting in front of the fireplace unfolded before her.

The clock on the mantle rang a late hour and she jumped,

becoming fully awake. Jack was asleep in the armchair, and Henry stared into the embers of the fire. His cheek was not far from her lips. A simple kiss seemed innocent enough. He turned his head and faced her, a softness in his glance. Her breath stilled and she waited for him to take advantage of the moment.

Instead, his jaw stiffened and he snapped to his feet like a soldier. He grabbed his cane and tapped Jack on the shoulder. As Jack groaned awake, Henry said, "We need to leave."

Evelyn rose, smoothing her hair and wishing her cheeks weren't so warm.

Without looking at her, Henry half-bowed. "Thank you for the evening. I will call again next Tuesday. Goodnight."

Before she could think how to respond, he rushed out the door, dragging his brother with him.

Ever since that night, the distance between them seemed to have doubled. She would lean over an old map they were discussing, her fingers brushing his. Where before his hand would have stayed, he now stepped away and became quiet.

Evelyn set down the scraper as she stretched her back. She had come to her father's tannery to avoid thinking. Glancing at the waste barrel as fumes of dead flesh mixed with acidic chemicals, she contemplated using the stink of the work as an excuse to cancel tonight's visit. She had once tried a similar excuse and Henry had sent her a short letter with a gift of a hearty shampoo.

With a wry laugh, she went back to scraping the griffinhide. Henry never sent or brought flowers. Instead, her small dressing table was covered in bottled ointments and cleaning solutions. There was also a growing collection of kitchen and household utensils. Henry handed her each gift with a mention of some brief comment or aside from their last conversation. His form of gallantry was more charming than flowers or jewelry, but now seemed empty as he kept an arm's length between them.

As she scraped away another layer of feathers, a voice nearby said, "What are you doing here?"

Evelyn looked up to see her father, John Havish, standing by her work table.

"You've been talking about how behind you are now that Talbot's shop's been picking up business," she said.

"All that means is I've got to hire some new workers."

"Who need to be trained." She wiped the tool off on the lip of the barrel and returned to scraping. "In the meantime, I can help."

"Mr. Kingston's coming to visit at seven. You've got other work to do."

"Julie promised to bake tonight's pie and Mom will have a bath ready at four."

Havish jabbed his finger at her. "It's your cooking he should be tasting."

"What difference is there between mine and Julie's cooking?" Evelyn decided not to mention Henry wasn't the sort of man to be won with food.

"You can't tell him, 'Here's a pie my sister baked cause I was too busy.'" Havish stepped over and touched her arm. "Will you stop a moment?"

She set down the scraper and looked at her rough-faced father. He pulled her gloved hands between his large palms.

"You've been trained to be a real lady, Evelyn," Havish said. "Don't be wasting your time around here. This is a rough life."

Evelyn smiled and kissed her father's cheek. "Dad, this is our life."

Havish looked away to hide his smile and grunted. "It's also ten to four."

Evelyn craned her neck to glance at the shop clock. The work may have cleared her mind too much.

Havish tapped the unfinished hide. "You run along and I'll finish up."

She smiled and kissed her father's cheek again. "Thanks Dad."

"You get going, will you?" He gently pushed her out of the workroom.

She left her gloves and apron in her cubby and ran for the door leading out of the workshop.

"What you in such a hurry for?" Dan, her eldest brother, leaned out of the office. He was nearly as broad and muscled as their father.

"Henry's coming tonight," she said.

"You're still running about with that pencil-legged fellow?" He grunted as he folded his arms. "I'd bet if you blew on him just right, he'd fly off. That's not the sort of man to keep my sister safe."

"From what, Dan?" she said. "What trouble will I run into in Pippington?"

"If there was trouble, you'd be the one walloping." Dan winked and jabbed his finger at her. "You need a man who can scrap in there with you. What'll Mr. Kingston do? Jab with his sharp intellect? It'll not keep him from a bloody nose."

Evelyn folded her arms. "He's a good man, and you know it."

"True or not, until you've made sure promises, I think you're better off to keep looking." Dan grinned. "I saw you talking to Roger Simmons this morning. He's a solid fellow."

"I am courting Henry." Evelyn shot a glare at her brother and marched out the door.

Roger Simmons was handsome and appeared to have better manners than most men Dan and her younger brother Charlie sent her way. However, for the past three weeks, Charlie had happened to invite Simmons to stop by right before Henry's visit. The excuses had adapted and evolved, until last week when her mother had dragged Charlie into the kitchen to lecture him on respecting his sister's choices in men. The walls had shaken several times and Charlie seemed an inch shorter when he came back in the parlor. The next day, however, Charlie and Dan were back to pushing.

Her brief conversations with Simmons were pleasant enough. If Henry persisted in keeping his distance, she might go on an evening out with Simmons just to stop Dan and Charlie from meddling.

Her frustration cooled as she walked the last few blocks and arrived at their home tucked in with other brick houses. She breathed in the fresh scent of the bright flowers her mother, Marjory, kept in the yard.

As Evelyn walked up the steps, Marjory opened the door. "What took you so long and what is that smell?"

"It will wash off."

"I may have to burn your clothes." Marjory waved her in. "Julie just put the pie in the oven. You get into the washroom and brighten yourself up."

Evelyn gathered fresh clothes from her room and went into the washroom. Settling into the washtub, she breathed in the scented oils her mother had dropped in. The aroma was a little overpowering, but refreshing after a day of smelling dead animal flesh.

Once she was clean, she stretched her sore muscles and pulled herself out of the bath. She dressed and arranged her long chestnut hair into a braid. Looking in the mirror, she contemplated which of her three jeweled hairpins she would wear with her dark skirt and lace blouse. She could wear one of the spoons Henry had given her instead and see if he noticed.

With a touch of color painted on her face, and her hummingbird hairpin set in her hair, Evelyn came down the stairs. She set the table in between sending her youngest siblings, Ron and Madeline, back to their chores. Julie and their mother laughed and sang together while they worked in the kitchen. As Evelyn finished, her cousin Maggie came through the front door with her youngest on her hip and her two toddlers at her side.

"So nice of your father to invite us over again while Howard's out of town," Maggie said before bustling into the kitchen.

She was soon followed by a parade of friends and relatives, punctuated by the arrival of Uncle Joe shouting over the din, "Good old Marjory always makes the best meal."

Men brought crates from the cellar for extra seats as the sitting tables were put beside the dining table. Evelyn pushed through the crowd and leaned in the kitchen with the latest count.

"Some nights," Marjory said as she added more flour and vegetables to the soup on the stove, "I think your father's going to invite the whole city."

Trying to manage the growing din, Evelyn went to the piano and played a jaunty tune. Cousins and neighbors joined in singing as the next song was requested. Evelyn used all her years of learning the great sonatas to play an old folk song about a farmer's war with a wily raccoon. She finished with a brief flourish on the piano and Mrs. Blanchard, their widowed neighbor, patted her shoulder.

"You've such a lovely talent. One day, some young man will whisk you away," the wrinkled woman said. "You'll not be an old maid for much longer."

Evelyn kept a polite smile on her face while ignoring a few of her cousins sniggering behind her. At twenty-one, she had already been an old maid in Mrs. Blanchard's eyes for four years.

The hum of conversation broke into greetings as Havish entered his home, his hands and face washed, but the rest of him stinking of the tannery. He gave each of his guests a hearty handshake and warm greeting while Marjory and Julie hefted the mounds of mashed potatoes, pots of beef soup, and piles of other fixings on the table. Evelyn ushered people onto seats, crates, and benches, with a few children sitting on knees. As she squeezed next to one of her cousins, and left a spot beside her for Charlie, she counted twenty-five people at the table. Only six lived at the house.

Havish gave a quick grace for the food. Then began the cacophony of silverware clinking, plates thumping, and voices humming. The conversations laced over each other, with comments shouted at topics passing by.

"I'm telling you, magic is real!" Havish pounded the table with his fist, sending a shudder along the plank of wood.

"I've seen no elves and sparkles in my shop." Uncle Joe jabbed his fork toward Havish and the two men went again through their circuitous debate. This was one of the few areas where Evelyn sided with Uncle Joe. Her father's passion about magic had grown ever since Talbot's Boots had picked up more business. Magic was a silly notion and not worth hoping for when rolling up one's sleeves and doing a bit of work would do more.

Evelyn's forehead began to throb from the overlaying voices and she half-listened to her cousin Harvey talk about his job at the carpentry shop. She jumped as the front door slammed open and Charlie entered, followed by Roger Simmons.

Across the table, her mother whispered, "What is that man doing here?"

Evelyn placed her hands firmly on the table, trying to stop the churning of her stomach. Havish had gone quiet and was glaring at his son, even while Uncle Joe blustered on about more reasons why elves couldn't be real.

Leading Simmons into the dining room, Charlie shouted, "One more for dinner, Mom!"

Havish leaned back in his chair. "You're late, Charlie. You two might have to sit outside and eat scraps with the dog."

Charlie covered his nervous grin with a laugh. Pulling out the chair beside Evelyn, he said, "Simmons, why don't you take my seat."

Evelyn's jaw was firm as she met her mother's eyes.

Marjory stood and rolled up her sleeves. "Mr. Simmons can have my seat. I've got to start cleaning up anyway."

"Don't you worry about that, Mom." Charlie waved for her to sit. "I can take care of it. I'm the one who's late."

Taking the seat beside Evelyn, Simmons said, "I'm sorry to disturb, Mrs. Havish, but your cooking's too good to turn down when Charlie invites me."

Evelyn focused on her plate. Simmons was everything a man should appear to be. He had a strong physique and a closely cropped beard to emphasize his square jaw. She had seen many girls swooning as he passed by. If she wasn't careful, she would be distracted by his musky scent and warm glances. However, she knew better than to fully trust the flirtations of men who worked for her father.

"It was nice to talk to you this morning." His blue eyes watched Evelyn, a warm smile on his lips. "I'm surprised to see you there so often. That's rough work for a fine lady like yourself."

"I don't mind the work." Evelyn spared a glance at the clock on the mantle. It was 6:30. Only a half-hour until Henry's arrival. She could rid herself of Simmons by then. Marjory would take care of most of the other guests.

"I'm sure you do a fine job." He leaned toward her. Evelyn tried to scoot away, but stopped before she accidentally pushed her cousin off his chair. "But, you have lovely hands. They shouldn't be ruined by tanning."

Evelyn tucked her hands into her lap as she sat up straight.

"There's a band coming from Willington to McBriar's next Saturday," he said. "Charlie and I've been talking of going. There'll be some good dancing."

Evelyn had spent too many evenings in the smoke-filled pub. The dancing could be fun, but, by the end of the night, her date was sweat-drenched, drunk, and embroiled in a fight. Most evenings at McBriar's ended with her walking home alone.

"I do love dancing," Mrs. Blanchard said. "My husband and I went as often as we could while courting."

"Someone's going to a dance?" Maggie looked up from wiping a layer of mashed potatoes off her infant's face.

"This young fellow and Evelyn are going," Mrs. Blanchard said.

"Oh, really?" Julie said as she leaned forward with a broad grin. Her eyes told Evelyn she would ask for all the details later. Evelyn shook her head and Julie's shoulders slumped in disappointment.

Havish's conversation with Uncle Joe cut off and his voice deepened as he said, "What's this?"

"Nothing," Evelyn said as she tossed down her napkin and stood. "Mr. Simmons was just—" She clamped her teeth together and turned to her mother. "Do you need some help cleaning up?"

"Yes, please." Marjory stood and began gathering the barren serving dishes. Together, they retreated into the kitchen.

Marjory placed a pot of water on the stove. "I don't know what Dan and Charlie see in that man. All he wants is to cozy up with the eldest daughter of John Havish."

Evelyn sighed as she pulled on an apron. At least Henry had no connection to her father. They had met when she was dragged to yet another lecture by yet another man trying to prove his intelligence. The evening's date had been Murray Phelps and the lecture had been on the advances of electric energy.

At the reception afterward, Phelps had droned on about his own ideas and opinions. Somehow, Henry had inserted himself in the conversation and shifted it, so Evelyn's voice could be heard. As the evening drew to a close, she found herself giving Henry her card, and the next day he called. They went for a stroll and spoke of science and industry. The conversation turned to small stories of home and he returned her to her doorstep with an invitation to come again. His interest in her had been clear then, not like the muddle it was now.

Marjory paused from her bustling as she glanced at Evelyn. "You're looking pale. Why don't you go upstairs and rest until Mr. Kingston comes?"

Evelyn felt a knot rise in her throat, but she clamped her mouth shut and stacked dishes beside the sink.

"Evelyn," Marjory said, her voice softening as she walked toward her daughter, "Is everything alright?"

"It's—" Evelyn raised her head and wished she hadn't. Looking in her mother's eyes always seemed to force things out of her. "I don't know. A few weeks ago, I thought, maybe—" She swallowed as a tear broke. "He'll barely touch my hand, Mom, let alone—" Her lips clamped together.

Marjory put her hands on her hips. "Has he kissed you yet?"

Evelyn's cheeks blushed as she shook her head.

"You mean to tell me," Marjory said as she slapped her towel onto the counter, "that all the times your father and I made sure to get everyone out of the parlor, he hasn't kissed you?"

"No. These last few weeks, when we're alone, he just grows quieter and stays in the chair across from me."

"He doesn't even cozy up next you? Put his arm around you?"

"Mom, he's a gentleman."

Marjory's brow furrowed. "Your father and I did things properly, but we still snuck a good number of kisses before we were engaged. I don't know what fool ideas young folks have about 'propriety.' There comes a time, if a fellow really likes a girl, that he should show it."

Evelyn took in a breath and the rest of her tears broke. Marjory put her arms around Evelyn and held her close.

"I like him," Evelyn said, taking in the warmth of her mother's embrace, "And, I think I could love him, if he would only let me try."

"Maybe he needs a bit of pushing." Marjory stepped back and lifted Evelyn's chin. She smiled, a twinkle in her eye. "I'm not sure of Simmons, but an evening out with him might spur Kingston on a bit."

Evelyn gasped and then let out a laugh. "You didn't raise me to be that sort of girl."

"Just one night to help Mr. Kingston along might be worth it." Marjory gave her daughter a wink.

"I don't think—"

Evelyn stopped as the door opened and Julie and Maggie carried stacks of dishes in.

"Why don't you go freshen up?" Marjory squeezed Evelyn's arm. "I'll take care of things here."

Evelyn returned to the chaos of the dining room as crates and chairs were put away and dishes collected into the kitchen. She glanced at the clock. Only ten minutes until Henry arrived. Even with her mother's help, too many people would still be here.

She moved to go up the stairs, but Simmons stepped in her path.

"Charlie says you've a fine talent for the piano," he said, his thumbs tucked in his belt loops. "I'd love to hear you play."

"Perhaps another night." She moved to step past him.

"Come on." He leaned in her way. "One rollicking song."

Her heart thudded as she thought of her mother's suggestion. Maybe, if Simmons was still here when Henry arrived, it would work as her mother hoped. Evelyn quieted the thought. It was rude and cruel to both men.

Instead, she turned and said, "Mrs. Blanchard, would you play for us?"

"I've just the song." Mrs. Blanchard patted Evelyn's arm and crossed to the piano. She sat and swept her fingers across the keys as she played *Roberta's Rescue*. The guests and family joined in singing the jaunty tune as Roberta's dashing hero attempted to rescue her from a tower. Evelyn's youngest brother Ron leapt about as if he were fighting the villains.

Most evenings, Evelyn joined in the singing, sometimes playing a duet with Mrs. Blanchard. Tonight, she took the distraction to grab a shawl from the hook by the front door and escape to swing on the porch. Sitting within the sight of the neighbors would still be more secluded than the parlor.

She pulled the shawl over her shoulders and rocked on the porch swing, listening for the tap of Henry's cane. Soon he would arrive, his narrow, angular face pinched in thought, his suit tailored to his slim, bony frame. His dark hair would be as polished as his shoes, every hair combed and accounted for. He certainly wasn't as good looking as Simmons, but he took great care in his appearance. Evelyn didn't need a handsome man. Just a good one.

The clock tower at the old church chimed the hour and Evelyn stood. She leaned on the railing and looked down the street. Henry was always at least at the door by the time the last chime faded, not a minute or two later. Perhaps the trolley had been delayed, or Henry had worked late. He would be coming around the corner any moment.

Minutes dragged on as the daylight continued to wane. Evelyn glanced down the other way, but there was still no Henry. Something was wrong. He was never late.

Crickets were beginning to chirp as the front door opened.

"There you are, Miss Evelyn." Simmons smiled as he leaned against a post. "Nice spot to wander to."

She kept her eyes focused on the street and tightened her shawl over her shoulders. She shut away thoughts of the news stories of missing young men. Any moment now, Henry would come around the corner and she would know he was safe.

Strolling toward her, Simmons said, "You seem a smart girl, Miss Evelyn. I'm sure you've figured out I haven't been coming around just for your brother's company."

She raised an eyebrow. "Is it my mother's cooking?"

Simmons laughed. "Her cooking is grand, but it's not what keeps me coming back." He sat on the railing and leaned toward her. "I'm sure I'm not the first man to tell you how beautiful you are."

She glared at him. "Henry Kingston and I've been courting for several months."

"But are you spoken for? From what Dan and Charlie've told me, it doesn't seem you are." Simmons folded his arms. "If he's not spoken up yet, then you deserve a better man."

"He is polite and a gentleman." A thickness filled her chest as the clock tower marked the quarter hour. Henry would have at least sent a note.

"He might be." Simmons shrugged and smiled. "However, if there's no understanding between you and the fellow, I'd like to take you on an evening out. Nice dinner, a bit of dancing. What do you say?"

She looked at him, his handsome face outlined in the soft evening light, her mother's suggestion echoing in the back of her mind. He seemed better than many men she had been on evenings with, and, a few months ago, she would have accepted.

Tonight, she said, "No, thank you," and walked to the front door.

Before she could touch the handle, Simmons opened the door for her. "Let me know if you change your mind."

She held back a sigh and passed through the small entryway beside the stairs and into the dining room and parlor. The singing had ended and everyone scattered about chatting in small groups. Marjory was speaking with several women, leading them slowly toward the door.

Havish broke from his conversation with Uncle Joe and walked to Evelyn's side. Keeping a sharp eye on Simmons, he asked, "Where's Kingston?"

"I don't know. He's late."

Havish frowned. "He's never late."

She glanced at her father, trying to ignore the tightness in her chest. "I know."

He smiled and squeezed her shoulder. "He'll turn up."

Feeling Simmons follow her, Evelyn inserted herself into a conversation between Maggie and Julie. She took Maggie's daughter on her knee and bounced her while only half-listening. The couch was tightly packed, with no space for Simmons to approach. He joined a conversation with Charlie and some of their cousins.

Out of the corner of her eye, Evelyn watched the minutes tick by on the clock. Each movement of the second hand thudded in her ears, but Henry still did not come. She tried to listen to the conversation and join the laughter around her, tried to quiet the brief images of Henry lying injured in the street flashing through her mind.

As Marjory finally succeeded in getting the first guests to leave, Maggie began gathering her children. The infant's missing shoe, however, slowed her progress. Havish took the child in his massive arms as Evelyn joined the search.

Evelyn was crouched behind one of the couches, when her father said, "Good to see you, Mr. Kingston!"

A thump followed. Havish had probably punched Henry's shoulder. Her father could throw Henry across a warehouse if he wasn't careful. "Where've you been tonight?"

"I am sorry, sir," Henry said. "I was delayed by unexpected business."

"No need to worry. You're always welcome under my roof. Evelyn's been chomping to see you tonight."

Evelyn wished her cheeks didn't feel so warm as she stood. Henry walked quickly toward her, his limp heavier than usual, his pants splashed with mud, his vest and coat askew, his face slightly red from exercise.

She thought to ask him what was wrong, but felt everyone's eyes watching them. Henry adjusted his spectacles and said, "Evelyn, is there somewhere we can speak?"

"Yes, just—"

"Have you found it yet?" Maggie shouted from the other end of the dining room.

"I'm sorry. Maggie's son lost his shoe," Evelyn said. "Do you mind waiting a bit?"

Henry's face looked more pinched than usual, but he nodded. "May I help?"

"No. I'm sure we'll find it in a moment."

Henry stepped away, when Uncle Joe clapped him on the shoulder. "I was hoping to see you again, Kingston. Now, I've got a bit of an investment I'm looking at. Wanted the thoughts of a money-man like yourself."

"I'm an auditor, not an investor," Henry said.

Uncle Joe didn't seem to hear and went into a long explanation of another one of his schemes. Evelyn glanced around the room for someone to rescue Henry, but her mother had an eye on Ron and Madeleine while she spoke to Mrs. Blanchard, her father was herding Maggie's children, Julie and Charlie would say something rude to Henry, and no one else knew enough to help. Her chest eased as Havish made his way to Henry's side and began to steer the conversation to better territory.

Evelyn moved to the next armchair. She jumped out of the way as Madeleine leaped on top of Ron and began pounding him. He laughed as he kept hold of her porcelain doll.

Havish shoved Maggie's youngest into Henry's arms and marched across the room. The infant broke into a wail as Henry held him in the crook of his arm. Havish grabbed his twelve-year-old daughter and ten-year-old son by their collars and dragged them out the back door. Conversations went silent as his bellows shook the walls.

Evelyn tried not to listen as she knelt and looked beneath the chair. Ron had done something similar last week, just to get a rise out of Madeleine in front of a crowd. She glanced at Henry, pinned in the corner by Uncle Joe, rocking the crying infant in his arm. He might be a gentleman, but he had grown up on a farm. He would understand.

She pulled aside a cushion and there sat the shoe. As she rose, Henry came to her side.

"Maybe I should call tomorrow." He hefted the infant.

Putting the shoe on the child's kicking foot, Evelyn said, "Things will be quieter in a moment."

She finished strapping the shoe on, when the infant gagged.

Evelyn reached to grab the baby, but was too late. A cascade of yellow-white liquid ejected from the child's mouth and spread over Henry's suitcoat. Evelyn cringed as she took the infant from Henry. "I'm so sorry. I—"

"It's fine." Henry made a valiant attempt not to wrinkle his nose as he patted at the mess with his handkerchief.

"There's your little shoe," Maggie said as she took her youngest from Evelyn. "Thank you, Evelyn, and thank your parents too. I've not had a night like this in a long time." She leaned a little closer and looked over at Simmons. "That young man of yours is quite a charmer."

Evelyn held back a groan as Maggie herded her children to the front door.

"May I use the kitchen?" Henry whispered.

"Yes." The kitchen seemed a safer place than the parlor or front porch. "I'll go with you."

Henry's shoulders relaxed a little as he nodded. She took in a breath as they came closer to the door and a chance to talk. Then, her cousin Harvey stepped in their way.

"Thank you for the evening." He grabbed Evelyn's hand and gave it a hearty pump. "We'll have to have you and your beau over for dinner some night. Simmons seems to have bright prospects."

"He's not—" Evelyn said.

Harvey seemed not to hear as he stepped away to say goodnight to Charlie. Evelyn rushed for the kitchen and was through before Henry could hold the door for her. Piles of clean dishes lay out to dry and rags sat abandoned on the counters.

"Set your coat on the table and I'll take care of it." Evelyn filled a cup with water before grabbing the canister of baking soda from the cupboard over the sink.

She carried the cleaning supplies and a handful of rags over as Henry laid his coat on the table. He slid an envelope out of a pocket and set it away from the mess. The corners were embossed with gold and a floral design was hand-painted across the back. She leaned for a closer look while setting the supplies on the table.

As she opened the baking soda canister, Henry pulled out one of the chairs. "Sit, please."

"No, I can—"

He pressed his hand to her arm and motioned toward the chair. Her heart skipped a beat as she met his brown eyes, a warmth she had been missing filled her. He was always more relaxed in these small moments, where he matter-of-factly took care of a task most men would see as beneath them.

She sat down as he sprinkled the baking soda over the smear of vomit, the chemical scent of the powder diminishing the stink. He rubbed the wet rag on the stain, creating a paste. She leaned her chin on her hand and smiled. "It seems you've done this before."

"The summer I broke my leg, Mother set me to getting stains out of clothes." He squinted as he scrubbed at a spot. "It's been useful."

"You told me she had you learning numbers."

"She did, but only in the afternoon and evenings. Mornings, I had to do my share of chores." He stretched his back and surveyed his work. "Mother always works hard and expects the same of everyone else."

Evelyn laughed. "How did Jack put it? That she even darns socks in her sleep?"

Henry gave a light chuckle. His cheeks tensed and he looked away.

Evelyn sat up. "What's wrong?"

Henry wiped his hands on the clean rag before pulling off his spectacles and rubbing his eyes.

She touched his elbow. "Henry, is everything all right?"

Henry sat down as he said, "Jack's missing."

Evelyn's breath froze in her throat. She and Henry had discussed the news stories about disappearing young men with a distant interest, even with a few of her father's workers joining the names of the missing. The thought of Jack going missing sent a shiver down her arms.

"How long?"

"Only a few hours." Henry put back on his spectacles. "He missed his afternoon work at the Bradford School. A young woman I ran into told me she saw Jack wander off with some girl. This could be true, but I'm not sure." Henry tapped his hand against the table. "If it is true, he's probably out at some dance hall and will turn up by morning."

"That's not like Jack."

"It used to be." Henry's fingers wrapped into a fist.

"Dad can help look for him." Evelyn stood. "Charlie and his friend Mr. Simmons are here. They know the dance halls. I'm sure they could find him."

Henry glared at the door as he shook his head. "If he is just out dancing, let him. He'll be home by morning. If he's in trouble, I doubt we'll find him tonight." A paleness crept into his face. "And I'll have to go to the police. I don't want to waste your father's time."

"Dad would be happier knowing he can help." She touched his hand. "Please, Henry."

She waited for him to draw his hand away as usual, but his fingers wrapped around hers. His hand shook, yet he held steady. She sat back down, tendrils of hope sparking even as she tried to quiet them.

"If you wish it, then I will ask." He leaned forward, his eyes seeking hers. "First, I—" He pursed his lips before picking up the gilded envelope with his free hand. "I won these tickets from work today, and I thought it would be nice, that you would like—" He took in a steadying breath. "Will you come with me this Saturday?"

She tried not to give him a quizzical glance. They had gone out on Saturdays before, and for tickets he had won from work. The lectures and small concerts had been fine evenings, and Henry, as always, was courteous and attentive. There was no reason for him to be so anxious. Perhaps his worry over Jack was wearing through.

Trying to calm his nerves, she said with a laugh, "Only if it is another lecture on using electricity to create sound."

He blinked at her. His cheek twitched as if he were about to smile, but it never came. "I stopped entering for those after the third time we went." His eyebrows lowered. "This event is far more—"

The kitchen door thudded open and Mrs. Blanchard leaned in. "Miss Evelyn, your handsome young man is leaving. Aren't you going to wish him a sweet goodnight?"

Evelyn stared at Mrs. Blanchard, the words foreign at first. A coldness filled her as Henry's hand slipped away and Mrs. Blanchard stepped closer.

All Evelyn could say was, "Thank you."

Mrs. Blanchard laughed and patted Evelyn's cheek. "Now, don't let a man like Mr. Simmons wander off."

The door swung shut as she tottered away.

Evelyn rubbed her forehead as she stood. "I'll get Dad so you can tell him about Jack."

She moved toward the door. As her fingers were on the handle, Henry muttered, "You're better than such men."

The words were quiet, but shot out as if from a misfired pistol and ricocheted through Evelyn's mind as she turned to face him. He stood, gripping the back of his chair to keep himself steady, his shoulders tense.

"What did you say?"

"I'm sorry. I'm tired. I did not mean to speak." He ran his hand over his hair before grabbing his cane. "Let's go see your father."

She stayed in the doorway. "Are you talking about Simmons?"

Henry's mouth clamped shut as his eyes met hers. Looking away, he said, "You have done nothing, but his presence has been common over the past few weeks."

"He's Charlie's friend. I never invited him." Her brow furrowed. Simmons could be why Henry had been colder the past few weeks. However, Henry didn't seem the sort to be jealous.

"As I said, you have done nothing." Henry's hand shook as he leaned on his cane. "But, the way your cousins speak of him, and not just tonight, make it clear I am not—" His lips tightened as he fought against the words. "They see Mr. Simmons as a better match for you, and you—" He raised his head and squared his shoulders. "You are better than a man of his station deserves."

She stared at him, her mouth slightly open as she tried to decide how much of his statement was a compliment. "I've no interest in Simmons, but his station's no better than my family's."

"I respect and admire your parents." Henry tapped his hand against his leg. "All I mean is, with your education and intelligence, you deserve better than to be associated with Mr. Simmons, as well as most of tonight's guests."

She tilted her head, trying to understand where his final statement had come from. Keeping her voice even, she said, "Those guests are my friends and family."

"Yes, but, they don't see you as anything more than a tanner's daughter."

"But that is what I am," she said. "Just as you're a farmer's son."

He looked at her, a glint of hardness in his eyes. "I have worked hard to become more than a farm boy from Craggsville. And, your parents have sacrificed much to give you an education." He nodded at the door. "You cannot allow people to think a man like that is worthy of you."

"I didn't invite him." She gritted her teeth.

"I understand, but people in our position must be careful who they are seen with." Henry pointed at her and then at himself. "You and I must have the right connections if we are to rise above the poor circumstances we come from."

Her eyes flared wide and her fingers balled into a fist. "Being a Havish isn't some 'poor circumstance'."

"That's not what I meant." Henry rubbed his neck as he glanced away. "Your family is respected in their own circles. However, they are holding you back from—"

"What you meant is clear." Her throat clenched around her words as she said, "Is this really how you see my family?"

He ran a hand over his face before picking up his coat and envelope from the table. "It's been a long evening. I should come back tomorrow."

She remained standing between him and the door, her glare hard. He was not escaping her question.

Tiredness hung in Henry's shoulders as he looked at her. His mouth unclenched and he said, "They mean well, but many of them are proud of being ignorant and can't see the damage they can make to your future." He took in a breath. "My own family is no better."

She glared at him, wondering if he would say this if were standing in front of either of their families. Given the stories he had told, his family was as loud as hers, their work as rough and dirty. Even still, both his and her parents had fought to prepare them for a better life.

His cheek tightened before he said, "I do like a few and I tolerate the rest because they matter to you."

Her jaw shifted as her neck tensed. The words were spoken as if they were an appeasement for insulting both their families. Had he been sitting near her, night after night, thinking this?

"Having an education isn't an excuse to look down on our families," she said, keeping her voice low.

"I didn't mean to offend. I just—" He shifted his feet before holding out the envelope, his hand shaking. "Please, consider the invitation tonight and we can talk tomorrow, after we've both rested."

"You don't need to come, Mr. Kingston. If this is how you feel about my family, I think we're done."

"That's not—"

She avoided his pleading gaze as she opened the door. "Goodnight, Mr. Kingston."

His lips tensed as if he were about to say more. Instead, he placed the envelope on the counter, he said, "These are yours."

He half-bowed before marching out of the kitchen, his limp slowing his pace. She slammed the door shut and pressed her head against it. A tear slid down her cheek as every hope and sweet moment from the past few months seemed tainted now.

"Kingston, where are you going?" her father said.

"I have personal matters to attend," Henry said.

"Why don't you just take a seat? There's pie in the kitchen for you. You can't go before having some."

"I'm sure it is a quality pie. However, I must leave."

The front door thudded shut and Evelyn stared blankly at the envelope on the counter. She felt as if her heart were being squeezed through a laundry press as she recounted the conversation. Anger mixed with a thread of doubt as she thought through all their evenings together. His disdain for her family must have always been there, driving him away over the past month.

"Evelyn Susan Havish," Havish bellowed. She slid the envelope into her pocket as she stepped into the parlor. Fortunately, the guests were gone and the rest of her family had left the room. "What happened with Mr. Kingston?"

Evelyn pressed her lips together. Her father's red face and furrowed brow warned her to speak carefully. "We had a disagreement."

"That bloke Simmons scared him off, didn't he?" Havish jabbed a finger toward the door. "Simmons is a decent worker, I'll give him that, but he isn't a gentleman like Kingston is. There's a man who's going to give you a good life, Evelyn."

Henry might be able to give her a good life, but she couldn't stand knowing he looked down on her family.

"It had little to do with Simmons," she said.

Havish waved his arm. "I'll be chewing on Charlie later, but you've got to think of what you've been doing. Letting the man flirt with you, encouraging him—"

"What have I done to encourage Roger Simmons?"

"You've been letting him sit all close and cozy. If you would just try with Mr. Kingston—"

Evelyn let out a tired laugh. "Dad, I have tried for months with Mr. Kingston. I might find more warmth hugging a lamppost."

"I didn't pay for you to go off to the Bradford School and learn to be an accomplished lady only to see you marry a man who sweats for a living."

She threw her arm back and pointed. "I don't need some fine house in a North Town neighborhood with a man who doesn't respect me or my family."

"Respects you?" Havish shook his head. "You're not going to find a man who respects you more than Kingston. He stopped by my shop the other day and ended up helping me with a few accounts. He's not much of a talker, but what he did say was all about how smart you are, how hard you work, how witty you can be. Other fellows would have asked why you stepped out of the kitchen."

She glared at her father, wondering if Henry had been helping with accounts because he didn't trust Havish to think for himself. Her jaw trembled.

"He's ashamed of us, Dad." Tears fell down her cheek. Havish's brow softened and his fists loosened. "And his own family. He's been sitting here, judging us."

Havish wrinkled his nose before shaking his head. He stepped closer, placing his hands on her shoulders. "It'll be all right. Even your mom and I have our fights. Give him a few days. Then, when your head's clear, decide what to do."

"I don't want to see him again," she whispered.

"Don't count the fellow out yet."

Evelyn pushed away from her father and ran up the stairs. A sob broke as she remembered the night at Dan's apartment, Henry's arms around her, so close, so comfortable, and then he pushed her away. Was it shame at himself or of her?

Once she reached the top of the stairs, she dove into the room she shared with Julie.

Her sister looked up from a book as Evelyn fell onto the bed. "What happened?"

"Henry left early." Evelyn wiped her cheeks before pulling the envelope from her pocket. She cut it open with the letter opener and removed the pair of gold-embossed tickets.

"That can't be what Dad was shouting about," Julie said.

Evelyn dropped the tickets onto the nightstand before pulling a pillow over her face.

"Was he jealous of Simmons?" Julie nearly hid the giggle from her voice.

Evelyn removed the pillow and narrowed her eyes at her sister.

Julie leaned against the bedpost. "Evelyn, every time you and Simmons are in the same room together, it's just—" She shrugged. "I get goosebumps all over my arm. He might not be as—" It took Julie a long time to reach the word, "Polite as Henry, but there's clear romance in the air." She giggled. "Not to mention how handsome he is."

Evelyn threw a pillow at Julie before shutting her eyes. Simmons was another problem she would figure out later.

"Dad likes Henry better."

Julie sniggered. "When he walks in the room, all I want is a nap."

Evelyn curled onto her side. Usually she would defend Henry, but not tonight. Despite her growing headache, she picked up the tickets and looked at them more closely. She gasped.

"What is it?" Julie said.

Evelyn held the tickets out to Julie.

"Does that say the Morveaux Theater and Ballroom?" Julie squealed as she jumped onto the bed for a closer look. "But, Henry—he's so boring. Do you even have a dress fine enough?"

"I have some money saved up."

Julie looked again at the tickets. "If you don't want to go, I'll go with Henry."

Evelyn snatched the tickets back. At the Morveaux, she would be among the highest class in the city. This must have been why he had been spoken of station. Most of her family wouldn't fit in at such a fine place, but it didn't excuse him calling them 'ignorant' and a 'poor circumstance.'

Henry's opinion of her family was clear now. Slapping the tickets onto the nightstand, her decision was sure. She was better off without worrying about Henry's opinion and find a man who had genuine respect for her and her family.

Chapter 3

Henry glared into his own bloodshot eyes as he slid the razor over his chin, smoothing away his stubble. Going through his morning routine always cleared his head and prepared him for another day in the safety of ledgers and charts. Numbers were predictable, clear, and did not have emotions.

Wiping off his face, he tried to shut away the lingering dream of Evelyn in Roger Simmons' arms as they danced and laughed. He had spent the whole night fleeing this vision, cycling between lying awake on his bed, and pacing his apartment. He ended up sitting in his armchair, staring out the small window. He finally dozed off a few hours before dawn. His sleep broke as the front door thumped open and Jack stumbled in with a drunken giggle.

Jack now lay sprawled on his bed, still in his rumpled clothes, sleeping with a peace Henry envied.

Henry combed his hair as he ran through the conversation with Evelyn again. He stood by his opinion of her extended family. They were common people, with their dreams limited by ignorance. His own family didn't understand Henry's accomplishments of graduating from a university and gaining employment with a respectable firm. Whenever he visited home, his elder brother Richard would sit with his latest child on his knee and say, "No man's meant to be a bachelor so long. Where's your girl?"

Today, Henry would have to say he lost her. He should have held his tongue and not let his tiredness rule his words. Speaking the truth had gotten him a few black eyes back home, but nothing like last night. In a few minutes, his honesty had undone everything he had dared hope for these past few months.

He had spent so many hours reading papers and magazines, seeking topics for conversation. Every Tuesday night, he sat across from Evelyn, his tongue clamped to the roof of his mouth. He listened as she spoke with intelligence and wit. The conversation became easier and she sat closer, the light of the fire highlighting her warm brunette hair. His sweating palms pressed to his legs and his pulse pounding, pushing away his ability to think.

Henry rubbed his shoulder, remembering the night he had dared put his arm around her, drinking in the scent of her hair, her head nestled against his shoulder as she slept. All he had wanted to do was raise her chin and engage in a rather improper kiss.

He had fled that night and made sure to keep his distance in the few moments they had been alone these past few weeks. Even then, every touch of her hand sent a thrill in his chest and a desire to brush her soft cheek with his lips. However, she was a lady, and he would not endanger her honor.

Buttoning his vest and coat, he decided he would write a letter. A careful apology could persuade her to forgive him and let him escort her to the Morveaux on Saturday. Then, he might not waste the three months of working late to help Nathaniel Bronhart increase his new account numbers high enough to win tickets to the Morveaux.

Once he and Evelyn were at the Morveaux, he could put to use the last six weeks of dancing classes. Evelyn would be charmed and everything he had set in place could run its course. In the end, he would no longer have to worry about competitors for Evelyn's heart.

First, however, he needed to address the culprit behind his tiredness and ill temper the night before.

Henry tightened the knot of his tie and approached the foot of

Jack's bed. "Where were you last night?"

Jack snorted as he rolled on his back, his eyes groggy and faded. With a yawn, he said, "I'm not sure you'll believe me."

Henry kept his glare steady, preparing for Jack's latest tale of excuses.

"I was doing an extra job for a fine lady at a mansion on the corner of North Lane and Pinafore." Jack smiled wistfully. "She's beautiful, her hair just like gold, her voice warm, and—" Jack sighed.

"Does she have blonde hair, blue eyes, and pink lace?"

"Yes." Jack sat up. "How'd you know?"

Henry flicked lint off his cuff. "I found your bicycle outside her mansion."

"Oh," Jack ran his hands through his hair. "I was wondering where it was. Did you bring it home?"

"Where were you last night?"

Jack pointed absently. "The girl, Cassandra, asked me to clean out her well. I climbed down, but then slipped and hit my head. Knocked me out. I had the wildest dream where I turned into a frog and—"

Henry pulled out his pocket-watch as his jaw hardened. The young woman had lied to him. He wasn't sure he was angrier at her or Jack. "How did she get you out of the well?"

"Her gardener was in the front yard, so she had him come help. They set me in a guest room—" Jack's grin broadened. "And then I woke up to her kissing me. Seems she couldn't resist."

Snapping his watch shut and sliding it in his pocket, Henry said, "And how long did you engage in such activity?"

"I came straight home."

Henry's fist tightened around the head of his walking cane. This Cassandra should have told him the truth. He would have collected Jack and taken him to a doctor. Jack would be better off forgetting the girl. However, Jack was unlikely to accept Henry's advice on the matter.

"Breakfast is on the table," Henry said. "In the future, tell your clients to inform me of any accidents."

"I'm always careful, Henry. No need to worry."

"I wasn't worried." Henry straightened his shirt collar. "You missed appointments and risked your reputation."

Jack's eyes narrowed. "I could have drowned."

"If you had been more careful, you wouldn't have fallen." Henry pulled off his spectacles and cleaned the lenses. "And climbing down to retrieve her child's toy isn't cleaning."

"It was her mother's. I couldn't leave her there crying."

Henry stamped his cane on the ground. "I spent my evening looking for you and was late to my visit with Evelyn."

Jack's eyebrows pinched together as he tilted his head. Eyeing his brother, he grabbed the edge of his nightstand and pulled himself to his feet. "And how is Evelyn?"

Grinding the point of his cane into the floor, Henry said. "She is well, but I doubt I will continue wasting her time. If you'll excuse me, I must go to work."

With a snap-turn, he marched to the front door.

Jack's feet pounded on the wood floor as he ran after Henry. He skidded to a stop as his shoulder hit the wall beside the door. "That can't be all. You look at her like you'll be sick without her. What happened?"

Henry pulled on his overcoat and hat as he tried to forget Evelyn standing in her parents' kitchen, glaring at him. He gritted his teeth as he opened the door.

"And what about that fancy ball this weekend?" Jack said. "Don't tell me we've been going to all those stuffed up dance classes for no reason."

Henry went to step out of the doorway, but Jack jumped in his path.

"All you need to do is to buy her flowers. Then you go stand on her doorstep and give her a sad look. She'll be so flattered and charmed, she'll forgive anything you may have done."

"I doubt she will forgive me."

Jack prodded his finger into Henry's chest. "It's that attitude which keeps men bachelors."

Henry snorted as he pushed past Jack and marched down the stairs. As soon as he reached the street, Henry let out a breath. Walking would give him time to think, to form the words he would write to Evelyn.

Jack appeared beside him, hopping as his bare feet hit the cold pavement.

"I'll even prove it to you," Jack said as he kept pace. "I'll take flowers to Cassandra at her mansion and I'll bet you a week's wages she'll be my girl by today's end."

"Flowers will not assist me," Henry said.

"Then send her chocolates. Girls love chocolates."

Henry stopped and faced his brother. "The truth is I offended her, and she appears to have another suitor she prefers over me."

Jack stood still and frowned. "Who?"

Henry's cheek twitched. "Roger Simmons."

"Roger Simmons?" Jack's voice cracked. "Why would any girl want that brute?"

"It appears he has some charm," Henry said. "And, he works for her father. Her relatives seem to admire him."

"She's too refined for a man like Roger Simmons. I've run into him at the dance halls. He's got charm in front of the ladies, but some fellows have told me stories. The man's a bully."

Henry shook his head. "Evelyn is a woman of intelligence. I trust whatever decision she makes."

"I've told you before, Henry, if you like the girl, you've got to tell her. You can't just sit there staring at her."

Henry busied himself with buttoning his overcoat. "I have left the decision to her."

Jack slapped Henry's shoulder. "When you've got a rival, you punch his nose in. You let the girl know she's wanted and fight for her. You don't just shrug your shoulders and say 'Well, the other bloke's handsome'!"

Stepping past Jack, Henry said, "Should I play hero and climb down wells to fetch a lady's toy?"

Henry turned the corner as Jack called after him, "At least I got a kiss out of it!"

Henry quickened his step. Jack did not understand these matters. He was not giving up. However, if Evelyn read his letter, and was still finished with him, he would respect her choice. He would not become a burden.

An evening wind carried Jack and his bicycle down North lane to his last, most important stop. He ran his day's tasks through his head again. Everything was completed, including his apology to Mrs. Hunter at the Bradford School. The headmistress had been stern, but hadn't sacked him, so the conversation had gone better than he had hoped.

He halted at the vine-covered fence and peered through the opening where he had first lain eyes on the beauty of Cassandra. There she was again, now sitting and dabbing a paintbrush on a set of glass marbles, creating ornate patterns. Her deep purple, satin dress hugged her slender waist, giving her a more refined air than the pink lace from before.

The memory of her kiss warmed Jack's lips as he nestled his bicycle into the vines. He pulled the bouquet of flowers from the basket and tucked it in his belt. After rubbing his hands together, he climbed over the fence. Unaware of his rustling, she picked up one of the marbles and raised a silver-inlaid scope to her eye. With a grin, Jack dropped down, careful to land softly.

Keeping low and quiet, he approached from behind. He edged up to her side, her sweet scent filling the air. Leaning close, he whispered in her ear, "Good evening, Cassandra."

She sprang to her feet, knocking over her chair, her arm flailing back and whacking Jack's chin. The glass marble flew from her hand and cracked on the walkway beside her. A plume of fire rose. Jack shouted and threw his arm around her to protect her. He pulled her with him as he dodged to the side. She shouted as they fell into one of the shrubs lining the path.

Shoving away from him, she stood. Jack pushed himself out of the bush as she snapped and gave a short whistle. The plume of fire spiraled back down to the broken glass and then puffed away. Jack panted as his mouth hung open. He had only seen a magic trick like that before in a carnival. Illusions were a strange hobby for a young woman of her wealth, but seemed more exciting than sitting in a garden alone all day.

He stepped over to the small table. The glass marbles sat on cotton padding inside a polished box with the lid open. Glowing lights circled in the marbles, giving a cloud-like aura. He had seen similar glowing under the cracks of doors while mopping at the Bradford School. Mrs. Hunter had dismissed his questions and said they were only experiments with electricity.

He reached out to prod one with his finger. Cassandra snapped the lid shut.

"Mr. Kingston, most men knock and ask permission to enter." Her tone was soft and a smile was on her lips, but her eyes were as cold as a frozen lake.

Jack stepped away while rubbing the back of his neck. This was not the reaction he had been hoping for. "I thought hopping the fence would be faster." He forced a smile as he held out the bouquet. Maybe she liked to keep her hobby a secret. "I wanted to thank you for getting me out of the well last night."

She took the bouquet, but set it on the table.

"Sorry about interrupting your work." He nodded toward the box. "Where'd you learn tricks like that?"

"It's a hobby I took up from my mother," she said. "Did you leave something behind?"

"No. I—" There was a growing chill in the air. He had come this far, however, and had to complete his mission. Forcing a lopsided smile, he moved toward her. "Actually, yes. I left you all stuffed up here, alone. I was hoping you'd step out with me."

She glanced at the upper floors of the mansion. "I doubt my father would approve."

"Then let me meet him and persuade him to let you go out." Jack tucked his thumbs in his belt and gave a friendly nod. Her coldness was probably caused by her father scolding her the night before. If she was afraid, he needed to make sure she felt more comfortable.

Cassandra blinked, her eyebrow twitching up. "With a young man who prefers sneaking in rather than entering through the gate?"

Jack shrugged. "I'm sure he remembers being young and losing himself around a pretty girl."

She lifted her skirts and began walking toward the gate. "I am flattered by your visit, Mr. Kingston, but I would be far less worried if you left before Father knows you're here."

Jack hopped to her side and touched her hand. A spark of electricity stung his fingers as the gas lights around the garden ebbed. He pulled his hand away, and the lights returned to their full brightness.

Cassandra wiped her palm on her skirt while she kept her tight smile and led him to the gate. Jack rubbed his fingers on his shirt, trying to lighten the sting. Maybe the spark had been caused by some buildup from painting the electric marbles. He would have to go by the university library and see if there were any books on magic tricks. She might warm up if they had something more to talk about.

"Your brother, Henry, came by yesterday to ask after you," she said. "How is he?"

"Henry?" Jack tucked his hands in his pockets, his lips warm. He would probably be better off venturing for a peck on her cheek. "Best as he can be. Had some trouble with his girl." He nodded toward the gate. "I'm sure your father wouldn't notice if we happened to stroll down to—"

"What sort of trouble?" She stepped toward him, her blue eyes searching his.

Jack scratched his head. Maybe she had been cooped up alone too long and looked for any sort of gossip. Henry and Evelyn's problems might interest her, and her lips were soft and full in the evening light, but he wasn't going to use his brother's personal life to get a girl.

"That's between him and Miss Evelyn." He jerked his thumb toward the street. A more relaxed setting away from her father's gaze might help. "There's a new cafe on Garnum Street, and—"

A warm tingle ran along Jack's arm as Cassandra touched it. The touch was far more pleasant than the spark before. He found a genuine smile growing. All he needed was to get her out of the garden, go have a bit of fun, and he would see the warm girl from the night before.

"Your poor brother must be so worried," she said. "Tell me about this Evelyn. Perhaps I can help."

He tipped back his cap and rubbed his forehead. A woman's perspective on the matter might provide a clean view and help Henry win Evelyn back. First, he needed to know her better.

"Why don't we talk over a nice drink?" He offered his arm.

"Oh, no." She patted his arm and the gas lamps dimmed again. "I was in terrible trouble for everything yesterday."

Jack frowned as Cassandra pulled her hand away and the gas lamps returned to their steady light. Scratching his head, he said, "Have you had anyone look at your lamps recently?"

"They are always a bit unsteady," she said. "What is your brother's girl like?"

"Evelyn's a fine woman." Jack put his hands on his hips and stared at the nearest lamp. The flame seemed steady. "I've got my tools on my bicycle. If we turn the lights off, I can see about fixing them."

He took a step toward the gate. Cassandra grabbed his upper arm, her grip as strong as his brother Richard's. Jack stopped.

"What sort of family does she come from?" Cassandra released her hold and ran her fingers along his arm. His heartbeat quickened as a warmth followed her touch. He began to smile as he leaned toward her, forgetting the lamps and the garden. His mouth was nearly to hers, when she placed her finger over his lips and whispered, "What is her father's trade?"

"Tanning." He pulled her hand into his. He cried out as a sharper zap stung him, a green flash sparking out from where his hand touched hers. The glass on the gas lamps shattered.

Jack stared down at his hand, the electric shock clearing his brain. There was no mark, but it still stung. He had seen a similar green flash before, while in the greenhouse at the Bradford School. One of the teachers thought they were alone and the green flash shone as some student's plant seemed to revive itself. She had asked him to keep her secret. He had marked it down to another experiment with electricity, but he often wondered if he was missing something.

The croaks of the frogs in the well seemed to grow louder as Jack glanced back at the broken glass from the marble. The fire could just be some fine parlor trick and the gas lamps could just have a bad pipe. Yet, the frogs' croaking rose and an uncomfortable certainty filled him.

The dream of dropping into the water and staring at webbed hands was far too real. He rubbed the back of his head as the vague memory came into focus of being pulled up in a net, kissed, and then whacked on the head by a bucket. It was almost too ridiculous to believe, but the memory didn't feel like a dream.

Henry already thought Jack had fanciful ideas and silly notions about how the world worked. Her touch from a moment ago had dulled his mind, but everything was converging into two truths: magic was real and he was in trouble. If he didn't want to be a frog again, he needed to get out of the garden.

Forcing a smile and walking toward the gate, he said, "It's been good to see you. I'll tell Henry you asked after him. Good night."

Cassandra stepped in Jack's way, all false smiles lost in a cold glare. He moved toward the gate. She threw her arm around his shoulders and pulled him into a kiss. A shock thudded in his chest as he tried to push away. Then, there was the softness of her lips, the warmth of her breath, the sweet smell of her hair. The pressure and fear of a moment ago ebbed away as he leaned into the kiss. A longing filled him as she let go and stepped back.

His mind felt dull as his grin broadened. He tried to remember what he had been so worried about a moment ago. There was something about frogs, but it must only be from her need to clean the well. He laughed as he leaned toward her again. She stepped to the side and opened the gate.

"Go. Before my father sees you."

Jack giggled as he tottered out. He turned around right as she shoved the gate shut. Leaning against the gate, he said, "I'll be back tomorrow."

She reached through an opening and touched his hand. He stood numbly, absorbed by her beauty.

"You will go home, Jack Kingston," she said, "and you will not come back to see me. However, you will tell your brother to visit."

Jack nodded and winked. "We'll find a way to meet again. Don't you worry."

Her voice deepened. "I am far from worried, Mr. Kingston. Good evening."

Jack whistled to himself as he sauntered over to his bicycle and climbed on. He sped through the city, laughing as he swerved around carts and motorcars. There'd be nothing better than Henry's face when he learned Jack had gotten a second kiss.

Cassandra wiped her lips with a handkerchief as she marched back to her worktable. She grabbed the bouquet and tossed it to the scorch marks where the fire had risen. With a melodic whistle, she gathered wisps of magic remaining around the broken marble. There was just enough to build a small flame, but the flowers burned.

Jack had seen too much. The devotion spell would dull his mind a little while, but she needed to move quickly if she was going to gain hold of Henry. This Evelyn might be a problem as well, but Cassandra could not worry about her until she knew more.

She opened the wooden case. To the naked eye, all the marbles glowed with an almost-electric light. They made a nice show but hid the real power.

She raised her silver spectroscope and the glow became a layer of vibrating waves. With a twist of the lens, the light and sound waves faded away, leaving only a glowing spectrum of magic waves. The pulsing lines had multiple colors twisting together, capturing threads of power to perform the tasks she needed. Waves arched around each marble and the threads of light inside the glass braided together, waiting for their power to be unleashed. One marble had a trail of energy seeping out. She lifted the brush and painted another swirl on the outside. The glow inside shifted and the trail pulled into the marble.

With the magic secured, she closed the cotton-lined box. Her ability to gather magic in the moment was growing more inconsistent. She hadn't sensed Jack coming and some of her power had leaped out by accident. She needed to pull more power into objects, but she had to keep an eye out for passers-by looking in. She had enough frogs and didn't need anyone asking questions.

She set the box in a crate and carried it into the empty mansion. Her shoes echoed on the marble floor before she stepped onto the carpeted runner. When she had been a girl, these halls had been full of servants, guests, and excitement. Now she felt trapped in her own mausoleum.

Once on the second floor, she stopped outside of the engraved double-doors leading to the room where the old man lay. Even with the doors shut, she could hear his wheezing. Each rasp of his breath stung, warning her his time was soon ending. He could not go and leave her with so much left to do.

She swept past the doors and entered her own chambers. With the crate locked in a cupboard, she sat at her gold-inlaid desk. All the reports she had requested in the morning were collected and stacked neatly. As the clock rang the evening hour, she pulled out paper and a fountain pen. This work was far simpler than magic, but just as key to securing Henry Kingston, and, with time and patience, her freedom.

Chapter 4

Late Thursday morning, Henry read the letter again, hoping the words would somehow change.

Dear Mr. Henry Kingston,

I apologize, but I must decline. It would be wrong of me to use the tickets without you. I have enclosed them for your convenience.

Sincerely,
Evelyn Havish.

Henry tossed the paper down. She had first sent the tickets back Wednesday morning. The question in her note about Jack's safety had given him a slim hope. Wednesday afternoon, he had returned the tickets with a note answering her question and ending with, "I would be honored if you would reconsider and allow me to escort you this Saturday."

Here were the tickets again and now the matter was settled. Evelyn had made her choice and he needed to respect her wishes and close their account. His hands shook as he scratched down a reply and tucked the note and tickets into an envelope.

He removed his spectacles and rubbed his eyes. Dreams of Evelyn dancing with Roger Simmons had haunted his sleep again last night, probably spurred by Jack's boasting over Cassandra kissing him a second time. Jack had dashed about the apartment, telling Henry, "Just go to Evelyn Havish's door and give her one good kiss."

Henry turned back to the ledgers piled before him, filling his mind with the sureness and truth of numbers. He doubted he would find another woman of Evelyn's quality, but he had to carry on. He was twenty-five and in a solid career. If he continued his efforts, he would find a suitable wife, begin a family, and establish himself. She would not be Evelyn Havish, but she would be satisfactory.

Henry looked up as knuckles tapped on his door. Nathaniel Bronhart stepped into the office and leaned his tall frame against the door. The dark-haired man had only been with the firm for two years and had an excellent fiancé. Perhaps, if Henry had followed more of Bronhart's advice, he would not be staring at a rejection letter.

Repressing a wry grin, Bronhart said, "A fine lady has come to see you about opening an account."

Henry adjusted his spectacles as he frowned. "I am an auditor. I do not open accounts."

"She presented your card and said she would only speak with you."

Henry's frown deepened as he stood. "There must be some confusion."

"She was quite insistent." Bronhart's eyebrow arched up. "Mr. Mackabee said to follow her wishes."

Henry sighed and followed Bronhart into the main office. The room was a grid of desks with financial clerks hunched in rote copying and careful calculations. Dozens of fountain pens scratched in near-unison, each a cog in an efficient machine churning out records and reports. Henry had sat for three years among them at his own anonymous sliver of a desk until his promotion to Assistant Auditor two years ago. Bronhart had been at the firm only two months before being promoted to Account Manager. He and Bronhart had earned their promotion through education and precise attention to detail.

Their merit, however, did not prevent the hidden glares of passed-over clerks as they walked to the lobby.

Henry's view of the lady was obscured by Mr. Mackabee's wide girth as he arrived in the entryway. She wore a rich blue gown made of sheening fabric and a long, pointed hat curving over her head with a plume of peacock feathers. Her voice was young and lively as she spoke to Mackabee. The broad man shouted things like, "Did he now," and "I'd never expect."

Bronhart tapped Mackabee's shoulder and Mackabee stepped back. Henry's hand clamped on his cane as his collar seemed to close around his throat. There was nowhere to escape as Cassandra swept past his employer and held out her lace-gloved hand.

"Mr. Kingston, I'm so glad to see you again," she said, a rose hue filling her cheeks as if on cue.

Bronhart let out a snort and covered it with a cough.

His voice like a tuba, Mackabee said, "Kingston, Madame Astrellar was just telling me of how you met." He pounded his hand on Henry's shoulder as he laughed. "I'd never have believed you could be so gallant."

The name Astrellar itched through Henry's mind, a recognition forming without explanation. The hinting arch of Mackabee's eyebrow was not helping his memory.

"Good afternoon, Madame." Henry barely touched her waiting fingers as he half-bowed. She stepped closer, placing her palm against his. Standing and drawing his hand away, he said, "Mr. Bronhart mentioned you want to open an account?"

"Yes." Her voice carried a calculated melodiousness. "My father and I have been looking for a new accounting firm. When you gave me your card the other evening—" She paused to blush and bat her eyes. "I just knew this must be a good firm."

"We're excellent, Madame, excellent," Mackabee said. "You'll not find a more honest and accurate firm in the city."

"I can help you open an account," Henry said. "However, I am not an Account Manager. Mr. Bronhart here is one of our best, and would be better able to assist you."

Cassandra pressed her round, full lips into a pout. "But, I so hoped you and I could work together."

Mackabee's hand tightened on Henry's shoulder. "A word, Kingston."

Henry was barely able to swing his cane fast enough to maintain his balance as Mackabee pushed him inside. Once in Mackabee's office, the broad man slammed the door shut.

In a whisper loud enough to reverberate on the walls, Mackabee said, "Do you know who Cassandra Astrellar is?"

"It is clear she has some wealth, sir."

"Some wealth? Her father is Arturo Astrellar. He may be a recluse no one has seen in five years, but he still has fingers in two-thirds of the businesses in this country. I'd doubt there's a man with more wealth. I've been trying to woo Astrellar's business manager, Albert Hedley, but the man's stone.

"I don't understand how or why, but that girl's taken a fancy to you. She is legal executor and co-owner of her father's entire estate."

"She is?" Henry tried not to wince, imagining what dangerous and vain frivolity could be done with so much wealth.

"I had it checked when she first walked in. I am not sure what she finds charming about you, but you are key to getting her account. That means you do whatever she asks. If she tells you to climb up a balcony and sing to her, you do it. If she tells you to feed her dog with a silver spoon, you do it. If she asks you to wear ribbons and dance around with a blasted tambourine, you do it. Do you understand, Kingston?"

Keeping his shoulders square, Henry said, "Sir, auditing is my specialty. I can manage my current workload, but have time for no more. There are better men for the job."

"She doesn't think so. You will be her personal account manager and I'll have other men take over your regular work."

Henry grit his teeth. Given Mackabee's reddening face, now was not the time to make further protests. He would find a way out later. "I will see what can be done."

They returned to the lobby where Bronhart was using his charm to attempt a conversation. Most women melted before Bronhart's lopsided smile and smooth voice. Cassandra busied herself with batting her fan and analyzing the bland landscapes hanging on the walls. Seeing Henry, she stepped around Bronhart and beamed.

Henry motioned toward the door. "This way, please."

Cassandra's fashioned curls bounced around her head as she slid her arm through his. "Oh, thank you, Mr. Kingston."

All pretense of work disappeared from the main floor as Henry walked past with Cassandra. Pens fell and mouths gaped. Henry pushed toward his office as Cassandra's hip brushed against his. Henry's hand clamped on his cane as he tried not to smell her pervasive perfume. Once in the safety of his office, he pulled out a chair for her. As she sat, he shot a quick glare at the many pairs of staring eyes and shut the door.

A file already rested on his desk with the new account forms. Settling into his old wood chair, he said, "Madame Astrellar, what sort of services were you considering?"

"All of them, I suppose." She waved a hand.

Henry pulled out the selection form. "We have many services. They range from basic bookkeeping, accounts payable, payroll, accounts receivable, auditing, among other services designed to fit the needs of your organization. May I recommend—"

"Thank you again for your assistance the other night." She scooted to the edge of her seat. "I don't know what I would have done had you not rescued me."

Henry glanced up at her, wondering how pulling a ball from a well was rescuing. He drew out another form. "Before we begin, I will need to see a copy of your annual financial reports for the past three years."

"Ah, yes," she said. "I have them here."

She picked up a large handbag which matched her dress and pulled out a thick folder of papers. Her fingers brushed his as she passed them over. He wanted to jerk his hand away, but held his composure. If he kept this meeting on point, it would be over quickly and he could return to his real work.

While he looked through the documents, she let out a sorrowful gasp, turning her head aside. It was well-outlined by light coming from the small window in his office. "I hope you can forgive me. I told you the most horrible lie. I did know where your brother was. He was in my house, injured from falling while trying to clean the well. If my gardener had not been at home, I know the poor young man would have drowned."

Trying not to let his eyes bulge at the long lines of digits in the list of assets, Henry said, "You should look into getting a cover."

"A what?"

"A cover for your well. It would keep frogs and other things from falling into it."

"Oh!" she cried in delight. "How clever, and simple too."

He tried not to glance at her.

"I do hope you understand why I didn't tell you your brother's whereabouts," she said. "The house servants had all gone on holiday and I was alone. I was afraid of what you would think of such an improper situation. I am dreadfully sorry, Mr. Kingston."

Henry busied himself with shuffling through her papers. Looking at her eagerly waiting expression, he decided a direct approach was his best option.

"Madame Astrellar," he said, "My brother and I may not always agree, but he is my brother. I spent much of my evening searching for him and in grave concern for his welfare. I would have preferred to know my brother was safe instead of wasting my evening on a pointless search.

"And, your situation would have been quite proper if your gardener had stayed, and if you had not—" Henry stopped as he tried to think of how to speak of her kissing his brother.

"Do you mean how I woke him?" A blush flushed across her cheeks. "How poorly you must think of me. Let me explain.

"My father's doctor is a man of great wisdom, and told me that a shock to the physiognomy can wake nearly anyone. Apparently, a kiss creates a current of energy between two people. When done between strangers, the shock is small, but effective." A tender smile formed. Henry returned his eyes to the papers. "When done between lovers, I hear it is magnificent."

Henry shifted. Perhaps he needed to open the small window and let some fresh air in.

"So, you see, Mr. Kingston, I was administering a medical technique on your brother to wake him. After meeting you, I felt so horrible for lying. I knew I had to wake him as soon as possible. It was a last, desperate attempt. I do not know what I would have done if it hadn't worked. Please forgive me. I am not normally so full of indiscretion."

Henry glared at the folder. He doubted her and Jack's kiss last night was also a "medical technique".

Holding out a form, Henry said, "If you will check off which services you would like our firm to provide, I will have a contract drawn up by the end of the day. Will that be satisfactory?"

"One small thing." She batted her eyelashes while raising a finger. "I've heard your employer likes to charge a percentage of the wealth managed. Considering the assets I am placing in your care, I think an established fee is more reasonable, and will avoid hidden charges. The payment will be fair, of course, but no more than the market rate." She reached in her bag and pulled another portfolio. "I sent inquiries to other firms in the area and have some remarkable offers. Given your fine character, I am sure you and I can come to a mutually beneficial arrangement."

There was a glint of intelligence in her eyes as she set the portfolio on the table.

Leaning back, she flipped open her fan. With a glance around the room, she said, "This office is too drab for a man of your admirable character. I shall send over a decorator."

Henry glanced at his bare, off-white walls. The simplicity helped him concentrate on numbers and calculations. The room would be unbearable if decorated with plumage similar to the feathers flaring from her head.

"I receive few clients," he said. "It would be wasteful to decorate my office."

Cassandra let out a pattering giggle as she leaned toward him. "It would be my gift."

Henry searched the floor for an undiscovered hole he could climb into. "I prefer not to accept gratuities."

"Then let me do it to thank you for your assistance, and to complete my apology. It is a small sacrifice."

Henry shut the folder detailing her wealth. "If you will finish signing the paper, you may be on your way. I am sure you have much to attend to."

She tilted her chin up as she sighed, the angle emphasizing her long neck. "If only I did."

Her hand was limp as she signed the form. Once the paper was in his hand, Henry stood. Cassandra looked up at him, tears dabbing the corners of her eyes.

He tried not to groan as she said, "If only I had friends. Growing up, dear Papa moved me from boarding school to boarding school. I can speak six languages, but can hardly tell you the names of any girls in my classes. The few who would speak to me soon turned against me, unable to bear my beauty when compared with theirs.

"Once I came to this city, I hoped my father's business manager would introduce me to others. However, Mr. Hedley is a hard and jealous man. He seeks to control me and keep me in the mansion. It is he, not my father who locked the gate. He is cruel and mad and—"

Henry pulled his sleeves straight. "Have you notified the police?"

"How could I? Though I have recently turned twenty-one, and am equal partner with my father, Mr. Hedley has secret books, which contain business dealings essential to our continued wealth. He uses them to keep his position. I am nearly helpless against him."

"And where is your father in these matters?"

"Papa is ill. His heart can no longer bear such worries, which is why I must take up his business affairs. I cannot sit idle and watch my poor papa waste away.

"When you came the other evening," she said, her smile soft and sweet, "You broke Mr. Hedley's chains and showed me what a true gentleman is. Since that moment, I have determined I shall make my presence known in the city."

Stepping toward the door, Henry said, "I am sure you will find many opportunities."

"I received an invitation to a gala this Saturday, but—" She dabbed the corners of her eyes with her handkerchief, "I know no one except you, Mr. Hedley, and the few servants who spy for him at my house."

"You know my brother Jack."

She laughed. "He is hardly suitable for such a fine event." She stood and touched Henry's hand. "Please, Mr. Kingston, be my escort."

He stepped back and tucked his arm behind him. "I do not believe in mixing personal life with business."

She turned her head away as large tears dropped. "You would abandon me, forcing me to hide from society?"

"There are many good men in the city." He approached the door again. "I am sure your father has connections who can make an introduction."

"But you will not join me, even to celebrate the beginning of our business relationship?"

The room felt smaller, the walls becoming tighter around him. On them, he imagined written the profits and fortunes of the Astrellar accounts. Mackabee's red face hovered over him, glaring down with eyes boring through Henry.

If he wanted to remain employed, he had to go. Attempting a polite smile, though it was more a grimace, he said, "For business purposes only, I will escort you."

"Oh, thank you!" She gripped his arm. "I shall return at one tomorrow. Then, we will go to the tailor for your suit."

Henry tried not to grind his teeth. Despite his limited funds, he worked hard to maintain a fine appearance. However, she was a client, and he had to be gracious. "Thank you, Madame Astrellar, but I already have several fine suits."

"Oh, posh." She tapped his shoulder with her fan. "We shall make sure you look very grand indeed."

Henry stabbed his cane into the floor with each hurried step as he escorted her out of the building. On the front stairs, he scanned the street for her motorcar. Instead, a carriage, drawn by four horses adorned with plumage matching Cassandra's hat, stopped in front of them.

Squeezing Henry's arm, she said, "Papa thinks it silly of me, but I prefer the elegance of a carriage to these modern contraptions. Don't you?"

Henry muttered something he hoped sounded like neutral agreement.

The driver wore a dark suit, his shoulders slumping, his empty, dead eyes staring at nothing. He dropped down, moving as if powered by steam, each motion stilted and mechanical. Henry stepped back without meaning to.

As the driver opened the door, Cassandra said, "Thank you, Marvin," and entered. Once inside, she held her hand out the window and smiled. "Till tomorrow, dear Mr. Kingston."

As the carriage rolled away, Henry's fingers curled around his cane handle. He attempted to push away a flood of dread as he imagined what ridiculousness tomorrow would bring.

Chapter 5

Evelyn ran a hand across the rosettes at the top of the dress's bodice. For months, she had eyed the maroon dress with a white lace overlay, dreaming of going to an event fine enough to wear it. At last, she stood wearing it, but the soft silk felt heavier than it should.

"You do look lovely," Mrs. Chancey said as she straightened the hem of the skirt. "Many girls try on dresses this fine, but don't carry them quite as well."

Evelyn looked in the mirror and sighed. It was a beautiful dress. She had done the right thing and had one of her father's messenger boys carry the tickets back to Henry on Wednesday morning. When Henry had sent them again Wednesday afternoon, she had barely looked at the note before returning them. Thursday afternoon, the envelope came back like a persistent odor. She had only glanced at the tickets before shutting the envelope and deciding to take the opportunity to go to the Morveaux. It was unlikely she would ever have the chance again and it would end her correspondence with Henry.

"I'll take the dress," she said.

Mrs. Chancey carefully folded the gown and wrapped it in paper while Evelyn changed back into her regular clothes, the cotton feeling cheaper than before. The package weighed in Evelyn's arms as she stepped outside, though her purse was lighter. Months of savings were now gone and in the till.

As Evelyn walked down the street, she tried to picture herself dancing with Simmons tomorrow night, among all the fine society from North Town. She had considered inviting other men as her escort, but decided to give Simmons' his chance. He had been polite to her and deserved that much. And, if his behavior was poor, Charlie and Dan would stop playing at matchmaking.

She skirted around the crowd now almost always surrounding Talbot's Boots and headed into Lapidary's Jewelry Shop. Her purse was lighter than she liked, but she could still buy something nice to complement the dress.

"Evelyn!" Stacey Foster bounced from the counter. Evelyn laughed as she embraced her childhood friend. "How are you? I haven't seen you in ages."

"It's only been a week," Evelyn said.

Stacey bore a bright smile as she raised her eyebrows. "I hear you are going to the Morveaux for a concert and dance tomorrow night. I imagine you need something."

Evelyn raised an eyebrow as she wondered how Stacey could know. She had barely mentioned it in Chancey's shop. Simmons or her father could have gone around announcing it. Though, Stacey had always been a hub of gossip.

"I don't have much," Evelyn said, "but I wanted to get a pair of barrettes and a necklace."

Stacey returned to the counter and pulled out several worn, velvet-lined boxes. Evelyn told her the budget and Stacey began arranging pieces of jewelry. "Pewter is nearly silver, you know. And, in the right light, copper can look like gold."

As Evelyn looked in the mirror on the counter and tried on some pieces, Stacey said, "I've only been to the Morveaux once for a concert. It is magnificent. I can't imagine how grand the ballroom will be. The man must be working hard to impress you. Do you think he will propose?"

Evelyn raised an eyebrow as she pulled out another necklace. "Why would he propose? This is our first time out."

Stacey frowned. "I thought he had been visiting for months."

"He has only been coming over for the past few weeks."

"Really? That is not what he said last time he came to make a payment on the—" Stacey's mouth snapped shut.

Evelyn looked up at her friend. "The what, Stacey?"

"The— He bought nothing." Stacey waved her hand as she pretended to dust the counter. "He was just visiting."

Evelyn put down the necklace and leaned toward her friend. All she had to do was keep her glare steady for long enough.

"Oh, all right," Stacey said. "I shouldn't show you, but you will love it."

From a locked cupboard, she pulled out a ring box. Evelyn's heart stilled as Stacey opened the box. The gold was real and three small diamonds decorated the band. The ring was beautiful in its simplicity.

"How can he afford it?" Apparently, she had underestimated Simmons' intentions. It was far too early for such a gesture.

"I don't know, but he made a sizeable down payment on it."

"I know what my father's workers make. He can't afford it."

Stacey frowned. "I thought he worked for Mackabee and Sons."

Evelyn felt as if her heart dropped and thudded onto the floor. She could not have heard the words right. "Henry Kingston bought this?"

"Yes," Stacey said. "Who did you think—"

"Roger Simmons. He's who I'm going to the concert with."

Wrinkles creased Stacey's brow. "Who's Roger Simmons?"

"He's one of my father's workers. Charlie and Dan have kept sending him around, and—"

"I thought you'd sworn off the men your brothers send your way. Don't they always end up drunk at McBriar's?"

Evelyn set aside the barrettes she was considering, their luster suddenly less interesting. Still, Simmons seemed better than the other men, and it was no good going back on her word now.

"Only usually," Evelyn said with a forced smile.

Stacey laughed, but then pressed her lips together. Tapping the ring box, she said, "I was so hopeful for Mr. Kingston. The man may be less than handsome, but he clearly has taste. I may have made a few hints once he mentioned it was meant for you. I often do when a man is going to—" Stacey's voice trailed off. Pointing at one of the necklaces, she said, "I think this one highlights your eyes."

"When a man what?" Evelyn said, already knowing the rest of the sentence.

"There is usually only one reason a bachelor buys a lady's ring, Evelyn. I've been told by Mr. Lapidary to hold my tongue better, and let the man surprise her. But, I can't help it!" Stacey closed the ring box and placed it back in the cupboard. "And his plans seemed so romantic."

"What plans?"

"I shouldn't say." Stacey's large eyes glanced at the door. "But no harm in spoiling a surprise that won't come." She leaned toward Evelyn and whispered loudly, "He came in nearly a month ago to pick the ring. When he found out you and I are friends, he asked what you liked to go out and do. He then made a deposit, and left."

"When he came back a week later to make the first payment, he brought a paper with an entire plan laid out. He read it to me and asked for any suggestions. I gave him a few, but his plan— I was bursting to tell you, but I wanted to have you tell me as he swept you off your feet."

"What was the plan?"

Stacey shimmied with delight. "First, the concert and dance at the Morveaux, then, a week later, an afternoon ride in an open carriage to Chasley Park. There, you would enjoy a picnic, serenaded by a string quartet. Later, on Abeyance Night, you would sit together to dinner on the balcony of the Charmant, overlooking the lake. And then—" Stacey leaned her chin on her hand and sighed. "As the fireworks shimmered down over the water, he would bend his knee and propose."

Evelyn waited for Stacey's bout of giggles to quiet before saying, "Really, Stacey. This is the same man who considers foot ointment romantic."

"All I suggested was Abeyance Night, but the rest was his plan."

"If you are so impressed, then perhaps you should try charming him."

"How could I? I see dozens of men come in for engagement rings. Few are as smitten as Mr. Kingston."

Evelyn prodded the barrettes on the counter, hoping to cover her sudden nausea. "Mr. Kingston is a practical man, he wouldn't—"

"I suppose he won't now that you are going with this Mr. Simmons."

Evelyn rolled her eyes at the friendly dig. Stacey walked over to the boxes Evelyn had been searching through. She laid out a pair of barrettes and a necklace with red and amber glass set in brass. They had caught Evelyn's eye earlier, but cost more than she wanted to spend.

"These will complement your eyes," Stacey said, "and highlight the details in your dress."

"How do you know what my dress looks like? I just bought it."

"Mrs. Chancey sends me a note whenever a girl is purchasing a gown. If a lady is looking for a dress, she will be looking for jewelry. She sends ladies my way and I send future brides her way. It's a nice arrangement."

"I can't afford these. If they were a little less, I might."

Stacey smiled as she mentioned a lower number. They played the game of bartering until Evelyn agreed and passed the money over to her friend.

While Stacey wrapped up the jewelry and chattered on about other gossip, Evelyn pulled the envelope out of her handbag. An emptiness throbbed through her as she removed the embossed tickets and set them on the counter.

"Those are beautiful." Stacey placed the jewelry box next to the tickets. "No matter who you go with, you'll have a fine night."

Evelyn gave a brief smile and thank you as she picked up the tickets and slipped them back in the envelope. She frowned at a folded piece of paper hiding inside. A weight pressed against her chest as she pulled it out. Stacey leaned forward with interest. Evelyn gave her another smile as she picked up her packages and left the shop. She was not going to read Henry's note in front of Stacey.

Her purchases grew heavier with each step as she walked down the street. Henry had to have selected the ring at Lapidary's right after the night at Dan's. His distance over the last few weeks could then be from nervousness and not disdain.

She reached the small park on the corner of Gridhorn and Willow and sat on a bench beneath a tree. She unfolded the paper and smoothed it on her lap. His words would either confirm her anger or prove her wrong. Holding her fist to her mouth, she read the scrawled writing.

Evelyn,

What can a farmer's son do to regain your favor?

Henry Kingston

Evelyn carefully folded the letter and looked out at the green lawn without seeing anything. Tuesday evening ran through her head again. Henry had already been in a foul temper because of Jack going missing, and then there had been Maggie's baby and everyone saying Simmons was her fellow. Had it troubled Henry she hadn't corrected them? She had ignored them so she could try to have a conversation with Henry. She thought he knew better. How many times had he asked to come the next day, when he had rest and everything was calmer? She hadn't listened. He hadn't been wholly right, but neither had she.

She began to walk the few blocks home. The trolley clanged as it approached a nearby corner. Making peace would only take a moment.

Her decision made, she held her packages tight in her arms and hurried her pace. The trolley reached the corner as she did. She grabbed the railing and pulled herself on. The trolley lurched into motion and rattled through the city.

Evelyn watched the familiar brick houses and streets of her neighborhood pass. Then came the granite buildings of midtown, full of banks and law firms. Each second brought her closer to Henry's office. She gripped a handle to steady herself as she wondered what she would do if she and Henry made peace. Was she too late to cancel on Simmons and go with Henry to the Morveaux?

Once at the stop closest to Henry's work, she got off the trolley. She lifted her skirt with one hand and broke into a jog. Dodging around street vendors and businessmen passing between meetings, she approached the stone steps of the gray building marked, *Mackabee and Sons*. She panted as she grabbed the banister and ran up the stairs.

Pulling together her best composure, she entered the dim interior of the lobby.

"May I help you?" the stern-faced receptionist said from her raised desk.

Evelyn ran her hand through her hair as she glanced at the sterile landscapes on the walls. "I'm here to speak to Henry Kingston."

The receptionist raised her painted eyebrows and muttered, "Popular young man lately." She picked up a pen. "He is out with a client. If you wish to open an account, Mr. Bronhart and Mr. Flemhold are available."

Evelyn held her packages to her stomach as she stared at the mole on the receptionist's chin. "Mr. Kingston doesn't meet with clients."

Tapping her pen on the desk, the receptionist said, "You are welcome to leave a note, in case he comes in. However, his schedule says he will be gone for the rest of the day."

Evelyn glanced at the opaque, stained-glass doors dividing her from Henry's office before taking the offered paper. She quickly wrote, *I need to speak to you as soon as possible. I will be home all evening..*

She lifted the pen before adding, *There is some hope*, and signed her name.

After folding the paper, she handed the note to the receptionist. The woman pursed her lips and plucked the paper from Evelyn as if it were carrying something contagious. Her thin, painted lips curved into the semblance of a smile.

"I'll leave it on his desk."

Evelyn gave a quiet thank you before exiting the building. Her stride was quick as she walked back to the trolley stop.

Once there, she leaned her chin on the package holding her dress. Henry was an assistant auditor. He didn't see clients. Perhaps Mackabee was adding to Henry's duties so he could grow.

The trolley heading toward her neighborhood arrived and she climbed on. She sat on the polished wood bench as the trolley bumped along Carter Avenue. From her handbag, she pulled her calling card and a pencil. All she needed to do was write a note and leave it at Henry's apartment.

A weight began to lift from her shoulders as she tapped the pencil against her hand, waiting for the conductor to announce Dronan Street. She had only been to Henry's apartment once. It was three months ago, on a bleak day full of sleet, when Henry had stopped in for a coat and an umbrella.

She hopped off the trolley as it came to the corner of Dronan and Carter and walked in the direction she believed he lived. After three blocks, she stopped. Ahead of her was row upon row of tightly packed apartments.

From her purse, she pulled the envelope. The return address was his office.

She stared at the rows of buildings. It would take hours to search for Henry's apartment, and she had already been out longer than she planned.

Walking back to the trolley, she tried to remember any detail which could help her find Henry's apartment. Nothing came.

Though the sun shone as she climbed aboard the trolley, a coldness settled on her skin. She would look through her box of notes at home, but it seemed everything had either been sent from his office or given in person.

She soon returned to the familiar streets leading home, past houses, which each had their own identity. Once at her parents' home, she opened the front door and followed the scent of fresh-baked bread into the kitchen.

Marjory glanced up from kneading and smiled. "Which dress did you get?"

Evelyn set down the package, which seemed much heavier now. "The maroon one with the lace overlay."

"Oh! That's a lovely one."

"I suppose." Evelyn sat at the kitchen table and leaned her chin on her hand. She wished she could spin her chair and go back in time to Tuesday night. Things would be simpler if she could change their conversation and accept his invitation.

Still pounding the dough, Marjory said, "Is everything alright?"

Evelyn stared at the chair where Henry had been sitting a few nights before. Her voice quiet, she said, "Henry, he—"

Marjory slapped down the mound of dough. "What did he do?"

Evelyn pulled out Henry's note. "He sent this to me, but I didn't see it until an hour ago. When I turned down the tickets, I was still angry, and now—" She pressed her lips together. Now was not the time to tell her mother about the ring at Lapidary's. Instead, she said, "I'm going with Roger Simmons, but I'd rather go with Henry." She groaned as she placed her hands over her face. "I sound like Julie talking about her beaus."

Marjory wiped her palms on her apron before pulling Evelyn's hands between hers. "Are you going to talk to him?"

"I left a message at his office, but he won't be back all day. I went to leave a note at his apartment—" She shrugged as she gave a tired laugh even as a tear threatened. "But I don't know where he lives."

Sitting in a chair, Marjory said, "If you really want to talk to Mr. Kingston, I'm sure your father can find out where he lives."

Evelyn shook her head. "I think matters'll be worse if Dad gets involved."

"John can get a bit too excited." Marjory smiled. "But he can help."

Standing and picking up her packages, Evelyn said, "It's too late to cancel on Mr. Simmons now. I'll go with him tomorrow. Hopefully, Henry'll stop by his office tonight." She looked in her mother's eyes. "What he said was wrong, but he meant well, and I—"

"We all get cross sometimes." Marjory pressed her firm hands to Evelyn's shoulders and looked her squarely in the eyes. "You're a grown woman, Evelyn. If you don't want to go with Mr. Simmons, you don't have to."

Evelyn squeezed her mother's arm. "I made a promise."

"Well, if you happen to catch a cold, or get some other illness tomorrow night, you let me know."

Evelyn laughed and kissed her mother's cheek. "I'll remember that if I need it."

Henry fumbled with his keys, as he tried not to yawn. The afternoon appointment for a suit had dragged out as Cassandra had gone to Cathedral Corner and stopped in to visit all four churches at the intersection. She bowed before each statue of the Dalthonian Council ruling the heavens and muttered a prayer.

"You can never be sure which is correct," she said before tightening her grasp on Henry and pulling him into a dinner engagement and a brief carriage ride.

She had prattled the whole evening, her eyes and attention scattered by the wonders around them. All he could think about was the joy of returning to his apartment, enjoying a warm cup of tea, and reading the paper.

At last released, Henry arrived home and reached to turn the key in the lock. The door slammed open and Jack stormed out. Henry stepped to the side to avoid being knocked out of the entryway and down the stairs.

"You act like you've got no interest in her." Jack slapped his fist against his palm. "Then I see you two strolling around town."

Jack shoved Henry's chest. Henry's shoulder hit the wall as he stared at his brother. His eyes were bloodshot, his face lacking color.

"What's the matter, Jack?"

Henry slipped out of Jack's path and edged toward the stairway. Jack couldn't have been out drinking. A drunk Jack would be laughing and making jokes. Henry had only seen Jack this angry when their cousin Rupert had locked their youngest sister in the outhouse overnight.

"You've stolen my girl!"

Jack pushed Henry's shoulders. Henry's feet slipped as he grabbed for the banister. He shouted as he lost balance and tumbled down the half-flight of stairs. His jaw knocked on a step, sending a jarring pain up through his teeth. The fall ended as his back thudded against the wall, his legs dangling in the air. A numbness was already spreading along his arms and ribcage. More pain would come in a moment.

He rolled onto his side as Jack pounded down the stairs. Henry began pulling himself away.

"Henry!" Jack grabbed Henry's coat. Henry tensed his leg, ready to give a sharp jab with his knee. He stopped as he looked in his brother's eyes. They were less bloodshot and color seemed to be returning to Jack's face.

"You alright?" Jack rubbed his eyes as if waking. "I'm sorry. I saw you with her, and— I couldn't think. I was just so—" He glared at his brother. "How could you do this to me? I told you how much I like the girl."

Henry blinked as the numbness left his chin and it began to throb. "You are speaking of Cassandra Astrellar?"

Jack folded his arms. "Who else would I be talking about?"

"She is only a client for my firm. We were out on business."

Jack narrowed his eyes. "There was a lot of laughing for a business meeting."

"I cannot help her behavior." A warm trickle of blood ran down from a scrape above his eyebrow. He pulled out a handkerchief and pressed it to the wound. "Let's step inside so I don't bleed out on Mrs. Flossom's carpet."

Jack nodded. Henry held onto the banister with one hand, his bent leg more sore after the fall. At the top of the stairs, Jack picked up Henry's cane and handed it to him.

"I didn't mean to rough you up so much," Jack said. "It's just—you know how crazy I am about her."

Henry glanced at his brother, but decided not to question the level of sanity needed to be attracted to a vapid beauty like Cassandra. Instead, he said, "I have no such interest in her."

Jack's eyes remained narrow as he nodded. He led Henry inside the apartment and put a kettle on the gas stove. As the water heated, he joined Henry at the card table they used in their dining area. He handed Henry a towel and sat down.

Henry switched out his handkerchief for the towel. "I don't understand your interest in the lady, but I will help you however I can."

Jack snorted before stabbing his finger at the table. "I'll win Cassandra. You'll see. And if I can do that, you can get Evelyn back."

"My acquaintance with Evelyn is over." Henry breathed in, pushing back the image of her final letter.

Jack sat forward, his eyes watching Henry. "You're supposed to be the smarter one out of the two of us." He pointed at Henry. "I bet you could walk up to her door tonight and work things out."

Henry shook his head. "I insulted her. I did not mean to, but it is done."

The teakettle whistled and Jack rose with a grunt. A moment later, he returned with the tea tray, some bandage plaster, and a bottle of brandy.

Mixing the hot water with the plaster, Jack said, "You told me to work for what I want. Despite what you might think, I've followed your advice." Jack slabbed a splotch of plaster on Henry's scrape and smoothed it with the towel. "Over the last couple months, between work and school, I put in an application to become an officer of the law." He leaned back and looked Henry in the eye. "And, just the other day, I found out I got in."

Henry blinked as he straightened his spectacles. "I didn't know you wanted to be a police officer."

Jack scratched his ear. "I was hoping to drop it on you and brag." He slapped down the towel. "But I think I've done enough to you tonight."

Despite his sore jaw, Henry smiled. Their mother had sent Jack to live with Henry to have a better life. Henry had watched Jack grumble through his studies, wondering what sort of profession Jack wanted. He would be miserable in Henry's firm, no matter the opportunities. Jack was far better suited to the packed life of a police officer.

"Congratulations." Henry rose and poured the brandy into two cups. He raised his, but Jack put his hand on Henry's arm.

"You've got to think about what you want and I doubt it's to be stuffed up in your office at Mackabee and Sons." Jack let go of Henry's arm and picked up his cup. "She's not lost to you yet, Henry."

Chapter 6

Evelyn tried to ignore Simmons' light snore as the soprano's final song rose toward its climax. Leaning forward, Evelyn hoped the vibrant tones of the woman's voice would drown out the rest of the evening. Dinner at the Copper Spoon had been full of Simmons repeating, "McBriar's a good dancing place. So is Jasper's," in between his eyes following the swinging hips of the waitresses. Once at the Morveaux, he snuck winks to passing young women as he escorted Evelyn inside. When she and Simmons were seated, he tried to slide his hand around her waist. She pushed his arm away but he leaned close, whispering, "Come on. You know you're my girl."

She glared at him, wishing she had accepted her mother's suggestion of sudden illness. "I am no one's girl, Mr. Simmons."

He gave her a grin and wink, and then the show mercifully began. With Henry, the conversation before the curtain rose would have turned toward the engineering of the elegant building. The concert hall was sculpted out of the ground, going at least three stories deep. Above the arched ceiling carrying the sweet voice of the operatic singers was the marble floor of the ballroom.

With Simmons, she slid deeper into her chair, seeking to forget him and lose herself in the swelling music, the elegant ballet, the grand costumes, and the gilded sets.

Now, the soprano's final note dissipated in the air, filling the hall with her aching sorrow and tragedy. Evelyn grinned as she joined the standing ovation. The applause and bravos grew louder as the curtains cascaded closed and the players made their bows.

Simmons started awake with a snort. Blinking away his bleariness, he straightened his rented vest and clapped loudly. "Good show. Good show."

The audience lights brightened, revealing the upper class sitting in their filigreed boxes, displaying their best fashion. Evelyn's own dress was nothing next to the ladies' ruffled and beaded gowns. She tried not to compare the men's tailored suits to Simmons' rumpled jacket and trousers. He had done the best with what he could afford, just as she had.

The chatter in the upper floors quieted and everyone gazed toward the rear of the theater. Evelyn frowned and followed their stares. Her heart jolted as there, standing at the center of everyone's focus, was Henry.

Their eyes met, but he looked away. Still clapping, Henry leaned over and said something to the woman beside him. Evelyn twisted her fan in her hands as a chill spread through her.

Henry's companion was like a statue of a goddess come to life. Her dress was emerald green satin, gleaming as if the fabric were made of jewels. A glittering, gold scarf fanned across her middle, accentuating the exquisite curves of her frame. Her skin was smooth and perfect, her blonde curls arranged in elegant fashion.

Evelyn forced herself to keep her eyes on Henry. Other than the yellowing bruise across his jaw, Henry's face was gray and pinched. The woman grabbed Henry's arm and whispered in his ear. He nodded blankly as his eyes scanned the box, seeming to seek a way out. Evelyn gripped her skirt as her hands tensed. Was he bothered Evelyn was there or did he not want to be with his companion?

"Ladies and Gentlemen," came the booming voice of the announcer. "Please, join us on the dance floor for the rest of the evening's festivities."

A set of gilded white stairs appeared as the red curtains drew back. The evening's singers lined the stage and broke out in a cheerful song. With a flash of sparks and lights, the first group of couples walked up the stairs and to the ballroom above.

"Bunch of poppycock," Simmons muttered as he lurched to his feet. He leaned toward her and shouted over the voices and music, "We don't belong with these swans. McBriar's is open for a few more hours. They've got that band from Willington and some good whiskey."

White gossamer curtains floated down on the stage to create an archway into the hall. Beyond was the sort of dance Evelyn had never experienced before. She was not going to give up standing on the ballroom floor due to Simmons' discomfort.

"Mr. Simmons, I might never be able to come here again," she said. "I will go on alone if I need to."

"No." He cleaned his ear out with his pinky. "I'm a gentleman and I promised you a good night out. I just think we'd have more fun at McBriar's."

He wiped his finger on his pants and offered his arm. Taking a breath, she placed her arm on his. One half-hour in the hall beyond, then she would end the evening and never give Simmons her time again.

They joined the other guests filing out of the rows and into the ballroom. Simmons grunted as he looked over the crowd, and then grinned.

"Who's that girl with Kingston?"

"I don't know."

"We'll have to say good evening, won't we?" He straightened his tie with a wink.

Evelyn glanced back as Henry and his companion arrived on the ground floor. Women shook the arms of their dates, trying to wake them from a beguiled stupor. Once the emerald-gowned woman passed, the men grabbed their dates by the arm and followed. Men shoved against each other, trying to edge closer.

Henry glanced at Evelyn as he passed her row, a bewildered plea in his brown eyes. Before she could begin puzzling what he was trying to tell her, Simmons dragged her with him and elbowed his way through the crowd. Evelyn held onto Simmons' arm, trying to slow the large man down while other women cried out at the rudeness of their escorts.

Simmons threaded through the crowd until he and Evelyn were right behind Henry and his companion. As they walked up the stairs to enter the ballroom, Evelyn wanted to touch Henry's shoulder, but held back. When they reached the ballroom, the woman pulled Henry away to the dance floor.

Stepping out of the entryway, Evelyn took in the ballroom. The ceiling was covered in white, sheer fabric with lights twinkling across it. Acrobats and aerialists swung and spun as streamers wrapped around them. Costumed men breathed fire, creating an archway for the incoming guests. Several tables were laden in a spread of fine pastries and foods she hardly recognized. At the end, was a tower of champagne flutes quickly being pulled apart by impressed guests.

A man shoved against Evelyn before moving past, leaving his date behind. Evelyn kept hold of Simmons' arm as she stepped out of the main path. Simmons moved with her, but his attention was on the growing swirl of dancers in the center of the gold-hued ballroom.

In the center was Henry and his companion. His face wrinkled in concentration as his head bobbed with the rhythm, his steps stilted and behind the beat. His companion glided with him, her small feet barely moving. She was the calm center of a torrent of staring men colliding into each other, forgetting their dance partners.

Gripping Evelyn's arm tight enough to bruise, Simmons said, "We've got to dance."

"Let me go," she said, pushing him away.

Simmons looked at her almost as if he didn't know her. The first song ended and his eyes cleared. Letting go of her arm, he rubbed his head, "Sorry— er— I—"

Other men were shuffling, trying to appease their scowling companions.

The melody of the second dance began. Simmons straightened his too-tight jacket and said, "Since we're here, let's try one dance, ay?"

Evelyn hesitated before placing her hand in his. The dance was rough and quick, though other dancers looked smoother. Even the finer-dressed men, however, were sweating as much as Simmons. As they did a second dance, Evelyn felt she should be having a better time than she was. Perhaps it was the way Simmons hammered through each step, or how he kept craning his head to follow Henry's companion.

He invited Evelyn to a third dance, but she said, "I need a moment to rest."

He grunted his assent and kept his arm in hers as they went to the tower of champagne. He chugged a glass and wrinkled his face. "What's this spit? It probably costs more than my month's rent."

Evelyn looked up at the carved molding and murals lining the walls. If only she had accepted Henry's written apology. Then, he might not look so miserable as he tried to keep up with the dance, and she could enjoy the Morveaux without keeping a wary eye on her escort.

Taking another glass of champagne, Simmons said, "Look at these men in their spit-polished boots. They probably don't even know how to pull their own pants up. Been pampered all their lives, and think it's their right to have these grand parties while men like me sweat our lives out making them money." He placed the empty glass on a passing servant's tray and took another. "These women probably wouldn't know a real man if they saw one."

He downed his next drink and pulled out his pocket watch.

"McBriar's is still open, Evelyn. Let's go join—"

His voice trailed off as Henry and his companion danced by again. Simmons stepped forward, joining the growing crowd of men gaping at her.

Evelyn set her full champagne glass on a waiter's tray, deciding some fresh air might clear her head. She pulled her shawl over her shoulders, covering her muted dress as she skirted the edge of the crowd. The room glittered and pulsed with a class and magnificence just beyond her reach.

Arriving at the double-doors leading to the garden, she looked back. Henry bobbed alongside his date, his face pinched as he tried to keep pace. He was drowning in the crowd, the circle of men tightening, trying to push him from his companion. Their dates were only a means of approach, an opportunity to bask in her aura. Despite their fine suits and slicked hair, these men were no better than many men Evelyn had gone on evenings with.

She walked outside and followed a small sign reading "Roof Open" to a narrow staircase. She climbed up to the roof and strolled around the large dome at the center of the building. Several couples sat on shadowed benches, their lips engaged in improper public conduct.

At the end of her circuit, she went up another few steps and onto an empty balcony. A light breeze blew as she leaned on the railing, music lilting up from the ballroom. The city lay below her, a pattern of lights stretched out, curving along Chalice Lake on one side, fading into the forest leading to Craggsville on the other. The corner of lower town where she had grown up was just a few dots, a small box she rarely had the chance to venture from.

Resting her chin on her palm, she inhaled the cool night air. Simmons could stay down there, gawking at Henry's date. She would absorb this canvas of quiet beauty, holding onto it for future days of washing dishes, scraping hides, and scrubbing floors. Tonight, she could be a lady without the daily cares of a tanner's daughter.

Footsteps and the familiar tapping of Henry's cane approached. She stood fully, her hands gripping the brass railing to steady herself.

"Evelyn," he said as he reached her side, his forehead dotted with sweat. "The woman I am with, Madame Astrellar, is only a business client." He took a deep breath to slow his panting. "I didn't know she was bringing me here till we arrived."

Evelyn rubbed her thumb along the railing before turning to face him. His skin was gray and his eyes bore heavy shadows. All she had wanted to say yesterday rushed away from her. He had never looked so tired and miserable before.

"I am sure Mr. Simmons will be here soon." Henry shifted his grip on his cane and turned to walk away. "I'll let you return to your evening."

Evelyn swallowed, hoping to clear the tightness in her throat. "He isn't coming."

Henry's arms went rigid. "I can retrieve him for you, if you wish."

"No!" Evelyn clamped her mouth shut. She hadn't meant to shout., "I'd prefer if he stayed downstairs."

Henry's voice lowered. "If he has done anything—"

"It's not—" She glanced at Henry, his brown eyes hard as he watched the stairway. "He's spent the evening grumbling and I decided I'd rather be alone."

The corner of Henry's mouth twitched up, but the smile faded. "Then, I'll leave you to enjoy the view."

As he took a step, she touched his arm. He leaned on his cane and stared at her hand as if he did not know what it was.

Pulling her fingers away, she said, "I've been thinking about last Tuesday and I— I'm sorry." She pressed her hand to her stomach, hoping to give herself the courage to finish. "With your brother's disappearance, my family interrupting, and—" She couldn't help but give a small laugh. "Maggie's baby, it was a poor evening to discuss anything."

Henry nodded, yet his hand clenched the head of his cane.

"I was wrong to say what I did." He glanced at the short stairway leading to the balcony. "After these past two days of assisting Madame Astrellar, I have realized—" His eyes turned back to her. "You are fortunate to have your family."

He seemed about to say something more, but moved again to walk way.

"I spoke with Stacey at Lapidary's yesterday. She showed me— She said—" Heat rose in her cheeks. She had spoken too hastily. She should have been more careful about bringing up the ring.

Henry looked at her, a stiffness in his shoulders.

"It's beautiful," she said. "I just wish I'd known what you were planning." She swallowed. "But, you have given no sign except—"

She stopped. She could not bring up the evening at Dan's apartment. Nothing wrong had happened, yet she felt awkward mentioning it.

Henry knocked his cane against the railing as he gazed out at the city. "I don't know how to be charming. When I try, I—" He shook his head as he looked down.

"You are a good man," she said. "And don't need to be anything else."

Evelyn's breath stilled as he stood straight and faced her. She waited, her lips pressed together. He needed time to think and balance things in the charts and ledgers he seemed to have in his head.

"May I— It'd be nice to—" He held out his hand. "I'd like to dance with you tonight."

She smiled as she placed her hand in his. His fingers wrapped around hers, his hold firm and strong. He set his cane against the short wall before pressing his trembling hand to her waist. He steadied his feet and straightened his posture. Her smile broadened as she looked up into his face. Apparently, he had taken classes.

A waltz played below and he led her into the first few steps, his leading just firm enough to guide her. On the third step, his crooked leg faltered. She grabbed his elbow as he caught the railing.

His feet slipped before he stood. Brushing off his jacket, he said, "I'm sorry," and reached for his cane.

Evelyn touched his arm. "Just one dance."

He took a steadying breath before taking her hand once more. She gave him an encouraging nod and they danced again. With each successful step, his breath eased into a steady rhythm, his grip on her hand loosening. The stilted steps turned into a smooth waltz, though his rhythm was a touch behind. The beat didn't matter as a soft smile warmed away the worry on his face and they floated together across the balcony. He steadied his feet a few times to release her into a twirl. She laughed as he held his arm above her and guided her spin, and then they came back together.

The music faded and applause echoed below. Henry seemed not to hear and Evelyn decided not to tell him. Their waltzing steps slowed into a gentle swaying. She rested her head against his shoulder and drank in the smell of his cologne. Their steps stilled, his hand pressed to her back as he held her close.

A bouncy tune started in the ballroom below and Evelyn raised her head. His gaze held hers and she could almost feel his aching longing as everything he never spoke filled her. A heat rose in her face.

She rested her palm on his cheek. His breath became quick and short as their swaying stopped. He placed his hand on top of hers while his other hand remained on her waist. She pressed her lips together, trying to quiet their throbbing. The moment needed to be savored.

Her breath caught before he kissed her, the touch of his lips soft and tentative. A thrill shot through her breast and she wrapped her arm around his shoulders. Her whole body felt light, as if barely tethered to the ground.

An emptiness grew as Henry broke away and gasped in air. His eyes were wide and his face pale as he stared at her. He ran his fingers through his hair as he glanced at the stairway. "I'm sorry."

She laughed before covering her mouth. "For what? I thought it was quite nice."

Henry's cheek nearly twitched into a smile, but he frowned. "Your father. He'll kill me." He rubbed his forehead. "I'll be smashed with one fist."

"I don't think he will." She stepped closer and took his hand. Henry stared at their hands together. "In fact, I think both my parents will be very happy to hear we've made peace."

"Jack will be glad." Henry groaned. "But he will gloat."

She smiled and kissed his cheek. He blinked before leaning down and kissing her once more. This time, the pressure was sure and deep, sending electricity through her. He held tightly to her, as if letting go would mean losing her.

They both breathed hard as he drew his lips away. Adjusting his spectacles, he said, "Jack was right."

She giggled and Henry let out a laugh. His arm around her, they walked to the railing. Once they were at the edge of the balcony, she rested her head against his shoulder. She shut her eyes, enjoying the soft breeze as the music lilted below.

"Abeyance Night is a long time from now," she said.

"It is only two months." He tapped his free hand on the railing. "Actually, I have reservations at the Gormand. I was hoping—" He tilted his head. "How much did Miss Foster at Lapidary's tell you?"

"Far more than she should have," she said. "But it all seems quite nice."

A cool breeze blew in from the lake and he pulled her closer, using his back to block the gust. She smiled as she nestled her head against his chest.

"There you are, dear Mr. Kingston!"

Henry jolted away. Evelyn reached for his arm, startled by the fear in his eyes.

"And who is this acquaintance of yours?"

Henry grabbed his cane as he gasped in air. Once his cane was steady on the ground, he squared his shoulders and his composure fell over him like a cloak. Evelyn kept hold of his arm as she turned to face Henry's companion for the evening.

"Madame Cassandra Astrellar," he said. "Allow me to introduce Evelyn Havish."

"Enchanted." Cassandra held out her hand, letting it dangle from her wrist.

Evelyn accepted Cassandra's limp handshake, ignoring the diamond-tipped glare in the woman's eyes.

"Mr. Kingston." Cassandra batted her fan. "Would you be a dear and ask the orchestra to play the Falsay Minuet? It is my favorite and I should hate to end the evening without it."

Henry half-bowed to Evelyn. "May I call tomorrow?"

She restrained a smile. "Yes, Mr. Kingston."

Henry almost reached his hand out to touch hers, but stopped. Pivoting like a soldier, he faced Cassandra and offered his arm.

Cassandra patted his arm with her fan and gave the pretense of a smile. "No. I'd like to follow Miss Havish's example and get some fresh air."

Henry looked to Evelyn. "Is there a song you want?"

Cassandra turned her head away and batted her fan.

"No," Evelyn said with a grin. "But I'll look forward to seeing you tomorrow."

Henry returned her smile before glancing at Cassandra. His face hardened, though a polite smile remained. "I'll return as soon as I can."

Henry nodded to both women. Cassandra watched him disappear down the stairs before joining Evelyn at the railing.

"It's a beautiful view from up here," Evelyn said. Silence seemed a dangerous state with this polished stranger.

Cassandra snapped her fan shut as she leaned on the railing. "You and Mr. Kingston seem quite close."

Evelyn knew the woman's cool, uninterested tone. The wealthy snobs at the Bradford School used it when circling their latest prey. She would not fall into whatever trap this woman was trying to lay.

"We are."

Cassandra tapped her fan on her arm as her blue eyes took in Evelyn's appearance. The tight corners of her mouth hinted at disdain. "He is a remarkable man, isn't he? Honest. Candid. Ambitious without being audacious. A true gentleman. It is no wonder you desire his attentions."

"He'll give his attention where he wishes." Evelyn looked down at her hand, picturing the ring from Lapidary's on her finger.

"And yet, what assets can a lady of your standing offer a young man seeking position?" Cassandra leaned back, letting the lamp light highlight her fine profile. "Your beauty is satisfactory, though unremarkable. I presume, from your dress and the quality of your evening's companion, that you live in comfortable surroundings, but nothing of note. I am sure you must work for your living, given the calluses hidden on your hand. When Mr. Kingston is raised to higher spheres, I fear the drabness of your upbringing would drag him from his full potential."

Evelyn raised her head. The snobs from the Bradford School were never so direct in their rudeness.

"If he is interested in you, he will court you." She pushed herself from the railing and walked away.

"And you will stand aside?" Cassandra said as Evelyn reached the stairs.

Evelyn hesitated her step. "No. I will let Henry do as he chooses."

Cassandra walked toward her. "It will be better for you if you give in now. Mr. Kingston has a strong mind, but he will succumb to my charms."

Evelyn knew she should keep walking, yet she turned around. "You could have any other man here tonight."

"Those men are worthless to me and could be replaced by a thousand others. There is only one Henry Kingston and I have claimed him."

"Henry is not some property." Evelyn stepped toward Cassandra, her fist tightening. She had never punched a woman before, but it was becoming more probable by the moment. "He will make his own choices."

Cassandra pressed her fan to Evelyn's throat. "I have suffered too much to find a man as pure as Henry Kingston. If you stand in my way, I will destroy you and everything you hold dear."

Evelyn huffed out a grunt as she moved to step around Cassandra, but the woman blocked her.

"Bully me again and I'll do more than stand in your way." Evelyn shoved Cassandra's wrist away. The woman was mad. She had to warn Henry. "Good night."

Cassandra snarled as she pushed Evelyn against the half-wall. Evelyn swung her fist, but Cassandra caught the punch in her hand and squeezed Evelyn's fingers until she cried out. Evelyn shook her hand, her fingers aching.

"What are you—"

Cassandra grabbed Evelyn's jaw with one hand and squeezed, forcing Evelyn's mouth open. Evelyn pushed against her assailant's shoulders, but Cassandra was as immovable as stone. With her other hand, Cassandra shoved a piece of chocolate into Evelyn's mouth. Evelyn tried to spit it out, but Cassandra covered her mouth. Her nostrils flared as she sucked in air, until Cassandra pinched her nostrils and held tight. Evelyn's chest burned as she tried to open her mouth, to get fresh oxygen. Her reflexes took over and she swallowed.

The chocolate was thick and syrupy as it slid down her throat. Cassandra whispered a chant in a strange tongue, the pitch high and shrill, and then let go. Evelyn gasped in air as she fell to the ground. She leaned over a potted plant beside her and spat out her chocolate-filled saliva.

Cassandra crouched down and grabbed Evelyn's jaw again, this time forcing Evelyn to look at her. The blue eyes were hard, far from the vapid snob of before.

"Do not test what I am capable of." Cassandra's fingers dug into Evelyn's face hard enough to bruise. "If you want your family to be safe, if you want to protect Mr. Kingston, then you will step aside."

She snapped with her free hand. Evelyn jerked back as a vision rose in her mind of her home burning, her mother fleeing from the fire.

Cassandra stood and smoothed her dress. The drapery of pretense returned to her face as she smiled and said, "Do enjoy the rest of your evening."

Evelyn wheezed in air as Cassandra glided down the stairs. Using the railing, she pulled herself to her feet and said, "She is a madwom—"

The word cut off as her stomach gurgled and something slimy crawled from her throat into her mouth. Her face wrinkled as she ran to one of the nearby planters and wretched into a bush. A frog plopped from her mouth and onto the soil. Bile rose in her throat as the slimy creature's bulbous eyes looked up at her. It croaked and then hopped away.

Evelyn fell onto her knees as she pressed her hand to her head. There was some drug in the chocolate which made her see things. She whispered, "I'll go home and sleep it off and—"

She stopped as something else began to climb its way out of her throat. Evelyn's whole body shook as she spat a small salamander into the bush. She dropped against the half-wall and covered her mouth. Henry had to be warned, but a terror wracked through her, pinning her there.

Chapter 7

Henry hurried toward the orchestra conductor. Each step distancing him from Evelyn made him more ill. He doubted Cassandra wanted a casual conversation. However, Evelyn was intelligent and strong and Cassandra was vain but harmless.

He passed the request to the conductor with a few folded bills. The conductor glanced at the money and said, "In two songs."

Henry muttered his thank you and hurried back toward the stairs. He was nearly to the door, when someone gripped his shoulder. His feet slipped and he shoved his cane down to keep from falling.

"Who do you think you are?" said an alcohol-sodden voice. "Taking the finest girl here like you're some flouncy high-to-do."

Henry turned to face Simmons and his meaty fists.

"I only had one dance with Miss Havish," Henry said.

"Who?" Simmons shook his head. "She's nothing. I'm talking about that other girl."

Henry frowned, his own fist tightening on his cane. This man was more than unworthy of Evelyn. "You are welcome to dance with Madame Astrellar."

"You're not even going to fight for her?"

"I do not see the need."

Simmons jabbed his finger into Henry's chest, and leaned close with his fermented breath. "Too afraid to fight for her? You're just a scrawny little dog yapping. I'll show you what a man should be."

His elbow cranked back. Henry leaned to the side, considering his options of escape. As Simmons was about to release his fist, another man grabbed Simmons' wrist.

"Sir," Nathaniel Bronhart said as he let go of Simmons' arm. The pressure in Henry's chest eased. If Bronhart could take care of Simmons, Henry could return to Evelyn. "Your choice is to leave now peaceably or to be escorted out by security."

Simmons snarled and lurched forward. Before Bronhart could step in the way, Simmon's fist connected with Henry's face. Henry's spectacles cracked as he fell onto his back. Bronhart bowled his shoulder into Simmon's chin and followed with a right hook to the gut. Simmons snarled and swung for Bronhart's face. Bronhart dodged and brought his left fist into Simmons nose. A crunch was followed by a trickle of blood.

Security officers scrambled across the floor and dragged a fuming Simmons out the door. They moved to take Bronhart, but several women who'd been watching protested. As the security officers walked away, Bronhart helped Henry to his feet.

"You should have taken boxing in college." Bronhart brushed off Henry's shoulder. "I thought coming from a farm would have made you handier in a fight."

"I'm usually better at dodging." Henry tried to adjust his bent spectacles.

"Who was that fool?" Bronhart said.

"He was Miss Havish's date." Henry placed his cock-eyed spectacles on his face.

Bronhart frowned. "You let another man bring your girl? And a man like that?"

Henry squinted out of the one good lens. "It's been a complicated week."

"Right." Bronhart grunted and thumped Henry's shoulder. "Be

careful of Madame Astrellar. She may be wealthy, but I don't trust her." He paused as he glanced at the doors leading to the garden. "Although, I don't trust my own date tonight."

Henry rubbed the bruise forming above the one Jack had given him. "I thought you were here with your fiancé."

"I thought I was too. She seems to have forgotten that and is off with some author fellow." He gestured toward the dance floor.

Through the haze of his tilted spectacles, Henry saw Adeline Winkleston float by in the arms of a tall, dashing man with golden hair. He looked as if he had stepped out of one of Jack's ridiculous books. Henry squinted again and realized he had seen the man before in Jack's collection of autographs.

"That's Alvin Westengaard, isn't it?" he said.

"I believe he is," Bronhart muttered as he folded his arms. "And that he'll be escorting her home."

Henry's good eye followed Adeline and Westengaard as they broke off from the crowd of dancers and went through the doors leading to the gardens. They walked up the wide stairs to the roof while Cassandra's skirt swooshed around her as she came down. Henry winced. She had already spent the whole carriage ride here petting his arm and moaning over his bruised jaw. He had only told her he had fallen down the stairs. He did not need her fawning over his eye, which was now swelling closed.

Gripping Bronhart's arm, Henry said, "Tell Madame Astrellar I had to leave on urgent business."

"Is she so difficult, Henry? You never lie."

Henry stumbled to the nearest flower arrangement and dove behind it. Men flocked to the door as Cassandra swept into the room. Bronhart reached her first and directed her attention toward the front entrance. Henry dove through the door behind her and clambered up the stairs, nearly tripping in his hurry. Evelyn should have already come down.

He passed the couples whose lips were still engaged in far less proper conduct than he and Evelyn had enjoyed. Adeline and Westengaard had already taken residence on a dimly lit bench. Henry's fist clamped his cane as he considered intervening on Bronhart's behalf. The thought broke off as quiet sobs echoed from the balcony above.

Scanning the darkness, Henry jogged up the short set of stairs. He followed the sounds of genuine weeping until he found Evelyn. She sat on the ground, her face pressed to her knees, her makeup smeared on her dress and sleeve.

Gripping his cane to steady himself, he knelt beside her. His heartbeat thundered away his words and he pressed his hand to her arm. "What happened?"

She turned her head away, her hand clamped over her mouth. With a shallow breath, she said, "I want to go home."

Henry offered his hand. "I'll take you."

She raised her head and her eyes widened. Touching his bruised cheek, she said, "Are you all—"

Turning away, she made retching noises. Henry looked away as she vomited into the bush, the end marked by a plopping sound.

"Mr. Simmons and I had a disagreement." Henry held out his handkerchief. "Let's get you home."

"Madame Astrellar will be looking—" Her cheeks bulged and she cringed.

"My friend Mr. Bronhart is accompanying her for the moment." Henry tried not to wrinkle his face. "He has told her I have left for urgent business."

He shut his eyes as Evelyn retched into the bush once more. After wiping her face with his handkerchief, she gripped his hand and stood. Her whole body shivered, her skin cold. Leaning against the rail, Henry pulled off his jacket and put it over her shoulders. She held tightly to his arm as they walked to the steps leading back to the ballroom.

Henry paused at the top of the stairs, keeping in the shadow of a marble statue. Cassandra stood beside the door leading to the patio, tapping her fan on her arm. Bronhart talked animatedly, keeping her facing the ballroom. Henry would have to thank him later.

Hoping to find an exit away from Cassandra's line of sight, Henry pulled Evelyn with him and into the gardens. He thought of slowing his step and strolling among the hedges and flowers, Evelyn leaning on his arm. However, Evelyn's face was nearly green from her sudden illness and every passing moment risked Cassandra discovering them.

His shoulder relaxed as he found a side gate leading to the street. Once on the curb, he hailed one of the cabs waiting for the couples to trickle out. Evelyn held to his hand as he helped her inside. He joined her on the bench seat and kept his arm around her as the motorcar puttered away from the Morveaux.

Evelyn burrowed her head against his shoulder and let out a sob. His cheeks went tight. There had already been too many improprieties between them during the evening. Yet, he put his other arm around her and held her tightly. For the first time, he wished all those fairy tales Jack read were true and a single kiss would clear away whatever was ailing her. However, this was reality and what she needed was a good tonic.

The motorcar rolled to a stop in front of her house. Henry paid the driver before helping Evelyn out of the cab and then up the porch stairs. The door slammed open, John Havish's broad build filling the frame.

Evelyn's sobs erupted into wheezes as she fell into her father's arms. Havish glared at Henry as he held his daughter tightly.

Havish's eyes narrowed. "What happened to your face?"

"Roger Simmons, he—" Evelyn stopped as she made another retching noise.

"Not in your mother's bushes." Havish said as he and Henry looked away, avoiding the wet plopping noise.

Marjory Havish appeared at the door and ushered Evelyn inside. Henry leaned against the banister, watching through his one good lens until Evelyn disappeared into the bathroom with her mother. His hand tightened on his cane as he tried to quiet the desire to follow them, to be with Evelyn, and make sure she was safe.

"Why don't you come in for a drink?" Havish said. "Tell me what happened tonight."

The blood drained from his face. How could he explain how improper he had been with the man's daughter? His unbruised cheek was far from safe.

"There is not much to tell, sir," Henry said, his pitch higher than he expected. "Evelyn is ill, and Mr. Simmons—" He rubbed the thick mass of a bruise forming around his eye. "Could use some manners."

"Those're a couple of fine shiners. Did you get a good punch in?"

"No. I should be going." He swallowed as he looked up at the large man. "May I check on Evelyn in the morning?"

A sly grin formed on Havish's face. "Only so long as you explain how she left with Simmons and came back with you."

Henry blinked. The bulging muscles of Havish's folded arms were about three times the thickness of his own. It would be best to make things clear. "Actually, I will accept that drink."

"Glad to hear it." Havish gave a friendly pound on Henry's back as he escorted him inside. "I'd also like to know how her lipstick ended up on your collar."

Cassandra forced a placid smile as she pretended to listen to Bronhart. Other men eyed him with jealousy, jostling to come closer. Cassandra kept her gaze on him, not daring to give anyone else an invitation. The allure spell had worked and Henry had passed the test, but she would be relieved to return home, away from these prying eyes.

Bronhart paused mid-sentence as his own date for the evening floated by in the arms of another man. Glancing at this Westengaard, Cassandra wouldn't doubt the man had an allure spell of his own.

Whatever the cause, the matter was Bronhart's to deal with. Cassandra had enough challenges of her own.

Evelyn Havish had an unfortunate strength of character and would be a graver obstacle than expected. The curse would silence her for now, but Cassandra needed a more permanent solution. She would not let this girl interrupt her plans.

Henry had probably made his escape by now and she needed to make hers. There was no purpose to participating in this pathetic menagerie any longer.

Bronhart attempted a joke and Cassandra forced a laugh.

"So clever, Mr. Bronhart." She tapped his shoulder with her fan before fluttering it. "I must confess all the grandeur of this evening has left me quite exhausted. If you would excuse me."

He glanced to the back of the room where Henry must have escaped and offered his arm. "Let me escort you to the door, at least."

Cassandra smiled and patted his arm. "Thank you, but I don't want to steal you from your evening's companion."

Bronhart's teeth grit together as he held his forced grin.

She swept part of her skirt over her arm and sashayed for the door. Men tumbled toward her as she walked alone. A few fists hit flesh and shouting soon mixed with women screaming and the thud of fainting. The servants rushed to break up the mob while Cassandra walked on.

With her shawl retrieved, she exited the Morveaux. A crowd of drivers stepped forward, each man offering a ride as their eyes glistened with hope. She bestowed a smile on them, but pressed on, forcing them to step out of her way.

As she approached her carriage, Marvin opened the door. She was nearly inside the sanctuary when an arm swung up in her way and a man stinking of alcohol grinned at her.

"One dance before you go," the muscled young man said. "What do you say?"

As Marvin's arms tensed, Cassandra reached in her pocket and fingered one of her glass marbles. She let go. There were too many eyes watching.

She looked at the man again and raised an eyebrow. He was Evelyn Havish's escort. This drunken fool might prove useful.

Holding out her hand, she fluttered her eyes and smiled. "Cassandra Astrellar."

He grabbed her fingers and slopped his lips on her hand. "Roger Simmons."

"I was just leaving," she said, pulling back her hand, trying to ignore the layer of saliva on her knuckles. "But, I am missing my evening's companion. Would you be kind enough to escort me home?"

Simmons pulled down his too-small vest and grinned. "I'd be happy to."

As she climbed into the carriage, she flexed her jaw, stretching her cheek muscles. Her face was going to be sore with the many forced smiles she would have to give on the way home.

Jack rubbed the chill from his arms as he crouched in the bushes outside the entrance to Cassandra's mansion. He should be back at his apartment studying, but he couldn't bear his textbooks any longer. He had done his best to read, trying to ignore his body throbbing for one glimpse of Cassandra. Giving in, he had come here. All he needed now was a few words with her and she would be in love with him.

At last, plumed horses pulled her gilded carriage up the drive of the mansion. Jack began to rise, but paused when Roger Simmons exited the carriage and assisted Cassandra out. Her light and airy laughter chimed through the air, fueling Simmons' broad smile. Jack's chest burned and he ground his heel into the dirt.

Keeping her arm through Simmons' elbow, she said, "And tell me, who supplies Mr. Havish with the skins he turns into leather?"

Simmons grinned at her as he listed slaughterhouses and escorted her to the door. Jack pounded his fist into his palm. She was blind if she couldn't see through Simmons' charm.

The couple reached the porch and Cassandra rested her fingers on the door handle. Simmons leaned close to her, his lips puckering. Cassandra patted his cheek.

"Why don't you come inside?"

The door opened and Jack leaped out from the bush, his pants snagging on a branch. Jack's feet were nearly to the porch stairs, when the door slammed shut. He panted as he glared at the crystalline glass in the door, dividing his rival and his love from him.

Jack crouched along the edge of the house, trying to keep his boots from squelching in the mud. Watching through the windows, he followed Cassandra and Simmons' to a large parlor. A fire burned in his stomach as Simmons put his arm around the woman. Cassandra gave him a teasing laugh and pulled away. Once at the mantle, she lifted the same gold bauble Jack had rescued from the well. Jack stood fully, his heart thumping as he considered breaking through the window.

With a warm smile, Cassandra placed the bauble in Simmons' hand. The broad-shouldered man leaned in for a kiss, but she put a finger on his lips. Jack rubbed his palms together. Maybe she needed something else from Simmons.

Simmons held the bauble up to the light before setting it on a nearby table. As he released the gold sphere, he disappeared in a flash of green light. In his place, a frog plummeted to the floor.

Jack slipped in the mud and dropped flat on the ground, his heart beating off-rhythm. He rubbed his eyes, wondering if he was seeing things from a lack of sleep. Sitting in the well as a frog had only been a dream.

Footsteps echoed toward the window. Jack scrambled across the slick grass and slid behind a topiary bush. Through the leaves, he watched as Cassandra opened the curtains and looked out. He tried to remain perfectly still.

Cassandra pulled the curtains shut and Jack scrambled back to the street. He began to pull his bicycle from its hiding spot in the vines. One of the mansion's doors slammed opened and Jack's whole body jolted.

Crouching, he stared through one of the decorative holes in the fence. Cassandra crossed the yard, holding a large frog in a towel. She reached the well and lifted a wooden cover before dropping the frog inside.

"Goodnight, Mr. Simmons." Letting the cover clang shut, she wiped her hands on the towel and strode back inside.

Jack rubbed his forehead, seeking any signs of warmth from a fever. He followed with a quick slap to his jaw, ensuring he was awake. His skin stung, warning him this was no nightmare.

The green sparks, the flaring gas lamps, and the long set of hours living as a frog were all true. The only lie was his insane attraction to Cassandra.

Once the door shut and the light went off, Jack was on his bicycle and speeding down the street. He had never pedaled faster in his life.

He reached his apartment and threw open the door. "Henry!"

No answer.

Jack ran a hand through his hair. Henry might be stuck as a frog anywhere in the city. No matter what state Henry was in, this trouble was Jack's fault. He should've ignored Cassandra's crying and pretty face. If he had, Henry would be here, safe, and Jack wouldn't be calculating how many of the missing men were stuck in Cassandra's well.

He marched in his room and dumped his box of books across the bed. If magic did exist, the stories in adventure books might be true. Several had men turning into frogs. There might be an answer, a cure, anything to stop Cassandra.

He kept an eye on the door as he flipped through his books, tossing away his textbooks on science and history. Much good they did with a girl who could turn men into frogs.

The clock in the living area clanged after one and Jack paced the apartment while trying to read. Was this how Henry had felt last Tuesday? If Jack had to, he would search the whole city for Henry in frog-form. He didn't know how he would be able to tell Henry from the other frogs. Maybe a frog-Henry would have a tiny pair of spectacles.

Jack ran his hand over his face. He needed to stop and think logically. Yet, nothing was logical in this whole mess.

He jumped as the door opened and Henry entered. Jack shouted as he embraced his brother, glad to see him in full-human condition. Henry stiffened as he pushed Jack away.

"Are you all right?" Henry said. "Have you gone out drinking?"

Jack smiled as he slapped Henry's shoulder. "I'm just glad to see you."

Henry grunted as he tossed his broken spectacles on the table and rubbed his tired eyes. He cried out as he pressed against his swelling black-eye.

Wincing, Jack said, "What happened tonight?"

Henry dropped into an armchair and stretched out his legs. "Roger Simmons punched me."

"Did you get a good punch in?" Jack pulled at his ear. At least Simmons deserved to be a toad.

"No." Henry leaned back as he shut his eyes. "Mr. Havish recommended some techniques for future encounters, but I'd rather avoid the whole matter."

"I don't think you'll have to worry much about Simmons." Jack leaned against the table as he frowned. "Wait, when did you talk to Mr. Havish?"

"After I took Evelyn home."

Jack traced invisible lines on the table with his finger. "But she was at the Morveaux with Roger Simmons, and you were out with Madame Astrellar—" He scratched his head before grinning. "Evelyn's a fine girl to fight over."

"Simmons fought me over Madame Astrellar." Henry glanced at Jack. "I don't understand your fascination with the woman. She was alone with Evelyn for a few minutes and I came back to find Evelyn ill and very upset."

"What sort of ill?" Jack stood up. "Was she green and clammy?"

"A bit." Henry raised an eyebrow. "I thought you were training to be a police officer, not a doctor."

"It's for one of my exams next week." Giving himself time to think, Jack walked into the kitchen and filled the dented teapot with water. "I'll tell you, Madame Astrellar isn't the girl for me after all."

Henry pointed at Jack. "It's good to see you becoming wiser."

"Of course."

Jack lit the gas stove and set the pot on the burner. Leaning against the cupboard, he thought of a dozen ways to begin what he had to say to Henry, but none felt right. He shook his arms and stretched his neck before venturing back into the living room and sitting across from his brother.

"How much do you believe in magic?" Jack looked into his brother's unswollen eye.

Henry snorted. "Magic is just a bunch of children's stories. Why are you asking?"

"What if I were to tell you I didn't dream of being a frog the other night, but I really was one?" Jack licked his lips as he watched the rising tide of skepticism in his brother's eyes. "And I saw Madame Astrellar herself turn Roger Simmons into a frog?"

With a huff of a laugh, Henry said, "I'd say we're both exhausted and should get to bed."

"I've heard John Havish say magic is real."

Henry's lips pressed together as his brow furrowed. "Have you been reading your adventure books again?"

"Not until the last hour or so." Jack stood and rubbed his neck. "I'd rather not admit this, but I went over to Madame Astrellar's place earlier."

Henry slammed his cane on the floor. "You what?"

"It was foolish, but I was under her spell, her charm. I went, and I looked in the window, and one moment, there's Roger Simmons, and the next—" He snapped. "Poof, there's a frog on her carpet."

Jack stepped back from Henry's glare.

"How much have you had to drink tonight?"

Pointing at the pile of textbooks on the table's corner, Jack said, "I've been studying, as I should, but couldn't keep myself from—"

"You will stay away from Madame Astrellar," Henry said as he stood, leaning heavily on his cane. "She is already meddling enough in my business. I don't need you giving her an excuse to make matters worse."

"She didn't see me." Jack held his hands up in surrender. "I ran off right when Simmons became a frog."

"Stop trying to distract me with that ridiculous story."

"Everything I've said is the truth. You've got to believe me."

"Oh, I'll believe you, but only if you can grab a passing frog and he can confirm what you've said."

"Frogs can't speak. Not even enchanted ones."

The whistle blew in the kettle as Henry's face started to turn red. Jack scurried to the kitchen and poured tea into two mugs. He rested his head against a cupboard as he let the tea cool.

Henry didn't believe in magic and he was wise enough to not trust Cassandra. As long as Henry was safe, there was no reason to convince him of a truth he wouldn't believe. Jack stirred sugar into the tea as he planned how to dodge his way out of this conversation. Henry had to trust him.

Carrying the mugs into the main room, Jack forced a smile. "Sorry about ribbing you. I fell asleep with my head in my books, and the dream of Madame Astrellar's mansion and that brute Simmons turning into a frog seemed real enough I might convince you." He set a cup in front of Henry. "I thought it'd be a fun distraction after having to sit down with Evelyn's father."

Henry stirred in a cube of sugar as he glared at Jack. After yawning, he took a long drink. Shutting his eyes, he said, "Maybe you wouldn't dream of amphibians if you hadn't fallen in the well."

Jack gave a false laugh as he sank into his chair. "I think you're right." He scratched his chin. "By the way, did you patch things up with Evelyn?"

A smile broke across Henry's face as he kept his eyes closed.

Jack leaned forward as he grinned. "Did you kiss her?"

Henry's smile dropped away. "Those matters are between Evelyn and myself."

Jack pointed "What about those lipstick marks on your shirt?"

Henry frowned as he rubbed at the pink smudges on his collar. "Let's just say, despite her illness, the evening went quite well and I will be visiting her tomorrow."

Jack raised his mug. "I'm glad to hear it. Here's to Evelyn, and may I find a girl half so fine."

A corner of Henry's mouth turned up as he raised his cup to Jack.

They both drank. Henry set his cup down and leaned back in his chair with his eyes shut. As he drifted into a light snore, Jack shook his shoulder and helped guide the exhausted man to his room. Henry fell onto his bed and began snoring again. Jack chuckled as he tugged off Henry's boots, just as Henry had done for him a few nights before.

He tossed a blanket over Henry before leaning in the doorway. At least Henry had Evelyn. She was a fine woman, but even she might not be enough to send Cassandra packing. Her illness was troubling and was likely the result of Cassandra and her magic.

Jack went back to his room and stared at the mound of books on his bed. After setting aside three books, which might help, he shoved the rest back into the box. He didn't have any answers yet, nor solid enough evidence to prove to Henry magic existed. With a bit more study, however, he would find a way to keep his brother safe. It was no less than Henry would do for Jack.

Chapter 8

Evelyn stared into the bowl of porridge, trying to forget the newts and frogs wriggling on her bed when she woke. Julie had screamed and tried to smash them. Her father was still upstairs banging on the walls, checking for whatever holes the creatures had crawled through.

Marjory pressed a hand to her daughter's forehead. "Still no fever."

Evelyn forced down another spoonful, though her stomach churned and blurped. All she wanted was to tell her mother about dancing with Henry and the kiss she had been waiting for. Instead, she was silenced by whatever Cassandra had done to her.

Havish spoke of magic as if it were real. He claimed Talbot's shoes were made with the help of elves. Evelyn always shook her head and laughed when he talked of such things. Magic was a childish superstition until amphibious creatures crawled out of your mouth each time you tried to speak.

"It's probably just food poisoning. It will pass," her mother said.

A knock pounded on the door. Julie went to the window and shouted, "It's Mr. Kingston. Should I send him away?"

Evelyn's cheeks reddened. She was still in her nightgown, her hair pulled back in a loose ponytail. He couldn't see her like this.

Marjory rubbed her shoulder. "I'll tell him to come back tonight."

Before Marjory could move, Havish clomped down the stairs and threw open the door.

"Don't—" A creature slithered into Evelyn's mouth. She considered letting it fall to the table and explaining everything. As the muscles of her jaw moved, the vision of the house in flames rose again. Clamping a hand over mouth, she ran to the washroom and shut the door. Her cheeks bulged as she spat a newt into the washtub.

"You're here bright and early, Kingston!" Havish's voice boomed through the house. "Evelyn's still not feeling well. Why don't you come back later today?"

"I brought a tonic the pharmacist said would help," Henry said. "And some warm socks."

Evelyn began to laugh, but gagged as a frog climbed out of her mouth. She leaned her head against the door, trying not to let tears fall. She had tried to write him a letter when she couldn't sleep last night, but even writing brought frogs to her throat. Somehow, she had to warn him about Cassandra.

"We'll see you this afternoon, then?" Havish said. "Marjory's making a fine soup."

"Oh. I—" Henry paused. "Yes, Mr. Havish."

Evelyn pulled her knees to her chest as she listened to his cane tapping across the porch. When he returned, this illness might be gone. She would be able to sit beside him, his hand holding hers as they talked of nothing. If he was feeling bold enough, they would steal another kiss. However, such things couldn't happen if she was still spitting out frogs.

Henry joined the Havish family for dinner, but Evelyn's chair remained empty. His palms sweated as he smiled politely, attempting to answer questions and ignore Julie's giggles. Charlie sat across from him, glowering while everyone crammed around the table chatted over each other.

Mrs. Blanchard leaned toward Marjory. "Is Miss Evelyn ill because that handsome Simmons fellow didn't come?"

Henry glared down into his soup. Havish tapped his shoulder and gave him a wink before pounding his hand on the table like a gavel.

The room quieted as Havish stood. "I've been thinking I haven't made proper introductions." He clamped his hand on Henry's shoulder. "This here's Mr. Henry Kingston, who's courting my Evelyn. He's a good man and I'd not be surprised if we'll be announcing a wedding soon."

Havish slapped Henry's back, nearly knocking him through the table. The crowd, except Charlie, stomped and whooped. Henry rubbed his chin, glad any redness was partially covered by the bruise from Simmons' fist.

Dinner ended, the dishes were cleared, and all the extensions to the table were put away. Henry adjusted his spectacles, wishing his new ones weren't broken, and approached Evelyn's father.

"This might not be proper," Henry said. "But I was hoping to sit outside Miss Evelyn's room and read to her."

"Sounds grand." Havish hooked his arm around Henry's shoulders. "I'm sure it'll help her quite a bit."

Soon, Henry was seated on a chair beside Evelyn's door. He pressed his palm to the wall between them.

"Evelyn?" He pulled at his collar and cleared his throat. "I thought it would help if I read to you."

A weak "Yes" came from behind the door, followed by gagging and retching. Henry cringed while he pulled the book out of his coat pocket. He opened it and stared at the title page.

A Voyage of Hearts by Alvin Westengaard

He had not paid attention when Jack had handed him the book.

Henry opened to the first chapter and tried to read without skepticism as a swashbuckling pirate fell into an impossible romance with a princess. The story was full of ridiculous magic and foolish heroism. As the pages passed, Henry wondered how Jack could enjoy such delusional tales.

"And as the waves crashed over the ship and the hull cracked apart," Henry said flatly. "They clung to each other.

"'If I am to drown, at least it is with you,' he said.

"'We shall not drown, my love,' she said. 'Drink this potion and it will save you.'

"'Take it first. I cannot live if you shall die.'

"'I have already drunk some. We will be saved together.'

"He drank the potion, and watched as his fingers became webbed and long, his head widened and view changed. Next he knew, he was falling into the water as a…"

Henry slammed the book shut. "Ridiculous."

"What is?" came Evelyn's voice followed by vomiting and a wet sploosh.

"The man turns into a frog," Henry said. "They are in the middle of the ocean. Frogs absorb water through their skin. It would die within moments. I can tolerate the other fanciful details, but the science should at least be reasonable."

"It's about a pirate and a prin—" She spat something into the bucket.

"Pirates and princesses can survive in sea water." Henry thumbed through the book, glancing at the etched illustrations. "There's a fight between a sea monster and a mermaid later in the story. And someone gets to ride a giant sea turtle. This would be far more plausible if they turned into turtles. At least turtles can live in the ocean." He continued flipping pages. "Maybe Jack read this book before his dream."

"What dream?" Evelyn gagged again.

"Last night, Jack tried to convince me a dream he'd had was true. He claimed Madame Astrellar had turned both him and Simmons into frogs. He even claimed magic is real." Henry grunted. "Jack usually has a better wit, but I think his fascination with Madame Astrellar is wearing on him."

Evelyn panted as she said, "What if he was telling the truth?"

A long series of retching followed. Even if her breath smelled horrible and she looked sickly, Henry wished he could sit by her and grip her hand. However, they were not married yet.

"Hen—" Evelyn's gagging was followed by the starts of words broken by retching and panting. Henry placed his hand on the door as he stood. There was nothing more he could do for her tonight.

"Get some rest. I'll send your mother up." His fingers brushed the doorknob. He was breaking enough propriety just standing here. Opening the door would do nothing to help. "Goodnight, Evelyn."

"Don't. I—"

Henry forced himself to march down the stairs. He would come tomorrow with a better tonic. Evelyn had to heal quickly. No woman would want to be proposed to while she had the stomach flu.

The gray of dawn lingered as Evelyn stood on a lake dock and poured the bucket of frogs and newts into the water. If Evelyn didn't speak of or to Henry, the creatures came less often. The threat was still enough to churn her stomach.

Walking toward her father's shop, she wondered how she would try to explain everything. She had tried again to speak to her mother the night before, but her jaw had clenched up, her mouth unable to move. Marjory had wrapped Evelyn's head in warm towels and sent her to bed.

Her father might be easier to explain to, especially while alone in his office. If anyone was going to believe her ailment was caused by magic, her father would.

Then she had to find Jack. Any other day, she might dismiss his dream as nonsense. Today, his dream had to be true. If he had been turned into a frog and then back into a man, he might know some spell or cure to help her. Even if he couldn't help, he could at least confirm she wasn't going mad.

Charlie looked up from scraping dragon hide and waved to her as she entered the back door of her father's shop. The walls shook as their father bellowed from his office.

Evelyn motioned for Charlie to stay as she ran down the narrow hallway. Her father's office door opened and a small man shuffled out.

"I'm sorry, Havish. You're a good bloke, but it's just business. Unless you match the price, I'm going to sell it to Mr. Hedley."

"That's gouging, Simpter! Are you trying to bleed off my business?"

"You'd do the same if someone offered a higher price."

"We've got a contract."

"I'm very sorry, Havish."

Mr. Simpter slinked out the front door as Havish shouted, "Go run off with the rest of you bleeders!"

Evelyn stepped into her father's office. Papers were scattered and furniture knocked over.

"What're you doing here?" he said, the redness in his face draining. "You go home and rest."

She swallowed, holding the bucket firm in her hand. "What happened, Dad?"

Havish snorted. "I run an honest business and do a good turn to folks out of their luck. And how do I get repaid? By some scum-sucking blaggard buying up all my suppliers. We've got enough hide to cover orders for the next week, but I don't know what we'll be doing later this month. There's no shortage of cows being skinned, but there is a shortage of intelligence. Can't they see Hedley's trying to snuff out my business?"

"Who is Hedley?" Evelyn pressed a hand to her stomach as it felt like something took a swim inside. For once, nothing climbed out.

"Some business manager for some rich folk. They're not even opening a rival tannery. They're wasting good cow hide just to ruin me."

Havish pounded his fist into the wall, leaving a dent. "They're cowards who can't see past their own fat noses." He growled before looking at her. "Don't you worry about it. I'll sort the matter. You get home and rest."

Evelyn pressed her lips together. She needed her father's help, but now was not the time.

She stepped outside and considered going directly to Henry at Mackabee and Sons. No. The conversation, if she could even speak, would go better with Jack confirming the truth.

Walking down the street, she tried to remember places Henry had mentioned Jack doing handyman work for. Most of them were mansions and residences in North Town, but she didn't want to go too close to Cassandra's territory.

A pulse of hope rose in her chest as she remembered Jack worked almost every day at the Bradford School.

She hurried to the next corner and made a silent prayer as she got on the trolley and rode across Pippington. Once at the stop, she jumped off the trolley and walked quickly to the school.

The brick buildings with steep roofs still stood just as they had during her school days. Girls sang a pleasant melody, the music echoing from the open windows of the choir room. The girls stopped as Miss Billow tapped her conductor's wand and said, "Together, girls! Together!"

The girls sang again as Evelyn opened the gate and stepped onto the well-manicured grounds. She strolled along the path lined with bright daisies and gerberas, remembering running around the yard with her friends during their play hour. However, there was no sign of Jack.

She looked to the tall double-doors. She could try talking to the headmistress, Mrs. Hunter, yet a chill ran through her. The two times she had been called into Mrs. Hunter's office had left her trembling. She hadn't been in trouble either time, but had been terrified all the same.

There was rustling on the roof and a voice muttered out a few curses. She stepped back as she looked up. Jack lay across the roof, his feet against the rain gutter, his arm stretched out for a bird's nest sitting in one of the eaves. He covered his head as two sparrows circled and dove at him.

"It's a bad spot for your nest!" He waved them off. "I'll go put it in a nice tree. Don't you worry."

Evelyn cupped her hands around her mouth. "Mr. Kingston!"

Her cheeks bulged before she spat a frog into the bucket.

Jack leaned up on his elbow and looked down. He frowned and tipped back his hat. "Miss Evelyn, what brings you here?"

Evelyn opened her mouth to speak, but she didn't know how to begin to explain. Jack waved his arm and said, "I'll be down in a blink."

She scratched her head as she tried to plan her words, hoping she could get enough out.

Jack cried out in triumph as he snatched the nest from the eaves. Cradling it in the crook of his arm as the sparrows swooped at him, he crawled along the roof to the ladder. Evelyn held the ladder steady as Jack climbed down.

"I—" She took a breath. "I have a problem."

She raised the bucket just in time to catch the salamander slithering out of her mouth. Jack's foot slipped and he slid down the last three rungs of the ladder. The nest wobbled in his hand, but he steadied it before it fell.

His mouth hung open as he stared into the bucket.

Evelyn swallowed before saying quickly, "I heard you were turned into a frog."

Jack pulled off his hat and ruffled his hair. His eyes met hers as he whispered, "She did this to you at the Morveaux, didn't she?"

Exhaling a breath of relief, Evelyn nodded.

Jack glanced at the school before nodding toward the large sycamore tree. "Walk with me. Mrs. Hunter doesn't like me to stand around and chat."

Evelyn carried the ladder as she followed Jack across the yard. She helped him set the ladder against the sycamore tree while he waved away the sparrows diving for the nest.

"I've been thinking as I've been going through all my books." He climbed up the ladder with one hand holding the nest. "It seems there're many types of magic. But, I have no idea how any of it works, nor what type Madame Astrellar uses."

He set the nest in the crook of a pair of branches before looking down at her. "What exactly did she do to you?"

Evelyn waited until he climbed down before she said, "She shoved a piece of—" She gagged before spitting a frog into the bucket. Jack cringed. "Of chocolate—" Another frog followed.

Jack folded his arms and wrinkled his forehead. "Did she see you with Henry beforehand?"

Evelyn nodded.

Jack's tongue pushed out his cheek as he tapped his foot. "When I went back to her garden like an idiot, she asked me all these questions about you and Henry. There's something about her. Makes me a blind fool when I'm around her. But, her questions— they were odd."

He rubbed his forehead. "Henry has no idea how deep of trouble he's in."

"Mr. Kingston!"

Both Jack and Evelyn jumped as Mrs. Hunter appeared from around the corner, her hair pulled back in her usual tight bun. She arrived beside them and Evelyn kept her head down just as she had as a girl.

"Mr. Kingston, why you are meeting young women in my garden?"

"This is Miss Evelyn Havish, my brother's girl. You see, Henry's in a spot of trouble, and we're trying to help."

Mrs. Hunter raised her pointed chin, as she looked Evelyn up and down. Evelyn felt as if her whole self was being cataloged and judged.

"How urgent is this personal matter?" Mrs. Hunter said.

"Very urgent, ma'am."

Mrs. Hunter folded her hands together. "Then go see to the matter, Mr. Kingston, and come finish your work when it is resolved. There's no worth in paying for slow, distracted work."

Evelyn's shoulders eased as Mrs. Hunter turned to leave.

Jack said, "I don't mean to pry, Mrs. Hunter, but I've seen a few odd things while working here—"

Mrs. Hunter raised her eyebrows as she blinked at Jack.

Jack pulled off his hat. "Do you happen to know anything about, say, people turning into frogs?"

Evelyn frowned, wondering why he would ask the headmistress.

"People transforming into frogs?" Mrs. Hunter gave him a disdainful shake of her head. "If such preposterous things happened, don't you think it should be taken up with the authorities? You could always speak to Inspector McCay. I'm sure she would handle the matter."

Mrs. Hunter's dark skirt swept around her as she turned and marched back to the school.

"That made me look a fool," he said as he tugged his hat on.

Evelyn touched his arm and nodded toward the gate. They were wasting time. They had to tell Henry the truth and hope he would accept it.

Jack offered his arm and gave Evelyn a firm nod. "Let's go save Henry."

Chapter 9

The city was still waking as Henry stepped out of his building and onto the street. He whistled as he strode to work, tapping his cane along with the rhythm. Tonight, Evelyn should be well when he visited again. If her house was full, they would go to the porch. He would sit close beside her, enjoying the evening air.

He ran through his plans once more. The deposit on Friday's dinner and string quartet remained. Thursday, he would have the final payment for the ring. There was no need to wait another two months for the fireworks of Abeyance Night, especially after the shop girl at Lapidary's had ruined the surprise.

If all went well, soon he and Evelyn could begin a peaceful life together. He would be a respectable auditor with an intelligent, beautiful wife.

Henry began to smile, but stopped as a passing man gave him a quizzical glance. Henry's whistle cut off and he returned to his regular, steady step. He was near the office and needed to maintain dignity.

As he stepped into Mackabee and Sons, a few clerks were already ticking numbers away at their desks. He approached his small office, envisioning the firmness of putting pencil to paper. Today would bring another steady day of work and none of the chaos from Saturday night.

He opened the door and his heart stopped. He shut the door again. This was only a bizarre vision. He shut his eyes, wincing as bruised muscles tightened. He adjusted his spectacles and opened the door again.

What lay beyond may have been sliced out of the Morveaux and placed where his office should be. The walls were draped in blood-red velvet curtains with gold fringe. The ceiling had been replaced by a nine-piece painting divided by gilded molding. In each square were frescos of the sky and ocean, several containing cherubim. His scratched and worn desk was gone, replaced by a polished wood table, inlaid with silver and gold filigree. A pair of red velvet chairs sat on one side of the table and his creaky, tattered chair had been replaced by a small throne.

He stepped in, trying not to stare at the dizzying pattern on the Gathrayan carpet. Turning around, he sought any sign of his files. Even if he found them, no one could get anything done in this mausoleum.

He rubbed his forehead as he leaned on his cane. Maybe one of the clerks had removed his files. He turned to step out, when he saw the wall adjacent to the door. He cried out as he jumped back, nearly falling over the table.

What had once been a plain, off-white wall was now a portrait of Cassandra Astrellar dressed in a green, velvet ball gown. She sat nobly, her chin high, her face clever, but serious. Behind her were impressionistic details implying ships, clouds, and waves. With a gasp, Henry forced himself to take in air.

Henry's door opened and a man of small, though thick stature entered. The face behind the broad mustache was serious, the eyebrows heavy and cheeks drooping. Pools of gray were under his eyes as he looked Henry over.

"You're the one she has chosen?" He shut the door before taking a slow stroll around Henry as if surveying a race horse. "Not as handsome as other men, but that is not what she usually seeks."

Henry held onto his cane to stay on his feet. "Who are— did you— what is—"

Stopping in front of Henry, the man held out his gloved hand.

"Albert Hedley, Mr. Astrellar's business manager."

Henry shook the man's hand. He needed to remain calm and polite, even with Cassandra's portrait gazing down at him.

"Mr. Astrellar and I have worked together a long time, and it always concerns me when Madame Astrellar decides to take matters into her own hands." Mr. Hedley folded his arms behind himself. "I wish I could say something to help you, but I fear I have discovered her escape too late. Instead, all I can offer is some advice to minimize the damage."

"I doubt a girl of twenty-one can cause much damage," Henry said as he opened the drawers of the table. His trusty fountain pen was gone, replaced by some gold-plated atrocity.

"She appears so young, doesn't she?" Hedley said, glancing up at the portrait. "I have known her so long, I forget how she looks to an inexperienced eye."

Henry frowned. Considering her lies about Jack, he would not be surprised if Cassandra masked her true age.

"There is no need to worry, sir," Henry said as he tapped the table, looking for any secret drawers. "My relationship with Madame Astrellar is only a matter of business."

Hedley's eyebrows raised. "What about the concert and ball you escorted her to?"

"It was a formality."

"Quite a formality. And do you have any pending 'formalities' with the lady?"

"No." Henry glanced around the room. There were no papers anywhere.

"Keep it so. She already has one rope around you, and it will be best if you do not let her attach another."

Henry frowned at the stranger. "Sir, I have no intention of welcoming Madame Astrellar into my personal life, nor do I have any plans to steal her wealth. If you will excuse me, I need to find my files."

Hedley crossed the room and pulled aside part of the velvet curtain. There sat shelves full of Henry's files.

"Thank you," Henry said as he walked over.

Hedley stepped in Henry's way, his gray eyes firm. "I do not mean to question your integrity, sir. As I said, I came to warn you. Your only hope is to be completely cold to Madame Astrellar. If she persists, cut everyone out of your life. It'll be the only way to protect them from being used to ensnare you."

Henry carefully lifted the first box. "I can manage Madame Astrellar, sir."

Hedley tilted his head as he eyed the gilded room. "I hope you can, but I have my doubts. I will do what I can to help, but I fear it is not much. Best of luck, Mr. Kingston."

The odd man strolled out of the room and Henry grunted. He could manage keeping his distance from Cassandra. His pending engagement to Evelyn might even help.

Henry pulled off his coat and began laying out the boxes of files. He gritted his teeth as he rifled through the papers and folders, seeking the ledger he had been working on. On Friday, he had left with everything carefully stacked and organized, and now it was jumbled into a mess. Once he had things sorted, he would talk to Mr. Mackabee and demand someone else be made Cassandra's account manager.

He finally found the ledger and sat in the throne. The cushions were stiff and he kept sinking back against the tilted backrest. The table itself was higher than he was used to and the edge pressed into his arm. He set out the papers, pencils, and fountain pens, glad everything masked most of the inlaid surface.

The room disappeared around him as he returned to the normalcy of numbers. He had barely fallen into his steady rhythm of re-calculating costs, when the door creaked open.

"What do you think?"

Henry stiffened at the breathy voice. His fingers clutched his pencil, nearly breaking it. Cassandra leaned against the doorway, one arm covered in a fur muffler, the rest of her draped in radiant blue.

"Good morning, Madame—"

With a gasp, she leapt across the small space to his side. Before Henry could stand, she shoved everything off his desk and sat on it, her bosom too close to his face. He tried to draw back, but the throne would not budge as she bent down and looked at his swollen eye.

"You poor dear." She cupped his face with her hands, her full lips close to his. "Is this why you left so suddenly? Were you ashamed? Did you think I would be troubled by the brutish nature of men and unable to look upon your poor, damaged face?"

"I left to attend to personal business." He gripped the armrests and pressed his feet to the ground.

"I was so saddened to leave alone," she said, her lower lip protruding. She tapped his shoulder with her fan. "You shall have to make it up to me tonight. I have dinner reservations at the Charmant. You must join me."

"I have other arrangements for this evening." He pushed himself to his feet.

Cassandra rose from the table and ran her hand down his arm. "We can discuss my accounts over dinner, if you wish. I have so many to talk about."

He drew his arm away. "If you wish to discuss them, we can discuss them now."

"Oh, no. I'd rather wait till tonight."

Limping away from his desk and grabbing his cane, Henry pointed to the portrait. "Madame Astrellar, I cannot work with all of this!"

She smiled as she glided to a long tassel beside the portrait. As the curtains shut over it, she said, "I told the workers I was much too beautiful for you to concentrate. Do not worry, dear Mr. Kingston. I will leave you to your work, and we will meet tonight."

"It is not the portrait. It is everything. I am a simple man, Madame

Astrellar. My life is only numbers within small lines. I do not need such grand surroundings."

She leaned toward him and placed her gloved finger on his lips. He stepped back, falling until his back hit the wall. He grabbed the curtain, but it ripped beneath his weight and fell with him. Kicking at the curtain, he untangled himself. Grabbing onto one of the velvet chairs, he pulled himself up.

Cassandra pressed against him and whispered in his ear, "These are only the seeds of what is to come, Mr. Kingston. You are a greater man than you can see. Soon, you will be quite at home with all this finery."

She squeezed his arm and then swept out the door. He pressed his hands to the desk to steady himself. One of his hands landed in a pool of spilled ink. He wiped it on his shirt, leaving a black streak. With a grunt, he grabbed a piece of the broken curtain and wiped off his hands and desk. He tossed down the stained cloth and marched out of his office and toward Mackabee's. The man might yell until the roof came down, but Henry could not tolerate Cassandra any longer.

As Evelyn and Jack stood across the street from Henry's office, Evelyn's cheeks bulged. She pressed her teeth together, trying to keep the creature down. Jack stepped in front of her, blocking her from view as he raised her bucket. Evelyn spat out the frog and wiped her mouth.

"We'll find a way to stop all this," Jack said as he squeezed her arm.

The doors of Mackabee's and Sons swung open and Cassandra swept down the stairs. Jack pulled Evelyn with him behind a parked motorcar while a carriage with plumed horses rushed down the street.

As soon as Cassandra was inside her carriage and the vehicle had turned the corner, Evelyn and Jack hurried across to the building. Climbing up the stairs, Evelyn gripped Jack's arm as she tried to hold back her growing nausea.

Once in the lobby, Jack leaned on the receptionist's desk and said, "Miss Greenberg, looking more beautiful than ever."

The stern-faced matron glared at Jack. "Can I help you, Mr. Kingston?"

"Just dropping off some messages for my brother." He winked. "Important leads, you know."

"Leave them here and I will deliver them."

Jack grinned as he shook his head. "I'd love to, but he said to tell him directly." He leaned closer. "It's to help the Astrellar account."

Miss Greenberg glanced at the front doors before waving Jack and Evelyn through. Evelyn followed him into the dim main room. Men and women hunched over their tiny desks, almost as if there were chains holding them there. At least her father's workshop had daylight and his workers smiled instead of sitting sour-faced.

"Jack!" A tall, handsome man put his hand on Jack's shoulder and gave Jack's hand a friendly shake. The man glanced down the hallway and nodded toward a nearby office. "Henry just went into Mackabee's office. I think our employer's about to blow. You'd best hide in my office."

"Thanks." Jack slapped the man's back.

The man led them into a narrow office brightened by a painting of a landscape and a rug to cover the worn floor. He closed the door as Mr. Mackabee's shouting shuddered through the entire building.

Holding out his hand to Evelyn, the man said, "Nathaniel Bronhart, miss."

She took his hand and opened her mouth to speak, when Jack said, "This here's the famous Evelyn Havish. She'd tell you herself, but she's got a horrible sore throat. Can barely get out a word."

Evelyn glanced at Jack and nodded her thank you.

Bronhart gave her a broad grin. "I'm glad to finally meet you, Miss Havish. Henry doesn't speak of much at work, but he's told me quite a bit about you."

Evelyn attempted to return the smile as she tried to understand what Mackabee was yelling.

"What brings you two here?" Bronhart said as he sat in his chair.

"We've been working on a surprise for Henry," Jack said. "We wanted to steal him during his lunch break."

Bronhart frowned as he glanced at his wall clock. "Lunch isn't for another two hours."

"We got excited," Jack shrugged. "And, wanted to make sure we got to Henry before Madame Astrellar did."

Bronhart laughed. "She's a persistent woman. I just hope you've arrived in time."

The clock ticked away while Mackabee's voice still rumbled. Evelyn stared down at the bucket, glad the frogs were quiet. Bronhart and Henry seemed to be good friends, but she didn't want to explain everything more than she had to.

Breaking the silence, Bronhart picked up a newspaper from his desk with a bitter laugh. "Jack, I'm in the paper again."

Evelyn glanced at the front page of *The Rosetown Journal.* The headline read: *Heiress Leaves Accountant for Author.*

Bronhart tossed the paper to Jack. "Be glad neither of you are famous enough to have your private affairs splashed out for the rest of the public."

"I thought you and Miss Winkleston were quite solid with each other," Jack said as he flipped through the paper.

"I did too. Then, last Saturday, I found her in the arms of Alvin Westengaard." Bronhart picked up a letter. "At least she had the decency to officially break off our engagement." He tossed the letter onto the table. "Let this Westengaard have her. I'll find myself a girl who won't be stolen away by a few turns around the dance floor." His sharp eyes looked to Evelyn. "I am sure you are wiser than to break things off with a good man like Henry."

Evelyn blushed as she looked away. A few days before, she had chosen Simmons over Henry. If only she had gone with Henry instead. Then, he wouldn't have escorted Cassandra and all of them might be safer.

"I met Miss Winkleston a few times back when she worked at the Bradford School," Jack said as he folded *The Rosetown Journal* closed. "She doesn't seem the sort of girl to do this."

"I didn't think so either." Bronhart leaned back in his chair. "It's the money she inherited. All that wealth has gone and ruined a wonderful girl."

"I'm sorry, Bronhart," Jack said. "You're a good man. I'm sure you'll be all right."

"I'll be fine," Bronhart muttered. He picked up a pencil and pointed at Evelyn. "Don't you worry about Madame Astrellar and Henry. He can easily see through her vanity. Besides, she's just like every other wealthy beauty, trying to play with men like toys. Her fixation on Henry will pass and she'll be off to pursue some new trend."

"I don't know," Jack said. "She's got a lot of money."

Bronhart waved his hand. "I ran into her father's business manager this morning. Mr. Hedley mentioned something about cutting back her allowances."

"Hedley?" Evelyn sat up, but then clamped her lips together. No creature came, but her tongue was feeling thick and heavy.

"Yes," Bronhart said. "Do you know him?"

Evelyn shook her head as she glanced at the door. Cassandra must have sent this Hedley to buy up hides and ruin the tannery. Her teeth ground on each other. Apparently, it was not enough to curse Evelyn. Cassandra Astrellar was another level of cruel and selfish.

"Seems a smart man," Bronhart said. "He's got a good handle on her father's business."

Evelyn's stomach gave a warning churn, and she swallowed, trying to keep everything down.

Several doors slammed and Bronhart stood. "Things seem to have quieted down. Let me escort you, just in case."

Dizziness waned and ebbed through Evelyn as she followed Bronhart. Jack gave her a concerned glance as he carried her bucket and kept his hand on her elbow.

Bronhart knocked on the faded door marked, *Henry Kingston, Auditor.*

"Yes?" came Henry's voice.

Putting on a grin, Bronhart opened the door. Evelyn caught a glimpse of red velvet before Bronhart stepped back and slammed the door shut. He frowned as he looked at the door again and ran his fingers over Henry's painted name.

"What in the light of—" he muttered. Turning to Jack and Evelyn, he said, "Maybe you should return later."

"It's pretty urgent," Jack said.

Henry cracked open his door and leaned out, a smear of ink on his chin and nose. "Bronhart, what can I—"

His eyes met Evelyn's and his face grew paler. Jack pushed past his brother and shoved open the door. He blinked before leaning against the door and bursting into laughter.

Evelyn felt numb as she stared at the rich velvet interior. This was hardly what she envisioned as Henry's office. She had expected only a slender desk and beat up chair. This seemed grander than the powder room at The Morveaux.

"My office does not usually—" Henry scratched his forehead. "It was like this when I came in this morning."

Jack fell onto one of the plush armchairs as he wiped tears from his eyes and gasped for breath between chuckles.

Henry hurried to button his jacket over the ink stain on his shirt.

"Miss Havish, er—a, what can I—" He shook his head before motioning for her to enter. "Please, come inside."

"I'll leave you to manage your business," Bronhart said with a repressed smile.

Evelyn entered and accepted the velvet-lined chair Henry pulled out for her.

"Has Mackabee finally put some money into redecorating?" Jack wheezed between laughing.

Henry shut the door firmly. "It was a gift from Madame Astrellar."

Jack's laughter stopped with a snort. Evelyn felt as if the curtains would wrap around her and suffocate her. She pulled her hand from the armrest, a dirtiness lingering on her palms. Jack was already on his feet, approaching the strip of canvas visible among the red velvet. He pulled back the curtain, revealing a massive portrait of Cassandra. Jack let go as if his hand burned. As the curtain cascaded shut, Evelyn felt her throat close.

"I must get to work," Henry said as he tapped his fingers on the table. "How can I help you?

Jack grimaced as he looked to Evelyn. "I think the only way he'll believe is if we show him."

"Show me what?" Henry said.

Evelyn raised the bucket and opened her mouth. She began to say his name, but was cut off as dry heaves wracked through her, but nothing came out. She forced out a cough, but her throat was still constricted.

Henry limped over and knelt beside her. Pressing his hand to her forehead, he said, "You're burning up."

He reached into his pocket and pulled out a few bills. Holding them out to Jack, he said, "Get a cab and take her home."

Jack pushed Henry's hand away as he crouched on the other side of Evelyn. "Why aren't they coming out?"

Evelyn shook her head as she tried to say anything, but only a wheezing whine came out.

"What are you doing?" Henry shoved the money into Jack's hand. "She should be home resting, not here."

"Cassandra Astrellar put a curse on her." Jack grabbed the bucket and shoved it toward Henry. "Look! Miss Evelyn's been puking frogs and the like—"

"There's only mud in the bucket."

Evelyn's eyes widened as she stared at the slopping mud inside. What had happened to everything she had been spitting out?

Jack dropped it with a grunt. Mud splattered onto the desk and carpet. "She probably figured we'd show you."

Evelyn's chest ached as she tried to wheeze in air. Henry gripped her hand.

"Jack, go call a cab."

"We're not lying, Henry!" Jack jabbed a finger toward the portrait. "That woman isn't what she pretends to be. The dream I thought I had wasn't a dream! She really did turn me into a frog. If you don't believe me, go try to find Roger Simmons. You'll find he's missing because he's now a toad stuck in her blasted well."

Evelyn's wheezes were reaching a higher pitch. She tried to move her tongue, to form a word, but could not.

Henry let go of Evelyn's hand and turned to his brother. "You told me you were not interested in Madame Astrellar."

"I'm not. I'm trying to warn you."

"Are you? Against what? How dare you use Evelyn to try to prove your ridiculous story."

"Everything I've told you is true."

"These children's stories do not happen in reality, Jack. Men do not turn into frogs. People do not put spells on each other." He pointed at the money in Jack's hand. "Go and hire a cab for Evelyn."

Evelyn gripped at her throat as her wheezes grew worse, spots filling her vision.

Henry touched her shoulder. "Maybe we should take you to the doctor."

"Oh, dear Mr. Kingston! Is everything all right?"

Henry's fingers dug into Evelyn's shoulder as Cassandra swept into the room. Evelyn's throat cleared and she gasped in air. Henry grabbed her before she could fall.

"I am so sorry to intrude," Cassandra said. "I forgot my glove when I was here earlier. Do ignore me."

Holding onto the table, Henry bit out, "Jack, please get a cab."

Eyeing Cassandra, Jack said, "Right."

Cassandra gasped and covered her mouth as she looked down at Evelyn with wide-eyed, supposed-compassion. "Miss Havish, what is wrong?"

The burn of vomit rose in Evelyn's throat. This time, it was not due to some frog or newt. She narrowed her eyes and firmed her jaw.

Laying a hand on Henry's arm, Cassandra said, "My carriage is outside. Let me take her home."

"I'll take care of it," Jack said as he jogged out the door.

"She is such a dear." Cassandra leaned her face close to Henry's.

Evelyn's fists trembled. One good slug across the woman's face would not solve anything, but it would make the day better.

"I so enjoyed her company at the Morveaux," Cassandra said. "I am so sorry she fell ill. I am glad your brother brought her to you when he saw her walking about. I was worried when I passed her earlier. Her eyes were so faded and fevered. I wasn't sure she even knew where she was. I am sure her heart is broken now Mr. Simmons has gone missing, what with—" She placed a hand over her mouth. "I am sorry, Miss Havish. I did not mean to share any indiscretions."

Evelyn grabbed the bucket and threw its contents at Cassandra. The woman squealed as the mud splattered across her dress. Evelyn stood and smashed her fist against Cassandra's fine jaw.

"Evelyn!" Henry said.

He wrapped his arms around her and dragged her out of the office. She pulled against him, wanting only to rip those gold curls from the woman's head. Her elbow pounded into Henry's stomach and she darted for another attack. Cassandra raised her head and flicked her hand. Evelyn halted as her throat closed for a few seconds. Cassandra flicked her hand again and Evelyn dragged in air.

"Please," Henry whispered as he held onto the wall and held out his free hand to Evelyn. "Let's just step outside."

Cassandra raised her eyebrows, inviting Evelyn's next attack. Evelyn wanted to bare her teeth and growl, but stopped herself. She would not feed into Cassandra's games. Instead, she held onto Henry's arm and let him escort her outside.

Once on the front steps, Henry kept hold of her arm and said, "What she said about you and Mr. Simmons is a petty lie. Jack will take you home. I'll stay here and talk to Madame Astrellar."

Evelyn gripped Henry's hand and shook her head. He frowned. "What has Jack told you? Is he playing games?"

She shook her head harder. She started to point, but stopped. What could she gesture to? He hadn't believed Jack and he thought she was mad with a fever.

As a cab slowed and pulled to the curb, Henry helped Evelyn down the stairs, his own legs shaky.

Assisting her into the motorcar, he said, "Please. Go home and get better. I—" His lips pursed as he stared down at their hands. "I might not make it to visit tonight, but I'll do my best. However—" He took a breath. "May I take you out on Friday?"

Tears sprung down Evelyn's cheeks as she tightened her hold on Henry's hands. With a few words, she could confirm Jack's story and warn him. However, she couldn't even tell him what Cassandra was doing to her father.

Henry pulled his hand from hers and shut the door. Jack slid into the seat beside Evelyn and they both stared back as the motorcar rolled away. Evelyn's blood heated and boiled as Cassandra stood at the top of the steps, shoulders back and chin high, like a queen watching her rival being destroyed.

"We'll stop her," Jack whispered as he punched his fist into the seat. "We'll find a way."

Chapter 10

The clams and oysters stared back at Henry. They had been safe in their tight shells until dropped into boiling water and forced open. Now they waited to be consumed. A single, massive octopus tentacle stretched across the platter, its strength clear even as steam rose from its boiled hide. Cassandra cracked apart a lobster claw, red skin splitting open to reveal the soft meat inside.

"How delicious!" She stabbed her fork into the white flesh, maintaining the dainty angle of her wrist.

A shudder ran through Henry as he met the lobster's dead, beady eyes. Neither of them could escape this evening. The lobster had already been boiled and buttered and Henry was one tenuous thread away from being fired, all for this false beauty skewering them both.

"When my mother was ambassador to Barthan," Cassandra said as she raised a rounded fork, which Henry had still not discovered the use of, "The Consular would never have sent out these drab pieces of steel. Only real silver, or, on dinners with the head of state, gold."

Henry kept his eyebrow lowered with great effort. They were at the Espadon, one of the finest restaurants in Pippington, but still below the lavishness of some of the places Mackabee boasted about attending in Willington. Cassandra would surely find her pure silver cutlery there. If Henry could convince her to go and visit her old childhood haunts in the capital, he might have a few days of peace.

As she took another bite of the unfortunate lobster and fluttered her eyelashes, Henry doubted such an escape was possible.

Four nights of being dragged to grand restaurants and pretentious evening gatherings were too many. He should be with Evelyn, holding her hand to give her strength as she sat silent, deep shadows under her eyes, an exhaustion in her shoulders. The past three nights, he had used his one spare hour to sit with her in her parents' parlor. When he got up to leave, she clung to his arm, shaking her head, her eyes pleading for him not to go. Pulling away was like ripping away a piece of himself, yet he did it. If he wanted to pay for the ring and provide a good home, he had to go to dinner with Cassandra.

Henry had spoken up twice already to Mr. Mackabee, only to have his protests bellowed away. Speaking up once more might end with no employment and years of loyalty and hard work gone to nothing. Yet, as Cassandra bobbled her fork through the air and babbled on about some new art trend, he wondered if his employment was worth this.

Tomorrow night was his only anchor of hope in this sea of vacuous drudgery. Even if Evelyn was still ill, he would take her out for the carriage ride and open air. When he bent his knee and held out the ring, she would surely accept, even if she could not speak. Once he was engaged, Mackabee would not expect him to attend dinner with Cassandra alone.

"And tomorrow," Cassandra said with a tittering giggle as she brushed her fingers on his arm. "I have planned for us a grander evening than ever before! I shall expect you to be ready by six and to look your most dapper."

Henry prodded the rubbery tongue of a clam. "Madame, I cannot join you tomorrow. I have personal matters to attend to."

"You shall have the day to yourself in your little office." She smiled and laid her hand on his. "And, you cannot call our delightful evenings purely business."

Henry drew away his hand. "They have been tolerable, but still business."

"Oh, Mr. Kingston!" She laughed, her head tilting just enough to highlight her chin. "Must I remind you what great service you have done to me? I have no other friends in this city. I am not only entrusting my financial affairs, but also my hopes to gain social connection."

She lifted a piece of lobster on her fork and held it near Henry's mouth. "Do try this. It is delectable."

He pushed away her wrist. "There are other men in the firm better for meeting higher social circles."

"Which is where we can help each other, Mr. Kingston." She set down her fork and rested her chin on her hand, her perfect curls framing her face. "My wealth and beauty draw strangers to me and they flutter about to gain favor. You are an honest and sensible man and can help me find those who have my best interests at heart."

"I am hardly—"

Cassandra leaned forward, her smile remaining, but a touch of vapidness evaporating. "Do you not see we are made to be allies? I knew it from the moment you rescued my mother's bauble out of the well. You are a remarkable man, Mr. Kingston. Help me ascend social circles and I will help you rise in this capitalist little game of yours. You do not need to be a mere pawn in Mackabee's business."

Henry tapped his foot while slowly taking a drink of water. Setting down his glass, Henry said, "I have earned every advancement. I will not have things handed to me."

She leaned close and whispered, "Speak the word and my wealth can be yours."

He started and gripped the armrest of his chair as her hand brushed his knee.

"Imagine," she said, her breath on his ear. "What a man of your intelligence and ambition could do, given free reign of my wealth. You would become the pinnacle of both business and society. I am willing to place all I have into your stewardship: my wealth, my beauty, my heart. Our business and our lives could be made one."

Henry's fists clenched as he pushed back his chair, creating a respectable distance between them. "You are only a client."

She laughed and ran her finger along his arm. "I know your heart. You do not need to hide what you truly desire."

Henry tossed down his napkin. "My only desire is to conduct my business honestly and without distraction."

"A bachelor cannot be interested in business alone."

Flexing his hand, he tried to slow his rising pulse, "I am courting Evelyn Havish."

Cassandra tossed her head with a laugh. "Miss Havish is pleasant enough, but wholly unremarkable. What is there to gain from such a union?"

Forcing his tongue to separate from the roof of his mouth, Henry stood. "There is much to gain. Evelyn Havish is the most intelligent and beautiful women I have ever met."

Cassandra's smile turned into a hard, thin line. "Those are the assets which lead you to favor her over me?"

"Yes." He swallowed, his collar seemed to press in around his throat. He grabbed his cane, holding tightly to the handle.

Cassandra forced a smile as she ripped some of the meat from her lobster. "What a fortunate girl to have your loyalty. How am I to compete with such a lady?" She gestured with her fork. "Sit. Others are looking."

"Thank you for the evening." Henry gave a rigid bow. "But I think it best I return home."

"What of Mr. Mackabee's invitation to join him and his wife for cards later tonight?" Her eyelids fluttered again. "It would be a shame for you to miss such a fine diversion."

Henry's hand trembled as it clamped on his cane. Walking away would free him of Cassandra for a moment, but it would also free him of being employed. Proposing to a woman while unemployed was poor form. He sat, his stomach feeling as rubbery as the octopus leg across his plate. He could endure a few more hours for Evelyn's sake.

A fog hung in the air as Evelyn watched Jack spring up the vine-ridden wall. Glad she had worn breeches and braided her hair, Evelyn stepped back and took a breath. With a running start, she jumped up and grabbed the vine. She dug her toe to find a foothold, but her grip slipped. Her fists tightened, but the vine was slick. She slid down, barely keeping her feet beneath her.

She squared her shoulders, readying to try again. Straddling the top, Jack said, "I don't remember it being this slick. I'll try opening the gate."

Keeping an eye on the dark street, Evelyn waited as Jack fumbled with the gate. Her pulse beat a drum of warning in her ears. They had spent the past few evenings sitting on her parents' porch, reading books on transformation and magic while Cassandra wound her net tighter around Henry. Their plan should work, as long as they were not caught sneaking into Cassandra's mansion.

The gate creaked open. Evelyn slipped inside and shut the gate with a firm clang. They approached the well while Jack lit his small lantern.

"It's simple," Jack said. "We rescue the other blokes from the well, and then we figure out how to turn them back into men. She won't be able to hide from all that."

Doubting things would go so simply, Evelyn helped Jack remove the well's cover. He hooked the lantern to his belt, lowered the bucket, and then slid down the rope. She crouched beside the well, watching the mansion for any signs of movement. The windows were dark, the building feeling as if no one had lived in it for decades. Yet she could not trust the silence.

Splashing sounds echoed from below as Jack grumbled to himself. He pulled on the rope and she cranked up the bucket. Frogs were packed in the small container, climbing over each other and filling the garden with a cacophony of ribbits. Wondering how many were actual frogs, she lifted the lid of the picnic basket and poured them inside. She sent the bucket down again, Jack filled it quickly, and she pulled it back up. As she tugged the last frog out and dropped it in the basket, she called down, "Is that all?"

She cringed as a salamander climbed out of her mouth. She tossed it away.

"Wait," Jack said.

Chains clanked below, echoing up the shaft. Evelyn frowned as she stared into the well. The light from Jack's lantern disappeared.

"Jack!" she whispered. "Where'd you go?"

"Hold on!"

Her breath stilled as the light of a passing motorcar shined through the decorative holes of the fence. With her eyes on the house, she waited for Cassandra's arrival. Cassandra seemed to prefer a horse and carriage, but she might be traveling by motorcar on this cold, damp night.

A light appeared in the far corner of the garden. Evelyn grabbed the basket and sprinted for the gate. Footsteps sped toward her. She dodged behind a bush and crouched down, hoping the fog could help hide her.

"Evelyn?" Jack whispered as he stopped a few feet away. She peered around the bush and he pointed toward the well. "You've got to see this."

She held the basket close as they crossed the garden. He replaced the cover on the well before nodding toward the corner by the shed. The mansion loomed over them as they scurried across the wet grass, its curves dark and menacing in the moonlight peeking through the clouds of fog. Jack led Evelyn behind the shed and to a trap door open in the ground.

Jack began to walk down the slim, brick stairs, but Evelyn held still.

"We have enough—" She stopped to spit out a newt.

He wiped his forehead with the back of his hand. "There could be more evidence down there. If we can get enough, the police might help."

Evelyn pressed her lips together as she raised an eyebrow. As Mrs. Hunter had said, the police weren't going to believe in magical curses. However, there might be something below she and Jack could use to convince Henry.

As they walked down the steps, the stone chilled the air further, sending goosebumps along Evelyn's arms. A mineral smell thickened as they entered a narrow tunnel, the echo of water lapping surrounding them. Slivers of moonlight shined through cracks in the ceiling until Evelyn and Jack went down another set of stairs and into a natural cavern.

Jack raised his lantern, illuminating the space. One side was bordered by a lake, the expanse of water dark and endless, mist hovering over the surface. A skiff was tied to a small dock, the lip of the boat carved with strange symbols mixed with waves. Evelyn stared at it, an uneasiness resting in her chest.

Pointing at a small tunnel in the wall behind them, Jack said, "This leads to the well."

He looked around the main cavern before approaching a large wood cupboard. Evelyn cringed as Jack opened it and the stink of moss and decomposing flesh mixed with the mineral scent of the cavern. The cupboard was a full of frogs and a few pieces of meat dangling from a butcher's string, flies buzzing around them. Evelyn held a hand to her mouth, hoping to not add bile to the things coming out.

"How many do you think there are?" Jack said as he shut the cupboard. "Another fifty? We can't carry all of them out."

Stepping further along the walkway, he raised his lantern, illuminating a spiraling set of stairs heading up. "What's this way?"

Evelyn pulled on his arm and shook her head, pointing at the basket of frogs. They had enough. They needed to leave.

"We can't go now. She's probably got a room of bubbling cauldrons up there. Maybe she's got people still in human form, locked away." He looked up the stairs as he half-smiled. "We might find her source of power and stop her tonight. That's worth going a little further."

The shadows hiding the top of the stairs glared down at Evelyn. She and Jack could also be caught or trapped. Yet, they had already broken into the woman's yard. If they were going to find or do anything useful, they had to go further.

Evelyn looked to Jack and nodded. Jack grinned and slapped her shoulder before running up the stairs. Evelyn hurried to keep up with his long stride. They reached a wooden door, the edges carved with waving lines and small star shapes. Evelyn held onto Jack's shoulder as he gripped the handle and turned it. The door opened in silence and Evelyn allowed herself to breathe.

They stepped into a bare cellar, a few boxes and barrels piled along the far wall, a layer of dust coating the floor. Jack walked up a small set of steps and opened the plain door leading into the mansion.

"Shall we explore, then?" Jack said.

Evelyn held tightly to the basket as she followed Jack. Beyond was a long hallway lined with lush carpets and carved archways fit for a cathedral. The air had the musty thickness of a mausoleum.

Jack opened the first door they came to and raised his lantern. Inside was stacked furniture covered in white dust-cloths. Jack watched the hallway while she lifted the cloths. The furniture beneath was polished with fine marquetry, but there were no signs of cauldrons or spells.

They checked the rest of the rooms along the hallway, but each was either empty or storing piles of boxes and furniture. Somewhere, they would find the small wing where Cassandra lived in this sprawling place.

They reached the end of the hall and went up a wide, polished mahogany staircase. Their feet tapped against the wood and a few steps creaked.

Jack's lantern lit the next floor. The hallway was identical to the one below, except for a set of double-doors set in one wall. Jack approached the doors and turned the handle. It did not move. He jiggled the handle and pulled on the door.

A moan full of elderly pain echoed from the room. Evelyn flattened herself against the wall, her heart pounding in her chest. She waved her arm and nodded toward the stairs. With the glint of a grin in his eyes, Jack shook his head. He pulled out a set of lock-picks and set down the lantern.

Hurrying over, Evelyn whispered, "Someone's in there." She cringed before spitting a frog into the basket.

"Could be a prisoner." Jack crouched down and squinted at the key hole. He pried the lock while gritting his teeth. "Henry was always better at this."

She frowned at him, but had no time to ask questions as the lock plinked and the door creaked open.

A hacking cough broke out on the other side, followed by wheezing.

"It must be her Papa," Jack whispered as he opened the door.

"Don't—" Evelyn said, but it was too late.

Jack removed his hat and stepped inside.

"Good evening, sir. Sorry about barging in, but I was wondering if we might be able to help each other."

Evelyn picked up the lantern and stepped inside as the old man broke into a wheezing laugh, ending in a coughing fit. She and Jack were here together and would see this through, even if he was being careless.

The room was lit by a fireplace, the light flickering around them.

Seated in a high-backed armchair beside the fire was a man with a gnarled face, his jowls stretched from too many years alive. He glared at them with his dark, sunken eyes, drooping red rims beneath them. His gray hair spread thin across his mottled scalp. A dressing gown hung over his hunched shoulders, draped over his frail body.

"You are Cassandra Astrellar's father, correct?" Jack said as Evelyn shut the door.

"I am Arturo Astrellar." The old man grunted a laugh. "But Cassandra is certainly not my daughter."

"She is an imposter?" Evelyn cringed before a salamander slithered out of her mouth. The old man's face wrinkled in disgust as Evelyn tossed it into the fire. There was a wet popping and cracking sound, and then it was gone.

"I see you've gotten in Cassandra's way," the old man said.

"And some men who're now frogs," Jack said. "Can you help us?"

"You have come for Cassandra Astrellar's secrets?" Arturo's eyes glittered in the firelight. "Do you think the truth will help you defeat her?"

"We'd like to try," Jack said.

Arturo leaned back in his chair, his mottled hands resting on this cane. "I have learned over the past sixty years it is safest to step out of Cassandra's way. I suggest you go home and stop interfering with her business."

"Sixty years? How can you have known her—" Evelyn stopped as another frog climbed its way out of her mouth. She looked to Jack. Cassandra was only twenty or so. Arturo could not have known her so long. Maybe he was locked away due to his lack of wits.

Sitting on the bench seat across from the man, Jack said, "We can't step away. The lady's out to destroy our lives, sir, and doesn't seem to be treating you much better. Help us and we might be able help you get free."

"You're fools to be here. If she finds you—"

"Tell us the truth quickly and we will go." Jack leaned toward the man. "We came for answers, and not just for ourselves. Tonight, she's out with my brother. I don't know what she wants with him, but I don't think it's for his good."

"Is he the new man she has chosen?" Arturo sat up, his dark eyes becoming more aware. "What are his qualities? Is he very handsome? Clever?"

"He is an honest man with a good heart." Evelyn barely forced out the last words before spitting out another frog.

"A pure heart? Incorruptible?" The eagerness in his eyes sent a chill through Evelyn.

"He's the stodgiest man I know and wouldn't do anything with even a hint of wrong to it," Jack said. "All the same, he's my brother and I want him safe."

"Then let him be. Cassandra will play her game, and if your brother is all you say he is, he will return safe and well. If he is not," Arturo lowered his chin as he stared at nothing. "Then, I am sorry for you."

Evelyn stood. "I will not abandon him." She tossed a salamander away from her mouth. "You see—" She felt another creature crawling out, but kept on. "What she has done to me." Pointing at Jack, she said, "He was turned into a frog. There are countless more transformed men down—" She gagged before spitting out the latest frog.

"Cassandra does not wish to be cruel," Arturo said. "I have done what I can to limit her means and force her to find another way, but we have searched for the last forty years to make things right. At first, she did not sacrifice others, but my time is running short and she is afraid. If you understood her, you would forgive her."

"I was a frog for less than a day," Jack said, grabbing the basket of frogs and opening it. "But how long have these fellows been kidnapped and trapped here?" He pointed at Evelyn. "Cassandra's threatened her family. What excuse can she have? I don't know what she has planned for my brother, but it can't end well."

The old man tapped his fingers on his armrest before pointing to a white and gold nightstand. "There is a book in the top drawer. Bring it to me."

Hoping for any answer, Evelyn opened the drawer and pulled out a leather-bound journal, the pages weathered and yellowed.

"She has tested many men before," Arturo said as Evelyn handed him the book, "But none have had friends loyal enough to risk themselves." His hands shook as he turned over a few pages. "She has kept her secrets from each of the men and each has failed. Perhaps, a bit of truth can help us all."

He looked up from the pages, his eyes boring into Evelyn and Jack. "I will tell you who Cassandra Astrellar truly is and what she seeks from your brother in the hope you will understand her better and consider helping her."

Evelyn shook her head, but Jack put his hand on her arm. Their eyes met. They needed the truth to help Henry.

Taking their silence for acceptance, Arturo motioned for Evelyn to take the book. She picked it up and sat beside Jack, the page still opened. Glued to the paper was a small, cracked portrait of a handsome, dark-haired man of twenty standing arm-in-arm with Cassandra. They looked at each other with warm smiles and bright eyes. On the opposite page was pasted a marriage certificate.

I hereby certify on this day, Arturo Astrellar and Cassandra La Mer were by me united in marriage in accordance with License issued by the Clerk of Valar, Court of Justice, Nation of Castallar, numbered 11456.

Evelyn looked again at the year. It was marked sixty years before. The picture seemed old enough, based on the cracking and yellowing. Maybe Cassandra looked similar to the grandmother she was named after.

"Cassandra La Mer Astrellar is not my daughter," the old man said.

"She is my wife, and while I do not agree with her methods, I must do what I can to help her."

"This is impossible," Jack said as he leaned closer to the book.

"She turned you into a frog and cursed this young lady and you think her lack of age impossible?" Arturo took a drink of water from the glass by his side before smacking his lips.

"How is her age possible?" Evelyn said, trying to hold back a salamander.

Arturo Astrellar kept his sharp, intelligent eyes on them. "To explain, I must go back to when we met, over sixty years ago. I was only twenty-one, alone with my elder brother Hernan on a hunting trip off the coast of Castallar. We pulled Cassandra from some wreckage. She was the only survivor."

"She was only on our boat for a day, and I spent most of my time worrying Hernan would lose his head over such a charming beauty."

The corners of Arturo's wrinkled lips rose into a smile as Jack's cheeks flushed a little. Evelyn raised an eyebrow and Jack shrugged.

"You've got to admit, she is beautiful," Jack whispered. "And can appear charming."

Evelyn's eyebrow rose higher, but she kept her eyes on the old man. She was too close to the truth to say anything to stop him.

"In the evening, we sat on the deck and talked. I didn't notice when Hernan abandoned the conversation and went to bed. I myself became wrapped in her wit and intelligence, her friendly repartee. We sat closer as the night went on.

"By dawn, I longed for her kiss. When I finally dared the approach, she laughed and kissed my cheek. I fell back, and next I knew, I woke with Hernan shaking me as a storm brewed around us, Cassandra gone."

"Must've been quite a kiss," Jack said.

Evelyn glanced at the door, wondering when Cassandra would next appear here. They couldn't ask too many questions. The sooner

Arturo finished his story, the sooner they could get out of the mansion and decide how to save Henry.

"There was no time to look. The storm grew, and our ship broke, and my brother and I were lost at sea." Arturo rubbed his hands together. "Out in the open ocean, waiting to drown is when I saw Cassandra again."

Evelyn found herself joining Jack in leaning forward and letting the old man's story carry them to sixty years before, on the seas beyond Castallar.

Chapter 11

60 Years Earlier

Another wave battered at Arturo, shoving him deeper into the ocean. Arturo barely kept hold of his brother as he sank. Kicking his legs, he pulled Hernan up. His brother was a dead weight, yet Arturo could sense himself approaching the surface. Another swirl of waves tossed Arturo back under.

Growing up on the shores of Castallar and traveling across the ocean in his father's merchant ships had taught Arturo how to swim and hold his breath a long time. Right now, it wasn't long enough.

An arm wrapped around Arturo's middle. Arturo kicked harder. There were rumors of strange creatures in these waters, laughing as they dragged men down to their death. He reached for his hunting knife. A hand swatted his arm while pulling him to the surface.

He gasped in air as his head breached the water. His unknown rescuer dragged him onto a piece of broken timber. Coldness filled his chest as Cassandra's voice said, "Hold on."

His mind had to be broken by a late night followed by a shattered yacht.

Arturo panted, trying to pull his brother further onto the beam. He shouted as another wave crashed, pulling Hernan from him. As he tumbled, he held onto the wood beam with both arms. The beam bobbed to the surface, pulling Arturo with it.

Scanning the water as the rain pelted and the ocean churned, Arturo prayed for a sign of his brother. The deepening hollowness in his stomach told him his brother was dead.

Arturo cried out as a wet rope slapped across his face and Cassandra's voice yelled, "Grab on!"

Some impossible creature must have stolen her voice. Hernan was dead and Arturo was not going to join him. Keeping his arms around the timber, Arturo kicked. His own survival was most important now. Someone had to tell his parents how Hernan had drowned.

The rope slapped across his arms again. Arturo wasn't sure if all his kicking was just sending him in circles, but he couldn't trust the rope.

The splashing of someone swimming mixed with the crash of waves. A pair of feminine hands pressed to the other side of the timber. Arturo's heart jolted as Cassandra rose out of the water. Her blue eyes sparkled in the moonlight and her blond hair hung around her in a wet mass.

"Are all men this stubborn?" she said. "Or do you prefer to drown?"

Arturo shouted as he shoved off the timber and swam with all his strength, fighting against the swelling water around him. He would rather take his chances being battered by the waves. The woman was a witch of the sea, known by more romantic people as mermaids. They sat on rocks, drawing men with their beauty and song. These creatures drowned the men for sport and then divided whatever spoils of gold and jewels were left.

Her arms wrapped around his torso and she dragged him with her. He rammed his elbow into her stomach while his other arm reached for his hunting knife. She tightened her hold on him, squeezing his ribs. Her muscular fish tail splashed out of the water as she increased her speed, the scales slick and glittering. His fingers were on the handle of his knife, when she tossed him into the air. He flailed his legs until he landed on a wooden plank.

Rain pelted down as the plank rode up a growing wave. The mermaid pushed the broken piece of ship along the crest. Arturo held on with both arms as the former deck glided along the wave and then bobbed into a still patch of water. He raised his head. Beside him lay an unconscious Hernan, tied to the plank. Arturo kept one hand on the lip of the plank as he knelt and pressed his hand to Hernan's chest. His skin was cold and clammy, but he was breathing.

A wave crashed over them, shoving the plank underwater. Arturo grabbed the rope holding Hernan. He thudded down onto the wood as they came back up.

"Hold still!" Cassandra pushed the plank.

Water sprayed as she drove them away from the storm and the remnants of his light yacht. Arturo stared ahead, wishing events hadn't turned out this way. He and his brother should have been on their way home to Castillar, where Hernan would be stuffed into a suit and married off to Rosa of the Mercado family. The hunting trip to the islands on the coast of Castillar was only supposed to be a final adventure of bachelorhood. Now, both his and Hernan's survival seemed doubtful.

The sun was breaking through the dark clouds as Cassandra pushed the plank over a set of crashing waves and to the still shore of an island. Arturo began to slide off the plank, when she grabbed his shoulder.

"Do not touch the land." She picked up the loose end of the rope tied around Hernan. She swam into the shallows and looped the rope around a boulder.

Arturo looked out at the green island. They couldn't be too far off course, despite the storm. Here would be fresh water and game. They could survive until rescued.

Arturo sat up, letting his feet hang over the side. The water was shallow enough for him to walk onshore. He started to push himself off, but Cassandra shoved him back onto the plank.

"Any human who touches the island will be executed, or worse," she said.

"Why should I trust a witch of the sea?" He kept one hand on his brother. "You lied to us."

"I never told you what I was or was not." She pushed back her hair from her face and smoothed the collar of her sharkskin vest. "I'm a northern mermaid, not like these southern ones. They would have let you drown."

"How'd you end up in the wreckage, and with legs?"

Her tail splashed in the water. "We've enough magic to have legs when we need to. As for my captors, they were fools who thought they could manage selling a mermaid."

She placed her hand on top of his, but he jerked away.

"I didn't tell you because we try not to announce ourselves to humans. Most either fear us or don't believe in us, and the whole conversation gets messy." Her blue eyes searched his. "I did need your help. I was unconscious and couldn't escape from human form. I would have drowned if you hadn't saved me."

Arturo kept his glare on her as the plank bobbed in the water. "If I can't touch the ground, can you get me a paddle?"

"We both know this bit of wood will fall apart before you reach the mainland."

"I just need it to stay together long enough for us to be found."

"Stay here. I'll find a boat."

Cassandra slipped back into the water and swam away. Sitting cross-legged, he stared at the beach as the plank floated on the small waves hitting the shore. The sea creature could be lying. Their conversation from the night before had felt real. Her laughter and smile had been so genuine, not like the barmaids who flirted with Hernan.

He was being a fool, but he would give her a few hours. If she wasn't back by noon, he would take Hernan onto the shore. Their chances were better on the island.

The hours crept by, filled only with the lapping of the waves, the wind in the trees, and the cry of birds on the island. Arturo watched his brother sleep, a massive bruise across Hernan's face. Despite the periodic spray of water, the sun dried Arturo's skin, leaving a layer of salt. Sweat formed along with the desire for fresh water.

Hernan groaned as he opened his eyes and blinked in the bright sunlight. Arturo pulled the rope off Hernan as he sat up. He laughed and clapped Arturo on the shoulder.

"We made it!"

Before Arturo could grab him, Hernan rolled off the plank and splashed into the water. He ran to the beach and jumped onto the sand. Arturo stood and began to shout at his brother. The uneven vessel tilted, dumping Arturo into the water. Arturo's toes dug in the sand as he prayed Cassandra had lied.

Arturo joined his brother on shore. Hernan pointed at the green trees filling the island.

"I'll bet we can find some good fruit out there." He rubbed his stomach. "Or a fine pig."

Hernan ran to the rocks and grabbed the rope holding the plank. "Help me. We can trap a whole herd of pigs."

"We should get back on the plank."

"What for?" He licked his lips. "If we get to shore, we'll have a full meal by tonight."

Arturo glanced at the beach. There was no sign of humans nor merfolk. His lack of water was getting to him. A drink and a hearty meal would do both of them good.

Just then, a net sprang out of the water and wrapped around him. As he fell, he grabbed his knife and tried to cut through the thick cords. Hernan ran for him, but another net caught him.

A shirtless man stood over the pair of brothers, a tri-cornered hat on his head, his legs covered by breeches made from fish-like skin. He cried out in a high-pitch and kicked the knife out of Arturo's hand.

"To the cages!" He snapped to a half-dozen hunched-over men in rags running from the trees.

The men in rags had sunken, defeated eyes, their hair and long beards matted, their skin layered with grime. They lined up like a team of horses and took the ropes holding the nets wrapped around Arturo and Hernan.

The dull-eyed men dragged Arturo and Hernan across the hot beach. Arturo shut his eyes and mouth, grains of sand filling his ears and scraping his skin. They reached wet, stony ground and the men in rags lifted the brothers onto their shoulders. The shirtless man snapped a whip on the ground and shouted at them, pushing them faster up a steep hill, their bare feet sliding against the stone.

"We are the sons of Gonzalo Astrellar!" Hernan said. "Our uncle is Admiral Ricardo Astrellar of the Castallar Navy."

Chains clinked and the brothers were tossed onto a metal floor. The nets were ripped away. Arturo tried to ignore the sand grains in his eyes. His vision cleared as the cage door clanked shut. The cage rose, swinging as it was pulled into a dimly lit cavern.

"Welcome to Marveth," the shirtless man said. "Your trial will be held shortly."

Hernan shouted and threw himself against the wall of the rusted cage. Arturo stared down at the lagoon, his eyes meeting those of the crocodiles swimming below. Had the mermaid led them into a trap or should they have listened to her? It did not matter. He needed to make sure he and Hernan did not die.

Arturo patted his pockets until he found his penknife. Glad it hadn't been lost to the waves, Arturo pressed his hand to Hernan's shoulder.

Chest heaving, Hernan stopped his pounding and glanced at

Arturo. With one hand gripping the bars to hold himself steady, Arturo leaned against the cage and tried to pry the knife into the lock.

"The man's lying," Hernan said as he glared into the darkness. "Marveth's only a sea dog's legend meant to scare children. Who do you think they really are? Pirates?"

Arturo paused to glance at his brother. The truth set a chill through his chest. "I think we are in Marveth."

"All that sea water's gotten to your head."

The cage creaked as it swung over the crocodile-laden lagoon. Arturo rubbed his forehead.

"I don't know what's true or not anymore. Cassandra—" He felt an idiot to say the truth aloud, but Hernan needed to know. "She saved us from the wreckage and brought us here."

Hernan held out his hand for the knife. "You sit down and rest. I'll get us out."

Arturo passed the knife to his brother and scooted back. "She's a mermaid."

Leaning against the cage, Hernan laughed. Clapping his hand on Arturo's shoulder, he said, "And I'm the one who got knocked in the head? You've listened to too many stories."

Arturo pressed his teeth together, preparing a protest. In Hernan's place, however, Arturo wouldn't believe either. With a grunt, he dropped into a sitting position and leaned his head against the cage. He shut his eyes, hoping he would wake and all this would turn out to be just a nightmare.

Arturo jumped awake as the cage rattled and shook. Hernan shouted as the door swung open, nearly pulling him with it. He slammed it closed and grinned at Arturo.

"We'll give them a bit of a surprise," Hernan said. "Just wait till the guard gets close."

Trying to swallow to clear the dryness in his mouth, Arturo stood. The cage rose through the darkness. Light grew as the rocks glowed around them. Several men wearing tri-cornered hats and holding spears waited at the entrance. Arturo crouched behind his brother, ready to spring. They had one chance. All he needed was to grab a spear, then they could fight to shore. From there, he had no idea how they would get back to the mainland, but they had a better chance there than locked away.

The cage shuddered to a stop over the ledge. Two of the guards approached, spears pointed forward. Hernan threw open the door, knocking back a spear. Arturo leaped out and rammed his elbow into the guard's stomach and moved to twist the spear out of his grip. The guard's hold was stronger than expected. Arturo pushed harder. Something wet splatted on his chest. An electric charge shuddered through his body, leaving him hot and cold at the same time. He fell to the ground, his arms and legs twitching.

A guard picked up a quivering eel and dropped it into a sack at his side, water splashing out. Arturo heard another zap behind him followed by a thud.

"The High Witch has summoned the one with a mark," a guard said. "Leave the other."

A guard hefted Arturo's limp body over his shoulder. Sharp pricks zipped across Arturo's skin. He tried to count the guard's steps as they went down the stone stairs and into a corridor. He lost count by the time he was dropped on a pile of seaweed beside a pool of water.

The room was lined with white marble. Several statues of mermaids rose out of the pool, their tails gilded with gold. A few divots sat along the edge of the pool for mermaids to rest. Whoever had ordered him brought here was probably not going to help him.

The water frothed as a wide, barnacle-covered hat rose. Sea

urchins decorated the brim as a crab or two scuttled across. If decorated in feathers and jewels, it would have made a fine ladies hat, though larger than most would wear.

With a flash of a fishtail, the mermaid wearing the hat appeared. Her face was older than Cassandra's, with faint lines of age, yet she had a similar cool beauty. The lens of her over-sized monocle made one eye appear larger than the other, but did nothing to soften her piercing gaze. Any warmth Arturo had felt was sucked away by those eyes. He wondered how many sailors she had lured into dashing themselves into the sea after her.

She raised her hand, her fingernails encrusted with jewels and half-as-long as her fingers.

"I told you I wanted to speak with him," she said, flicking Arturo's numb face.

"He attempted to escape, High Witch Randala," the guard said, a crack of doubt in his voice.

She snapped her fingers to dismiss them.

"I cannot keep Madame La Mer waiting." A thin smile crossed her face. "I suppose I'll just have to make you more pathetic."

She drew back her hand and scraped Arturo's cheek. He wanted to yell as the stinging spread and blood dripped across his face, but could not move.

"We'll see how she responds to her poor, pretty little pet, won't we?"

The blowing of a conch shell echoed and Randala swam to the highest of the underwater seats. Her torso was draped in gold chainmail decorated with living sea creatures. She leaned back, her head raised high, her arm draped over a statue's tail.

Cassandra rose on the opposite end of the pool, wearing the same sharkskin vest as before. She held both arms across her chest and bowed.

"Here is your prize, Madame La Mer," Randala said, "As tidy as we could make him after his efforts to escape."

Cassandra glanced at Arturo. Her face remained as calm as the best diplomats Arturo had seen. "Where is the other?"

"He does not have your mark."

"They are both my guests. They saved my life and I returned the deed by bringing them here. They did not know where they were and would have returned to Castallar as ignorant as they left it."

"How can two humans spare your life?" Randala tilted her chin up. "Was it the little mishap with the ship you were hiding on? You could have returned to your true form and been fine."

"With assassins chasing me?" Cassandra's eyes hardened. "It's not my fault the Witch of Tiria hired them. My cousin realized her deception on his own."

"Your cousin would be wise to take the alliance."

"To a mermaid two centuries older and an eye only to overthrow my uncle?" Cassandra waved her hand. "You would never accept such an offer."

"I would never need to." Leaning back, Randala said, "I protect my people by upholding our laws. This human has your mark and I will let you keep him in whatever form you wish. In return, you will release all claims on the other and he will remain prisoner."

"Have a little mercy. They are not thieves or pirates. They are gentlemen of Castallar, and they—"

"I am being generous." Randala pressed a hand to her chest. "In honor of your position as ambassador, I have kept them from being traded as workers. If you take the matter up with our Court of Justice, I will not be able to keep them from a worse fate."

Cassandra's arms remained relaxed even as the tendons in her neck flexed. "This is your generosity? Then I must choose the Court of Justice."

"Cassandra, we have known each other a long time. I cannot believe—"

"I have given you my choice. These two men are now mine until the Court meets."

Randala's eyes narrowed. "Do not be foolish. I lead the Court."

"We both know the laws. The statues in the Hall of Justice will fall if you go against the truth and the ancient laws the tribes agreed on. We shall see if these innocent men will receive their just reward."

"You are being childish. You cannot—"

Randala broke off as Cassandra pushed herself across the pool and pulled herself up until she was sitting on the edge.

"Pardon me, Your Excellence, but my pet and I must take our leave. I will expect his brother as soon as possible."

Randala glared as Cassandra pulled an armband from the satchel tied to her hip. As soon as the armband was on, her sharkskin vest and scaled fishtail transformed into a blue, velvet gown. She stood up, tottering a moment before whistling and circling her hand. A bubble rose from the pool and surrounded Arturo, lifting him off the ground.

He stared out from the bubble, everything warped by the shield of water carrying him through the air. They passed through a carved tunnel and over a clear surface. Beneath, merfolk flitted about, some stopping to chat just as humans chatted on the street. A few guards stood along the edges of the tunnel, but Cassandra ignored them as she marched on.

She stopped at one of a series of archways carved in the walls and sang out a few high-pitched notes. The stone blocking the opening rolled aside. Once Arturo was carried through, the stone rolled back. The bubble lowered Arturo onto a stone bench beside a pool smaller than Randala's, and then popped, the water spraying.

Tingling grew sharper through Arturo as he flexed his fingers.

Cassandra bent down beside the pool and opened a cupboard. "I usually have better accommodations for human guests, but this will have to do."

From the cupboard, she pulled a glass bowl with several glowing creatures in it. She returned to Arturo's bench and sat beside him. Her face softened with concern as she brushed back his dark curls and looked at the scratches Randala had left on his face. The stinging was hard to feel over the numb tingling in the rest of his body.

"I don't think there's poison," she said as she lifted a starfish from the bowl, a halo of blue light around the creature. She set it on Arturo's wound, the stinging doubling as the starfish clung to his skin.

The numbness ebbed from his body, leaving a throbbing on his face and a sting on his chest where he had been struck by the eel.

Cassandra wrapped her fingers around his. "I'm so very sorry, Arturo. I left the yacht to keep you and your brother out of danger, but it seems I made things far worse."

Arturo inhaled as he regained control over his own muscles. Drawing his hand away, he sat up. He flexed his jaw, his tongue still feeling fat.

"They won't let us go, will they?" He stretched his mouth, hoping the words weren't too slurred.

Her face was close, her eyes searching his. He clamped his hand against his leg, unsure if his chest was throbbing from pain or from desire for this creature of the sea. Facing the fullness of her lips took remembering every tale of mermaid treachery.

"There is little chance," she said. "But requesting an audience with the Court of Justice may buy us some time to smuggle you out." She pressed her lips together as her eyebrows lowered. "How do you feel about being a sea turtle?"

"I'd rather be a man."

"It would only be a temporary condition. I would help you return to Castallar and turn you back."

She moved to touch his uninjured cheek but he leaned away. "Please trust me. I know I kept my true form from you, but every word I spoke the other night was true. I have not been able to speak so freely for a long time.

"I cannot watch you become yet another slave or pet. You've a noble heart and are meant for better things. Let me repay your kindness and help you get home."

Arturo kept hold of the bench to keep himself steady. He had already been taken in by her beauty once, yet the earnestness of her voice stirred something within. He wanted to give in and trust her, but a sliver of doubt kept a wedge between him and the hope she attempted to give.

Cassandra pressed her hand to his knee before rising. "I wish I could just be the girl you thought I—"

The stone at the entrance rolled aside and a guard shoved Hernan in. He stumbled and nearly caught hold of the bench before falling in the pool of water. Arturo tried to shove himself from the bench, but his legs were still numb and he fell. Cassandra bent down and caught Hernan by the back of his collar. As easily as lifting a puppy, she pulled him from the water. She rose and set him on the bench before helping Arturo sit up.

Shaking water out of his hair, Hernan said, "Cassandra, you're a prisoner too? Arturo told me some mad story about you being a mermaid." He let out a laugh before frowning. "How'd you get here? Did these pirates steal you off our ship in the middle of the night?" His gaze turned to Arturo and his eyes widened. "What's that glowing thing on your face?"

"It's a starfish," Cassandra said, laying her hands against her skirt as a coolness filled her eyes. Gone was any illusion of youthful innocence. "I enchanted it to heal him."

Hernan wrung out part of his shirt. "Both of you need some rest. I'll keep watch. Then we can find a way out. Once we get to shore, we'll light a fire to help Uncle Ricardo and the navy find us."

"The navy won't find this island," Cassandra said. "Even if they did, the sailors would be in danger."

Hernan pushed himself up from the bench and took a hobbling

step toward Cassandra. He lifted her hand and placed it between both of his. Arturo would have taken a step back under the glare Cassandra gave.

"There's no need to play brave." Hernan smiled and Arturo held back a groan. "Arturo spent a few years in the navy himself and I'm not too bad with a sword. We'll escape and you can come to Castallar with us.

"Our mother will welcome a beauty like you." He winked as he added, "And, I'm sure Arturo won't mind having you around a bit longer."

Cassandra pulled her hand away and moved to the edge of the pool. "Do humans ever take beautiful women seriously?" Walking down the staircase into the water, she said, "I often long to be old, wrinkled, and listened to."

She pulled off the armband and dropped it in her satchel. Hernan jolted back and fell onto the bench as Cassandra's velvet skirt morphed back into a long fish tail, the shark-skin shirt replacing her bodice.

"Arturo," Hernan said, tugging on his brother's sleeve, his voice hoarse, "She's a mermaid!"

"She's trying to help us get free," Arturo said as Cassandra leaned back in the water, letting her golden hair spread around her. He watched her fins splash as she stretched. Unsure he believed his own words, he said, "We'd be wise to listen to her."

"Mermaids can't be trusted, if the stories are true." Hernan ran his hands through his hair. "Maybe a fever's spreading."

"I wish it were." Arturo looked up at his brother and repeated a summary of Cassandra's discussion with Randala. "Cassandra says our best chance is to escape before we're at the Hall of Justice. I've no idea how to do it, but we've got to try."

"I could turn you into something more portable." Cassandra rested her arms on the edge of the pool. "Arturo already turned down sea turtles, which might be too large anyway. Now, frogs—" She slapped her fist against the stone. "But Randala would sense the transformation."

Hernan scratched his head. "I think Arturo and I'd be better help if we can get some fresh water and food."

"You are right. I'll have some sent immediately, along with clean clothes." Cassandra pushed away from the wall and disappeared into the pool.

Hernan whispered, "Do you really trust her?"

"I don't know. She did save our lives, but—" Arturo tapped his fingers, trying to decipher how he felt. The attraction was there, but he could be blinded by her magic.

Pressing a hand to Arturo's shoulder, Hernan said, "We're best off finding a way off the island on our own."

Arturo nodded as he pulled the starfish from his cheek. It stung, but his head felt clearer. "You have any ideas how?"

"No." Hernan gave a half-smile. "But, we are sons of the House of Astrellar. We'll find a way."

Arturo returned a weak smile as he clapped his brother on the shoulder. They would have to find a way or end up as the dead-eyed slaves who had dragged them from the shore. He would not accept such a fate.

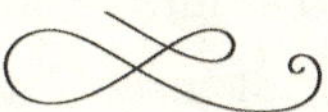

Arturo knelt and rolled up his over-long pant legs as the platters of roasted kelp and fish was removed. No utensils had been given, meaning no new tools for escape. The opening was currently uncovered. He and Hernan could try to run, but they wouldn't get far. They were better off waiting and finding a quiet route out.

As dead-eyed men and women carried the trays out, a guard entered, his tri-corner hat tilted jauntily. He crossed his arms over his chest and bowed.

"Madame La Mer, the Hall of Justice has decided to be generous and give your guests an immediate trial."

"I thought I had at least three days."

"You have one hour."

Cassandra glared at him. "Thank you. If you will pardon us, I need to prepare."

"I was ordered to stay and assist you."

Hernan and Arturo glanced at each other. Assisting was only another word for watching.

In the small time provided, Arturo and Hernan took turns pacing. Cassandra went to a cupboard along the edge of the pool and pulled out a music box made of glass. Strange music echoed from the box and Cassandra changed the spool a few times. With each melody, the empty space in the glass glowed. Sometimes Arturo thought he saw a few figures and distinct shapes. Concentrating was hard with the dark-eyed guard watching them, his eyes unblinking.

"It is time," the guard said. "They will meet you there."

Cassandra looked up at Arturo, a flash of worry in her eyes. This was soon covered by a perfect calm.

The guard led the brothers on another set of winding staircases, this time going down. The path turned from carved steps to natural rock formations as they went further down.

"Welcome to the Hall of Justice," the guard said as they stepped through a carved archway and onto a paved platform.

The Hall of Justice was almost a cathedral, with four giant statues of merfolk serving as pillars along the dome, staring down with stern faces carved from stone. The water reflected on the gold ceiling along with glowing lights hanging above dozens of floating candelabras. Merfolk crowded in the water, each peeking over each other's shoulder for a better look. At the head of the room, carved out of the tails of one of the statues, were a set of five seats sitting just beneath the surface of the water. In them were two mermen and three mermaids, including Randala, who sat at the highest seat in the center.

Cassandra waited at the end of the paved platform, her hands on a stone podium rising out of the water. Arturo and Hernan followed the path and stood behind her.

With high-pitched singing, Randala opened the trial. Arturo and Hernan put their hands over their ears as the high pitches of the mermaid's native tongue pelted at them. Through his growing headache, Arturo could tell the five judges were asking questions while Cassandra calmly batted off whatever they threw at her.

"She could be selling us for her own safety," Hernan said, leaning close to Arturo. "We should speak for ourselves."

"We don't know their laws."

A silence broke, but Arturo could still hear ringing. Cassandra turned toward the brothers and motioned for them to come closer.

"It doesn't look well," Arturo whispered as he and Hernan knelt beside her.

"They claim you are human and so do not even have a right to innocence." She glanced at the merfolk. "They are calling for you to either be added to the labor camps as prisoners or be transformed into a more tradeable form."

"Tradeable?" Arturo said.

"I'll not be bought and sold," Hernan grunted.

"You might not have a choice." Her cheek twitched. "If they decide to, they will turn you into something they can cage and carry to the gambling hall."

Arturo frowned. "We'd be used to make a bet?"

"What do you think happens to all of the drowned sailors?" she said. "It would be wasteful to let them die."

"If we agreed to be transformed, could you keep us?"

Cassandra shook her head. "Randala would auction you off. I might try to win you back by gambling, but one creature is almost impossible to tell from another." She swallowed as she looked him in the eye. "I will not let you be lost forever."

Arturo glanced out at the hall. There were no friends here. He and Hernan should have agreed to be a pair of sea turtles back in Cassandra's room.

"Let me speak," Hernan said. "I can persuade them."

Arturo shook his head while Cassandra raised an eyebrow.

"No," she said, when Hernan stood up.

"Honorable Justices," he said. "And good Merfolk, my brother and I apologize for anything we did to offend. We are shipwrecked and only wish to go home. We will keep your island secret, even from our uncle, Admiral Ricardo Astrellar of the Castallan Navy. However, if we're not set free—"

Cassandra tugged at Hernan's pant leg and shook her head.

He kicked her hand away. "If we're not set free, the whole of the Castallar Navy will be looking for us. Your secret will be lost, along with many lives."

"Madame La Mer," Randala said. "Please remind your humans to respect this court."

"Of course, Your Excellency," Cassandra said.

Randala wrinkled her forehead before leaning close to one of the other members of the council. Arturo flexed his hand as he glanced at the sunlight gleaming through a hole. If he jumped in the water now, he might make it out of this lagoon. He doubted, however, he would get much farther.

The five justices went silent and Randala said, "We have heard enough. We will have your decision shortly."

The justices dove into the water and swam out. The merfolk broke out in high-pitched chatter while Arturo and Hernan were marched out to a holding room. Arturo sat on a rock and held his head between his hands while Hernan paced.

"They'll have to let us go now," Hernan said. "Uncle Ricardo's probably already found the island and is getting the cannons ready. Before morning, we'll be on a Castallan battle cruiser, sailing back home."

"We'll be frogs," Arturo said. "Or worse." He looked up at Hernan. "If you'd let Cassandra speak for us, we might have had a chance."

Hernan jabbed his finger toward Arturo. "You're blinded by her pretty face. A man's fate is better in his own hands."

Arturo jumped to his feet and grabbed Hernan by the shirt. "If they imprison or transform us, we're lost. There might be a way off the island, but it could be years before we find a way."

Hernan shoved Arturo back. "Where's your hope? With this sham done, we can start finding a real escape."

Arturo tightened his fist, wondering if a bloody nose would make his brother wiser. Before he could swing, a guard appeared and ushered them back to the supposed Hall of Justice.

It only took moments for Randala to pronounce, "Imprisonment for life."

Hernan shouted and fought against the guards. Arturo stared, a chill spreading through him. The guards grabbed his arms and he began to fight, until his eyes met Cassandra's. Tears dripped down her cheeks. He squared his shoulders and raised his chin.

"We should've kept the knife hidden," Hernan said for the fifteenth time.

Arturo rested his head against the edge of the cage and stared back down at the crocodiles. Perhaps one of them had been a man. What would life be like as a crocodile? Could he swim all the way to Castallar as one?

The chains rattled and the cage swung.

Arturo and Hernan stood, holding onto the cage to steady themselves. Watching the walls, Arturo wondered how much give the chain had. They might swing the cage enough to loosen the chain and grab onto one of the ledges or stalactites. They would have a better chance with the crocodiles than the merfolk.

The cage jerked to a stop at the glowing opening. Six guards stood with pikes as another two pulled Hernan and Arturo out of the cage. The guards pushed them into a nearby alcove. In the pool of water, Randala sat glaring from beneath her over-sized hat, Cassandra beside her.

"Madame La Mer has persuaded me to have some mercy." Randala motioned for Cassandra to speak.

"High-Witch Randala has agreed to the release of one of you. Whichever is set free, he will forget being here and only believe his brother has drowned." She inhaled as if to calm herself. "The choice is yours."

Arturo's heartbeat quickened as he saw himself running up the steps of his family's old hacienda and embracing his parents, greeting his younger sister, laughing with his friends. Guilt filled him as he imagined holding his parents' hands as he told them of how he abandoned his elder brother, the heir of the House of Astrellar. No matter Hernan's faults, he was the one to carry on the Astrellar name. In time, he would bring it honor. How could Arturo bring it honor if he betrayed his only brother?

"Go home, Arturo," Hernan said. "I'll find another way."

Cassandra released a pent-up breath. Arturo ignored her as he turned to his brother.

"You're the heir," Arturo said.

"You'll carry on the Astrellar name better than I can," Hernan said. "And, I'd rather miss my own wedding."

Facing the two mermaids, Arturo stepped forward. "Hernan must go."

Cassandra's eyes flicked to him and she gave a subtle shake of her head.

"Madame La Mer, I don't know why you bothered. It appears they both want to stay."

"He is the elder brother. As second son, I do not matter. For the honor of our family, let him go."

Hernan opened his mouth to protest, but Arturo grabbed his arm. Arturo met his glare and Hernan shook his head before hugging his brother.

He ruffled Arturo's hair and whispered, "I'll remember the truth and we'll find you."

Arturo forced a smile, though he knew this was a lie.

Hernan stepped forward and said, "He's right. I will go."

Randala's frown deepened. "This is your choice?" She turned to Cassandra. "Strange creatures, these pets of yours."

"Yes," Cassandra whispered.

Randala snapped to the guard. "Give him the potion and put him on the boat."

Cassandra touched Randala's arm. "Let them say goodbye."

"What for? One will forget the other and the other will wish he could forget."

Hernan gave Arturo one last embrace, but it could not ebb Arturo's rising numbness.

The guards pulled them apart and Arturo kept his head high as he was taken back to the cage. Here, on this forsaken island, he might spend the rest of his days, his plight quickly forgotten by his brother, himself left for dead by his family.

He would have to find a way to escape.

Chapter 12

Hours or days passed. Neither mattered as hard loaves of bread and half-rancid water were tossed into the cage. Arturo tried to swing the cage as he reached his arm out toward a stalactite. The cage arched a bit, but never close enough. Once he was worn out, he curled up on the floor. He wondered if or when he would become one of the hunched-over men who'd carried him and Hernan from the beach. His fate might be worse.

He listened to the echo of crickets telling him it was sunset in a world beyond this dark tunnel. Lying against the side of the cage, he wished he could feel wind on his face.

The cage shook as the chains chinked into motion. He peered into the darkness. He shouted as the cage dropped like an anchor. He slammed against the sides as it splashed into the lagoon. Water surged in, surrounding and suffocating him. He pushed his feet against the cage door. Drowning was better than being prisoner, but he would rather live.

The door gave under his feet and he pushed himself down. He kicked as hard as he could to be clear of the cage and swam to the surface. As his head returned to open air, there was a snap of teeth followed by a thud and whimper.

A hand wrapped around his and drew him away from the thrashing behind him. He was pulled down and through an underwater tunnel. As he bumped against stone walls, his lungs burned. His head broke through to the surface and he gasped in air.

Paddling to keep his head above water, he looked up at the island's dark shadow. He kicked himself back as Cassandra rose in front of him.

"I arranged the deal for you," she said, grabbing his shirt and shaking him, "Not your brother."

Arturo's eyes followed the line of starlight highlighting her cheekbones, leading down the soft curve to her chin. He shut his eyes to clear his thoughts.

"Thank you," he whispered.

"Wait till you've escaped."

She grabbed his arm and pulled him to a small sailboat waiting near the shore. Arturo dragged himself over the side. As he unfurled the sail, Cassandra climbed aboard, her fishtail slapping against the hull. Arturo untied the rope holding them to the rocks as she put on the armband and had legs once more.

He wanted to doubt her, yet she had been true in every action. Even now, she could easily return to Marveth and claim he had escaped on his own.

"You shouldn't come with me," he said.

"If I'm going to be punished, I want it to be worth something." She grabbed the mast and pulled herself to her feet.

Arturo used an oar to push the boat off the shore and they inched into the water. He almost fell as bells clanged and high-pitched whistles erupted around the island.

"Guide the rudder." She moved behind the sail. "I'll give you some wind."

Arturo frowned as he gripped the rudder. Cassandra took a deep breath before singing a strong, operatic note. A soft breeze sent a ripple along the sail, but nothing more. The note rose in pitch and Cassandra held out her palms toward the sail, a green light forming around her hands. The boat jolted forward as a tunnel of wind hit the sail. Arturo clung to the rudder, steering the ship around rocks jutting out of the water.

"I don't know the way," Arturo shouted over the wind. There was no compass or map to guide him.

"Picture your home," she said before letting out a series of lower notes.

Arturo pictured the marble halls, his mahogany framed bed, the frescos along the hallway, and his brother, sister, and parents out in the main garden. A clearness filled his mind and he looked forward. His hands moved the rudder with precision, guiding him to home and safety.

His concentration slipped as something thunked against the boat. He glanced to the side and a massive shark fin rose from the water, promising a mouth full of teeth.

"Focus on me." Cassandra kept one palm facing forward and twirled her other hand. She continued singing as clouds formed around them, followed by flashes of lightning. The thunking increased until one of the bolts hit the shark. The beast jumped out of the water, gnashing its massive jaws, before splashing back into the ocean.

The clouds followed them as they sped across the ocean. Arturo wasn't sure how long they sailed as he crouched in the bow of the skiff. Shadows and outlines became visible. Then he saw the lighthouse's lamp shining out from the shores of his hometown.

The skiff rocked and wood cracked as a silver trident shoved up through the floor. Cassandra glanced back, fear in her eyes. Arturo held to the rudder and aimed for the beach. Another trident stabbed through, splintering the wood.

Cassandra sang out strange words, the rhythm hurried, her voice full and rich. Green light sparked and glowed around her as the boat sped. An invisible force shoved the bottom of the boat, sending the vessel into the air. Arturo barely held on as they crashed back down, water spraying around him.

With a crack, several planks flew off the ship's bow. Arturo jumped from the rudder and threw his arms around Cassandra, pulling her into the water with him. She ripped off her armband and kept hold of him as her fishtail returned. With a powerful kick of her tail, she drove them through the water. Arturo's knees hit sand and Cassandra let go. He dug his feet in and pushed toward solid land.

Something grabbed his ankle and began to drag him back. Cassandra slammed her tail into what held him. Arturo splashed through the shallows. At last, his feet touched hardened, dry sand. Breathing hard, he spun around.

The shallow water churned as Cassandra battled a merman. Arturo glanced around the beach before picking up a sizeable rock. Holding it with one hand, he ran back into the water. He kneed the merman's back, narrowly missing Cassandra. The merman released Cassandra long enough for her to slide off. The merman dove toward him. Arturo swung with the rock, hitting the merman's jaw. The merman slopped into the water. Arturo didn't wait to see if he was unconscious or not as he threw his arm around Cassandra's waist and lifted her. She clung to his shoulders as he carried her to shore.

Once on dry ground, Arturo dropped to his knees, losing hold of Cassandra. He collapsed forward while Cassandra's tail slapped against the sand.

Leaning onto his side, he looked at her. His chest eased. She had a few scratches, but no major wounds.

He brushed aside the hair covering part of her face. "I'll go find your armband and then bring you inside."

"The armband's lost," she said between breaths. "Even if it wasn't, the magic only lasts a few hours at a time."

"There's a nice pond in the gardens." He pushed back his hair, trying to picture her swimming in the pond among lily pads and reeds. "Could be a good place for you to rest."

She rolled onto her side and stared at him. He tried to smile, but his exhaustion was catching up with him. A shock went through Arturo as she leaned forward and kissed him. He was still aware enough to put his arm around her and pull her closer. The soft press of her lips made him almost forget her fishtail.

Pulling away, she ran her hand along his cheek. "I should be wiser than to love a human."

Before he could speak, she kissed him again and rolled into the water. The last he saw of her was her tail flashing through the air as she dove beneath the waves.

Arturo ran into the surf, the warmth of her hand still on his cheek, his lips pulsing. He kicked at the water and marched toward the town and home. Tonight he could do nothing. Tomorrow, after he was welcomed home, he could pull out the charts, find the island, and see if Uncle Ricardo would help battle a horde of mermaids.

Arturo tapped a stick against his leg as he walked along the beach, the wind rustling through his dark hair. Ahead, his mother and her entourage surrounded Rosa Mercado and Hernan. The women chittered and laughed. Arturo wished he could be riding his stallion through the hills, lost in the quick trot, his mind focused only on the movement of the horse.

For the past few weeks since returning, riding helped exhaust him, giving him a few hours of sleep before the nightmares came. Merfolk with shark-like teeth surrounded Cassandra as she was curled up in a pit, weak and beaten. Arturo ran toward her, swinging a sword to fight, but could never reach her.

Instead, he woke in a cold sweat and spent the rest of the night in his family library. He stared again at old charts, comparing them with current maps, but never finding a piece of land where Marveth should be. All he had told his family was he had been rescued by some girl who had been lost at sea.

Whatever spell the merfolk had placed on Hernan had wiped any memory of Cassandra's existence. The spell appeared to have wiped away some of Hernan's wisdom too as he flirted with every pretty girl who wasn't his fiancé.

As celebrations and gatherings filled the hacienda, Arturo spent his evenings standing on the balcony, staring out at the ocean as the sun set. He would find Cassandra and rescue her from whatever punishment she had received for his sake.

Arturo was brought back to the moment as several cries broke out among the crowd. At least two women fainted. Arturo dug the toes of his riding boots in the sand and ran. His hand on his decorative sword, Arturo jumped onto the rocks overlooking the circle of women. His breath stilled.

Hernan knelt at the center of the crowd, beside an unconscious Cassandra in human form. She was dressed in a simple, white dress, her blonde hair a wet mess around her. Her face had the pale grayness of drowning. Arturo jumped down the rocks and sprinted to her side. He put his arm around her shoulders and lifted her. Her skin was frigid, a blueness to her lips.

He listened for breathing, but heard nothing. He pressed his fingers into her neck and felt the faint beat of her heart. It was slow, but it was working.

Remembering some tricks sailors had shown him, he rolled her onto her side and pounded his fist against her back. After several hits, she spat out a mouthful of water and coughed.

The crowd broke into applause and gasps of relief. Arturo wished he were alone with her. If he were, he would have kissed her and held her tight against his breast, relieved she was safe. With his mother and her guests watching, he helped Cassandra to her feet and put his jacket around her shoulders. She held onto him as she panted, her legs shaking.

"Who is she?" mixed with "Oh, the poor dear," and "Where did you come from?"

"I'll take her to the house to rest," Arturo said as he kept his arm around her.

His mother motioned to one of her servants. "Go with him and make arrangements. The poor girl will have the best care we can provide."

Arturo let the heavy-set woman scurry ahead as he helped Cassandra limp along, her steps shaky and unsure. Once they were a dozen paces from the staring crowd, he picked her up. Her tall form was heavier than expected. She gave a tired sigh as she put her arm around his shoulders and leaned her head against him.

"What did they do to you?" he said. "How did you escape?"

She kissed his cheek and then whispered, her voice hoarse and weak, "I am here and safe. What else matters?"

Arturo half-smiled as he carried her up the beach, glad for her closeness. When they reached the stairs leading up to the hacienda, the servant woman was nearly to the top. Arturo set Cassandra's feet on the ground and helped her stand.

"Where is your armband?" he said. "What magic allows you to—" He frowned, trying to figure out how to say it. "To have legs?"

Cassandra leaned against him as she held out her bare foot, the skirt falling and revealing her calf. "These are permanent."

"Permanent?" He scratched his head. "But won't you need to—"

She pressed her hand to his chin and turned his head to face her. With a smile, she said, "I am now human."

Arturo stared at her, the words not fully reaching his mind. He smiled and kissed her. She held tightly to his shoulders as she returned the sweet pressure.

The next few days blurred past, full of luncheons, banquets, and balls in celebration of Hernan's approaching wedding. Arturo was always at Cassandra's side, ignoring the jealous glances of other men and disappointed frowns of single young women hoping to attach themselves to the Astrellar fortune. Cassandra feigned amnesia from the shipwreck as she charmed Arturo's parents. When she and Arturo were alone, she spoke of the many lands and cultures she had visited in her life of diplomacy, learning all she could of humans in order to improve relations between merfolk and land dwellers.

The night before Hernan and Rosa traveled south to be wed at her family's estate, Arturo and Cassandra ducked away from the dancing and laughter to stroll through the gardens. They sat on a stone bench near one of the various fountains, enjoying the quiet night air.

"I cannot make any promises until after Hernan's wedding," Arturo said, holding her hands in his. "However, once they are sailing off to their honeymoon, I'd like to announce our engagement."

She leaned her head against his shoulder. "And how long would the engagement be?"

"I'm the second son. I'll not have all the pomp and circumstance Hernan gets." He kissed her softly. "I'd like the wedding to be as soon as possible."

She squeezed his hand. "Good. Quicker is better."

They talked quietly of their future until the crowd of the ball began to leave. Arturo escorted Cassandra to her room before floating off to his own. The world was dull and empty when away from her. Soon, they would be married and would not need to part.

He lay in his bed for a few minutes, trying to sleep while he dreamed of Cassandra's head on his shoulder, her sweet kisses. Shouting broke out in the hacienda and his eyes shot open. Still in his clothes from the ball, Arturo ran into the hallway. His parents passed him in their nightclothes, holding candles aloft. He followed the growing trail of people down to the courtyard.

Hernan held his decorative sword out as he wobbled drunkenly. Rosa's brother, Guillermo, was just as sodden with alcohol as he tilted toward Hernan, sword raised high. The two blades skidded against each other, both men's forms poor. Nearby, a young woman huddled in tears. The rumors flitting about the crowd confirmed Arturo's suspicions.

After the ball, Hernan had come to a shadowed corner of the courtyard to sneak a few kisses from this girl. Guillermo had found his sister's fiancé engaged in such unfaithful conduct and now both men were more likely to bloody themselves than each other.

Arturo jumped in front of his brother and grabbed Hernan's arm, twisting it until the sword clanged to the ground.

"Pick up your blade!" Guillermo said, slashing his sword through the air. "Or do you have no honor to defend?"

Arturo's parents broke into an argument with Rosa's parents. Arturo crouched, becoming a barrier between the two men.

"Set down the sword," Arturo said. "And we can clear the matter."

"He's betrayed my sister!" Guillermo lunged forward. Arturo spun out of the way and jabbed his elbow into Guillermo's stomach. The bigger man oofed.

Pointing his sword at Arturo, he said, "Do you wish to defend your brother?" He picked up Hernan's blade and tossed it to Arturo. Hernan moved to join the fight, but several men grabbed him and pulled him back. Arturo caught Hernan's blade by the handle, but pointed the tip down.

"I will stand in for my brother at dawn," Arturo said. Hopefully, the matter would be cleared by morning, and Guillermo would have slept off the wine. "Then, we can have a real duel."

Guillermo snarled and lunged. Arturo parried with his blade while bringing his left fist across Guillermo's jaw. Rosa's brother shook his head as he stepped back, but then charged again. Arturo deflected the weak swing of the blade and dropped into a crouch. Guillermo tripped over him and sprawled across the stone ground. Before Guillermo could rise, Arturo kicked the sword away and pressed the point of his blade to the man's neck. Guillermo glared but held still.

"Arturo, come," his father said. Arturo tossed away Hernan's sword and followed his father to his study, his mother close behind. His father lit the gas light before dropping into his chair.

"The Mercados have called off the marriage," Arturo's father said. He rubbed the side of his face.

Arturo sat down across from his father and gripped his mother's hand. His parents had spent months creating this alliance. He should have been at the ball, watching Hernan.

"Everything may be saved," Arturo's mother said, "If we offer them a different groom."

Arturo drew his hand away as he stared at her. "I am going to marry Cassandra La Mer."

His father leaned forward, his hands pressed to the table. "She has no fortune and no family. If we are to remain powerful, we must have one of our sons marry Rosa Mercado."

"I love Cassandra." Arturo stood. "If I marry any other woman, it will be a lie."

"We will find a good place for Madame La Mer, far from here, where you can forget her," his father said. "In time, you and Rosa will be comfortable and content, as your mother and I have learned to be."

Arturo glared at his parents. They both had done their duty and treated each other well, but were not happy. They could not understand what he felt for Cassandra.

"I will not punish Cassandra for Hernan's mistake," he said.

"Your duty is to our name and honor, not to her." His father pounded his fist against the table. "You've no idea what we risk if this alliance breaks."

"They will seek to block shipping lanes and ruin our business," Arturo said, holding his father's glare. "Their anger will be a challenge, but I will do everything to help our business succeed.

"What I will not do is give up the woman I love for some business alliance. Cassandra will be no less than my wife and will make a better ally than Rosa Mercado."

His father and mother looked at each other, a silent conversation passing between them.

"We must tell him," his mother said. "Arturo will keep his silence."

His father grumbled as he scratched at his mustache. Age seemed to cascade over his face as he looked to his son. "You are not the only one who's made sacrifices because of other's poor choices.

"Your Uncle Ricardo—" He rubbed his forehead. "Soon after he was named captain of his first ship, Ricardo conspired with a few others, including our father. Your uncle gave pirates the navigation plans of a freighter owned by the Mercados. He gave the pirates just enough time to take the Mercado's ship. With the shipment still on board, and pirates at the helm, Ricardo blasted them out of the water.

"With one maneuver, Ricardo damaged their business and gave himself a victory which led to a quick promotion."

Arturo's hand gripped his armrest to keep himself calm. Ricardo was a respected admiral, known for his honor and judgment. Arturo wanted to deny his story, but the weariness in his father's eyes betrayed its truth.

"One of Ricardo's lieutenants knew the truth and wrote a journal confessing everything. He died a year ago and sent the journal to the Mercados as some kind of penance."

Sitting up, Arturo tried to push away the chill pricking at his neck.

"The agreement is their daughter marries our son. Our family will give them a wedding gift, which equals the total of the lost vessel and cargo, as well as our business and political connections. In return, they will burn the journal."

Arturo stood, trying to keep his fists from trembling. He barely kept a growl from his voice as he said, "This whole marriage is blackmail?"

His mother looked away while his father said, "I am trying to be just while protecting our family name. If the truth is revealed, Ricardo will be brought to trial, we risk much of our wealth being confiscated, and our family name will be ruined."

"If this is the truth, then our family honor is a lie."

"No." His father slammed his hand on the table as he stood. "I knew nothing about this until the Mercados came to me. They are being generous, Arturo, because I was not a part of these lies.

"I am sorry your love for Madame La Mer must be sacrificed. However, if we do not protect our name, all of us, including your mother and your sister, could lose everything."

Arturo backed toward the door as he glared at his father. He stopped as his mother touched his arm.

"You have always done what's right," she said.

"This time, I don't know what's right," Arturo said. He forced his teeth to unclench. "I will give you my answer by dawn."

Arturo paced the grounds of his family's hacienda, feeling the weight of the generations of Astrellars who had walked the familiar paths. Following his heart would most likely strip these walls bare. The Astrellar name might be able to redeem itself in time, or fade into a scandal-laden legend.

If Ricardo had lied about this escapade, there were probably more conspiracies he kept hidden. Arturo couldn't run about marrying daughters of every slighted family. Nor could the Astrellar fortune, however large, stand to pay off others.

He stopped and looked up at the window where his younger sister slept. Isabella was only beginning the parades of balls and dinner parties, and had already proven herself a beacon of the Astrellar reputation. She was as innocent as Arturo. Once he said no, he would have to find a way to protect her.

He clasped his hands on his head. How could he provide for Cassandra once they married? No one would trust or hire him. He might be able to take on a false name, but where would he work? Wherever he went, he would always be hiding, watching for who might discover his secret.

Cassandra deserved a better life after everything she had sacrificed for him.

As the sun rose, he sat at his writing desk, each word he wrote jabbing into his chest. On his way to his parents' room, he slipped the letter beneath Cassandra's door. He pressed his fingers to the handle, but stopped himself. There was no time. She would understand.

He marched to his parents' room, entered, and stood at attention.

"I am a servant of the House of Astrellar," he said. "I will do what I must."

There was no fanfare, no rattling of execution drums as Arturo walked the long dock and up the ramp into the ship carrying him to the Mercado estate.

The morning was silent as the ship cast off. He stood on the deck, looking out at his home, his gray-faced brother on the dock, unable to meet his eyes. Arturo felt as if his heart would burst as Cassandra ran along the dock, still in her nightgown and robe. She stood at the end of the dock, the wind whipping through her hair as she stared at him. Unable to bear her stare of betrayal, Arturo turned away and entered his cabin. He sat with his head in his hands, wondering if the prison of this marriage was any better than the cage Cassandra had rescued him from.

The voyage was short and passed swiftly. The Mercado's bore false smiles as they welcomed him and his parents, and he took Rosa's arm. She was an unremarkable young woman, though a bit square in structure. If he did not picture Cassandra, he would be content with this dull-eyed bride.

Celebrations were held, a banquet served, and congratulations given. At last, Arturo escaped to the quiet of his guest room. He paced the small floor, trying not to picture the morning's wedding. He stared out at the ocean, the moon gleaming across the surface of the water. If he had not been captured, if he had not met Cassandra, he would be ready to do his duty.

Tiredness finally came and he lay down on the bed. As he dozed into a light sleep, he felt the shift of the mattress as someone sat beside him.

"Arturo."

He groaned and moved onto his side, trying to push away the memory of Cassandra's voice and the smell of the ocean.

"Arturo!"

He frowned as someone shook his shoulder. Turning on his back, he opened his eyes. He stiffened as he stared up at Cassandra, a pain in her blue eyes. Her arm was raised as she held a broad, curved knife, the point directed toward his chest. Her hand trembled, but the blade held still.

Arturo sat up and pushed himself back, keeping his eyes on the sharp tip of the blade.

"Is this all I am worth to you?" She threw a crumpled pile of bank notes at him while her other hand kept the knife high.

"I—I was trying to give you enough to start your life with," Arturo said. "I wanted to give more, but didn't have time to—"

"Do you think I wouldn't have resources on land?"

Arturo swallowed to bring a little moisture into his mouth. "I love you, Cassandra, but I must protect my family name."

Cassandra lowered the knife, but rested it in her lap, one hand keeping hold of the handle. "You have been bought, Arturo."

"I know and I am sorry." He wanted to reach his hand out to her, to move closer and try to comfort her, but had no right to. "Last night, when we spoke, I thought I was free. But, I am not. I must marry her to keep my family from ruin."

"Human lives are short." She tapped her fingers on the blade. "Yet you are willing to waste yours being miserable over money and family honor?" She leaned toward him. "And, how do you know the Mercados are fully innocent in the matter?" Gesturing to the rest of the hacienda with the knife, she said, "Powerful families are always infested with dark secrets. What will you do when the next scandal comes?"

"I have made a promise," he said.

"And what of your promises to me?"

"I meant everything I said." Arturo edged toward her. The glint of anger in her eyes was softened by pain. The blade worried him, yet he might be able to calm her. "But after you left, everything changed."

Though his hand trembled, he placed his palm on top of her hand holding the knife. He kept his eyes on hers as he wrapped his fingers around hers.

"I will be miserable," he said. "If I could, I would find a way to marry you and still protect my family, but that is impossible. The best I can do is to let you go."

She pushed away his hand and stabbed the blade into the bed. Feathers fluttered up and Arturo jolted back. His heartbeat thudded as he stared at her fingers on the handle.

Her voice was careful and measured. "I knew how grave my punishment would be when I broke the chain holding your cage. After I left you on the shore, I was captured. I had to use every connection and influence I had to make a deal with Randala that didn't leave me turned to stone, or worse."

She tapped the hilt of the knife with her finger. Arturo tried to look away, but could not.

"Our agreement was I would be exiled here as human. My life would be safe, so long as the man I risked everything for married me." Arturo's spine stiffened as her eyes bore into him. "I didn't bring the matter up, because you seemed interested in our marriage too."

"What happens if we do not marry?"

"I die."

"No." Arturo rose to his knees. "It must be a lie."

"On my way here," she said as she pulled the knife from the mattress, "My sisters found me. They traveled all the way from the north to give me this." She laid the blade between them. "They traded their hair to Randala. They've such beautiful hair, Arturo."

She looked him in the eye, her face serious and cold. "With it, I am supposed to kill you before you can marry another. Then I will return to mermaid form."

He stared down at the blade. "If I marry Rosa, you die, unless you murder me?"

"Yes," she said. "Mermaid law is rather unforgiving."

With his hands pressed to his knees to hide the shaking, he kept his eyes on the blade. Was his family honor worth more than his or Cassandra's life?

Raising his eyes to meet hers, he said, "If I choose to marry Rosa, what will you do?"

A gust blew outside, a tree branch tapping at the window, marking time.

"I have survived the fall of kingdoms and the rise of wars," she said. "I have woven my way out of assassination plots and countless conspiracies. I have always been sure what I needed to do to win." A tear glided down her cheek. "But, tonight, Randala has placed me in a position where I can only be defeated."

Arturo's breath was short as a few more tears followed, but

Cassandra's face remained calm. His voice hushed, he said, "You choose my life over your own?"

He pushed back a strand of hair from her face before cupping her cheek. His lips touched hers in a soft, short kiss. He wrapped his arms around her and held her close, his cheek pressed against hers. He shut his eyes as he shed a few tears for his sister, mother, and father, who would suffer for the choice he had to make.

"There will be chaos here," he said. "But we should go immediately. When we find a town far enough away, we can worry about finding a magistrate or priest."

Cassandra pulled away and slowly smiled, "We will add to the chaos."

She kissed his cheek before standing, taking the knife with her. She motioned for him to get off the bed and he stood. Arturo jumped back as she raised the knife and plunged it into the mattress. She dragged the knife down, creating gashes in the fabric, and then stabbed a few pillows.

From the washstand, she picked up the pitcher. She sang out some low notes as she sprinkled water on the knife, pillows, and torn mattress. She sang a few more notes. Deep red stains spread across the white fabric. She walked to the window and tossed out the knife.

"My family— They will think the Mercados did this," he said.

"But there will be no proof, and if the Mercados come forward with the story about your uncle, it will appear a petty cover-up and excuse for your death."

"We must at least tell my parents the truth."

"Even if we find and burn the journal, the Mercados know the truth about your uncle. This is the only way you and I can both live and your family name can survive." Her face softened as she walked to him and touched his hand. "Your parents' heartache will be a small sacrifice, and, in time, we'll be able to reveal you are alive."

Arturo looked in her eyes. This woman had already sacrificed her position and life among her people, including her family, for him. As soon as he could, he would tell his parents the truth. He raised her hand and kissed it. Tonight, he would make this sacrifice for her.

Chapter 13

Present Day

Evelyn rubbed at her throat, wondering how much of the tale she could believe. Cassandra being a witch or sorceress seemed more believable than her being a mermaid, yet it had to be true.

Jack sat with his elbows on his knees and muttered, "Sounds like a Westengaard novel."

"Did you ever reunite with your family?" Evelyn said between spitting out a pair of frogs.

Arturo wheezed through a cough before saying, "Cassandra and I settled in a fishing village in northern Castallar and lived happily for a few years. Then I read some disgrace or other ruined the Mercados, soon followed by news of my brother dying in a riding accident." The pain of years weighed in his face. "Cassandra and I returned home and I took on the role of heir."

He crouched forward as he stared into the fire, his eyes distant. "My children may have been safer if we'd stayed in that village."

"You have children?" Jack said.

Evelyn wondered how old the children were and how they felt with their mother looking so young.

The firelight deepened the shadows of Arturo's wrinkled face. "Randala stole our first two. Cassandra left for eight years to look for them, but returned with nothing. We hid the third as a child of one of our servants. He ran off to the Navy when he was fifteen. I hope he has lived well, but I know I'll never see him again."

Evelyn rubbed her hand on her leg, unable to picture Cassandra as a mother. If everything Arturo said was true, she almost felt sorry for Cassandra. The sympathy was limited by the bucket of frogs sitting next to her. Whatever pains Cassandra had lived through, her cruelty could not be excused.

"What about Henry?" Jack sat up, his arms folded. "What does she want with him?"

"I have aged naturally, but she has aged only a few years." Arturo pressed his fingers together, his hands shaking. "I suspect she's tired of watching me fall apart and she thinks your brother can help."

"How and with what?" Jack said.

"She doesn't tell me. She just finds men she thinks can carry off her plans, takes them away, and returns disappointed." He wheezed out a cough. "I hired Mr. Hedley to limit her resources, so she's forced to tell me everything, but she always finds her own way."

"And the frogs?" Jack said. "How do we stop her from turning Henry into one?"

"The men she becomes fascinated with never end up as frogs." Arturo pulled his blanket tighter around his shoulders. "They are ruined financially or socially, or they—" He waved his hand through the air and a shiver ran along Evelyn's spine. "Disappear."

"How can she—" Evelyn clenched her jaw before spitting out a salamander. "Ruin Henry?"

"If you can persuade him to help her instead of fighting, he might be saved." Arturo's hands clenched his armrests. "I've given you my story and the truth. If you help her, she will not need to hurt others anymore. She will finally be at peace. Please, have some compassion."

"I will not," Evelyn said as she grabbed the basket and stood. She opened her mouth to say more, but a salamander flew out.

"Neither of us are going to abandon Henry to whatever

Cassandra's plans are." Jack rose and jabbed his finger at the old man. "Even if your story is the truth, you need to wake up to what your wife's doing. Whatever she wants can't be worth—"

A door slammed somewhere in the mansion, followed by quick footsteps. Evelyn jumped and looked to Jack.

"If you will not help," Arturo said. "You should escape."

Jack blew out his lantern and Evelyn led the way to the hallway. Cassandra's silhouette appeared on the wall, etched with the flickering light of a candle. Each footstep sent Evelyn's heart slamming in her chest. She and Jack rushed into the nearest room, careful to shut the door quietly. They leaned against it, holding their breath to quiet their panting. The pool of light from Cassandra's candle spread beneath the door as she approached.

Henry tossed his hat on the table and dropped into his old armchair. Leaning his head back and shutting his eyes, he breathed out the foulness of the evening. The night had been far too long. Throughout the card game at his employer's, Cassandra made small talk and charmed the room. Henry watched her eyes, sensing the calculations stacking in her mind. Her unknown conclusions chafed at him, nearly as badly as remembering the painting in his office.

Rubbing his forehead, he groaned and let his head roll to the side. Tomorrow he would find a way free and spend his evening with Evelyn. Once he was engaged, things would be far simpler.

The front door shook as someone rammed their fist against it. Henry fumbled for his cane as the hammering repeated. He limped over and looked through the peephole. Bronhart stood on the other side, his skin an unhealthy gray, his jaw rough with stubble. Henry frowned as he opened the door and his friend rushed in.

Dropping a mass of folders on Henry's table, Bronhart said, "Those accounts you sent to me— there's some trouble."

Henry shut the door and made his way to the table. "I am sure we can look this over tomorrow."

"I won't be at work." Bronhart spread out the folders, sorting them into groups. "I showed some of my discoveries to Mr. Mackabee this afternoon, and he—"

Bronhart's hand shook as he scratched his chin. Henry twisted the point of his cane into the ground. He had brought questionable accounts to Mackabee's attention before. The echoes of their employer's shouting burned in Henry's ears. The man always finished with snatching away the file and humphing, "My son'll look into it."

"He sacked me." Bronhart slumped into a chair. He fingered through the folders before pulling out a file marked *Cordwainer* and handing it to Henry. "I should have been wiser than to question his most profitable clients."

Henry flipped open to the first page. Adjusting his spectacles, he looked over the tight column of numbers. He frowned at the accounts payable, especially where it had been circled with pencil.

"These numbers are low for such materials," Henry said.

"It stinks of stolen goods," Bronhart said. "Unless Mackabee's been working the numbers ever since his daughter married Cordwainer's nephew."

Henry shut the folder and handed it back to Bronhart. "There's not enough here to go to the authorities."

"I know." Bronhart slid over a different folder. "Here's the one which made him fume."

Henry lowered himself into a chair as he recognized his own handwriting. Inside were receipts and information on acquisitions. He sifted through a few pages before frowning.

"What does Madame Astrellar need with so many cow hides?" Henry said. "She has no tannery business and there are no signs of reselling them at higher prices." He looked again. "These are three times what a hide should cost. She could put all the tanneries in town out of business."

He dropped the folder into his lap and pulled off his spectacles. Cassandra could not be so petty.

No. She could, and it was Henry who had made Evelyn a target. He rubbed his eyes as he groaned. This must be why Evelyn had come to speak with him earlier in the week. Jack must have been trying to help, but Henry had been too busy to listen.

"I showed Mackabee the same thing," Bronhart said. "He tried to shut me up. When I stood up to him, he roared at me and told me to clear out my office." Bronhart ran a hand through his hair as a mad smile formed. "So, I did."

"These are stolen and confidential accounts." Henry snapped the folder shut. He had been sitting with her tonight, letting her play her games while she was secretly out to ruin John Havish's business. His arm shivered where she had brushed him. "You could be arrested." He looked down at the table. "I could be arrested."

"If we can prove the price-fixing," Bronhart said, "We can leave the materials anonymously with the newspaper or the police. They'll investigate and the truth will come out. We can keep our names out of it, but we can also stop all this corruption."

Numbers held truth. All Henry needed to do was weave his way through the numbers and leave signs for others to find the truth. He stood, pulled off his dinner jacket, and rolled up his sleeves. Pointing to a cupboard behind Bronhart, he said, "Pens and paper are in there. I'll put on some tea."

Evelyn pressed the lid of the basket shut, hoping to quiet the croaking frogs as she watched the door handle. Hopefully, the creak of Cassandra's steps on the wood floor would mask the noise. Jack pulled back a dust cloth, revealing a cupboard. He took the basket from Evelyn and shoved it inside.

Cassandra's footsteps paused outside their door, the light flickering through the cracks. Evelyn and Jack pressed against the wall. If only they could make themselves invisible for a moment.

They both let out a pent-up breath as the footsteps continued and the door across the hall opened.

"I thought I locked this," Cassandra said, her voice calm and sure.

"You were in such a hurry to leave," Arturo said. "I don't think I heard the key turn."

Her voice dropped an octave, its coldness sending goosebumps along Evelyn's arms. "Who was here?"

Evelyn winced, waiting for him to betray them.

"I thought I heard thieves, but it turned out to be nothing."

"How long ago did they run away?"

"Ten minutes or so."

Jack crouched down and peeked through the gap at the bottom of the door. Evelyn focused on quieting her pulse by breathing steadily.

Cassandra said, "Where are they hiding?"

"They are gone." A series of coughs followed, the hacking becoming more violent.

"You're coughing up blood again." The floor creaked as she moved toward Arturo. Real concern was in her voice as she said, "I will send for a doctor."

"Now!" Jack whispered.

Evelyn pulled the basket from the cabinet while Jack opened the door a crack. The door to Arturo's room was half-open, but Cassandra could not be seen. Hoping Arturo's coughing would cover the thump of their footsteps, they scurried for the staircase. The polished wood was slick, and Jack's shoes squeaked, but they kept moving.

Once on the lower floor, they hurried along the hallway.

"Do you remember which door it was?" Jack said.

Evelyn shook her head, scanning the darkness for anything to distinguish one room from another.

"We do have guests." Cassandra's voice boomed through the whole house. The doors to all of the rooms opened at once, one of them smacking the back of Jack's head. He yelped.

"Please, make yourself comfortable. I will be with you in a moment."

Evelyn and Jack ran. She wasn't sure if it was a newt or her heartbeat thudding in her throat. The floor shook as the furniture shuddered as if alive. A low table slid out of a room ahead of them, nearly tripping them. Jack dove beneath it while Evelyn climbed over it. Once they were both on their feet, they sprinted on.

"This way," Jack said as he grabbed Evelyn's arm.

They turned down a hall and reached a set of marble steps leading to a grand entryway. Furniture thudded from the rooms behind them while the dimmed chandelier cast eerie shadows along the walls. Evelyn reached the door first and yanked on the handle. It didn't budge. Jack rammed his shoulder into it, but yelled as he rebounded back.

With a plan forming, Evelyn shoved a vase off a stone pedestal. The vase crashed across the ground while Evelyn crouched to get a good hold on the pedestal. Hopefully, the hours of work in her father's shop would give her enough strength. She bowed under the weight, but picked it up.

Jack grabbed the other end as he said, "Battering ram? Excellent plan."

She shook her head and nodded toward the window.

"Better plan," he said.

They ran together and flung the pedestal through the glass. The window shattered, shards spilling out and knicking Evelyn's skin. She covered her face with her arm and jumped through. Jack tossed her the basket before tumbling out. Evelyn led Jack to the nearest bushes as Cassandra's heeled shoes clicked on the marble floor of the entryway. They crouched alongside the bushes before hopping over the waist-high front gate.

Once on the street, they broke into a sprint, Jack's longer legs outpacing Evelyn. She tried to push more speed and keep up with him as she huffed in air. Jack slowed and grabbed the basket from her.

"We can hide in the park," he said.

They ran down a series of alleyways, twisting right and left, until reaching a broad avenue. Across the street was Kamen Park, a dark green mass shadowed by trees. There would be plenty of places to hide.

The grass was wet and slick as they ran toward a grove of oak trees. Jack shouted as his foot slipped. His arms flailed and his legs knocked about as he went tumbling down a hill. The basket bounced after him, the top flapping open and frogs launching out. Evelyn's feet slid on the muddy grass as she chased the man and basket, trying not to fall and squish the escaping frogs.

At the bottom of the hill, Jack laughed and panted as he and the basket rolled to a stop. Evelyn grabbed a tree branch to stop her momentum before picking up the basket. Inside there were still a few frogs, but most had escaped.

She glanced up the hill. There were no signs of pursuit. Still, they needed to move quickly.

Running along the incline, she looked for frogs jumping around. Using her handkerchief as a net to trap them, she gathered frogs back into the basket. Her hands were soon sticky with frog slime. Jack's laughter stopped and he cursed. He scrambled across the hill, diving at the frogs and trying to snatch them. Both Evelyn and Jack slipped in the mud, their pants caked up to the knee, with grass stains on their shirts.

Once there seemed to be no more frogs to chase, they stood beside each other, peering in the darkness.

"I wish we knew how many we had grabbed." Jack wiped his hands on his shirt as he glanced up the hill. "We should test if you can kiss them free."

Evelyn grimaced. He had suggested this theory, since it was in so many stories. Part of her hoped it didn't work. However, if the men were to be free, she had to try.

From the basket, she pulled a small, slim frog and cupped it in her hands. Its chin expanded and retracted as it breathed, staring at her with its wet, bulbous eyes. She swallowed, forcing back whatever was rising from her stomach. It probably wasn't another frog. After a quick breath, she pressed her lips to the frog's slimy head.

Nothing happened.

"Kiss him again." Jack smoothed back his hair. "Maybe it needs a really good one."

She shot a glare at Jack before shifting her shoulders and kissing the creature again. It blinked, but remained amphibious.

"Here." Jack reached into the basket. "Try a different one. I'm sure we got some real frogs in the mix, or some of the ones you—"

He forced a cough and switched out the frog in her hand. Evelyn wiped her mouth with the back of her hand before pressing her lips to the creature.

The frog expanded and grew. Evelyn jumped back, dropping it to the ground. As it fell, the webbed fingers narrowed and the legs became longer. In a moment, a full-grown man in out-of-fashion clothes appeared. He blinked at her before grinning and smoothing his mustache.

"Well, what a lovely night." He leaned toward her with pursed lips.

Evelyn shoved the man back and Jack stepped in front of him.

"You get home, you drunken idiot!" Jack pushed the man. "What are you doing, trying to kiss my girl?"

"I— I'm sorry." The former frog backed away, his eyes wide and bewildered.

"Wait!" Evelyn said. "We need him!"

The man turned to return. Evelyn's cheeks bulged and she spat out a salamander. He cringed and stepped back, tripping over a bush before stumbling to his feet and breaking into a run.

"Don't we need him to—" She spat out another frog. "To tell the truth?"

"I'd say we have enough in the basket." Jack glanced at her and winced. "And I'd recommend you don't talk unless you must. We don't need any more frogs to mix up tonight."

She nodded.

"I think Madame Astrellar may have seen me. It might go better if we take them to your place." Jack picked up the basket. "I'm sure your sister Julie can help with the kissing."

Evelyn raised an eyebrow and Jack pointed at the basket.

"Kissing the frogs," he said. "Not me— No!" He grunted. "Let's get you home, hide the basket, then we'll both get some rest."

They reached the opposite side of the park. A cracking thunder rumbled in the clouds. As they came out of cover from the trees, rain poured down. They ducked under awnings the rest of the way, the wind howling at them, and water splattering their clothes.

Not daring to think how late it was, Evelyn approached her own doorstep. Jack passed her the basket before gripping her free hand and giving it a firm shake.

"I couldn't ask for a better companion in the face of danger." He grinned. "I'm glad you and Henry have made peace. You're a wonderful girl."

She smiled and opened her mouth to say thank you, but clamped her lips closed. There were enough slithering things already.

"You have a good night. I'll be by in the morning."

Evelyn waved at Jack as he began jogging home, his hair flat and dripping with water. Once he was around the corner, she ignored her own shivers and unlocked the door. The frogs seemed to croak louder as she slipped inside and began to sneak upstairs.

"Evelyn Susan Havish."

The gas lights sputtered on and Evelyn turned to face her father, his broad frame blocking the bottom of the stairway. Marjory was behind him, her arms folded and her eyes tight with worry.

"You've been sick all week, and then you go running about all night?" He glared, but her mother's uptick of an eyebrow sent a shudder through Evelyn. "Where've you been? It better be a good explanation."

Even before she opened her mouth to speak, she felt another creature coming up her throat. She cringed as she tried to go up the stairs. Her father's arm blocked her.

"What's in the basket?" Marjory said.

Havish ripped it from Evelyn's hand even as she tried to pull it away. He opened the lid and then shut it tightly.

"What are you doing with a basket full of frogs? Did you go to the lake?"

Taking the basket from her husband, Marjory said, "I'd expect Charlie to bring in something like this as a prank, but not you."

Marjory threw open the front door and began to swing the basket back to dump it out.

"No!" Evelyn's cry sent a newt flying onto her father's face with a loud splat.

Havish blinked before pulling the creature off his face and staring at it.

"They're men." Evelyn shut her mouth, holding back the next creature from climbing out. "We rescued them."

Shutting the door, basket still in hand, Marjory said, "Are you mad?"

Havish gripped Evelyn's shoulders and scowled. "Who did this curse to you?"

Evelyn pressed a hand to her cheek as her lips trembled. She put her arms around his shoulders and hid her face against her father's chest as tears threatened to fall.

"A curse? Really, John?" Marjory said. "I don't understand your fascination with magic. All those theories about the elves and Mr. Talbot have come to what? And now you say Evelyn is cursed."

Evelyn pulled away from her father and said, "It's true, Mom—" she stopped before gagging out a salamander.

Marjory screamed, dropping the basket of frogs. Evelyn cringed, hoping the transformed men were unharmed.

"Who did— How did—" Marjory put her fists on her hips. "What is going on?"

Evelyn sat on the stairs and leaned against the banister. How could she explain? She tried to say Madame Astrellar's name, but her throat constricted, blocking the words. Her next attempt brought visions of the house burning.

Pulling in a breath, she said, "Ask Jack Kingston."

"Did that boy do this to you?" Havish said. "Where is he? I'll wring him out for you."

Evelyn shook her head. "He— He's been helping me—" She pulled out yet another frog and sighed. Just one more sentence. "We're trying to save Hen— Hen—" Several creatures came out before she could say, "Henry."

"From what?" Havish said.

"Don't make her say anymore. Don't you see the curse is worse around his name?" Marjory said. "One more question, Evelyn: Where is Jack?"

Evelyn pointed at the door. "He just left."

"Charlie!" Havish ran upstairs to his son's room.

Charlie moaned groggily while Havish shouted at him. Marjory picked up the basket of frogs in one arm and put her other arm around

Evelyn as she guided her into the parlor. After stoking the fire, she put a blanket over Evelyn's shoulders. "Sit here while I get some tea to warm you up."

She brushed back Evelyn's wet hair and kissed her forehead.

Evelyn rested in the chair and shut her eyes as Charlie ran outside. As she drifted into a dazed sleep, the door slammed open and Charlie led Jack inside.

"Here, Mr. Kingston," Marjory said as she held out a towel and blanket.

Trying to hide his shivers, Jack wiped off his face and hair before wrapping himself in the blanket. He dropped into the chair in front of the fire as he said, "Everything all right? Charlie said something was wrong."

Evelyn pointed at her parents.

"What's this curse my girl's under?" Havish said.

Jack looked to Evelyn. "You want me to tell them what's going on?"

She nodded.

He winced. "Everything?"

With her second nod, Jack said, "All right." He rubbed his hands on his pant legs and repeated his own turning into a frog the night he had gone missing. Havish leaned forward with interest while Marjory scowled with disbelief. Jack told them of their encounters with Cassandra, finishing with their sneaking into Cassandra's mansion.

Jack glanced at Evelyn before saying, "While there, we got all the frogs we could, and we learned—" He pressed his lips together as his eyes widened. "She's a mermaid." He raised his shoulders. "How're we supposed to stop a mermaid?"

"Talcum powder," Havish said as he pounded his fist into his palm. "That's what my magical house guest book says. Dries them right up, and keeps the tiny ones from blocking the plumbing."

Evelyn groaned as she pressed her head into her hands.

"Your books are nonsense, John," Marjory said. "We'll need something better if she really is a—" She sighed, as if disbelieving her own words. "A mermaid."

"My books aren't nonsense." Havish folded his arms. "They're carefully researched. I'm sure we'll find something."

"Our plan is to go to the police," Jack said. "Show them the frogs, turn a few into men. We might be laughed out of there, but we've got to try."

Havish waved his hand. "The police won't believe all this."

Marjory glared at her husband. "We have to try. You told me what was going on at Talbot's. I didn't believe you, but—" She grimaced as she looked at the basket of frogs. "After tonight, I'd believe anything."

Chapter 14

Henry's hands shook as he buttoned his vest and coat. For years, he had planned each day precisely. Today, he did not know what the day would bring nor if he would be employed by the end of it. His brief hour of sleep would have to be enough to face whatever happened.

With his copy of the documents he and Bronhart had organized tucked securely in his briefcase, he left the apartment. Outside, the wind raged, sending rain pelting sideways. Henry pulled his scarf over his face, turned up the collar of his coat, and tugged his brimmed hat tighter on his head. He clung to his cane as he walked, leaning against a lamppost now and then to keep from slipping.

Once at Mackabee and Sons, his shoes squelched as he crossed the main floor. He entered his office and looked up at Cassandra's portrait. Giving up this gilded office was not much of a sacrifice.

The booming of Mackabee's voice announced his arrival. Henry straightened his tie and coat before venturing out. Reaching Mackabee's side, Henry said, "Sir, I have a question about the Astrellar account."

"Of course, Mr. Kingston." Mackabee slapped Henry's shoulder. "Come in."

Once inside his office, Mackabee hung his coat and moved behind his massive desk. "Fine work last night with Madame Astrellar. Seems you've realized the benefit of having favor with a lady of such wealth. Now, when I was a young man, I made sure to use my charm. I remember a Miss Handrell—"

"Sir." Henry's hands shook as he set the folder on the desk. He wasn't sure if his shirt was wet from sweat or rain. "I noticed a few strange expenses with the Astrellar account."

Mackabee waved his hand. "Let the lady spend money as she wants. She's got plenty coming in."

"Sir, I..." Henry wished there was moisture in his mouth. "I believe there is some price fixing going on."

"Price fixing, eh?" Mackabee opened the folder and raised an eyebrow. Shutting it, he said, "There's only one way to deal with that."

He opened the heating stove and tossed the folder in. Henry watched the fire flare, grateful Bronhart had a second copy and the originals.

Brushing off his hands, Mackabee said, "Anything else?"

Small pieces of ash escaped from the fire and floated in the air before scattering on the ground.

"Madame Astrellar and her manager Mr. Hedley are buying all of the hides from the slaughterhouses."

"Buying things is not illegal, Mr. Kingston."

"Buying out suppliers to destroy a healthy business is, sir. Given the size of the Astrellar fortune, I cannot help but wonder—"

"Who gave you permission to wonder?" Mackabee came around the desk and clamped his hand on Henry's shoulder. "Your job as account manager is to use your dim charms to keep Madame Astrellar interested, not to question how she uses her wealth."

Henry squared his feet beneath him. "I am an auditor, sir."

"On accounts who are behind on paying us. On accounts who threaten the livelihood of our larger ones." Mackabee tapped his nose as if letting Henry in on a secret. "Our business is to know where the money is flowing. If someone with enough wealth is doing something questionable, it's not our job to ask questions.

"We will ignore this little bit of price fixing and you will focus on planning your next evening with Madame Astrellar."

"Men's livelihoods are at stake, sir." Henry kept his eyes level with his employer's.

Mackabee waved his hand. "There are always other forms of employment."

"It is a clear maneuver to destroy a single man's business."

"Then, the man was foolish to make himself a target." Mackabee jabbed his finger into Henry's chest. "Forget this, Kingston."

Henry's knuckles were white as he held his cane. It was not merely some man. It was John Havish, Evelyn's father, and a good man. Jobs at his tannery fed countless families in the lower side of town. Havish worked hard to keep his business open and deserved better than to fall to manipulation and lies.

Henry's mouth and tongue clamped together. His heart knocked against his spine, shouting he was a fool, but he knew what he had to do. Other businesses had surely been destroyed by Mackabee's looking away. Henry was a man of honesty and honor. The words needed to be spoken.

"Sir." Henry forced his fist to unclench and his voice to remain level. "I cannot work for an employer who ignores dishonest and illegal practices."

"Come now, Mr. Kingston!" Mackabee laughed as he dropped into his chair. "I am sure you knocked other boys out of the way when playing games as a child. This is no different. The ones who fall have to learn to play the real game."

Henry ground the tip of his cane into the carpet. He had always been the one shoved out of the way.

Mackabee pointed a fat finger toward the outer office. "How many of the men out there did you shove aside to gain your position here?"

"I earned my position through honest and accurate work, sir."

"And how many were pushed aside to reach Madame Astrellar's side, and pocketbook?" He gave a hearty laugh.

Stamping his cane, Henry said, "I am not interested in Madame Astrellar, nor her pocketbook. I came here to—"

Mackabee's laugh deepened. "Come now, Kingston. She's a beautiful woman. Enjoy her and enjoy her wealth."

Henry's hands shook, but no longer from fear. He felt as if he were back at the farm, balancing on the fence as he tried to race Mick, his cousin. Mick shoved him off and Henry fell, his leg cracking as he landed on the ground. The phantom pain shuddered through his leg, Mick's laugh biting at his ears.

He was not going to be shoved aside. Not by men like Mackabee. Not by men like Roger Simmons. Not by Mick. He was a man and had earned his place in society.

"I must resign, sir."

Mackabee's laughter ended in a gagging snort. "You can't resign. You have too many years invested in this firm."

Henry turned to the door. "I have been here too long, sir, and I am resigning."

"But the Astrellar account—"

"Will be managed by someone else. Good day, sir."

Henry opened the door.

Struggling to pull his girth out of his chair, Mackabee shouted, "If you walk out of here, I'll make sure no one will hire you. You stand there, Kingston!"

Henry forced himself to breathe as he made his first step out of the office. He ignored the eyes of the clerks as he rushed past them. Mackabee escaped his chair and charged after Henry.

"Kingston! Kingston! You stop where you are. You're not in your right mind. Come back here!"

Henry grabbed his overcoat, hat, and scarf from his desk. Red-faced, Mackabee moved to block him. Henry slipped around him and hurried through the tightly packed desks.

"Just take the day off and we'll talk Monday," Mackabee said between huffs while running parallel to Henry.

Henry reached the double doors leading to the lobby. Once he stepped out this door, his decision was final.

He looked back at Mackabee and said, "Thank you for my employment, sir. Good day."

Henry walked out and Mackabee rammed through the doorway after him.

"What position did she offer? What salary? I can match it. Kingston!"

Henry crossed the lobby, pushed open the front door, and let it slam shut. He grabbed the railing and went down the slick stairs. Rain pelted down, but he did not take time to put on his hat or overcoat. Mackabee reached the top of the stairs as he continued shouting. A few painful, heavy thuds followed and Mackabee howled like a wounded dog. Henry did not dare turn around. Let other men attend to the man.

With each step, a lightness filled him. For so long, he had kept his head down and done his work with few questions. He was a respectable man and would be able to find honest employment out of Cassandra's grasp. All he had to do now was free Havish and propose to Evelyn.

Jack ran his hands through his still damp hair as he yawned. Dropping back on the bed, he was glad today was set aside for studying. He had gone to the police with the Havish family and watched the constable's eyes nearly pop from his head as Evelyn kissed a frog and a man appeared. She and the frogs had been rushed into a side room. Jack had gone to follow, but was shoved away like a nuisance.

"Go home and rest," Havish said. "We'll watch out for Evelyn."

Jack had hesitated but run home. Now, he had finally had a few hours of sleep. He stretched as he walked into the cramped living area and glanced at the old, bent clock. It was late morning. He would make something to eat and then stop by the Havish's and see what the police had to say. Evelyn had to be home by now.

He whistled to himself as he changed into fresh clothes and combed his hair. He and Evelyn weren't alone anymore. Evelyn's parents believed them and were willing to help. Soon Cassandra wouldn't be able to hide what she really was, and, finally, Henry would believe the truth.

Jack slapped butter on a piece of bread and pulled leftover bacon from the small ice box. As he chewed, a knock rapped on the door. Jack set down his food, wiped his hands on his pants, and looked through the peephole.

He nearly choked on his half-eaten food.

Cassandra's face was as beautiful as she had been when turning Jack into a frog. His eye lingered, noting how her bodice accentuated her curved figure. She was probably more stunning in her true form, with fins gliding in the water.

He pulled away from the door and ran his hand over his face. What had her kiss done to him? This was not some young, innocent girl. Whatever power she had over him, he had to fight it.

His heart thudded as she knocked again. If she had seen him last night, it was better to pretend not to be home.

"Mr. Kingston?"

He held his breath and watched through the peephole.

"You looking for Mr. Kingston?"

Jack held back a curse as his neighbor, Paul Billard, stepped out from his apartment.

"I saw him coming in with the mail a little while ago. He should be home." The rotund artist knocked. Jack leaned his forehead against the door, praying they would leave.

"Is there something I could help you with?" Billard said. "It isn't every day I can help a beauty."

Jack punched his fist against his leg, trying to stop a twinge of jealousy. He knew what she was. There should be no attraction.

Her voice soft and light, she said, "I have a gift for Mr. Kingston. I so hoped to give it to him in person."

Jack looked through the peephole again. Whatever this gift was, he would keep it from Henry. It could only be part of her trap.

"If you'll leave it with me, I'll tell him the loveliest girl left it for him."

Cassandra batted her eyes as she turned her head away with a giggle. Touching his shoulder with her fan, she said, "That would be so kind of you, but it is an intimate gift. If only I could leave it on the table for him."

Grinning dumbly at her, Billard said, "I happen to have a spare key."

Jack pressed his teeth together to keep from shouting. He had forgotten Henry had given Billard a spare key in case of emergency. Henry's studiousness and carefulness could now ruin Jack.

"Oh, would you?" Cassandra's words sang with delight. "That would be most wonderful."

"No trouble, miss."

Jack slid across the living area and jumped into his room. He shut the door as Billard turned the key in the lock.

"I don't mean to be presumptuous," Cassandra said as she and Billard entered. "But, I'd like to wait here for Mr. Kingston to return. Wouldn't it be a grand surprise?"

Jack cringed. It would be a surprise, but it wouldn't be grand.

"Er— I suppose," Billard said.

Jack threw off his shoes and pulled a blanket from the bed. Once Cassandra was gone, Jack would get the locks changed and take the key from Billard. He scruffed up his hair, threw the blanket over his shoulders, and stumbled into the living area.

Squinting his eyes and sniffing through his nose as if about to sneeze, he said, "Oh, Madame Astrellar!" He wiped his nose on his sleeve. "What are you doing here?"

"The lady's got a present for you," Billard said with a wink.

"It's for Henry Kingston," she said.

Billard frowned. "Henry? But he—"

"You know, Billard, I'm so glad you're here." Jack added a little hoarseness to his voice. "Henry dropped his key somewhere yesterday and had to borrow mine today. Can you lend me yours?"

Billard gazed at Cassandra as he slowly handed over the key. "Of course."

"Thanks. You're a big help."

Cassandra pretended to analyze her gloves while Jack leaned on the door. Billard grinned blindly as he smoothed back the triangle patch of hair above his forehead. Jack coughed into his hand and Billard jumped.

"Um— I really should be going. Got plenty to do today."

Billard stumbled into his own apartment, but Jack left the door open.

"I'm sorry if you came to see Henry." Jack blew loudly into his handkerchief, grateful for all the days he had practiced getting out of work as a child.

"I was so hoping he would be here." She pouted. "Do you know when he'll return?"

"He may have told me." If Jack didn't look at her directly, he didn't notice how perfectly her curls framed her face. "But I could barely think when he talked to me."

"I hope you weren't out in that horrid weather late last night." Her lips parted into a thin smile. "Running about in that rain would cause anyone to catch cold."

"This came on suddenly last night," he said, adding a cough at the end. "I was so ill, I couldn't have gone anywhere."

"You poor dear." She touched his arm. "You shouldn't be here alone. I will wait till Henry returns."

Jack didn't have to pretend to shiver. "I wouldn't want to bother you."

She patted his cheek with her gloved hand and let it linger as she whispered, "It is no bother for dear Mr. Kingston's brother."

A brief throbbing ran through Jack's lips. He stepped away and bent over with another false cough. It didn't help clear his head.

She removed her hat and gloves and set them on the table. Wiping dust from the back of a worn chair, she said, "I am surprised a man of your brother's caliber can live in such common surroundings."

"It's better than home, where chickens walk through the house."

"I will send some things along." Setting her coat across the chair, she said, "Do you have a tea kettle? I bought some tea to help my dear papa with his cough, but it may do you a bit of good."

Moving to the kitchen before she could, Jack said, "I think it's got a leak."

The kettle was sitting out on the stove. Before he could try to hide the dented tin kettle, Cassandra took it from the stove. He wished they did not have indoor plumbing as she walked to the sink and filled it with fresh water. She lit the stove and placed the kettle on it.

"You know, it isn't proper for a lady to be alone with a fellow," Jack said. "Rumors go around. Could be bad for your reputation. I can care for myself, and I'll send Henry your way when he comes home."

"We have already been alone at my house." She smiled far too sweetly at him. "How is this any different?"

Jack wanted to mention he wasn't a frog. Adjusting his blanket, he forced a loud sneeze, making sure to spray in her direction. "I'm so sorry." He rubbed his nose. "I hope you don't catch cold."

"I appear to be unable to catch things." She laughed, sashaying back to the table.

Despite the sweat forming under his shirt, Jack tightened the blanket around him. What would happen if he forced her out? No. It was better to play her game a little longer.

"Why don't you go back to bed and I will sit here and wait?" she said.

"I've got some studying to do. Don't know how much I can absorb, but it'll be better if I can get the reading done."

He picked his largest book and thumped it on the table. She delicately leaned her chin on her palm and watched him with a small smile. Keeping his eyes off her, Jack hunched over the book. He coughed and made sure to smack his lips wetly between reading loudly under his breath. His youth of irritating his sisters was at last coming to some use. He rubbed his nose, making sure to make sucking noises. However, she remained with the same demure smile and enchanting eyes. She looked ready to sit there for hours.

Chapter 15

Henry stood under the awning and shook off his hat and overcoat. His clothes were soaked, his white shirt nearly transparent. The rain had washed out most of the wax and polish in his hair, and it was starting to be as unruly as Jack's. Grimacing, he tried to smooth it, but his thick hair sprang back up.

Restraining a grumble, he entered the brick building and made his way down the narrow, dim hallway. His cane echoed on the bare floor, the boards creaking. Dust lay thick in doorways, handwritten "For Rent" signs in place of name plaques. A single light flickered, illuminating the area above an office marked, "A. Hedley."

Henry knocked.

"Come in."

Henry squared his shoulders and opened the door. The cramped space beyond made Henry's office look like a warehouse. Albert Hedley glanced up from something he was writing and squinted.

Rising to his full height, still at least a head below Henry's, he said, "Mr. Kingston. What can I do for you?"

"I wanted to let you know I have resigned my position at Mackabee and Sons."

"You did, did you? What for? Are you hoping your closeness to Madame Astrellar will persuade me to hire you?" Hedley folded his arms and barked out a laugh. "The men she chooses are all the same. They resist her at first, and then turn around and think her affection means they might control her wealth."

"No, sir. I came on another matter." Henry shifted his grip on his cane, giving himself time to find the right words. "I was looking over the accounts you sent over and I observed some questionable purchases."

Hedley picked up one of the papers on his desk. "Do you mean the three new hats she has bought this week, and orders for six new dresses, eight new purses, and—inquiries into a small dog?"

"I mean purchases of raw cowhide from slaughterhouses at triple the regular price."

Hedley's eyes narrowed. "What?"

"I have evidence you have begun fixing prices in the leather market, sir."

Hedley growled as he picked up the ledger again. Holding it out to Henry, he said, "Do not look at the items. Look at the numbers. Are they familiar?"

Henry tapped his fingers on his cane handle as he looked at the prices aligned with frivolous purchases. The fine items matched the sudden influx of money to the slaughterhouses.

"Are you related to, or friends with, anyone in the leather business?" Hedley asked.

"I—" Henry looked up from the ledgers. "I have been courting the daughter of John Havish."

Hedley leaned forward. "Does Madame Astrellar know you are courting this Miss Havish?"

"They met at the Morveaux on Saturday." Henry set the ledger on the table. "I do not like my personal affairs being brought into business."

Hedley laughed. "You think Madame Astrellar's interest in you has anything to do with business?"

"I am an excellent auditor, sir, but I do not understand her interest in me."

"Has Miss Havish been acting peculiar since meeting Madame Astrellar?"

Henry narrowed his eyes and adjusted his spectacles. "I have spoken enough of personal matters. Havish is an honest businessman and should—"

"Has your girl been particularly docile, angry, ill, or active?"

"She has had a stomach flu all week." Henry flexed his jaw before saying, "And, please do not refer to her as 'my girl'. She is a grown woman."

Hedley shrugged, his arms still folded. "Do you love this 'woman'?"

Henry cleared his throat. "That is a private matter."

Hedley pointed toward the small window in the dimly lit room. "You won't answer, but you would resign your comfortable employment and then come and accuse me of illegal activity to save her father's business?"

Henry swallowed. "It is my intention to marry the young woman, sir. Once we are married, her family becomes mine. I wish for their finances to be as healthy as possible."

"And why would you marry this girl, especially when you have Madame Astrellar willing to be on your arm?"

Henry's jaw tensed. "Pardon me, sir, but there is no comparing the women."

"You're a peculiar man, Kingston." Hedley twisted the end of his mustache as he thought. "Miss Havish might be the one thing which can save you, if she loves you in return."

"Sir, I did not come for romantic advice."

"No. You came to save her father." Hedley walked to the coat rack by the door and pulled on his overcoat. "I'll see what I can do about this cowhide business. Rest assured, matters will be set right." He paused from buttoning his coat and put his hand on Henry's shoulder. "Watch out for yourself, Mr. Kingston. Go home and get some rest. If Madame Astrellar arrives, do not let her in. I will come visit you once my business is done."

"I am going with you, sir," Henry said.

Hedley pulled his bowler hat from the coat rack. "If you want, but it'll be a tedious business." Squinting, Hedley glanced at Henry. "You'll need a bit of grooming first. Let's stop by your apartment, then see the matter through."

Henry smoothed his hair as he followed Mr. Hedley out, each step firm. Hopefully, Mr. Hedley was an honest man, and the matter would be settled quickly. There was still much to do before tonight.

The teakettle whistled and Cassandra danced into the kitchen. Jack looked again to the open front door, relieved not to see Henry. Hopefully, he could get rid of Cassandra before Henry came back.

Cupboard doors banged and Cassandra returned with the bent kettle and a mismatched pair of mugs. With a smile, she pulled a small packet from her coat pocket and dropped a fine powder into a mug. Jack watched the steam rise as the hot liquid drowned the powder. Whatever was in there, he would not touch it.

"This always helps my papa feel better."

Jack tried not to scowl, picturing Arturo's wrinkled face. How did the man feel about his wife calling him "papa"?

Dropping a packet of tea into the other mug and filling it with water, she said, "It is so difficult to talk with dear Papa these days. Ever since his mind went, he tells the wildest stories. I look so much like my mother, he sometimes confuses her with me, claiming she has hardly aged. It is heartbreaking."

She moved next to Jack and leaned against the table, her back to the open door.

"And the tales he concocts! They are so filled of fantasy. One time he told me he served on a flying ship when he was young." She sang out a tittering laugh. "Can you imagine? A whole clipper ship in the sky? Next you know, he will say I'm some siren." She placed her hands on her well-formed hips and tossed her blonde curls. "Such creatures cannot exist."

Jack dropped his chin and stared down at his textbook. Her beauty could not be questioned, but he wished it could.

Cassandra eyes remained on him as she spooned some sugar into her tea and stirred it. The thick aroma of her perfume enveloped him, quickening his pulse. He pressed his lips together, trying to quiet impulses.

"I was so worried about Papa last night," she said. "He is so frail and he was left all alone while his nurse was out sick." She inched closer to him, her hip touching his arm. "It is such a large house, but so empty. I often wish there was a man around to protect Papa and me."

The words on the page blurred. Jack rubbed his forehead and kept his head down.

"And last night—" She shuddered. "I fear I nearly lost Papa. Some thief dared climb over my fence and sneak into my house. I have not found anything stolen, but what if they had harmed Papa?"

She leaned down until her breath warmed his ear. Jack's hand clamped to the armrest of his chair as she whispered, "Who would do such a thing?"

Jack forced a cough and stamped his feet.

Standing straight, she said, "The thief got away. I saw him bravely leap through my window and have filed a report with the authorities. I gave an exact description. I am sure they will catch the scoundrel."

Jack's eyes drifted to the doorway, wondering if he should run. His heart skipped a beat as the top of Henry's head became visible as he clomped up the stairs.

The plan still forming, Jack rushed to his feet and tossed off his blanket.

"Madame Astrellar!" he shouted, grabbing her hands. She opened her mouth in shock, but the glint in her eyes spoke of triumph. "I can't stand it anymore. I know you like Henry more than me, but—" His mind raced through all the grand, romantic speeches from his adventure books. "I am more of a man than he could ever be."

The line was common enough to work.

"Oh, Jack," she said, gently pulling her hands from his. "If only things were different."

Jack grabbed her shoulders and smashed his lips against hers. If there was anything to cure him of his attraction to her, it was the wet press of her lips. She pushed him away, her strength greater than expected. He glanced over her shoulder and was glad the hallway was clear.

"Mr. Kingston! I am a lady!" she said.

"You certainly are." He gave her a wink. "I've tried to hold back, but, with you sitting so close, I knew what was needed."

She laid her hand on her chest, prepared to give the next line in their scene. Then she looked at the door. Her tone dropped along with her pretense. "You saw Henry, didn't you?"

"I saw him in your eyes and I couldn't stand it. How can you desire him? I—I—" It made him sick to finish with, "I adore you."

"Which is why you climbed my fence, crept into my house, and escaped out the window?"

She stepped toward the door. Jack scrambled over the table and jumped in her way. He forced a grin. "You came hoping Henry wouldn't be here. I know it."

"What fantastic story did my father tell you?"

"Nothing, but I'd love to meet him." He reached for her arm, but she drew away. "I don't have much myself, but it's not money you need. I can offer everything else. How can any man not love a girl of your beauty?"

He cried out as she grabbed his ear and yanked his head toward hers. Her whisper was harsh and stinging. "The game has ended, Jack. I warned you not to return to my house. I know you saw my father. You will tell me what he told you or I will turn you back into a frog."

They both jumped as someone tapped on the doorframe. Jack turned to face the stranger.

A jolt shot through Jack as a middle-aged woman rested the shoulder of her lean and hard body against the doorjamb, her hands settled in the pockets of her tweed coat. Her gray-blue eyes were narrow in her tight, square face. Jack had seen her in the paper, but never in person.

She said in her graveled voice, "Sorry to bother you lovers, but I need a word with a Mister Jack Kingston. Are either one of you him?"

"I am," Jack said.

"Inspector Gertrude McCay." She reached out her rough, dry hand.

Jack wanted to grin. He had pictured meeting her for so long while filling out his application to the officer academy. However, his smile was a weak grimace. This was not how he wanted to meet the famous inspector.

He took her hand and said, "I've seen you in the paper, Inspector."

Giving a firm shake, she said, "It's never a good picture." She turned to Cassandra. "And what's your name, ma'am?"

Cassandra snapped open her fan and batted it. "I think I am far too young to be called 'ma'am'."

"No one's too young, ma'am." Keeping her hand extended, Inspector McCay said, "Now, what's your name?"

"What have you come to bother this young man for? We were in the middle of a very important conversation."

"Was he proposing?"

"No."

"Then it can't be important."

"Madame Astrellar was just on her way out." Jack winked at

Cassandra. "I was hoping for a kiss before she left."

"Not Cassandra Astrellar?" Inspector McCay said. "I can't tell you how many times I've heard your name today. There's talk you had a break and entry last night." She looked Jack over. "How was the suspect described? Roughly six-feet tall, dark, scruffy hair, lean build?" Her eyes turned to Cassandra. "Been having a rough time finding the fellow."

"Mr. Kingston is right," Cassandra said. "I have so many things to do today, especially after the break-in. I really must go."

As Cassandra moved to walk out, Inspector McCay said, "You're going to leave your boy without a kiss? Don't be ashamed. I know what young folks do when left alone."

Cassandra eyed the inspector. She stretched up her head and leaned out her cheek. Jack gave the expected peck, ignoring her skin's coldness.

Without another word, Cassandra walked out and disappeared down the stairs. Inspector McCay leaned against the stairwell as she waited. Then, she called, "Herb!"

A paunchy, balding man in a wrinkled suit ran up from the flight below.

"Follow the lady," McCay said.

"Yes, Inspector."

As Herb disappeared down the stairs, Inspector McCay motioned for Jack to return to the apartment. Once the door was shut, she said, "I've had many strange reports today, Mr. Kingston. Madame Astrellar's case would be of little note, if her name hadn't come up in a report of frogs turning into the group of men the police have been looking for."

She motioned for Jack to sit. It wasn't a request. He slowly lowered himself into his chair.

Leaning on the table, she said, "I also have a note from Margaret Hunter, Headmistress of the Bradford School. There was your name again, in connection to transforming frogs. Three mentions of the same name are worth noting."

Jack nodded numbly, feeling as if his acceptance letter to the officer academy was burning away and disappearing into ash.

"Here I've been," the inspector said, pointing to herself, "Dealing with a case of missing children who come back with frosting and gingerbread crumbs all over their clothes. However, across town, there's a sudden increase in the amphibian population while men are disappearing." She tilted back her hat as her steely eyes turned on Jack. "Mr. Kingston, do you have any explanation?"

Jack stared at her stern, lined face, and winced. "Do you believe in mermaids?"

Inspector's McCay eye twitched. "If the case does involve mermaids, we might have greater trouble than I'd like." She stood, her hands in her pockets, and she nodded toward the door. "Why don't you come down to the station and make an official report?"

Jack smoothed back his hair. "Pardon me, Inspector, but no one's going to believe—"

"You'd be surprised what I'll believe." She pulled out a crumpled note from her pocket and glanced at it. "Especially when told by a young man who'll soon be an officer of the law, if everything turns out all right."

A coldness bristled across Jack's neck. He had worked too hard to get into the Officer Training Academy to have this whole mess with Cassandra stop him.

"Let me get on my shoes," he muttered as he walked toward his bedroom.

"Tuck in your shirt and comb your hair while you're at it," McCay called after him. "We need you to look presentable."

Henry dodged into the custodial closet as the beat of heels echoed down the stairs. He peered through a crack in the door and waited until Cassandra passed. Frustration burned across her face as she walked out of the building and slammed the door.

Right as Henry began to open the door, a frumpy man hurried down the stairs and followed Cassandra's path. Henry stepped out of the closet and kept a wary eye for any place she might be hiding.

Marching up the stairs, Henry practiced what he would say to Jack. The young man protested any liking for the woman, had avoided her at Henry's office, and now Henry caught him declaring his love. What game was Jack playing? If there was some secret conspiracy or romance, it had to be Cassandra's doing.

Henry reached the next landing as Jack came down the stairs, followed by a familiar-looking, trousered woman. His grip tightened on his cane as he remembered his and Evelyn's discussions of Inspector McCay's impossible cases.

"Jack, is everything all right?" Henry said.

"I've got to go to the station and report on something I saw the other night." Jack gave him a false smile. "Should be no trouble."

"I'd like a word with you before you go," Henry said.

"Inspector Gertrude McCay." The inspector stepped around Jack and held out her hand.

Henry gave her hand a brisk shake. "I'm Jack's brother, Henry Kingston."

"Normally, I'd let you have a few minutes," she said. "But, the case I'm on is urgent."

Henry frowned. "Jack, what happened?"

Jack opened his mouth to speak, but McCay gripped his shoulder and smiled. "Confidential information, sir. He'll explain after the matter is settled."

"Maybe we should tell Henry the whole mess." Jack glanced at the Inspector, his smile weak. "He might be able to help."

"If we need your brother, we'll send for him." She tipped her hat to Henry. "Good day, sir."

Before Jack and the inspector continued on, Jack touched Henry's arm. "There's some tea on the table. It's nasty. Don't drink it."

Henry frowned, but proceeded up the stairs, letting the inspector take his brother to the station. He needed to return to Hedley as soon as possible and solve the price fixing matters before worrying about anything else. Once he had everything prepared for his evening with Evelyn, and if Jack wasn't home, Henry would look into the matter. For now, Jack had to manage for himself.

The station clock marked late afternoon as Evelyn woke from another dazed nap on the hard bench. She stretched, her breeches and shirt stiff with mud and grass stains. Her corner of the police station buzzed with the crowd of men who'd been turned back from frogs, each bragging about how they got taken by Cassandra. Many had disappeared in the last two years, but a few were from outside Pippington and had been transformed over a decade ago.

Evelyn moaned as her head throbbed, part of her wishing she had left them in amphibian form.

"You can lean on my shoulder to rest." Roger Simmons gave her a wink as he sat beside her.

Evelyn stared straight ahead. Explaining the whole story to Inspector McCay had left Evelyn's throat raw. The Inspector had sat silent and calm as Evelyn paused to spit out creatures into a bucket, taking everything Evelyn said with grave seriousness. Now the Inspector was in her second hour in the interrogation room with Jack. All Evelyn wanted was to be excused, have a hot bath, and dress for her evening with Henry.

Simmons scooted closer to her, his leg brushing hers. "I don't know what came over me that night."

"You were turned into a frog." For once, she was disappointed she didn't feel a creature coming.

"Your kiss to restore me," he whispered, touching her arm and leaning close. "It was—"

She pulled her arm away and stood. "I only did what was—" She cringed as she felt something in her throat. She spat out a salamander into the bucket and finished quickly, "Needed."

Simmons mouth stretched in disgust as he shoved himself back. Evelyn tried not to smile as she crossed the waiting area and leaned next to a doorway.

"Evelyn, there you are." Her father's face was worried and tight, sweat beading on his forehead. "This is Mr. Albert Hedley."

The small, mustached man held out his hand. She shook it slowly, even though all she wanted to do was shout at him.

"I need a word with you before speaking to your father," Hedley said. He gestured toward one of the conference rooms. "Please, Miss Havish. Just a word."

Hoping he had come on Arturo's orders, Evelyn followed Hedley into the barren conference room. He pulled out a seat for her before sitting across from her, his small eyes appraising her.

"Miss Havish, I have just parted with Henry Kingston and I wanted to assess your feelings toward the man."

"That's between Hen—" She gagged before letting a frog plop onto the table.

Hedley's face wrinkled as he reached into his coat pocket. "Is this what she did to you? I am very sorry, miss. I tried to warn Mr. Kingston."

Glass clinked as he unrolled a small leather packet. Inside were at least a dozen clear vials filled with liquids of strange colors. He ran his hand along and pulled out one of the vials. Setting it in front of her, he said, "Drink this. It should resolve your symptoms."

She eyed the vial. He could be trying to trick her and use the potion inside to do something worse to her.

"I need to have a discussion with you, Miss Havish, and I would rather not do it in a swamp of creatures."

Evelyn was tired of spitting out amphibians, and Hedley seemed to work for Arturo, not Cassandra. She grimaced before tossing the thick, syrupy liquid into her mouth. The substance tingled and burned down her throat, stinging where she was sore.

She decided to risk speaking. "My feelings for Henry are between him and myself."

For now, no creatures came.

"Your depth of attachment to Mr. Kingston," Hedley said as he pressed his forefinger to the table, "Could be the key to escaping Madame Astrellar's plans for him."

Evelyn swallowed, wetting her sore throat. "What are her plans?"

"I am never sure." Hedley pulled at his mustache. "It's the men she doesn't turn into frogs that I worry for. I have worked for Mr. Astrellar for twenty years and I have yet to discover what she does with the men she seeks to conquer. Usually, she spends a few months to a year pursuing the man, and then, he disappears, and she and Mr. Astrellar move to one of their other mansions or manors."

"Why Henry Kingston?" Evelyn kept her gaze firm.

Hedley shrugged. "I gave up long ago fully understanding Madame Astrellar's reasons. My job is to minimize the damage she does." He reached into his briefcase and pulled out a thick packet of papers. "I fear she slipped some purchase requests past me while trying to buy out the local hide market. She forged contracts with my signature and sent them out Sunday night." He set down the papers. "If it weren't for the efforts of your Mr. Kingston, I might never have noticed."

"Henry helped you?" Evelyn frowned. "When?"

"This morning. I don't think he's realized the full scope of

Madame Astrellar's efforts, but he at least saw she was attempting to destroy your father's business. Your Mr. Kingston's got a noble heart. Once he saw what she was doing, he resigned from Mackabee and Sons and came straight to my office to resolve the matter."

Evelyn blinked, unsure she understood Hedley. "He what?"

"He came to my office."

"No. What do you mean he resigned at Mackabee and Sons?"

"Apparently, your father's business and Mr. Kingston's integrity led him to leave the place." Hedley straightened the vials on the cloth before rolling them up. "If he survives what Madame Astrellar has planned for him, I would be glad to hire him as an assistant. There are few men so honest." His brown eyes looked to her. "I'd rather he make it out all right. If you and Mr. Kingston's loyalty to each other can prove itself true, Mr. Kingston might be saved."

"Our loyalty?" She folded her arms. "How can that change anything when we're fighting a mermaid?"

Hedley rubbed his hands together as he leaned forward, an eagerness in his eyes. "I was already a great student of magic before Mr. Astrellar hired me. In my years of study, I have come to believe in the power of true loyalty."

She had seen frogs transform into men, had creatures climb out of her throat, and firmly believed Cassandra was a mermaid. Yet, she could not stop the rise of her eyebrow. "You believe in true love?"

"No." Hedley smacked his hand on the table. "True love is a lie for starry-eyed dreamers. It's a silly passion, which lasts three months into marriage and then fizzles into the grind of daily life. True loyalty, however, is far more powerful, and lasts much longer. It means, no matter what comes, you will do what is right for those you care for."

Evelyn felt as if a rock was slowly pressing on her, boxing her in. Last week, she forgot her loyalty to Henry and had gone to the Morveaux with Simmons. If she had not faltered, Henry would have had a better chance to escape from Cassandra's grasp and Evelyn would have never been cursed. If Hedley was telling the truth, she could not betray Henry now.

"I suspect," Hedley said, "Madame Astrellar is seeking a True Love to replace Mr. Astrellar before he passes away. No man deserves to be caught in her trap.

"I came here, Miss Havish, because I believe Mr. Kingston's loyalty to you protects him from Madame Astrellar's charms. You have two choices: Your first is to separate entirely from Mr. Kingston. Madame Astrellar will withdraw her attack on you and your family. Your second is to hold tightly to your loyalty and stand with him. In the latter, you have slim hope of survival, but you might be able to save him."

"I've already made my choice," Evelyn said. "As has Henry. We will stand by each other. What can you do to help us?"

Hedley's lips disappeared beneath his mustache as he pressed them together.

"I have already meddled too much," he said, gathering his briefcase and standing. "I have protections in place, but one step too far will make me too large a target for Madame Astrellar to ignore. My loyalty is to my employer and I must protect his interests."

"You are a coward, then?" Evelyn said, her arms still folded. "How many men have you watched her do this too? How many lives and businesses has she ruined, because you're too afraid to fight?"

Hedley buttoned up his suit coat as his eyes narrowed. "Miss Havish, I have spent twenty years trying to protect the world from Madame Astrellar. Because of my efforts, matters are manageable—"

Evelyn pointed toward the station lobby. "There are nearly forty men who Jack and I rescued from her well, and I know there are more she has hidden away. How is the kidnapping of forty men manageable?"

Hedley snapped down his lapel. "A bit of cowardice helps us all survive until we are in a position to win."

Before she could say anything, he marched out of the room. Evelyn slumped in the chair and pressed her hands to her head. Her loyalty to Henry was more firm than ever, especially after he had resigned his hard-earned position to protect her father's businesses. Yet, she could not see how her being loyal to Henry would stop a mermaid who probably had a whole arsenal of magic hidden away.

Sitting in this conference room, however, could not help Henry. She stood and walked briskly to the lobby. As she turned the final corner, Inspector McCay was up on a table and raising a vial with a purplish-gray liquid. The crowd of men looked up at her.

"You've all been discussing how you've been frogs," McCay said, "But I want you gentlemen to walk out of here knowing the truth. This liquid was poured in your drinks, causing you to sleep. In your sleep, there were hallucinations, which were tainted by your surroundings. All of you remember being frogs because of the frog infestation in the cellar where you were kept."

"But, I haven't aged," one of the men shouted. "And I was gone eight years."

"According to the Dr. Sonoros Principle, when you're sleeping, the electricity in your body calms down and your aging slows to a near stop." She pointed toward the door. "If you'll talk to Officer Dolores Kane at the front desk, she'll make sure you've signed your affidavit and will either send you home or to a hotel. We've booked rooms for those of you who've been gone longer.

"Most of you know my reputation. I'll make sure you receive justice and things will be set right. If you have any further questions, talk to one of my assistant detectives."

Much grumbling and shuffling followed as the men pushed toward their escape. Evelyn's eyebrows pinched together. The men seemed to believe McCay's lie, yet some had to see through it.

Judging by the redness in her father's face, Havish saw through the lie too. Evelyn moved to his side as he pushed through the crowd until he was next to McCay.

He opened his mouth to speak, but McCay said, "Someone always objects, Mr. Havish, and they're welcome to. Before you do, please consider how many people will believe such stories."

"If forty men confirm the same story, people'll know the truth," he said.

"These men will believe what they will, but I have given them a story their families will understand." She raised an eyebrow. "You know the truth, Mr. Havish, but it's not the sort of thing polite company discusses."

"I don't care about polite company," Havish said. "I care about people being aware of what can happen."

"And how many other people do you know who've been turned into animals?" McCay waited, her thumbs tucked into the pockets of her vest. Havish grunted and McCay said, "You're a bright man, Mr. Havish. Telling stories few will believe won't help these men."

She nodded toward the crowd of former amphibians. "Some of them are heading home to no prospects. You have a solid business and many connections. I'm sure you could provide a bit of help."

Havish grumbled before nodding. "I'll do what I can."

"Thank you." McCay's genuine smile faded as Havish stepped away. She pivoted to face Evelyn and jerked her thumb toward an interrogation room. "One more word. Then we'll get you home."

Not liking the grim lines on McCay's face, Evelyn followed the inspector into the room. Jack stood up, straightening his wrinkled coat while squaring his shoulders like a soldier at attention.

With the door shut, McCay leaned against the wall and folded her arms. "Here's how things stand: It appears I've got a mermaid to catch, but I also have two full confessions of breaking into her property."

"But we rescued the men," Evelyn said.

"You did, but without a badge or warrant." She raised an eyebrow. "Do you see now why those men had to believe me? The frog problem, most people'll dismiss as part of the trauma of being kidnapped. But—" She jabbed her thumb toward the door. "All those men repeating your names? Telling the papers how you broke in and pulled them out? There'd be too many questions."

"Wouldn't it be safer if people knew about magic?" Evelyn said.

McCay shook her head. "There'd be mass panic and charlatans on street corners. People would start looking at everyone with suspicion and everything would become a magical trap. It'd be chaos and trouble across the whole nation." She waved a hand. "Things are better as they stand."

"So you hide the truth?" Evelyn stepped forward. "If magic was commonly known, then Henry would have believed Jack and would be free of Madame Astrellar."

"Even if Henry Kingston was an expert in magic, he'd still be in trouble." McCay pulled out a chair for Evelyn, but Evelyn remained standing. "If what you say is right, we're dealing with a mermaid infestation. Not even the best mage, sorcerer, or warlock could keep from being tricked."

"Warlocks exist?" Jack's eyes widened as he lowered into his chair.

"Many things exist, but they keep quiet in Barthan," McCay said. "If their magic is harmless, they are left alone. It's when men start disappearing and greater dangers are suggested that matters need to be settled."

Leaning forward, Jack said, "Do you have special equipment? What about training?" His face brightened. "Are there secret magic people on your squad?"

Evelyn rubbed her forehead while McCay glared down her narrow chin at Jack. He attempted a smile before folding his hands together and fidgeting with his thumbs.

"What are your plans for us?" Evelyn said.

"Depends on what you'll agree to." McCay sat on the edge of the table. "By law, I should arrest you, but I'd rather not. You've done the public some good and I think you can do a bit more."

"I've done enough," Evelyn said.

Jack sat up. "Whatever you need me to do, I'm ready, Inspector."

McCay eyed them as she swung her leg. "All you need to do, Miss Havish, is go about the rest of your evening's business as you've already planned. My boys and I will tag along nice and quiet." She waved her arm. "You'll not even notice us."

"No." Evelyn kept her back straight as she clamped her mouth shut. Tonight, Henry might propose. She didn't need police officers with guns hiding in the bushes while waiting for Cassandra.

"Henry and Evelyn have done enough, Inspector, but I can stand in their place," Jack said. "Set me out as bait. Let me be turned into a frog if needed, but give them some peace, especially tonight."

"I'd accept your offer, Mr. Kingston," McCay said, "If Madame Astrellar had any interest in you."

"You saw her at my place earlier. I think if we set the trap right—"

"She was only there to find your brother." McCay rose and approached Evelyn. "I know you'd like a nice, romantic evening with your man. If we do everything right tonight, you'll have plenty of such evenings." The inspector's steel eyes were grave as she held Evelyn's gaze. "If we don't intervene, I'm afraid you'll not see your Henry again.

"I'm an officer of the law. I've got to stop Madame Astrellar from ruining people's lives. I need you to draw her out. Will you help me?"

Evelyn kept her eyes steady as she took in a few breaths. Her throat was scratched, her muscles sore, and her body exhausted. All she wanted was a few private moments with Henry. Yet, she was naïve to think she could have an evening with Henry without Cassandra's intervention.

Though her neck was taut, Evelyn nodded. With her single nod, any hope of Henry proposing tonight disappeared. The delay might be worthwhile if they could keep Henry safe.

Chapter 16

Henry's feet slipped on the wet sidewalk as he quickened his step. His crooked leg ached from walking across town with Hedley. The work was now done and Monday would resume normal shipments and prices for Havish's tannery. There was only one last task before spending the evening with Evelyn.

He tipped the water off his hat as he reached the door of Lapidary's Jewelry Shop. He gripped the handle and pushed, but the door was locked. Peering into the dim interior, he pounded on the window. It was only a minute after six. Someone had to still be here.

A light flickered on and Stacey stepped out of the back room. Swinging the key in her hand, she came to the window. Her face brightened as she unlocked the shop.

"Mr. Kingston!" She opened the door. "What can I help you with?"

Henry shook off his coat and stepped inside. Reaching into his pocket for the heavy envelope of cash, he said, "I have the final payment."

Stacey frowned. "Your friend came by earlier and made the last payment for you."

Henry blinked at Stacey. Bronhart and Jack were the only people he had told about the ring, but neither had the funds. He did not want to consider any other possibilities.

Limping to the counter, he said, "Then I'll pick up the ring and be on my way."

"It is tonight?" Stacey giggled. "After the carriage ride? How romantic."

"Miss Foster, I really must be going."

"Of course, but your friend picked up the ring when she paid for it."

Henry gripped his cane to keep himself from falling. "Who picked up the ring?"

"I can't say." Stacey grinned. "Beautiful lady, though. I told her it was against policy to release the ring, but she was so kind, I couldn't say no. She said it was meant to be a surprise, to thank you for all of your help."

Henry's jaw froze around the words, but he pushed them out. "Was it Cassandra Astrellar?"

Stacey's eyes widened as she giggled. She held a hand over her mouth and said, "Such a fine name for a lady."

"When did she take the ring?" He fought the urge to stamp his cane.

"This morning. We had the loveliest conversation. She spoke so highly of you, and—"

"Thank you, Miss Foster." Henry pushed past the young woman and hurried out to the street.

He had quit his employment to be free, yet she ensnared him again. Had she been at his apartment to blackmail him with the ring? He wasn't going to trade proposing to Evelyn for continuing to be her dog.

Knowing Cassandra's determination, he needed to be at Evelyn's quickly. There had to be a way to salvage the evening and keep out of Cassandra's grasp.

Evelyn ran out of the cab, up the front porch, and to the safety of her house. Inside would be a brief rest from men transforming into frogs, spitting up creatures, and other mermaid traps. She would enjoy the peace until Cassandra appeared and McCay and her squad broke from their hiding places along the street.

Bracing herself for the pounding of younger sibling's feet and the barrage of questions from her father, she opened the door. Inside, however, the only sound was the tinkling of a music box, the soft melody echoing through the house.

Water dripped from her hair and clothes as she walked into the dining room and parlor. She yawned. Naps on wood benches hardly made up for a lack of a night's sleep. She smiled as she found her father sprawled on the armchair, his mouth open as he gave a loud snore. Ron was asleep beside him. Marjory lay on the couch, one leg hanging off. Evelyn put a throw over her mother.

The night had been long for all of them.

She sprinted up the stairs. There might be time for a brief rest before Henry came.

As she reached the second story, Charlie fell out of his doorway and thumped onto the floor. Laying on his side, he snored. Evelyn shook his shoulder, but he just flopped over. She smelled his breath. Though foul, there was no trace of alcohol.

Forcing her eyes to stay open, Evelyn entered her own room. Madeline was curled up on the bed, snoring like a cat, while Julie was spread out on the floor, drool hanging from her mouth. Evelyn shook Julie's shoulder.

"Henry proposed."

With those words, Julie should have been up and bustling through questions. Unsure what else to do, Evelyn slapped Julie. Her sister didn't flinch, despite the red mark forming on her cheek.

Evelyn backed away, despite her faltering legs. She held tightly to the banister as she stumbled down the stairs. Smacking her own cheek to keep awake, she hurried to the kitchen. Cold water would clear her head.

She opened the door and a swell of anger rose in her breast.

Cassandra sat at the worn kitchen table, leaning back casually with a thin smile. Her satin, dark-green gown was fine enough for the best of galas and her wide-brimmed hat was cocked to the side.

"Such a quaint little house." Cassandra snapped shut an ivory and gold inlaid music box.

Evelyn's tiredness dropped away. She marched into the room, scanning for a good weapon.

"I'm sorry you've been caught up in this." Cassandra's tone was full of airs and pretense. "I wish I did not need Henry. I've used far less admirable man, but they all failed."

"What about your collection of frogs?" Evelyn moved toward the drawer where the meat pounder lay.

"I try to release them every few years, but some get left behind." Cassandra sighed. "I'd rather not turn them into frogs, but how else am I to test the quality of men?"

"I'm sure you could find a way without ruining their lives." Evelyn pulled on the drawer handle, but it did not budge.

"The frog test is the most efficient and I am running out of time."

Evelyn glared at the woman. "You're a mermaid. You have centuries."

Cassandra's eyes narrowed. "How much did Arturo tell you?"

"Enough." Evelyn grunted as she dug her fingers into the crack of the drawer.

"Come." Cassandra patted the table with her lace-gloved hand. "Let's have a civilized chat."

"I won't let you replace Arturo with Henry." Wiping her forehead, Evelyn stepped back from the drawer. She looked across the counter.

There were pots she could throw, but they might not be heavy enough to daze the mermaid.

Cassandra leaned her chin on her hand. "Is that what you think I am trying to do?" She tsked. "No, Miss Havish. There is no replacing Arturo. Besides, Henry's dedication to you is impossible to shake without the help of some love spell, and love spells are temporary and very messy."

"Then what do you want with him?"

"I need his help." Cassandra ran a finger across her cheekbone. "Every bit of me is as taut and tidy as when I walked out of the ocean sixty years ago. Do I appear fully human?"

"I don't care." Evelyn grabbed a ladle from the hooks on the wall and pointed it at Cassandra. "Whatever you want, you don't deserve. How many lives have you ruined in your selfish quest to do—" She gestured vaguely with the ladle, "Whatever you are trying to do?"

"I am trying to become fully human." Cassandra sat forward, her hands pressing against the table. "When my husband dies, his soul will remain on land. I will live on for a century or more, and then my soul will return to the sea." One of her hands balled into a fist. "There is your truth, Miss Havish."

"Truth or not, it's still selfish."

"You are in love." Cassandra stood. "What would you do to keep from losing him and living alone forever?"

"I wouldn't turn men into frogs."

Cassandra walked toward Evelyn, holding her fist to her stomach. "I am an exile. I have lost my children. I cannot lose Arturo."

Evelyn kept the ladle between herself and Cassandra. The mermaid's sapphire-blue eyes were softened by an edge of sorrow. Any thread of sympathy was gone as Evelyn felt the throbbing soreness of her throat.

"Persuade Henry to come with me," Cassandra said. "And I will do all I can to return him."

"He is a good man," Evelyn said. "But, after your threats and lies, he won't help you, and I won't send him into your trap."

Cassandra's cheek twitched. "I knew simply asking was a vain hope." She slid her hand into a hidden pocket of her skirt. "I'm tired of threatening people to get what I need."

Evelyn's grip tightened on the ladle's wooden handle. "I will not betray Henry."

Cassandra pulled a pair of glass marbles from her pocket, flashes of orange and yellow sparking through both. Holding them out on her palm, she pointed with her other hand. "If I drop this one, your house will set on fire, consuming everyone in it. This one will stop the fire, but might flood the house." The spheres clinked together as she closed her fist. "Everything will be much easier if you agree to help."

Evelyn's heart thudded along with a heavy knock on the door. Silence followed. Evelyn and Cassandra kept their sharp glares on each other. The knock came again and Henry called, "Evelyn?"

Deciding to risk Cassandra's spells, Evelyn swung with the ladle. It hit Cassandra's jaw with a satisfying whap. Cassandra's free hand grabbed Evelyn by the hair and threw her across the counter with impossible strength. Evelyn skidded, scattering pots and glassware to the floor. Landing on her feet, she grabbed a chair and threw it at Cassandra. Her feet slid on broken glass as she ran for the door. It flung open, smacking her face. She stumbled back, her nose numb. Henry pushed the door open and entered.

Henry huffed in air as he stared. The broken glassware and scattered pots explained the crashing, as well as the nicks on Evelyn's face and arms. They did not explain why Cassandra was standing in the Havish's kitchen.

"Mr. Kingston," Cassandra said, masking her surprise with a smile. "Miss Havish was telling me—"

"Madame Astrellar." His fists shook as he tried to keep his voice level. "Our business with each other is done. You will leave. Now."

Cassandra laughed as she teasingly shook her head. "I came to make peace with Miss Havish." She looked to Evelyn. "We have, haven't we?"

"Go find a bottomless pit to rot in." Evelyn gripped Henry's arm and pulled him with her as she stormed toward the front door.

Henry stumbled before matching Evelyn's quick pace past her snoring parents.

"What happened? Is everyone all right?"

"Nothing is right." Evelyn glanced out the windows. She dropped her voice to a whisper. "Police are waiting outside."

Henry's frown deepened. Bronhart must have left the price fixing materials with the authorities. Now Cassandra would be confronted.

"I am sorry you and your family have been caught up in all this," Henry said. "After today, your father's business should be safe."

"Dad's business is the least of our worries."

Evelyn reached for the front door's handle. Henry touched her arm and said, "Let me."

Even with police around, and whatever had happened in the kitchen, Henry would still be a gentleman. He reached for the handle. Something glass plinked across the ground in front of him. It shattered and noxious, green smoke swelled up. Henry jumped back as blue and green flames sprayed from the smoke.

"Get some buckets!"

Henry pushed Evelyn back as he ripped off his soaking wet overcoat. With a yell, he batted at the flame. The color had to be caused by an electric fire. His coat smoldered, white smoke rising. The cloth erupted in flames. He tossed it to the ground and stamped on it, leaving behind an ashen mess of fine wool.

"If you come with me, Mr. Kingston," Cassandra said. "This little house can be saved."

Evelyn snarled as she ran across the dining room toward Cassandra. The heiress raised her hand and a wall of flame rose in front of Evelyn.

"Turn off these theatrics," Henry said as he leaned on his cane. He scanned the ground for the wire Cassandra was using. "And I will discuss whatever you want."

Henry cried out as the front window imploded. Black marks etched the ceiling as the flame rose and the curtains lit on fire.

Cassandra had lost her sanity, or she had never had it.

"They are innocent," Evelyn said.

"Then tell Mr. Kingston to come with me."

Evelyn glanced at Henry, her cheeks taut, the tendons visible in her neck. "No."

The banister caught fire and Henry grabbed Evelyn around the waist. If the police really were here, they would break in at any moment. He would get Evelyn out and then help the police with her family. Evelyn pulled out of his hold. She tensed as if about to run, but Henry jumped in her way.

"Go get help," he said. "I'll get your father."

Evelyn grabbed Henry by the lapels. "She's a mermaid, Henry. She turned Jack into a frog and cursed me."

Evelyn's flu must have muddled her brain. Henry glanced at the flame going up the banister as he pushed Evelyn toward the window, but she did not yield.

"Go!" he said.

Evelyn let out a gasp of despair before pulling him to her and kissing him. Henry stiffened, the heat of the fire rising. He wanted to put his arms around her, but this was worth nothing if they died.

Pulling her lips away, Evelyn whispered, "You must go with her."

"What?" Henry pushed on her muscular shoulders again, wishing she hadn't spent so many hours at the tannery.

"Go with her." Evelyn shoved his hands off her shoulders.

"Good," Cassandra said. There was another plink. A torrent of water flew in through the window, crashing through the flame. The water moved as if it were a long snake, slithering and splashing across the line of fire. Hisses broke out where liquid ran over heat. The water deepened, growing into a wave. Henry threw his arms around Evelyn as the torrent crashed over them. He slipped and they both landed on the soggy carpet.

The water washed away, leaving charred walls and half-burnt furniture. Henry held Evelyn close. She was his only sign of reality. Water did not act as if it were some thinking creature, moving with enough precision to put out a fire. All of this had to be an elaborate parlor trick.

Cassandra held out his cane as she stood over him. "Things will go much easier tonight if you cooperate."

Henry snatched his cane from her, but remained sitting with Evelyn. Her skin was frigid as she shivered. He would not abandon her. He had also better propose tonight, considering the closeness of their position.

Reaching into a hidden pocket in her skirt, Cassandra said, "Miss Havish, I have more. Would you like me to test them?"

"Henry," Evelyn breathed as she kept her arms around his shoulders and leaned her head against his. "This was magic. Real magic. She can do far worse."

He stared at her, taking in her pleading eyes. She believed this.

"What lies has she told you?" he said. "Magic does not exist."

He used his cane to pull himself to his feet, his wet clothes hanging on his bony frame. Once his feet were steady, he helped Evelyn stand.

Keeping her hand in his, Henry said, "I have already resigned my position at Mackabee and Sons, Madame. I do not know what else to do to rid myself of you." He pointed toward the door with his cane.

"We are going to leave, you are going to surrender over to the police, and then your father will pay for repairs to this house."

"You are a remarkable man, Mr. Kingston." Cassandra tilted her head with a bemused smile. "After all of this, even the woman you love cannot convince you of the truth?"

Henry grit his teeth together as he let go of Evelyn's hand and approached the door. If the police were on the street, they had to be closing in.

"I suppose, then, only crude methods of persuasion should work," Cassandra said.

A mechanical click sent a shiver down Henry's spine. He had heard the sound too many times when his father raised his old hunting rifle, ready to strike some hapless beast. Henry spun around, falling against the door as he lost his footing. Cassandra pressed a gilded, old-fashioned pistol to Evelyn's forehead.

"Kill me and you have no chance." Evelyn kept her glare steady.

"I'd rather we didn't test the theory." Cassandra gave a false smile. "Now, Mr. Kingston, if you'll open the door, we can go to my carriage."

He wanted to say no, to use his cane to knock the gun from Cassandra's grasp. However, he could not risk the gun firing and Evelyn crumpling to the ground. The police out there might know what to do. He would bide his time and find an opportunity to get Evelyn to safety.

The springs in the motorcar seat squeaked as Jack tapped his leg. Inspector McCay took a long drink from a canteen, her unblinking eyes watching the Havish's house.

"Have you had trouble with mermaids before?" Jack said. Sitting next to the Inspector, he wanted to ask about her cases, about how much was true, and what the real source of mischief was. He had dared ask a few questions, but his mouth grew dry and his tongue numb as he met her hard glare. Her expression now was no better.

"All of my cases are classified," McCay said.

He tried to smile instead of scoot back in his chair. McCay scratched her nose as she looked him up and down.

"I don't like impulsive officers," she said. "They're jittery and liable to shoot their partner in the foot."

Jack slumped in his chair.

McCay pointed at his forehead. "You've got a quick and curious mind, Mr. Kingston, and a good eye for the truth. If you can make it through training, you're the sort of officer I watch. Whether or not I'll keep watching depends on what you do tonight."

"What do you need me to do, Inspector?"

She stabbed her finger into his chair. "Stay in the motorcar and keep quiet."

"Yes, Inspector."

Jack leaned back and blew out air while McCay turned her eyes toward the house.

"Henry's here." Jack began to point as his brother limped quickly down the street. McCay glared out of the corner of her eye. Jack dropped his hand and tapped his fingers on his leg.

McCay cracked her neck as Henry entered the house. Jack peered into the darkness as the rain slushed down. Cassandra and her carriage would drive up at any moment. The police would spring out and he would see McCay in action.

A bright blue light flashed in the house. Jack's hand went to the door handle, but he dropped his arm. McCay slid her pistol from her shoulder holster as she said, "She's already there."

McCay jumped out of the car and circled her arm over her head as the police converged on the house. They hid behind Marjory

Havish's trimmed flower bushes. At least two officers leaned up against the door, guns held in the ready position.

Jack grabbed the binoculars from the dashboard. The streetlights reflected in the lenses, blurring things. McCay crouched behind a bush and raised her fingers, counting down as the two officers by the door prepared to kick it in. Jack held his breath as he counted along with the Inspector.

As her last finger dropped, a serpentine stream of water erupted out of the street, gathering the torrent of rain with it. The water-beast swung and swerved. The police scattered, diving to avoid the wild swing of the liquid body. Water poured through the window while a wave of water rushed out, sending the officers and inspector tumbling.

Arms flailed as a knee-high flood rushed down the middle of the street. Jack threw open his door and ran out, the rush of water pushing against his legs. He lifted a foot and his shoe got sucked away by the water. To get steadier footing, he slowed his steps. This was no different than wading through fast streams while fishing back home.

The water quickened and Jack planted his feet on the ground. A door or two down the street, the stream split as if a motorcar were parked there. However, nothing was visible.

Jack walked toward the hidden object, each step quicker as the water ebbed. He was still ten paces away when Henry exited the house, followed closely by Cassandra holding a pistol to Evelyn's head. Jack squatted, hoping he wasn't visible. How good was a mermaid's vision in the dark and rain? As Cassandra stepped onto the sidewalk, her carriage and horses appeared where the water split.

Keeping low, Jack splashed toward the carriage. Henry and Evelyn entered first. Cassandra holding the pistol steady as she followed. Jack reached the carriage's side as it lurched into motion.

"Mr. Kingston!" McCay shouted as she ran toward Jack and the carriage.

Jack glanced back. "Sorry Inspector!"

He ripped off his remaining shoe and tossed it aside. His bare feet slapped against the wet pavement as he broke into a sprint. The unseen driver snapped the whip and the horses picked up speed. Jack jumped and caught hold of the rear ladder. His legs swung until he pressed the balls of his feet against the cold metal. He held on tight as the carriage swerved around a corner.

They reached a straightway and Jack stretched out his leg until his foot touched the ledge over the wheels. He was glad for his height as he kept hold of the railing along the roof and moved his weight to his foot on the ledge. He edged his way over to the door. The carriage shook and swerved, and his cold, wet fingers barely hung on.

Once at the door, he peeked inside. Cassandra sat across from Henry and Evelyn, her lace-gloved hands resting in her lap while keeping the gun pointed at Evelyn. Remembering how the heroes from his books did these things, Jack tightened his grip on the railing and tried to swing back. His hands slipped and he thudded against the carriage's side, one leg flailing.

The carriage jerked the opposite way. Jack held on with one hand and threw open the door. He grabbed the side of the opening and prepared to jump inside. The carriage swerved, sending him sprawling inside. His face smacked against Cassandra's lap. The gun fired and Evelyn cried out.

Jack's arms flailed as he tried to sit up. Cassandra grabbed his wrist placing something metal and round in his hand.

Henry jabbed his cane at Cassandra. She caught it and ripped it away. Shifting her grip, she smacked Jack's hand holding metal ball. He shouted out as he dropped it. The familiar golden bauble thudded across the carriage floor as a flash of green light filled the carriage and Jack felt himself falling.

"Not again," Jack said just before his chin expanded and he let out a ribbit.

Henry grabbed Evelyn's shoulders, hoping the wound wasn't too bad. Her torso was limp, her body swaying as he pushed. Without his cane, Henry had no weapon. He would rather take his chances jumping out and landing on pavement than going further with this madwoman.

There was a smack and a cry. Henry's breath halted as a green light flashed. Jack shrank, his skin turning mottled and green, his eyes growing rounder.

This was not possible. All of the tales were mixing with Henry's tiredness and making him see things. Yet, right where Jack had been, sat a frog.

The frog hopped toward the door just before Cassandra caught it. She dropped the frog into her purse before flicking her hand. A spark of green light snapped between her fingers as the open door slammed shut.

"Do help her sit up," Cassandra said as she leaned down and picked up her gold bauble and pistol from the carriage floor. "She should have quite a welt."

Henry pulled Evelyn up. She moaned as she held her hand to her breast. Readying himself to look, Henry moved to help put pressure on the wound. There was no blood. He gently pulled Evelyn's hand away and stared at the gray splatter of gunpowder on her shirt.

Her voice dazed, Evelyn looked down and said, "I felt—"

Cassandra waved the pistol before tossing it to the side. "I loaded it with blanks. I needed to persuade you, not kill you. We're almost to my estate anyways."

"You wouldn't have burned my house down?" Evelyn said.

"Only enough to persuade you." Cassandra leaned forward and looked out the carriage window. "Houses can be rebuilt. Murder cannot be undone."

Evelyn's eyes narrowed while Henry stared at the purse. He

gripped Evelyn's hand. It was real and sure. She and Jack had told him the truth, but he had been too blind to believe. There had been no evidence until now, with his brother locked away as an amphibian in a handbag.

"What are you going to do with my brother?" Henry said.

Cassandra patted the handbag. "Hold him until your task is complete."

Henry released Evelyn's hand and smoothed the lapels of his suit coat. "If you let Evelyn go, I will do whatever you need."

"No." Evelyn grabbed Henry's elbow.

Cassandra leaned back, her chin raised as she kept a small, pleased smile.

"I don't think you're in a position to negotiate," Cassandra said. "Still, I'll keep her as extra collateral."

The carriage passed through the mansion gates and lurched to a stop.

Cassandra held Henry's cane out to him. "After you, Mr. Kingston."

He snatched it away. When they were on the ground, he might sweep it behind her legs, giving him and Evelyn an opportunity to run. He would probably not make it far, but Evelyn would have a chance.

Marvin, her dull-eyed driver, opened the door, his shoulders slumped as the rain poured on him. Henry climbed down and turned around.

Cassandra grabbed Evelyn by the hair and shoved her face down into the seat. Evelyn shouted and fought as Cassandra placed her knee across Evelyn's back. Henry reached for the carriage handle. Marvin grabbed Henry by his collar and tossed him onto the wet pavement. Henry barely kept hold of his cane as he slid across the wet stone.

He rolled to his side and struggled to stand, his crooked leg shaking. Huffing, he hurried toward the carriage. The driver stood in his way. Henry clenched his fist, wishing he had Havish's bulk to put behind a punch.

"Stand aside gentlemen." Cassandra pushed Evelyn out of the carriage, Evelyn's wrists tied behind her. The driver caught Evelyn before she hit the pavement. She jerked out of his grasp and backed toward Henry.

Cassandra stepped down from the carriage, waving back the driver. Henry moved behind Evelyn and tugged at the rope, but there was no give.

Walking across the garden, Cassandra raised the handbag. "Are you coming?"

Henry wasn't sure if he heard a desperate ribbit. Leaning toward Evelyn, he said, "Run. I'll distract her."

"No." Evelyn's jaw was hard, a fierceness in her eyes. "We're going to make it out of this together, with Jack."

He stepped in front of her and tried to match the steadiness of her eyes. "Do you have any idea what we are walking into?"

"We're going to help a mermaid become human."

Henry wiped the water off his spectacles as he glanced at the garden entrance where Cassandra waited. This was all madness. He could not let the woman he intended to marry walk into unknown danger with creatures that should not exist. However, he seemed to have little choice. Cooperation with Cassandra was his best chance of saving his brother.

"If you are injured or—" His throat threatened to close around the words. "Do not return, your father will murder me."

"Are you coming or do I need to retrieve you?" Cassandra called.

Henry stamped his cane on the ground and straightened his shoulders. He placed his hand on Evelyn's elbow. Together, they walked toward Cassandra and whatever trap she was dragging them deeper into.

Chapter 17

Evelyn glared at Cassandra's elongated hat as they walked down the stone steps into the cellar. Her wrists pulled against the ropes as she flexed her fingers. She couldn't match the mermaid's strength, but she would still take the chance to strangle her.

Henry kept his hand on her arm as he followed her from the stairway and into the underground cove. Cassandra led them to the dock and motioned for them to enter the waiting skiff.

"Where are we going?" Evelyn said. If she moved her elbow just right, she might hit Cassandra in the gut.

"An evening cruise." Cassandra gave a false smile and gestured toward the skiff. "Come along."

Evelyn grunted while Henry stepped into the boat, using his cane to maintain his balance. He held her arm to help her climb onboard. Evelyn barely kept her footing, wishing she could use her hands to catch herself. She glared at Cassandra as she and Henry sat on the stern bench.

Cassandra hummed as she stepped onto the skiff. She approached the helm as she pulled Jack from her handbag. It consisted of a set of golden levers and cranks on a panel beside the steering wheel. Jack's eyes plead for help as Cassandra set him inside an empty lantern hanging behind the helm.

Evelyn eyed the dark water of the underground lake. She and

Henry might be better off jumping in and risking whatever could be in there. However, their escape would leave Jack abandoned in the lantern.

Marvin's feet thudded on the dock. He handed Cassandra a wire cage with at least a dozen more frogs. They jumped at the walls, their ribbits carrying desperation.

Marvin stumped back to the shore while Cassandra hung the cage on the hook beside Jack's. She pulled a stack of blankets from a box beneath the helm and set them on a bench to the side. She looked back as the squeaking of wheels echoed through the cavern.

"Where are you taking us?" Evelyn said as she and Henry sat together at the stern-end of the skiff. He kept his hand on her elbow, his arm tense as he watched Cassandra. If her hands were free, Evelyn wasn't sure if she would grip his hand or strangle Cassandra.

Cassandra ignored Evelyn as Marvin slumped along the dock with a slow, heavy gate, pushing a wheeled chair carrying Arturo. The old man's shaking shoulders and bony frame appeared frailer as Marvin lifted him from the chair and set him on the blanket-covered bench in the skiff.

As Arturo had another hacking fit, Henry leaned closer to Evelyn. "Why is she bringing her father?"

"He's not her father." A tiredness pulsed through her head as she wondered how to explain everything to Henry.

Marvin untied the skiff from the dock and used his foot to push the boat out into the lake. Evelyn's fingers clenched. Each second they drifted further meant a smaller chance of escaping.

Henry glanced back at the dock. "I think you have enough hostages."

"He is not a hostage." Cassandra sat beside Arturo, her face softened with concern. Evelyn wrinkled her nose. The worry had to be a lie. "He is my husband."

"You are married?" Henry let go of Evelyn's arm and stood,

rocking the skiff. "How can— You have been flirting with me, and—?"

"It was a test, Mr. Kingston. Nothing more." Cassandra wrapped a blanket around Arturo's shoulders.

"Let them go," Arturo said, placing a shaking hand on her arm. "We will find another way."

"We tried other ways." A pain flinched through Cassandra's eyes. "The damage was far worse."

"Then you must let me go. I will die soon. You can return to the ocean."

"No." Her back straightened. "We've discussed this, Arturo. Out there, I will have nothing."

"Our children—"

"They are grown and gone." She sat beside him and kissed him tenderly.

"I'm glad he's not her father," Henry muttered.

Evelyn looked away, trying not to wonder how rough and dry Arturo's wrinkled lips were.

"If you die before I am fully human, we will be lost to each other." She ran her hand over his silver hair and glanced at Evelyn and Henry. "Look at them. I've never brought a man in love before. It might give him a better chance."

Evelyn's fingers tensed. Hedley had said her loyalty to Henry would help. So far, it had only gotten them deeper into Cassandra's trap. She couldn't see how it would help them battle a mermaid.

Arturo pointed a trembling finger at the dead-eyed servant standing at the dock. "And what if he ends up like Marvin?"

"Then, for the sake of Miss Havish," Cassandra said as she moved to the helm. "I will steal back Mr. Kingston, just as I stole you."

A laugh burst out of Evelyn. "For my sake? Was that also why you tried to ruin my father's business?"

Cassandra flipped several of the levers. "If you had listened to my warning, Miss Havish, you would not be here."

"If she had listened, she would not be the woman she is," Henry said.

Turning, Cassandra seemed to analyze them. She flipped a lever on the panel in front of the helm and a series of gears cranked. A pearl about the size of Evelyn's head rose out of the enclosure.

"Love is a strange phenomenon." Cassandra leaned against the helm as she looked down at Arturo. "It catches you and keeps hold. It flourishes in moments of joy and sweetness. In times of darkness, you hold close the small sparks of love until they can be fully lit again." She reached into her pocket. "Does it make us fools or does it make us our better selves?"

She lifted a ring box. "Mr. Kingston, I am bringing you into grave danger. While I have lied to you to bring you here, I do not wish you harm."

Evelyn grunted as Henry's jaw clenched. She was glad to know he believed Cassandra as little as she did.

"I believe your love with Miss Havish is strong enough to protect you," Cassandra said, "But you need a symbol of your love to remain secure."

She flipped open the box, revealing the ring Stacey had shown Evelyn. Cassandra crossed the skiff and held the box out to Henry.

"Carry it with you and be safe."

Henry glared at the ring, his fingers digging into Evelyn's arm. Cassandra waited before setting it next to Henry.

She turned back to the helm and Henry slipped the box into his pocket. She pulled a few more levers and a buzzing rose. With the spin of a crank, electric light arched around the pearl. Singing out a high-pitched note, almost inaudible to human ears, Cassandra turned another lever. The pitch of her note lowered and the water sloshed and churned.

A vertical whirlpool of light rose in front of the skiff, blue electricity snapping through it. Henry put an arm around Evelyn and she planted her feet against the floor. Her skin tingled as they entered the circle and the boat lurched forward. Henry and Evelyn fell back, their feet flailing in the air. Evelyn grunted as her shoulder bashed against the bench.

The metallic scent of the underground lake was gone as the skiff jetted through darkness, only illuminated by sparks of light. Wind rushed, sending goosebumps along Evelyn's skin.

"This shouldn't be real," Henry said as he helped her back onto the bench.

Henry sat beside her, his hip against hers. She watched in the darkness, Cassandra standing at the helm, steering the ship through the strange tunnel. She shifted as Henry's fingers wrapped around hers.

"This isn't how I wanted to give this to you," he whispered. "But if she spoke the truth, and it brings safety, I'd rather you have it."

As Evelyn opened her mouth to ask what he was talking about, she felt the cool metal of the ring slip onto her finger.

"If we make it back alive," he said, his breath on her ear. "I'd like it if— I'd rather—" He swallowed. "I'd like you to be Mrs. Kingston."

She turned her head. In the brief flashes of light, she saw his earnest face, his spectacles slightly askew.

"I'd like it too," she said. "And, we'll make it back."

He began to smile, but was cut off as the boat broke out of the tunnel, sending up a splash of salty water. Evelyn rocked back, falling into Henry, her head knocking against his chin. He oofed while throwing his arms around her to stop her fall. She waited for him to let her go, but he held her close and cradled her head. Letting herself lean against him, she looked out at wherever Cassandra had brought them.

The air smelled of salt and brine. Gulls cawed as they flew overhead. The red hues of sunset were disappearing on the horizon. If they hadn't been brought here as captives of a mermaid, she would have liked to sit close with Henry and watch the sun reflect on the expanse of ocean. As they were, she dreaded sitting up to see themselves so far from Pippington with Cassandra as their only way home.

Evelyn raised her head, the wind snapping loose strands of hair. Jutting rocks spread ahead of them, stabbing through the skeletons of broken ships. The heaviness of death hung in the air. Beyond the rocks, a gray cliff loomed over the water.

Cassandra guided the skiff around the wrecks and toward a small cove.

"Is this Marveth?" Evelyn said. "I thought you were exiled."

"Arturo told you much." Cassandra spun a few cranks and the giant pearl lowered into its hiding place. By some unknown force, the skiff continued over the waves. "My daughter, Isabella, arranged for me to visit every three years on the night of a full moon." She looked back at Arturo. "I do not think we have another three years."

"What's on the island?" Henry said.

"My hope, Mr. Kingston." Cassandra plucked at the shoulders of her dress, re-puffing out the corners. "Every year, on this full moon, the merfolk of Marveth host a festival. Many spend the year collecting humans from shipwrecks so they can be traded. Most humans are transformed to make them easier to carry." She pointed to the frogs. "These are mine."

"What are you trading my brother for?" Henry said.

"Nothing. Jack will stay where he is." She tapped the side of the cage with her finger, letting the cage swing. "These men are the unsavory sort who'd be in prison if they weren't here. Their fate among merfolk will be little better. Jack, however, is a decent young man and will be restored when we're done."

"How is this festival supposed to help you?" Evelyn said.

"It is a game to see whose human will fall first to the pleasures and wonders." She glanced at Henry. "That is why I had to test you, Mr. Kingston. I need you to come with me inside Trisar's Hall and retrieve

Nereda's Tiara. All we must do is go in, stay focused, get the tiara, and I will take you home."

Evelyn glanced at Henry and was glad his frown was as deep as hers was.

"How long will this errand take?" Henry slipped his pocket watch out and flipped it open. He frowned as he shook it, water dripping from the casing. With a grunt, he snapped it shut and shoved it into his pocket.

"If all goes well and you listen to me, we will return to Pippington by morning."

"No man you have brought has returned, besides Marvin," Arturo said. "Take me."

Cassandra looked at Arturo. "You are too frail, my love. And, I will need you once I have the tiara."

The bottom of the skiff scraped the sand and came to be a stop. Cassandra pulled the cage of frogs from its hook and jumped onto the shore, the hem of her dress splashing in the water. She grabbed the rope attached to the bow of the ship. As she tied the skiff to a tree, Henry helped Evelyn stand. She stumbled, again wishing her hands were free to grab the side of the boat. He caught her, but nearly fell himself as his crooked leg slipped.

"Do take a seat, Miss Havish." Cassandra watched the trees. "You will be safer here."

Evelyn leaned against the side of the boat as it rocked. "Wherever you're taking Henry, I go too."

"Entering with two humans in their natural form will bring too many questions." She patted the bow of the ship. "Stay and keep Arturo company."

Henry kept hold of his cane as he sat down. "I will go no further without Evelyn."

Evelyn stood beside him, keeping her glare on Cassandra. Tapping her fingers on the bow, Cassandra gave a long sigh. She whistled, the pitch high and shrill. The boat lurched and knocked Evelyn off her feet. Her head banged against the side. Henry pushed off his seat to catch her. A slimy tendril of seaweed slid along her cheek. Several other strands burst out of the water and wrapped around her legs and torso. Her jaw was held shut as she and Henry stared at each other.

"Would you rather we leave her in this state, or with just the rope?" Cassandra said.

His mouth was tense, as if the words were foul as he said, "I will come."

"Good." Cassandra whistled and the seaweeds slid away. Evelyn grunted as she lay in the bottom of the boat. Henry gave her one last glance before stepping out of the skiff and following Cassandra onto the island.

All Henry could see as he walked behind Cassandra was Evelyn wrapped in seaweed and suffocating. He wished he would wake soon and find this all a nightmare. His sore leg and cold skin, however, warned he was fully awake and aware. His cane sank in the sand as he hurried to catch up, barely giving him support.

Cassandra tapped her foot as she waited at a faded wooden door at the bottom of the cliff towering over them. She reached into an alcove by the door and pulled out a fresh dinner jacket. "There's not much we can do about your hair, but I think you'll be presentable enough."

Henry glared as he took off his singed coat and pulled on the dinner jacket. He transferred his few belongings from his pockets before tossing his suit coat behind a hedge.

Cassandra gave him an appraising glance before opening the door.

The doorway led to a narrow spiral staircase, the steps carved out of the rock. As Henry followed Cassandra deeper, he had to lean on the wall to relieve the pressure on his crooked leg.

Henry stopped as his leg slipped on the wet stone steps. Cassandra paused from her quick pace and looked back.

"It's not much farther. Come along." She swept her skirt as she turned and continued.

A shiver ran down Henry's back, but he wasn't sure if it was from the cooling air or the trap he was willingly walking into. He pressed on. His cooperation was the only chance he, Evelyn, and Jack had to get home.

They reached a landing and Cassandra held out her arm. "Try to appear like you want to be here."

Henry grunted, but put his arm through hers.

The next flight of stairs was made of transparent crystal and led to a pair of engraved, silver doors. They gleamed in the ambient light. Beyond the doors echoed drunken laughter and the sort of frivolity Henry avoided.

Cassandra tapped the doors with her fan. A porthole slid open and a man glanced out, only his eyes visible in the slit. Cassandra raised the cage of frogs and smiled with a flutter of eyelashes.

"Madame Cassandra!" The man laughed. "What entertainment do you bring this time?"

"Reginald, I always keep such things a surprise. Do my little pets meet tonight's standards?"

"Of course."

The porthole closed and the doors opened as if they had no weight. Cassandra kept her arm in Henry's and said, "Keep close until we are near a door I'll point out to you. Play the idiot and do not join any of their games."

They walked through the gilded doorway and into an open hall more ornate than the Morveaux. Henry's stomach clenched as he stared at the glass floor. A broad fish tail attached to a human torso flashed through the water below.

Cassandra pretended to laugh as she gestured with her fan toward a balcony across the room. "The tiara is behind the white door. I can't enter, but you should be able to find our prize easily."

He attempted to smile as she batted her eyes.

They walked down the lush, red carpet to the main floor. Merfolk glided through the water beneath the glass to raised pools ringed by short, marble walls. Each wall was used as a gaming table, merfolk on one side, still-human men and women on the other. On the gaming tables were individual cages holding frogs, lizards, birds, and other small creatures, all being offered for bets. The humans leaned on their elbows, joking and flirting with the merfolk, ignorant of their own future inside the cages.

Some men wore suits, while others were in patched sailor clothes. The women wore a mix of fine dresses and everyday clothes. The mermen and mermaids wore shirts or bodices made of gleaming skins, their necks drenched in pearls and jewels. Many of the mermen had ornaments hanging from long, waxed mustaches, curving up into tight curls. The mermaids wore elaborate hats atop pillars of hair. Both were adorned with starfish, shells, and glittering jewels.

Pouring free-flowing wine among the humans were women in gowns, tri-cornered hats teetered at the peak of their towers of hair. A few men in fine suits wore the same hats. They all had the same cool eyes as the merfolk, despite their warm laughter and bright smiles.

The extravagance made Henry's stomach feel as if it were rotting, especially as the rich stink of brine mixed with perfume battered his nose.

Beautiful singing filled the air and Henry felt his head turn. Humans with blank and empty eyes stepped toward a group of merfolk in a pool. A tendril of desire rose in Henry, but he batted it away with a stamp of his cane. Cassandra's hand gripped his arm, her cheeks taut even as she smiled and greeted her fellow merfolk. Henry adjusted his spectacles and moved to hurry toward the white door.

Cassandra touched his shoulder. "Do not call attention to us. We will reach it soon enough."

He stifled a growl, allowing her to continue leading him. An auburn-haired woman swathed in sculpted gold satin stepped around the group of men drooling at her.

"Who is this?" she said, tapping her fan on Cassandra's shoulder.

Cassandra ran her hand along Henry's arm. "My latest pet, Vivian. Isn't he a dear?"

"A curious specimen." Vivian adjusted her tri-cornered hat as she smiled at Henry.

Henry met her cool eyes with a glare.

Vivian laughed. "And how spirited."

His teeth ground together. "I am Madame Astrellar's guest."

With a mocking pout, Vivian said, "You are still using that pathetic human's name?"

"It is how I am known on land." Cassandra's fingers dug into Henry's arm, her smile tight. "There, what does my name matter?"

Vivian tapped her fan on her arm before touching Henry's hand. His cheek twitched as he forced himself not to draw away from her cold touch.

"These gentlemen and I were about to embark on a game of roulette." She leaned closer, her green eyes the same as a snake preparing to coil around its prey. "Those men are fools. Come with me and I will guarantee your fortune."

"No." He tried not to snap the word.

Vivian leaned back and laughed. "So curious." To Cassandra, she said, "You have trained him well."

Cassandra nodded her thank you and Vivian led her entourage of men away. Once Vivian was out of earshot, Cassandra whispered, "Even before I was exiled, that mermaid was wretched."

Henry frowned. "She's a mermaid?"

"The hats." She gestured with her hand. "They have magic that gives merfolk legs for a few hours."

"Why aren't you wearing a hat?"

"I'm under a stronger spell." She tugged at his arm and focused her eyes on the door.

They walked on, but several other merfolk disguised as humans interrupted Cassandra and Henry's approach to the door. He kept his jaw firm and hand tight on his cane. His arm was sore where Cassandra's fingers continued to dig in, tightening each time one of the merfolk made some snide remark about humans. Each mermaid offered one trivial pleasure or another to Henry, but he kept his answer the same.

When they reached the bottom of the staircase leading to the door, Cassandra released Henry's arm. "They will notice if I go further. Do not speak to anyone once you are away from me. Especially if you wish to save your brother and Miss Havish."

Henry glared as he pulled his arm away. "I want nothing they can offer."

Cassandra's lips tensed as if she were about to speak, but she strode away. She put on a smile and approached a pool where merfolk rested. Henry looked up the stairs. He would enter the room, get the tiara, and Cassandra would have to honor their agreement.

His bent leg ached as he climbed the stairs, barely keeping his balance with his cane. The air did seem clearer as he reached the second floor. He hurried his step and approached the white door. His finger touched the handle.

A man in a simple, dark blue officer's uniform pressed his hand to Henry's arm. He was at least a head taller, with a square jaw and the honest eyes of a soldier. However, he wore a tri-cornered hat.

"Sir," the officer said. "I have watched this door for years. No man who enters ever returns."

"I must enter," Henry said. "Other lives depend on it."

The man narrowed his eyes. "Which of the mermaids sent you? It is one of their favorite tricks. They send a man to this door with lies of heroism, only to watch him die. You seem an honest man. Do not let them fool you."

"I know the lies well." Henry kept his eye on the hat. "I do not think this task is one."

"Who is in danger?" The officer glanced out to make sure no one was listening. He tapped the swordfish pin at his collar. "I was tricked into my position by the merfolk and trapped here. I have dedicated my life to saving others, knowing I cannot escape. Tell me why you want to enter, and I swear, on my honor as soldier, I will do all I can to help you."

Henry glanced back out at the casino floor, picturing the weave of lies Cassandra had wrapped him in. He had been so close to being free before, only to have her kidnap the two people he cared about most. He could not give her what she wanted. This man was a stranger. He might be as dangerous as the other merfolk or the only other sane person in the room.

"Even if I tell you," Henry said. "How can you help me?"

"I know the way to the Council. They want this place to end." The officer leaned closer. "Let me help you."

Henry kept the man's honest gaze and released the door handle. If the officer spoke the truth, he offered a better chance than Cassandra.

"I have been kidnaped and blackmailed," Henry said. "Can this Council offer me justice?"

The officer smiled. "Yes. Come with me."

Water lapped the side of the boat as Evelyn sat on the bench, her wrists sore from trying to loosen the ropes clasping her hands together. Arturo huddled in his blanket, shivering as he stared at her in silence. She ignored him as each heartbeat ticked away the seconds, each one growing the risk Henry would be lost.

"Mermaids are even better at tying knots than sailors," Arturo said, his voice wheezing. "You'll not get free by struggling."

Evelyn glared as she continued shifting her wrists. Doing nothing would not help anyone.

Arturo pressed his lips together before glancing up at the island. "She's made too many men disappear. She always claims to have the one who will succeed, but then comes back alone and disappointed." He pointed toward the lights glimmering in the distance. "I'm sure your Henry will last longer than the others. Those men got caught up in the simple temptations in that palace – beautiful women, the promise of wealth, gluttony, libation. However, the temptation changes the deeper a man gets. They always find something."

"Henry won't fail," Evelyn said.

Arturo's dark eyes watched her. "The ring might have helped, but he put it on you, didn't he?"

Evelyn clenched her hand, rubbing her thumb over the cool metal on her finger.

Arturo pushed himself up. He held onto the skiff as he moved toward the stern and collapsed on the bench beside Evelyn.

"I wish Cassandra had left you alone," he said as he reached into his pocket and pulled out a small, sheathed knife.

Evelyn scooted away, keeping a wary eye on the blade. His hands shook as he unsheathed the blade and sawed through the ropes. As they fell from her wrists, he said, "Go and help him. It might be his only chance."

Her brow furrowed as she stood. "You would betray your wife?"

Arturo's brown eyes met hers. "Cassandra will find a way to win.

She always does."

Evelyn's legs shook as she walked to the helm and grabbed the lantern Jack was stuffed into. With the first pulse of hope she had felt in hours, she jumped onto the shore.

Chapter 18

Jack pressed his flippers to the side of the lantern as it swung. He wished Evelyn would be a bit more careful as she trudged across the island. He would rather not discover the contents of a frog's stomach.

The swinging stopped as Evelyn sat down and set the lantern beside her. She opened the door and pulled Jack out once again. Jack hoped her kiss would work this time. She pressed her lips to his nose and he remained as froglike as before.

She sighed and set him on the ground. Looking into bulbous eyes, she said, "You remember who you are, don't you?"

He gave her a croak and the best nod he could manage with his large head. She glanced up at the cliff to bright lights shining out from crevices.

"I can't find a door." She ran her hands over her hair. "How did we get caught up in a mermaid's trap? I should be at home, just eating a pie with Henry."

Jack stared up at the wall, the rock gleaming in the evening dusk. The world had a strange roundness through his amphibian eyes, yet it was clearer than normal. He blinked as he noticed a vine hanging down. He opened his mouth, but remembered he couldn't speak. With a deep breath, he hopped across the dirt.

"Jack!" Evelyn chased after him. "Where are you going?"

Once he was underneath the vine, he hopped and tried to point. However, his arms didn't move at the same angles as when human.

Evelyn stopped, a deep frown across her face. Her eyes lit up and she jumped for the vine. Her fingers brushed the end, but not enough to grab hold. Jack jumped out of the way as she landed. She jumped again, her fingers catching the vine. It held until a whole yard broke off and Evelyn fell into the dirt.

Evelyn tossed away the broken strand in her hand. "Let's keep searching."

Jack hopped forward, scanning the wall for any opening. Evelyn ran to keep up. Jack stopped as they reached a weathered door. Beyond, the trickling of water mixed with grunts and huffs from animals.

Evelyn grabbed the handle and tugged on the door. It didn't budge. Jack squeezed himself through a gap at the bottom. Once on the other side, he glanced around until he found a good path. He hopped up a pile of stones before leaping to grab the lever-like handle. He soared through the air, hoping he wouldn't fall and splat across the ground.

The suction cups on his fingers gripped the handle. He hung on it, his legs dangling and swinging. The latch clicked and the door jerked open. Evelyn stumbled inside and slammed the door shut. The force knocked Jack from the handle and slapped him against the wall. He dropped to the ground and lay there, his chin expanding with each breath in.

Evelyn carefully lifted him from the floor. "Are you all right?"

He tried to nod. Nothing hurt as much as it should, but he certainly wasn't comfortable. He was unsure what feelings were pain and what were unfamiliar sensations due to his froggish condition.

She kept him in her hand as she ventured down the hallway they had entered. Water trickled along the stone walls, gathering into a small stream along the floor. The croaking of other frogs echoed around them, mixed with beasts huffing. Evelyn kept her free hand on the wall to guide her path in the dim light.

The smell turned from mineral to uncleaned stable as lamps illuminated the far-end of the corridor. Jack wished frogs didn't have such a strong a sense of smell.

Evelyn stopped at a corner and peeked around it, carrying Jack so he could see as well.

Two gruff-looking men paced the room, four donkeys and a cage full of frogs crammed into a corner. The bearded man pulled out a pocket watch as he scratched his chin. "Second batch should be coming soon."

"Let's not wait for the third batch tonight, Hank." The curly-haired man glanced at the door at the far end of the room. "One of these nights, they'll not let us go."

"We provide a needed service, Craig." Hank spat into the small stream of water. "We clear up their rubbish and make a profit on both ends. They might not like us, but they'll not ruin us."

A creaking echoed through the small space, mixed with squeaking wheels. A trap door opened in the floor and a platform rose, carrying a pair of men. They wrestled and kicked at each other, unaware of the rising platform. One had a set of donkey ears and the other had grown a tail. Jack decided he preferred being a frog to being a donkey.

Hank and Craig grabbed the two men by the back of their pants and pulled them apart. The fighting men opened their mouths to yell, but only donkey brays came out. The platform began to lower. Evelyn stuffed Jack into her pocket. He thumped against her hip as she sprinted toward the platform.

"Hey!" Hank shouted.

Evelyn's feet pounded on the wood and Jack felt the two of them fall. Before the men could grab them, the trap door thudded shut. The echo of laughter, roulette tables, and splashing water grew louder. Evelyn pulled Jack out of her pocket as she leaned over the edge.

The space they were in was small and dark. The platform shuddered beneath them. Evelyn crouched, watching the wall as they lowered. Jack ribbitted as he saw an opening she might be able to crawl into. Seeing it as well, Evelyn tossed Jack in before pulling herself into the small tunnel. He kept ahead of her as they slid down. Evelyn had to wriggle through a few spots.

They soon reached an opening. Jack looked out and his froggish jaw dropped. He had thought the Morveaux a fine place, but it was nothing next to the golden splendor before him. What he wouldn't give to be dressed in a fine suit among the other men, playing at a billiard's table with one of those women on the arm. He would wink at the mermaids and charm them all by the end of the night.

The echo of braying from above broke Jack's thoughts. He blinked and looked again. The humans laughed and flirted, but the merfolk kept their faces cool. They returned the laughter, but it was empty. The spectacle was just enough to keep the drunken humans in a soft lull until they fell into one trap or another.

"Henry," Evelyn said.

Jack glanced up. Henry stood on the walkway Evelyn and Jack were hiding over. He was in close conversation with a man in uniform wearing a tri-cornered hat. Jack swallowed. There was Henry's temptation: doing what he saw was right, no matter the consequences. This was not the place to report to the police.

Cassandra appeared on the staircase, laughing and talking with several gentlemen while her eyes stayed on Henry.

The man in uniform gave Henry a firm nod. Henry's shoulders relaxed as he and the officer walked toward where Evelyn and Jack were hidden. Jack held his breath, holding back any chance of a ribbit.

"How dare you!" Cassandra's voice echoed from the bottom floor followed by a sharp slap.

Evelyn glanced over as a group of men burst into a fight. Others gathered, cheering on the growing brawl. Cassandra disappeared into the crowd before running up the stairs, toward the officer and Henry. The officer turned away from Jack's hiding space and Evelyn dropped out of the opening. She waved to Henry and motioned for him to come. His eyes, however, remained focused on the officer. Evelyn ran toward him, but jumped behind a pillar as Cassandra caught up with Henry and put her hand on his arm.

"Do forgive him, Enrique." She laughed. "How my little pet likes to make up stories."

Enrique gave her a firm glare. "What game are you playing tonight?"

She laughed again. "As I've told you, these men fascinate me. Do you see this man's boldness?"

"Stop your lies." Henry stamped his cane. "I have been kidnapped, my brother's a frog, and Evelyn is your prisoner. This officer is a man of honesty and can give me justice."

Cassandra gestured to the men below them. "Don't you see? There's no justice here. Come, let's go back to our evening."

Henry pulled his arm away from her. Jack wanted to yell at his brother to not to be an idiot. All he could do, however, was let out a disappointed croak.

Cassandra touched Enrique's arm. He raised an eyebrow as she said, "Let him stay with me a little longer. I have only begun exploring his weaknesses."

"If you were a full mermaid again, and could be trusted, I would," Enrique said. "However, I will leave his fate up to the Council. Good evening."

Cassandra stepped back and gave a false smile. "Let them have their games."

Henry straightened his lapels before following Enrique down the hall. Jack's heartbeat quickened. He didn't want to abandon Evelyn, but Henry couldn't enter that unknown room alone. Even as a frog, there might be something Jack could do. With a nod to himself, Jack hopped down to the walkway and followed Henry.

Evelyn held her breath as she stayed behind the pillar and let this Enrique pass. There was something in his looks she didn't trust. She glanced down to check on Jack, only to see him hopping after Henry. Her lips tensed. She could follow them to this council and see if she might help Henry. The brawl on the first floor was growing, the merfolk watching it like some spectacle. The distraction would give her a chance.

A chill ran down Evelyn's spine as Cassandra leaned against the pillar, blocking her path. "Miss Havish, how is my husband?"

"Safe. Where is Henry being taken?"

"I did not expect such a temptation," Cassandra said. "He cannot go to the council. They will destroy him."

"Then we must stop him."

"Didn't you see me try? However, Mr. Kingston is quite stubborn." She straightened her gloves. "I may appear cruel, but I am nothing compared with the merfolk who run this island."

"What about the men you have turned into frogs?"

"All my debts will be settled once I am fully human," Cassandra said. "A temporary setback for a few is worth freeing myself from living forever in this horrid society." She grunted with disgust. "Look at them. Would you want to live among them?"

"What makes you better than them?"

Cassandra's blue eyes met Evelyn's as she raised her eyebrows. "Despite appearances, Miss Havish, I care."

Evelyn snorted.

Braying began to join the yelling. Cassandra unfurled her fan and said, "The evening is closing. If you wish to save Mr. Kingston, I must be saved first. The tiara I need is behind that white door. Run now, while the merfolk are distracted."

Cassandra stepped away. Evelyn pressed her lips together as her fists tightened. She could chase down the hall after Henry, but she didn't know where that would lead. As Arturo said, if Cassandra gained her wish, many men would be free. Henry was intelligent. He would find a way out of whatever trouble he was walking into. If he didn't, she would find a way to drag him out once she was done getting the tiara.

Evelyn broke into a sprint, expecting at any moment to find herself a frog, donkey, or who knew what else. However, in fewer strides than she expected, she reached the door and opened it.

The first part of the room appeared to be an ornate, yet normal office, with papers scattered on the table. The carpet ended, however, at the edge of a wide area of paved stone, leading to a lagoon surrounded by natural rock. A path of stepping stones led to a pillar of limestone holding a crystalline tiara set with sapphires.

At least the tiara was easy to find.

Evelyn stepped onto the first stone. A glow came from piles of gold coins mixed with relics in the water beneath her. This was probably just one more temptation. She didn't need wealth. She needed Henry.

With her eyes fixed on the tiara, she took the second step. A ripple ran across the surface of the lagoon. Evelyn hopped onto the third, and then the fourth. She stretched her leg to reach for the fifth, when tentacle twice as thick as her father's arm splashed up. Water sprinkled over her as she halted. Churning marked the movement of whatever beast was beneath her.

Holding her breath, she ran across the remaining stepping stones, her feet slipping on the slick rock. The sloshing grew and several tentacles rose around her, pelting her with waves. Evelyn reached the last stone step and stretched out her arm. Her fingers brushed the tiara. A tentacle splashed up and bashed into her stomach, sending her flying back. Evelyn gasped as she dropped into the cold water.

She kicked her way to the shore, despite her heavy boots. The tentacles, covered in massive suckers, slid past her legs. Evelyn dragged herself out of the lagoon. She panted as she sat glaring at the tiara. Gritting her teeth, she unlaced her boots and tossed them aside. No blasted octopus, no matter how large, was going to keep her from saving Henry.

She glanced at the office for any sort of weapon. The chair was made of a solid maple and was too heavy to break easily. There was a letter opener, but that seemed too small. Instead, she gripped the umbrella resting against the desk. She wasn't sure what use merfolk had with an umbrella, but it might help her against the beast.

With umbrella in one hand, she leaped across the stepping stones. She was only three away from the pillar, when the octopus struck again. Evelyn jumped to the side, keeping a firm grip on the umbrella. Once in the water, she kicked to the surface and took a deep breath. The dark, squinting eyes of the octopus seemed to glare at her just before it charged. Evelyn swam as hard as she could. Several tentacles reached out toward her. As one came close, she swung the umbrella. The movement pushed her further from the octopus, but right into the grasp of another tentacle.

The snake-like appendage wrapped around her torso, the suckers pressing against her skin. Evelyn's arms were barely free as the grip tightened, threatening to crush her ribs. She squeezed in a breath before the octopus dragged her beneath the water. Though the seawater stung, she kept her eyes open. A circular opening appeared beneath the octopus as she was drawn closer. Black ink spiraled out. Evelyn's chest ached, both from the pressure of the tentacle and from the want of air.

Evelyn's vision began to blur, but she held the umbrella in front of her. As her head was about to enter the octopus's belly, Evelyn opened the umbrella, blocking the octopus' mouth. The water shuddered, and the tentacle released. Evelyn kicked away and sped for the surface. She broke above the water and gasped for air. The octopus writhed, the tentacles pounding out waves. Evelyn kicked away, when a tentacle slammed against her head. She cried out as she fell beneath the water.

She dropped to the bottom, her hands brushing the gold. Out of the corner of her eye, she saw a jeweled trident. She grabbed it and carried the heavy object with her as she rose. The weapon would be worth the extra weight.

Another tentacle sped toward her. Evelyn knocked at it with the rod-end of the trident and the tentacle spun away.

Once at the surface, Evelyn kicked with all her might toward the pillar. She clumsily dodged the writhing tentacles, but kept moving. At last, she reached the pillar and climbed onto the slender ledge. Evelyn pressed the trident against a crevice in the rock and used it to steady herself as she stretched her arm up toward the tiara.

Her fingers wrapped around the tiara as a tentacle swung at her. Keeping hold of tiara and trident, she jumped onto the first stone. The tentacle swung past her and cracked into the water. She hopped from stone to stone as waves slushed around her, making her foothold ever more slippery. At last, she landed on the solid stone leading to the remarkably normal office.

She let her shoulders relax as she trudged onto the carpet. A wave surged out of the water, knocking her over. The tiara skidded from her hand. Evelyn grunted as she smacked against the floor. She was nearly on her feet, when a tentacle wrapped around her ankle. With a yell, she stabbed it with the trident. The metal bit in. The appendage released. Evelyn jumped up and ran forward. As she grabbed the tiara off the floor, the tentacle broke from the trident's hold. Evelyn cursed under her breath and threw open the door. She slammed it behind her as she dove out. She rolled across the ground, and stopped as her back hit the polished railing.

Cassandra kept her head high as she looked down at Evelyn. "Guards are coming." She tossed a satin cloak to Evelyn. "Cover yourself."

Evelyn held up the tiara as she panted. "How do we save Henry?"

Cassandra snatched the jeweled headpiece from Evelyn. She frowned and grabbed Evelyn's fingers with her other hand.

"He gave you the ring." Cassandra groaned. "No wonder he failed." She let go of Evelyn's hand and marched away from the stairs. Evelyn pushed herself to her feet and followed Cassandra.

The carpeted floor turned to blue tile gilded with gold ocean designs. Henry tried not to grunt at the continued marks of excess. Soon enough, this Enrique would lead him to the Council, whatever council it was, and all would be made right.

They came to a pair of mahogany doors covered in ornate carvings of merfolk with crowns and dolphins flying among the clouds and moon. It was just another mark of ridiculousness.

Enrique opened the door and motioned for Henry to enter. Beyond was a decorated cove. The tiled floor continued to the edge of a deep, broad pool. Carved into the stones above them were noble looking merfolk, similar to the ones on the door. At the bottom of their massive fins, just above the water, were thrones. Enrique approached a polished, brass bell and hit it twice with a wooden mallet. The gong echoed through the room, the tone changing as it circled up the spiral-like carving between the merfolk statues.

The water churned as the bell's tone was about to fade completely. Henry jumped back as a massive wide-brimmed hat atop a tower of hair rose out of the water. The rest of a middle-aged mermaid appeared, her torso covered in a breastplate woven of gold and abalone shells. She took the middle seat as two mermen and three mermaids appeared out of the water and filled the rest of the seats.

"Who has called us?" the mermaid with towering hair said.

Henry stepped forward, but Enrique motioned for him to stay.

"Madame Randala, Your Excellencies, The Exile has made another attempt at Nereda's Tiara." Enrique held out his arm, gesturing at Henry. "Here stands her latest, unwitting accomplice."

"I am not her accomplice," Henry said. "I have been kidnapped."

"Madame Randala," a mermaid wearing sharkskin said. "What shall we turn this one into?" She giggled. "He looks rather like a goat, doesn't he?"

Henry frowned. "I have come for your help." He nodded at Enrique. "He said you could set my brother and—" He swallowed, realizing he could call Evelyn this, "My fiancé free."

"Are they on the island?" Randala said.

Henry held her cold gaze, the pit of his stomach twisting. He was an honest man, and the truth was what was right. However, suggestions of transforming him into a goat did not bode well. If Jack were here, he would suggest Henry to only tell most of the truth. Jack had been telling the truth about every strange occurrence and Henry had not listened. Maybe it was time to listen to Jack.

Trying not to cringe, Henry said, "They could be. I am not sure where Madame Astrellar is keeping them."

Randala waved her arm toward the water. "Enrique, help this man bring his friends here, and we will settle the matter."

Henry's palms were slick, but he wasn't sure if it was from all the moisture in the room or from sweat. "How will the matter be settled?"

"You will be given justice." Enrique motioned for Henry to follow him.

"What sort of justice? I want a contract, in writing, before I bring them."

The merfolk and Enrique laughed.

"You are a human," Randala said. "You have no rights here. We are being merciful just speaking with you. Bring them."

"What will you do to them?" Henry glanced back at the tunnel. "Who are you and what is this council?"

Enrique stepped toward him and said quietly, "They are the Witches and Warlocks of the Sea, the true masters of the ocean. This island is the prison for any human who crosses them. Be careful how you speak."

"How did you become their prisoner?" Henry said.

Enrique smiled, letting the light glint off his white teeth. "I am no prisoner, and I am certainly not human."

Henry kept the gaze of the merman while his heartbeat quickened. He should have heeded Cassandra's warning. She had tried to stop him from entering this trap. Her motives may have been selfish, but she had been right.

His mistake was made. All he could do now as give Jack and Evelyn a chance to escape.

Raising his head, meeting the condescending eyes of the merfolk, he said, "I am not Madame Astrellar's accomplice, but I am her auditor. There are some curious matters regarding her account with you and I would like to see the original contract."

The merfolk laughed, but Henry kept his gaze firm. It was a ridiculous gambit and something Jack might do. However, he had to give Cassandra time to get off the island. Even if she abandoned him, she might have a bit of mercy on the other two. He stepped to the edge of the water, meeting Randala's eyes.

"I may not have rights myself, but as auditor for Madame Astrellar, you must show me the contract for her exile."

Randala raised her chin. "What do you know of merfolk law?"

"I know little, Your Excellency. However, I know truth is universal, and an auditor's job is to ensure honest and fair dealings. An organization so well-hidden from humans and capable of maintaining this island must have records and order. If your accounts with her are fair and honest, then I will be able to confirm them to you. If not—"

He thought of all the merfolk Cassandra had smiled and spoken to while walking through the casino. If her age was what she suggested, and her mother a former ambassador, Cassandra had connections.

"If not, what will you do?" Randala said with a condescending smile.

"Madame Astrellar will go to her friends and relatives, who will then send a whole army of auditors to fully analyze your accounts."

"Is that why she keeps returning?" Randala said, an edge of sarcasm to her voice. "To go through legal matters? Not to get Nereda's Tiara?"

"Her records, please."

Randala laughed. "Enrique, indulge the man. Let us see what he makes of it while we determine what to transform him into."

Enrique walked to the nearest wall and pushed aside a hidden door. Moments later, he returned with a jewelry box encrusted in abalone shells and edged with gold. He set the box on a flat rock at the height of his waist and opened the box. The tinkling melody echoed through the chamber as ghostly figures came into focus on the mirror embedded in the lid of the music box. Henry stepped closer as the music seemed to mold into words and the mirror held an ethereal image of Cassandra standing where he was now.

Chapter 19

Evelyn hissed as her bare feet hit the cold sand leading away from the cliffs. Cassandra continued her quick stride and Evelyn hurried to keep up. They reached the small cove where the boat and Arturo were hidden.

Pulling the cloak off her shoulders, Evelyn said, "How is the tiara supposed to work?"

"Patience, Miss Havish." Cassandra stepped into the boat and shook Arturo's shoulder. "My love, I finally have Nereda's Tiara."

Arturo grumbled awake and glanced at Evelyn. His frown deepened. "Where's her man?"

"He's been tempted away to the Hall of Justice." Cassandra sat beside him.

"You said the ring would protect him."

"The ring worked." She nodded toward Evelyn. "But, Miss Havish was wearing it." Cassandra held up the tiara. "Once we use this, we will see about rescuing Mr. Kingston."

Arturo's finger brushed the tiara. "Cassandra, how can this trinket be worth all the lives you've stolen?"

"I've stolen as few lives as possible and I have friends who have freed most of the frogs I brought here," Cassandra patted his arm. "Once this works, all will be set right."

She raised the tiara, moonlight glimmering in the blue stones. Evelyn held her breath as the sapphires began to glow. Cassandra shut her eyes as if settling into a bath after a long day and placed the tiara on her head. The glow brightened.

A high-pitched whine squealed from the tiara. Cassandra yelled out in pain as she tried to pull it from her head, but the metal stuck fast. The gems shattered. Cassandra jolted back and fell into the water.

Arturo lurched after her, but his foot caught and he fell into the bottom of the boat. He held his wrinkled hand out to Evelyn. "Save her!"

Evelyn looked over at Cassandra floating face-down in the water. Her arms hung there and her wet hair spread around her. For a moment, she considered leaving her there. However, she wouldn't be so cruel.

She dropped into the waist-high water and waded to Cassandra's side. Reaching her hand out, Evelyn frowned. Where Cassandra's feet should be was a gleaming fin.

Unsure what to do, Evelyn flipped the mermaid over. Cassandra's eyes fluttered open. The fire of malevolence in them made Evelyn jump back.

"They lied to me." Cassandra splashed her tail and pulled herself up to the side of the boat. "They sent me on a pointless hunt for forty years."

Arturo shook as he rose to his knees, his face level with Cassandra's. His withered hand pressed to her cheek. "Let's gather Mr. Kingston and go home. We don't—"

"Randala took our children. Then she planted lies to keep me from being truly yours." She pounded her fist against the skiff and the whole boat shook.

Cassandra looked at Evelyn. "We'll save your man and send you home. As for Randala, if I'm stuck as a mermaid, then she'll drown with me."

Evelyn stood in the water, staring at the shards of the broken tiara. She wanted to be glad Cassandra's plan hadn't worked, but her worry for Henry dampened any satisfaction. Besides, if Evelyn had been in Cassandra's place, what would she have done to restore her children and to be with her husband?

Evelyn pulled herself into the boat and stood at the helm. "How do we get there?"

"Follow me." Cassandra sang a high pitch song as she pushed away from the boat.

Evelyn gripped the wheel as an unknown force propelled the skiff toward the supposed Hall of Justice.

Henry tapped his fingers on his cane as he wound the music box's knob and watched the trial again. The phantom Cassandra projected in the mirror had a strength and purity to her, something he could trust. The same merfolk watching him spoke their sentence and Cassandra negotiated. Everything seemed clear, but his gut told him he was missing an important detail. He wound the knob and re-watched the final sentence.

The churning of water echoed through the cove. Henry glanced up as Cassandra entered in mermaid form, Evelyn and Arturo in the skiff following her. Cassandra's hair cascaded around her as she rose from the water, glaring at Randala.

A pressure weighed on Henry's chest. Evelyn should not be here. He needed to do something. He reached to shut the music box, but could not as he looked at her honest face within the mirror. He was too close to the truth. If he only took a moment more, he might get them all out safe.

The present and real Cassandra raised a broken tiara in her hand. "You lied to me!"

"I did not. Nereda's Tiara was only meant for full mermaids."

Randala leaned back comfortably. "If you had been in mermaid form, it might have worked."

"Might?" Cassandra swam to the center of the cove, tail splashing in the water. "If I cannot be human, then I will have your head."

Henry rubbed his forehead as he wound the knob on the music box. The sooner he found the answer, the sooner he might get them all free.

"Henry!"

Henry looked up as Evelyn steered the skiff toward the shore.

Randala sang out a few notes in a high-pitched whistle and flicked her wrist. A wave tossed up through the cavern, pushing Cassandra back. The boat tilted on its portside. Evelyn grabbed Arturo while wrapping one arm around the side of the boat. The wave subsided and the boat smacked back onto the water.

"Your human is about to drown," Randala said.

She sang again and the waves grew, tossing the boat higher. Henry's hand clutched his cane, his crooked leg throbbing. He was more likely to drown than help if he jumped into the water after Evelyn.

Evelyn held on to Arturo and grabbed the helm, somehow steering the skiff. Cassandra's muscular tail pounded through the water. A whirlpool formed, pulling at her. The skiff scraped against the shore. Evelyn kept hold of Arturo and leaped into the shallows. With a grunt, she pulled both of them onto solid ground.

Henry started to walk toward her, but stopped as he glanced at Enrique. He couldn't risk the music box being taken away. Evelyn was strong and on solid ground. She should be safe for now. He wound the knob again and turned his attention back to the box.

Another high-pitched whistle filled the cavern, breaking Henry's concentration. The water around Cassandra rose before slamming into Randala, breaking part of the rock. Randala and her massive hat disappeared into the water.

The water sloshed as the whines echoed into nothing. The two mermaids broke to the surface and swam toward each other. A crack filled the air as they slammed together. They bashed with their fists and tails. Despite being mermaids of apparent rank, the whole affair was an underwater bar brawl. The other merfolk merely leaned forward with interest, a grin on their faces as they waited for blood.

Henry glanced back at the music box. He bit his lip to hold back a smile. A way out finally became clear, if he could get Randala to listen.

He looked up as Enrique grabbed Arturo and pressed a broad knife to the old man's throat.

"Will you let your human die?" Enrique said.

Evelyn sped across the rocky shore and rammed her shoulder into Enrique's. The knife clattered across the ground and Arturo fell. Enrique reached for another knife on his belt. Evelyn slammed her fist into his jaw. She swung again, but he caught her fist with his palm. His other hand flashed forward and gripped her neck. Her eyes widened as he tightened his hold.

Henry slammed the music box shut and grabbed it with his free hand. Evelyn's face was paling. He was not going to lose her tonight.

His heart rammed against his ribcage as he swung his cane, trying to urge more speed out of his limp. Enrique grinned, his teeth glinting in the strange light of the cavern. Evelyn's legs shook, their collapse approaching.

Once close enough, Henry yelled and bashed the music box against the back of Enrique's skull. Enrique shook his head and turned. Henry raised his cane and swung it as hard as he could. It thwacked across Enrique's skull, the wood shattering, sending a tremor up Henry's arm.

Enrique bobbled a moment before tumbling unconscious to the ground, his hand releasing Evelyn's neck.

She dropped to her knees as she gasped in air. Henry moved toward her, but the foot of his crooked leg caught on a rock and he tripped forward. Evelyn jumped up and caught Henry's shoulders, steadying him. He wrapped his arms around her, pulling her close.

He kissed her cheek as she held onto him, her breath wheezing.

"Everything's going to be all right," he whispered.

She rested her head against his. "We can take the skiff and get out."

Henry pulled away as he looked at the thrashing mermaids. "No. They broke their contract."

"What?" Evelyn said.

Henry held onto her arm to steady himself as he bent down and picked up the music box. His arms trembled, but Evelyn's presence strengthened him. The merfolk might not listen, but he had to try. This was their best chance at surviving.

Raising the music box, he shouted, "High Witch Randala!"

The underwater battle continued, each mermaid trying to shove the other down.

Henry steadied his grip on Evelyn's arm. "High Witch Randala! I have found the truth!"

The sea witch panted as she broke out of the water, her hat askew as she held Cassandra in a chokehold. Dragging Cassandra toward the throne, Randala said, "What do you want, auditor?"

Letting go of Evelyn's arm, Henry limped toward the shore. "When your council exiled Madame Astrellar, you made a contract."

Her voice hoarse, Cassandra said, "I don't think—"

Randala tightened her hold around Cassandra's throat. "Go on, Auditor."

Henry opened the music box and held it out, letting the melody play. The natural acoustics of the chamber carried the notes as they formed words. Randala's voice echoed around them. "We have agreed to your punishment. You will be exiled among the humans."

"Will I be fully human?" Cassandra's voice joined the strange, musical echo. "Or a transformed mermaid?"

"What is your wish?" Randala said.

"If you are going to exile me, then it should be complete."

"You wish to be fully human?" Randala's voice let out a sigh. "Then, once you are married and legally bound to the human you are being exiled for, you will be fully human. However, if your pet marries another, you will die. Do you accept?"

"Yes, Your Excellency."

The rock thrones trembled and the six lower members of the council cowered. Henry slammed the box shut.

"You broke your contract," he said. "They are married."

"I did not break anything," Randala said. The other merfolk nodded as the statues trembled. "The contract was made under Merfolk Law. By our law, they have never married."

Henry kept his stance steady. This was the answer he had expected. He made a silent prayer before speaking.

"You did not clarify which type of law they had to be married under, so it is improper, and illegal under most law, to hold them to your standard." He stepped forward. "Even so, by any common-law definition of matrimony, they are husband and wife."

"If we use the common-law definition of marriage," the top-hatted merman said, "They are married."

Randala glared at him and he shrank back. Several cracks echoed in the Hall. A chunk of the ceiling crashed down, sending up a spray of water.

"We built the contract to give you a chance, Cassandra," Randala said, "To change your mind and return home."

"There is no home without my husband." Cassandra pulled against Randala's grip.

"You said the contract was perfect," shouted one of the mermaids, "And would keep Madame La Mer in her proper form."

Another chunk of ceiling fell.

"You broke the laws of our people," Cassandra said. "To keep the

Hall of Justice from falling on top of you, you must uphold what's right."

"I suppose so." Randala shoved Cassandra away. Leaning back and stretching herself into a regal pose, she said, "Council, do you accept what this auditor claims?"

Cracks rushed up along one of the statues and an arm crashed into the water. Six urgent voices cried out, "Yes."

Randala glanced up at the cracks. "Any against?"

The rest of the council shook their heads, a glimmer of fear in their eyes. Henry exhaled as the walls stopped shaking.

"The Council has spoken and Justice will be upheld."

Randala sang and was soon joined by the rest of the council. Cassandra remained in the water, her head held high. Waves frothed and glowed around Cassandra. Henry dropped the music box as Cassandra's golden hair turned gray and her smooth skin wrinkled.

"Remember, we tried to have mercy," Randala said.

Cassandra's face withered swiftly with age as she sank into the water.

"No!" Arturo jumped toward the water.

Evelyn grabbed his shirt and pulled him back. Henry moved to run into the water, but stopped. He had never been able to swim well, and now was not the time to test his limits. He hobbled toward the rope sitting on the floor of the skiff. Cassandra may have kidnapped him, but he couldn't stand still and let her drown.

He grabbed the rope and tossed it as far as he could. She was too deep to reach. Her dress floated around her and her eyes began to fade.

Jack leaned over the edge of the statue he had climbed. He had watched everything, his amphibious body too small to help. He had considered dropping down one of the mermaid's bodices. Though it might distract them long enough for the others to escape, Jack didn't like the thought.

Yet, as the aging Cassandra sank, he knew he had a better chance of helping her than Henry. He hopped down the statue and onto a ledge. Not sure what he could do, he leaped into the air, stretching out his long arms and angled legs. The sloshing water was coming far too quickly.

He landed with a small sploosh. The saltwater stung in his eyes and skin, almost as if a rash was spreading and catching on fire. He pushed on, pumping his webbed feet as the now-aged Cassandra's dress billowed around her, filling with water and dragging her down. She kicked and tried to rip away part of her dress, but her arms were too feeble. He pressed his teeth together, hoping they might be sharp enough to bite off her buttons. His vision began to cloud and all he could feel was the burning. With a few more kicks, his webbed fingers brushed Cassandra's.

Her hand wrapped around him and she pulled him through the water. She pressed her wrinkled lips to his head. Jack's vision blurred as she let him go and he tumbled away.

His stomach flip in on itself as he felt his arms and legs stretch out. The burning disappeared from his skin as his lungs suddenly ached. Opening his eyes, he stared at his very human hand. He began to shout, but his mouth filled with sea water. Cassandra's wrinkled face stared up at him, pleading in her eyes.

She might have gotten him into this mess, but she didn't deserve to die.

Ignoring the fire in his lungs, Jack reached in his pocket and found his penknife. He propelled his legs, pushing toward her.

Cassandra's eyes were clouding. Jack's heartbeat ticked away the seconds as he slid his penknife through the buttons on the back of her dress. The clothing floated off her, her body thinner than before. His lungs ached, begging for air, as he threw his arm around her. Each kick didn't seem to get him far enough and he wished he had kept the webbed feet for a little longer.

Breaking through the surface, he gasped in air. He listened for her breath, but nothing came. He shook her and she spat out water followed by a wheezing cough. Her bony frame pressed against his side as she clung to him, her gray hair hanging like a wet mop. He shook his head as he kicked through the water, trying to forget the warmth he had felt when he had first seen her. Next time he saw a girl in need of help sitting by a well, he would send someone else.

His bare, human, feet touched ground and he pulled Cassandra through the shallows. Henry splashed into the water and took her from Jack. His arms free, Jack crawled onto the shore. He let himself collapse on the solid ground as he panted in air.

Evelyn let go of Arturo and helped Henry lay Cassandra in the skiff. Arturo hobbled over, his legs shaking. Henry assisted Arturo into the skiff and the old man collapsed beside his wife.

Cassandra raised a trembling arm and touched Arturo's cheek. She pushed back her gray hair, revealing her wrinkled face bright with joy. "Arturo, I am old!"

"You are beautiful." He kissed her and they held each other close.

Jack rubbed the back of his neck as he pushed himself to his feet. He could feel the merfolk watching them. Best to be gone quickly.

Walking to Evelyn and Henry, he said, "How do we get out of here?"

Randala leaned back in her throne. "You are human. You do not get to leave."

Henry pointed to the music box. "Madame Astrellar is to live her days among humans."

"There are plenty of humans here," Randala said. "And she'll be with her little pet of a husband. I am being quite gener—"

She stopped as a golden bauble plinked from her sleeve and onto the stone behind her. She frowned before letting out a shout that was cut off in a ribbit.

As she shrank, the other council members pushed off their thrones and sped toward her empty seat. Jack looked away as the water filled with thrashing fins and bashing arms. He raised an eyebrow as Cassandra broke into a wheezing cackle.

Cassandra patted the boat and said, her voice cracked with age, "Shall we go before they notice?"

Jack joined Henry and Evelyn in pushing the skiff into the water before jumping in. None of them were going to risk this chance to escape.

As the skiff drifted toward the open sea, Evelyn said, "The boat's driven by magic, but you're not a mermaid anymore."

Cassandra rested her head against Arturo's shoulder as she pointed to Evelyn's hand. "There's power in true love, Miss Havish. Just raise the glass, whistle through the ring, and think of home."

Evelyn looked to Jack and Henry as she pulled off the ring. Jack gave her a nod while keeping a wary eye on Cassandra. Henry stepped to her side and gripped her hand.

With Henry's pull of the lever, the large pearl rose out of the helm's enclosure. Evelyn licked her lips before raising the ring and whistling. Jack held onto the side of the skiff and shut his eyes, picturing his warm bed and the long bath he would have once he was home.

Chapter 20

Two Months Later

Henry glared at the mirror as he re-knotted his tie for the fifth time. He huffed at the skewed knot and pulled it apart. Evelyn's laughter warmed the air as she placed her cheek against his, their faces both reflected in the mirror. With an expression to mock his seriousness, she said, "It's only a tie."

"I want to look respectable," he said.

She kissed Henry's cheek before tying his tie and adjusting the knot. Smoothing his lapels, she said, "You always look respectable."

Henry let himself smile before he leaned forward and kissed her. A tender warmth spread through him as she pressed closer.

"Mr. Kingston, we really should be going," she said as her lips parted from his.

"We could stay here, Mrs. Kingston." He leaned forward and stole another kiss.

"We made a promise." She stepped back and smiled. "And how else am I to show off the new stockings you bought for me?"

He offered his arm as they walked out of the apartment and to the trolley on the corner. She leaned against him as the trolley bumped across town. He kept his arm around her, holding her close. Here, there were no mermaids or other fantastic things to worry about. A part of him feared he might wake and have the past month evaporate into a dream. Holding her close helped him be sure this was real and she was here.

The trolley jerked to a stop and Henry forced himself to loosen his hold on Evelyn. Arm-in-arm, they walked down the street and joined a crowd funneling into the police station's courtyard. Evelyn rose to her tiptoes as she looked through the crowd. Henry didn't need to look as John Havish and Henry's father, Miles Kingston, took turns competing for who could holler the loudest. As the two men leaned on each other and laughed, Henry moved for the back row.

"They're waiting for us." Evelyn tugged him onward.

Once he and Evelyn reached the middle rows where their families sat, his sisters and sister-in-law crowded around Evelyn, shoving Henry out of the way.

Henry went to take a seat, when his brother Richard embraced Henry tight enough to squeeze the air out of his lungs.

Richard stepped back with a proud grin. "And how's business for my freshly married brother?"

Henry leaned on his new cane as he winced. He had hoped to avoid the subject. "I've enough clients to pay room and board."

He glanced at Evelyn, his chest feeling as if an anchor were dragging it down. She was working a few days a week in her father's shop to earn enough to help buy some necessities. Yet, her face was bright and her laughter warm as she chatted with his sisters as if she had no worries.

Richard gripped Henry's shoulder. "You've chosen well, Henry. She's almost as fine as my Hillary."

Henry began to smile, when Richard slapped his back. "And, soon enough, the children'll come."

All warmth left Henry's face. He had no time to reflect, however, as a dozen horns blasted out a fanfare. The crowd shuffled into their seats and the chattering lulled to a stop. Matching the beat of drums, the latest graduates of the Officer's Academy marched to the stage.

Jack stood among his classmates, looking sharp in his dress uniform, a brocade on his shoulder and polished badge on his coat. Evelyn squeezed Henry's hand. Henry found himself smiling. After all his work, Jack had completed his training and now stood as an officer of the law.

They sat through a half-dozen long speeches. Henry tried not to doze off and Evelyn nearly held back a yawn as she rested her head against his shoulder. He tried to ignore the women of his family giggling as they glanced over.

The graduates were announced by name and paraded through a circuit of shaking hands with the mayor, commissioner, and other officials. As Jack was announced, Henry joined the whole sea of Kingstons and Havishes who stood and cheered. Jack snuck a wave as he approached the line of shaking hands.

As Jack reached Inspector McCay, her face was stiff and the sharp jerk of her handshake seemed firmer than with other men. Henry gripped Evelyn's hand.

Jack had told them about McCay's instructions to not intervene the night Cassandra had kidnapped them. If Jack hadn't broken her commands, he wouldn't have been there to save Cassandra from drowning, and Henry and Evelyn would still be on Marveth. Now, Jack had no chance of joining McCay's squad. It was a grave price to pay for saving his brother.

The final graduate was announced, the ceremony closed, and the crowd rose and cheered.

Tables of pies and cakes were set out and the courtyard transformed into an open-air reception hall. The Havish and Kingston families gathered around Jack as he shook their hands and laughed.

As Jack reached Evelyn and Henry, he clapped them on the shoulders. "I watch you two and all I can think is I've got to find myself a girl." Evelyn raised an eyebrow and Jack held up his hands in defense. "A nice, normal girl."

As Jack continued his circuit of handshakes, Henry stood at the edge. A prickling ran along the back of Henry's neck as someone tugged at his elbow. "Mr. Kingston, a word?"

Henry's smile dropped as he turned and faced Hedley. The squat businessman nodded toward a less crowded corner. Henry grimaced but followed the man.

"The answer's still no," Henry said as he reached Hedley's side.

"The position pays well." Hedley nodded toward Evelyn. "Think of all you could provide your new wife."

"We will build our own future."

"Sir, I need your help more than ever." A heaviness weighed in Hedley's eyes as he removed his hat. "Mr. Astrellar passed away yesterday."

Henry stood straight. Cassandra had fought decades to be with Arturo, but now was left to live only with the hope they would be reunited in the next life. He supposed he should feel sympathy, but could not. Not after all the lives she had trampled.

"Madame Astrellar asked me to invite you to the funeral." Hedley pulled out a dark green envelope with embossing along the edges. "I told her you wouldn't come, but she insisted."

Henry kept his hands on his cane and glared at the envelope. "I want nothing to do with the Astrellars."

"Which is why I need you," Hedley said. "I am executor of Mr. Astrellar's estate until an heir is found. Madame Astrellar's house arrest has kept her contained, but I know better than to relax.

"I'm leaving in a few days for business in Castallar. I need someone I can trust to keep an eye on matters. You understand what sort of woman she is and won't bend under her manipulation. There's no better man I can turn to."

"She kidnapped my brother, my wife, and me. Even if you offered me the entire Astrellar fortune, I would not risk my family."

"Such integrity and stubbornness is rare." Hedley's jaw shifted as he eyed Henry. "A good man's hard to let go."

With a sigh, Hedley reached into a different coat pocket. "If you'll not accept the position, at least take my gift."

Hedley held out a thick envelope. Henry folded his arms and kept his glare on Hedley. Even if the money was from Hedley, the source was still the Astrellar fortune.

"It's for your wedding," Hedley said. "And to thank you and Mrs. Kingston for relieving me of greater trouble than you know." Hedley pushed the envelope toward Henry. "Take it and I promise not to bother you again."

Henry ground his teeth together before accepting the envelope.

"You know where to find me if you change your mind." Hedley tipped his hat and then wound his way out of the courtyard.

Henry glowered after the man as he tapped the envelope on his palm. He opened the unsealed edge and his heart jerked. He thumbed through the large stack of cash before shoving it in his pocket. His cheeks paled as he glanced at the crowd of officers. Nothing had been stolen, yet he felt they should arrest him.

With the envelope weighing down his pocket, Henry limped back to where Jack was reenacting one of his training exercises.

"And then Beauford tried to shove me off, but I dodged him, and his elbow smashed the sergeant in the nose!"

Jack bent over laughing, joined by guffaws from the Havish and Kingston men.

"Is that how Sergeant Carter broke his nose?" McCay appeared beside Jack, no humor in her steel-gray eyes.

Jack's laugh ended with a snort and he snapped to attention.

"I need a moment of your time, Officer Kingston," She glanced at Henry and Evelyn, "As well as your brother and sister-in-law."

Evelyn's hand was cold as she gripped Henry's. He squeezed her fingers, trying to reassure her even as dread spread down his spine.

McCay gave the Kingstons and Havishes a tight smile before motioning for Jack, Evelyn, and Henry to follow her into the building. The chattering of the crowd turned to a dull echo as she brought them into a conference room.

They followed her order to sit and she shut the door. Jack fidgeted in the chair while Henry kept his hand on Evelyn's shoulder.

"First, I want to thank you all for keeping your silence on the mermaid affair," Inspector McCay said as she leaned her palms on the table and kept her eyes on them. "I'm glad you're all intelligent enough to not announce strange happenings to the public."

She stood up and reached in her pocket. "I've spent the last few weeks, Officer Kingston, debating your merits. You're young, impulsive, and liable to get yourself tangled in a mess." Jack sat still as she pulled a palm-sized box from her pocket. "However, you have courage and a sharp eye." She opened the box, revealing a lapel pin with an encircled star. "In a year, you can wear this as part of my squad, if you prove yourself."

Jack's eyes widened as he leaned toward the pin. "How do I do that, Inspector?"

"I've arranged with the Chief for you to serve one day a week in my department. You'll work cases with some of my detectives and receive special training." She held up a finger. "But, if you take even half a step out of line, you'll be out permanently."

Jack jumped up from his chair and grabbed McCay's hand. "I'll do everything you ask, Inspector. You'll see I can—"

McCay pulled her hand from his grasp. "Sit down."

Henry rubbed his forehead as Jack thumped back into his seat.

"My squad is a hard duty, and I've never let an officer so green in before. I'm giving you this chance because you've already been exposed to the sort of work we do and Madame Astrellar spoke highly of your courage."

Evelyn's fingers dug into Henry's leg. Henry kept his hand firm on her shoulder as he narrowed his eyes.

"As a rule, I don't trust mermaids," McCay said before nodding toward Henry and Evelyn. "However, they confirmed the report."

McCay stood and put her hands in her pockets. "Now, Mr. and

Mrs. Kingston, the second reason I brought you here is because Officer Kingston will need your help. Most officers wash out from my squad because they've no one to talk to who understands magic." She pointed at them. "You've been through enough to not be too surprised and to know enough to keep things quiet."

"But if magic is real," Evelyn said. "People should know."

McCay raised an eyebrow. "Even if they're told, they'll not believe. No. It's better to keep the peace."

The inspector opened the door. "Officer Kingston, McBriar's going to be full of uniforms tonight. You'd best get there early."

Jack broke into a grin as he jumped to his feet. He grabbed McCay's hand and gave it another vigorous shake. "I'll not let you down, Inspector."

"Congratulations, Officer Kingston," McCay said as she slapped his shoulder. "But don't speak a word until I make the announcement."

"Yes Inspector." He grinned and gave her a salute before sprinting outside.

Henry kept tight hold of Evelyn's hand as they both nodded to Inspector McCay and exited. He placed his other hand on the envelope and stopped as they reached the doorway.

"What's the matter?" Evelyn touched his shoulder.

Henry glanced down the hall as Inspector McCay strode toward the door.

She paused beside them and raised an eyebrow. "The best cake goes quickly. I'd recommend getting in line."

"We need just a moment," Henry said.

She eyed the two of them before glancing out the window. "I remember what it's like to be young and newly married with the family crowding around." She tapped Henry's shoulder. "Take the time you need, but not too much."

Henry's cheeks burned as the inspector marched out of the

building and was soon surrounded by a group of young officers. As he reached for the door handle, Evelyn touched his elbow.

"What did Hedley want? Did he offer the position again?" Evelyn said.

"He did, but he also said Madame Astrellar invited us to—" He pressed his lips together as he met Evelyn's eyes. "Arturo Astrellar is dead. She wants us to come to the funeral."

Evelyn's eyebrows rose. She rubbed her temple before saying, "Really?"

Henry nodded.

"I pity her for losing her children, and her husband, but I can't excuse all the men she's kidnapped," Evelyn said. "You didn't accept, did you?"

"No." Henry's hand shook as he pulled the envelope from his pocket. "I turned down the job as well, but had to accept this as a wedding present."

He handed her the envelope. Her eyes widened as she opened it and stared at the stack of money.

"My business is growing slowly." He looked down at her hands, a few stains from her father's shop splotched on her skin, calluses on her fingers. "I cannot provide what you deserve. If we had waited to marry till I was fully employed, I could buy for you—" He swallowed as he looked into her brown eyes, the light from the window highlighting her soft features. "I could buy you everything – new dishes, furniture, even a fine house."

She looked down at the money as she closed the envelope. "Is that why you took this?"

"He promised to stop bothering us." He rubbed his fingers together, wishing they would feel less greasy from holding the envelope. "I don't want the money, but it might provide a better life until my business is stronger."

"We have enough to eat and a roof over our heads." She held the envelope out to Henry. "I don't need anything more."

"You deserve more."

Her smile was soft as she leaned close and kissed his cheek. "We have enough."

He pulled her into a tight embrace. Her body was warm against his as she nestled her head against his shoulder. He kissed her forehead as he pictured them on the porch of their own fine house, instead of their cramped one-bedroom apartment with leaking pipes and rusted hinges.

As he pictured himself inside the house, however, he felt as if Cassandra's portrait was on the wall, her eyes watching him as she ruled his life once more.

He released Evelyn and took the envelope from her. Eying a slot next to one of the office doors, he said, "How do you feel about donating to the widow and orphans fund?"

Evelyn followed his gaze and smiled.

Together they approached the donation slot. Henry crammed the thick envelope through the narrow opening. A relief rose in him as the envelope fell through and thunked into the box on the other side.

"How kind of Madame Astrellar," Evelyn said. "It's a fine memorial for her husband."

A smile slowly spread across Henry's face. Free of mermaids, transforming frogs, and Cassandra's manipulation, he took Evelyn's arm and escorted her outside.

The crowd, still thick in the courtyard, seemed far away, as he looked at his wife. With her, whatever hardships would come, where they would live, how many children they would have, what station he would rise to, didn't matter. She was everything he needed. He slipped his arm around her waist and pulled her into a kiss.

THE END

Author's Note: Discovering Pippington

When I wrote the first draft of The True Bride and the Shoemaker (The Pippington Tales Book 1) in 2010, I loved the story but didn't know what to do with the manuscript. Writing the tale of Peter Talbot and his discovery of magic had been just a diversion from working on a what I saw as a much more marketable YA fantasy adventure.

A year or two later, I joined a local writer's group and brought my super marketable YA adventure. The reaction was positive, but unenthusiastic. At the next meeting, I brought the first chapter of The True Bride and the Shoemaker. By the end, they were saying, "What happens next?" and asking for the rest of the story.

I knew then I had something people would be passionate about, but I still wasn't sure what to do with the book. My envisioned brand for myself was as an author of tales of sword fighting heroines and wizard battles. I worked on polishing the book, but continued focusing on more epic adventures.

In 2012, I decided to take a dive into National November Novel Writing Month (NaNoWriMo). This is an annual event where novice and veteran writers throw their sanity to the wind and race to write 50,000 words in 30 days. I wanted to try it at least once, so I followed the advice I had read online and made a thorough outline.

November 1st arrived and I had a full outline of a science fiction thriller involving betrayal and epic spaceship battles. On my hour-long bus ride home from work, I decided to take a nap to prepare myself for writing late into the night.

I was listening to the album "Baroness" by Sarah Slean, when the first scene of The Lady and the Frog appeared before me. (At this stage, Jack Kingston was genuinely helping Cassandra Astrellar, who I thought would later be revealed to be a princess in distress from some cloud kingdom from Jack and the Beanstalk.) Then, Henry appeared. And Cassandra became the villain. And the independent female in me said, "The True Bride and the Shoemaker has a male protagonist. Are you really going to write a second book without a strong female lead?" Thus, Evelyn Havish came to be.

In the forty minutes between this epiphany and arriving home, I had a full outline and a draft of the first chapter. I worked on the book feverishly, my mind wrapped in this story, plowing forward to get everything down. My muse decided to take a nap somewhere around the last third of the book (this may also have been due to getting the flu), but I kept writing. On November 30th, I dragged myself across the finish line and completed the 50,000th word.

The upside of this was I now had two books in the same world and the beginning of a series. The downsides were, first, the ending was terrible, and, second, I had a series without a name.

While cleaning up the first book and getting feedback for friends, I debated what to name the city. I was leaning toward Willington, when my friend Vanessa Haggard suggested Pippington.

With my series named, I drove forward with polishing The True Bride and the Shoemaker, revising The Lady and the Frog, and drafting the upcoming third book (which is based on Vanessa's question of whether or not Adeline Winkleston is a witch). During this time, I worked at a university while applying to graduate school, got into graduate school, and finished my first year there.

Since the release of The True Bride and the Shoemaker in June

2015, I finished graduate school, began the unexpectedly long journey to find post-graduate employment, and am now releasing the Lady and the Frog in February 2017.

When I finished The True Bride and the Shoemaker, many asked me if I was excited to have a book out. Honestly, I felt exhausted. It was my first book and I had independently published. Taking a first book from original draft to print book is a long process with a steep learning curve. By the end, however, I found myself a stronger writer and more knowledgeable about the art and business of publishing. Also, it doesn't hurt to be able to say I am a published author.

As I have approached the publication of The Lady and the Frog, I have been much more excited. The second book is the point where I know I can do this long-term, the point where I have proof I am committed. Also, the process has been easier because of what I learned while publishing the first book. I communicated better with beta readers and contractors. I knew how long each task should take and could plan for hiccups at all stages of the process. With all of this knowledge and work, I come out the other side as an author with two books.

The main reason I wrote this author's note is to help future authors know how to walk the same path. I started six years ago without any idea how to self-publish and now I have two books out. I may not be a bestseller yet, but I feel I have succeeded.

I hope you have enjoyed learning about the journey of writing this book and developing this series. If you have ever thought about writing a novel, I say go for it. Work at it, learn from more experienced people, and strive every day to move closer to your goal. The only way to succeed Is to take the jump and try.

Acknowledgements

First, thank you to my editor Tara Newland for your hard work, excellent revisions, and the long discussions of future Pippington Tales. You are a great friend and this book would not be what it is without your help.

Second, thank you to Michelle Allgood for your beta reading and proofreading support. Your enthusiasm for this book and general cheering-on skills have been a great help. Someday, however, we need to do a Star Wars Trivia rematch.

Third, thank you to the rest of my beta readers – Jenny Flake Rabe, Amber Darren-Hall, Daniel Honey, Heather Davis, Kara Russell, and Tiffany Whitsitt. Your constructive feedback and support was essential for polishing this story.

Fourth, thank you to my friends who have supported me – including the staff, faculty, and fellow students in the Masters in Public Administration program from 2014 to 2016, my Utah and California writer's groups, the many friends I made while living in Provo, Utah, the friends who live further away, and the ones close to my hometown of Ventura, CA. You have been supportive, encouraging, and willing to listen.

Fifth, thank you to all of the readers who bought the first book. Your genuine compliments and your requests for the second book have helped spur me on. An author's greatest pleasure is hearing someone tell them how much they loved their book.

Sixth, and finally, thank you to my family. Together, you have been incredibly supportive. There are a lot of you and I could probably fill this page with thanking each one of you. For brevity's sake, I want to thank Mom for being my best sales rep, Natalie for enduring many hours of giving feedback on story and writing issues, Julia giving me the opportunity for my most successful book signing, and Katherine for making the cover for both books. Dad, Michael, Kayla, Alexis, and the rest of our gang of extended and adopted family members, thank you for being great people and cheering on my writing efforts.

To everyone listed here and anyone I may have missed, a final big thank you. It takes a lot of people to make the book the best it can possibly be and I am extremely grateful for your support.

Other Works by L. Palmer

The True Bride and the Shoemaker

The Pippington Tales Book 1

Welcome to Pippington, where motorcars bump down old, city lanes, elegant shoes appear by magic, and an ordinary shoemaker can become a hero.

Peter Talbot could use a little magic. Cheap factory-made shoes are putting his shop out of business, his nagging sisters will never let him rest, and his efforts to find true love are constantly thwarted by worldly fickleness. However, the gift of a wild primrose and a shipment of rare griffin skin are about to change everything. When beautiful, handmade shoes begin appearing in his shop every morning, Peter is determined to find his secret helper. What he finds introduces him to adventure and the hidden world of magic in Pippington.

The True Bride and the Shoemaker is the first of The Pippington Tales, based on The Elves and the Shoemaker and other fairy tales.

 **To read a preview, visit <u>tinyurl.com/truebride</u>**

The Matchgirl and the Magician

The Pippington Tales Book 3

Welcome to Pippington, where motor cars bump down old city lanes, carpets can fly, and magic is a secret proper young ladies keep.

One fateful night, a child named Adeline lies alone in the snow. Fading into sleep, her only warmth comes from her matches and the embers of her hidden magic. As she succumbs to the cold of death, she is saved by Rompell, a stranger from a land of deserts and magic with secrets of his own.

Their lives intertwined, Rompell and Adeline become father and daughter. As Adeline becomes an elegant young woman, she fights to control and hide her growing magic in a world full of handsome young men, fine dresses, and her own grand romance.

When an enemy arises from the shadows of Rompell's past, with ancient spells and dangerous magic, Rompell and Adeline risk losing all they have built together. As Rompell fights to protect his daughter, it may be Adeline who must risk revealing her powers and losing true love to save her father.

Please enjoy this preview of **The Matchgirl and the Magician,** the third book of The Pippington Tales.

To read a preview, visit
tinyurl.com/matchgirlandmagician

The Mermaid's Apprentice:

Book 1 of The Pirate and the Mermaid's Tailor Trilogy

Mabel Sinclair never planned to become a pirate.

All she wanted was to escape her dull life as a debutante and conquer the world of fashion. One fateful night at a ballroom ends when Mabel's foolish brother is kidnapped and transformed into a toad. To save him, Mabel makes a bargain with a mermaid and travels with her to an unexpected realm of magic. Once there, Mabel must choose between being imprisoned by cruel merfolk or joining pirates.

Antonio Cortez never planned to fall in love with a pirate.

A sailor who dreams of returning to his quiet life as a tailor, Antonio's plans are knocked off course by a chance meeting with the dashing pirate Mabel Sinclair. Antonio bonds with Mabel over their love of fashion, only to become a target for Mabel's growing list of enemies.

Fighting for their lives and their future, Mabel and Antonio find they have only one ally to turn to: the treacherous mermaid who Mabel bargained with in the first place.

The Mermaid's Apprentice is an epic tale of pirates, mermaids, and adventures in high fashion.

To read a preview, visit
tinyurl.com/mermaidapprentice

About the Author

In between exploring the hidden magic of Pippington, L. Palmer works in public service and lives in San Antonio. She is an award-winning speaker and has presented on various topics at writing conferences, studied English and Film at The University of California Santa Barbara, and has a Masters in Public Administration at Brigham Young University. She developed her imagination and adventure skills through growing up in Girl Scouts, working at resident summer camps, teaching high school English, and reading great books of fantasy and magic. While she doesn't typically host tea parties, she does enjoy hosting some for dragons on Tuesdays. For the latest news, visit: lpalmerchronicles.com

To explore more of Pippington, visit: lpalmerchronicles.com/pippington_tales

To sign-up for L. Palmer's Newsletter, visit: lpalmerchronicles.com/about

For updates and free bonus content, visit: lpalmerchronicles.com/exclusive-preview

If you enjoyed this book, please take the time to leave an honest review on Goodreads, Amazon, or the bookseller site of your choice.

Follow L. Palmer on social media:

- Facebook: facebook.com/lpalmerchronicles
- Instagram: instagram.com/lpalmerchronicles
- TikTok: tiktok.com/@lpalmerauthor1

www.ingramcontent.com/pod-product-compliance
Lightning Source LLC
Chambersburg PA
CBHW061604190726
48288CB00007B/2164